SUSAN MALLERY

chasing perfect

HQN

Recycling programs
for this product may
not exist in your area.

ISBN-13: 978-1-335-08081-3

Chasing Perfect
First published in 2010. This edition published in 2020.
Copyright © 2010 by Susan Mallery, Inc.

A Fool's Gold Wedding
Copyright © 2020 by Susan Mallery, Inc.

HQN
22 Adelaide St. West, 40th Floor
Toronto, Ontario M5H 4E3, Canada
www.Harlequin.com

Printed in U.S.A.

Praise for Susan Mallery

"Susan Mallery never disappoints and with *Daughters of the Bride* she is at her storytelling best."
—Debbie Macomber, #1 *New York Times* bestselling author

"Susan Mallery brings her signature humor and style to this moving story of strong women who help each other deal with realistic challenges, a tale as appealing as the fiction of Debbie Macomber and Anne Tyler."
—*Booklist* on *California Girls*

"Mallery's latest novel is a breath of fresh air for romantics, a sweet reminder that falling in love is never how you plan it and always a pleasant surprise."
—*Library Journal* on *The Summer of Sunshine & Margot*, starred review

"In this poignant small-town charmer, Mallery beautifully illustrates the power of female friendship and the importance of reaching for one's dreams... This irresistible, heartfelt story will appeal to romance readers and women's fiction fans alike."
—*Publishers Weekly* on *Sisters by Choice*

"Heartfelt, funny, and utterly charming all the way through!"
—Susan Elizabeth Phillips, *New York Times* bestselling author, on *Daughters of the Bride*

"It's not just a tale of how true friendship can lift you up, but also how change is an integral part of life.... Fans of Jodi Picoult, Debbie Macomber, and Elin Hilderbrand will assuredly fall for *The Girls of Mischief Bay*."
—*Bookreporter*

"Soul-crushing revelations and old resentments are tempered by whimsy, sass, and belly laughs in a scrumptiously sexy, playful story from one of the genre's best. Touching, refreshing, and fun."
—*Library Journal* on *Why Not Tonight*

"Mallery skillfully weaves in tantalizing details from the sisters' pasts—romantic hurts, the emotional devastation of being abandoned by their mother when they were children— to make the heart-tugging happily-ever-after all the sweeter."
—*Publishers Weekly* on *The Summer of Sunshine & Margot*

CONTENTS

CHASING PERFECT

Francisco de León, first in his daughters' hearts.

CHAPTER ONE

CHARITY JONES LOVED a good disaster movie as much as the next person—she would simply prefer the disaster in question not be about her life.

The sharp crack of an electrical short, followed by a burning smell, filled the conference room on the third floor of City Hall. A thin wisp of smoke rose from her laptop, ending any hope of her PowerPoint presentation going smoothly. The presentation she'd stayed up nearly all night perfecting.

It was her first day on the job, she thought, breathing deeply to ward off panic. The first official hour of her first official day. Didn't she get at least a sixteenth of a break? Some small sign of mercy from the universe?

Apparently not.

She glanced from her still smoldering computer to the ten-member board from California University, Fool's Gold campus, and they did not look happy. Part of the reason was that they'd been working with the previous city planner for nearly a year and still hadn't come up with a contract for the new research facility. A contract she was now responsible for bringing to life. She would guess the unpleasant burny smell was the other reason they were shifting in their seats.

"Perhaps we should reschedule the meeting," Mr. Berman said. He was tall, with graying hair and glasses. "When you're more—" he motioned to the smoldering computer "—prepared."

Charity smiled warmly when what she really wanted to do was throw something. She was prepared. She'd been on the job all of—she glanced at the clock on the wall—eight minutes, but she'd been prepping since she accepted the position as city planner nearly two weeks ago. She understood what the university wanted and what the town had to offer. She might be new, but she was still damned good at her job.

Her boss, the mayor, had warned her about this group and had offered to put off the meeting, but Charity had wanted to prove herself. Something she refused to let be a mistake.

"We're all here," she said, still smiling as confidently as possible. "We can do this the old-fashioned way."

She unplugged her computer and took it out into the hall where it would no doubt stink up the rest of the building, but her first priority had to be the meeting. She was determined to start her new job with a win and that meant getting California University at Fool's Gold to sign on the bottom line.

When she stepped back into the conference room, she walked over to the dry erase board and picked up a thick blue pen from the small rack attached to the board.

"The way I see it," she began, writing the number one and circling it, "there are three sticking points. First, the length of the lease." She wrote a number two. "Second, the reversion of improvements on the land. Namely the building itself. And three, the freeway off-ramp signal." She turned back to the ten well-dressed people watching her. "Do you agree?"

They all looked to Mr. Berman, who nodded slowly.

"Good." Charity had reviewed all the notes on the previous meetings and talked to the mayor of Fool's Gold over the weekend. What Charity couldn't figure out was why the negotiating process was taking so long. Apparently the previous city planner had wanted to be right more than he wanted the research facility in town. But Mayor Marsha Tilson had been very clear when she'd offered Charity the job—bring businesses to Fool's Gold, and fast.

"Here's what I'm prepared to offer," she said, making a second column. She went through all three problems and listed solutions, including an extra five seconds of left-turn time on the signal at the top of the off-ramp.

The board members listened and when she was done, they once again looked at Mr. Berman.

"That does sound good," he began.

Sound good? It was better than good. It was a once-in-a-lifetime deal. It was everything the university had asked for. It was zero calorie brownie with ice cream.

"There's still one problem," Mr. Berman said.

"Which is?" she asked.

"Four acres on the county line." The voice came from the doorway.

Charity turned and saw a man entering the conference room. He was tall and blond, good-looking to the point of being almost another species, and he moved with an easy athletic grace that made her feel instantly awkward. He looked vaguely familiar, but she was sure they'd never met before.

He gave her a quick smile. The flash of teeth, the millisecond of attention, nearly knocked her into the wall. Who was this guy?

"Bernie," the stranger said, turning the megawatt grin on the group leader. "I heard you were in town. You didn't call me for dinner."

Mr. Berman actually looked interested. "I thought you'd be busy with your latest conquest."

Blond guy shrugged modestly. "I always have time for anyone from the university. Sharon. Martin." He greeted everyone else at the table, shook a few hands, winked at the old lady at the end, then turned back to Charity.

"Sorry to interrupt. I'm sure under normal circumstances you could deal with this problem without breaking a sweat. But the reason we don't have a deal isn't the lease reversion or the traffic light." He moved close and took the pen from her hand. "It's the four acres the university has been offered by a very wealthy alumni family. They want their name on the building and they're willing to pay for that privilege."

He flashed another smile at Charity, then turned back to the board. "I'm going to explain why that's a bad idea."

And then he started talking. She had no idea who he was and probably should have told him to leave, but she couldn't seem to move or speak. It was as if he projected some space-alien force field that kept her immobilized.

Maybe it was his eyes, she thought, gazing into their hazel-green depths. Or his sun-bleached lashes. It might have been the way he moved or the heat she felt every time he walked by her. Or maybe she'd simply inhaled some weird gas when her computer had sparked, flamed out and died.

While she enjoyed a boy-girl encounter as much as the next woman, she'd never been mesmerized by a man before. Certainly not during a professional meeting that she was supposed to be running.

She knew the type, though. Had seen the power of the havoc they brought with them everywhere they went. Self-preservation stated she should stay far, far away. And she would…just as soon as the meeting was over.

She squared her shoulders, determined to regain control of herself and the meeting. Then her mystery invader's words sunk in. A gift of prime real estate would be hard for any university to refuse. No wonder Mr. Berman hadn't been interested in her solution. It didn't address the problem.

"The research you're talking about is important to all of us," blond guy concluded. "Which is why the city's offer is the best one on the table."

Charity forced her attention to Mr. Berman, who was nodding slowly. "You've made some good points, Josh."

"Just showing you a few things you might not have thought of," blond guy said modestly. Blond guy who was apparently named Josh. "Charity's done all the work."

She frowned. He was taking over her nervous system and her meeting and trying to give her credit?

"Not at all," she said, relieved the power of speech had returned. "Who could compete with your excellent points?"

Josh actually winked at her, then reached for the folder on the table. "This is the letter of intent. I think the signing has been put off long enough, don't you, Bernie?"

Mr. Berman nodded slowly, then pulled a pen out of his suit jacket pocket. "You're right, Josh." Then, just like that, he signed the paper, giving Charity the victory she'd so desperately wanted.

Somehow she'd hoped it would be a tiny bit sweeter.

In a matter of minutes, everyone had shaken hands, murmured about setting up the next meeting to get the planning going and left. Charity was alone in the conference room, only the lingering smell of burned plastic and a signed document proof that anything had happened at all. She glanced at the clock. It was 9:17 a.m. At the rate things were happening around here, she could cure several diseases and solve world hunger by noon. Well, not her. So far her accomplishments seemed limited to frying innocent electronics.

She collected the paperwork, went out into the hall and picked up her cold, dead computer. Had it really happened? Had some guy blown into her meeting, saved the day, then disappeared? Like a local super hero or something? And if he was so in the loop, why hadn't he taken care of the problem weeks ago?

There was no way she could have known about a private donation—no matter how much research and prep work she had done. But Charity still had a vague sense of dissatisfaction. She preferred to win through her own actions. Not because of a rescue.

She made her way to her new office on the second floor. She hadn't had much time to get settled, what with moving to Fool's Gold over the weekend and the presentation preparation taking up all her free time. She'd brought in a box of personal items and dumped it on her desk shortly before six that morning. By one minute after six, she'd been in the conference room, going over her presentation, wanting it to be perfect. A complete waste of time, she told herself as she entered the second floor. Between the computer death and the mystery guy, she need not have bothered.

That morning, the open space in the old building had been empty and quiet. Now half a dozen women worked at desks. Doors to offices stood open and the sound of conversation spilled out to create murmured background noise.

She turned toward her office. Her assistant should have arrived, so they could meet face-to-face for the first time. Technically they'd been working together for a couple of weeks now, with Sheryl faxing and e-mailing information to Charity in Nevada.

Charity had visited Fool's Gold during her interview process. She'd met with the mayor and a few members of the city council, and toured the area. She'd never lived in a small town before. The closest she'd come was Stars Hollow, from watching Gilmore Girls while still in college. She'd liked everything about Fool's Gold and had been able to imagine herself putting down roots in the lakeside town. She had even been in this building, had looked around. But apparently she hadn't noticed the giant poster on the wall.

Now she stared into a larger-than-life-size picture of her mystery guy. He smiled down at her, a bicycle helmet under one arm, a tight shirt and bike shorts leaving very little to the imagination. The print underneath the picture proclaimed Josh Golden—Fool's Gold's favorite son.

She blinked, then blinked again. Josh Golden as in the celebrated cyclist Josh Golden? Second youngest winner of the Tour de France and possibly hundreds of other bike races? She'd never followed the bike racing circuit or whatever it was called. She didn't follow any sports. But even she had heard of him. He'd been married to somebody famous—she couldn't remember who—and was now divorced. He endorsed energy drinks and a major athletic brand. He lived here? He'd come to her meeting and had saved the day?

Not possible, she told herself. Maybe she'd fallen and hit her head and now couldn't remember the event. Maybe she was in a coma somewhere, imagining all this.

She walked past the poster and moved toward her office. Just outside the open door, she saw a thirty-something woman on the phone. The woman, dark-haired and pretty, looked up and smiled. "She's here. I gotta go. Love you." The woman stood. "I'm Sheryl, your assistant. You're Charity Jones. Nice to finally meet you, Ms. Jones."

"You, too, and please call me Charity."

Sheryl grinned. "I just heard you got the university to sign. Mayor Marsha will be doing the happy dance. They've been slippery little suckers, but you nailed them."

A flash of movement caught Charity's attention. She glanced over her assistant's shoulder and saw Sheryl's screen saver had come on with a picture show.

The first shot showed Josh Golden on a racing bike. The second showed him shirtless and grinning. The third photo was a very naked guy in a shower, his back to the camera. Charity felt her eyes widen.

Sheryl glanced over her shoulder and laughed. "I know. He's gorgeous. I downloaded these from the Internet. Want me to put them on your computer?"

"Ah, no. Thank you." Charity hesitated. "I'm not sure naked pictures are appropriate for a business office."

"Really?" Sheryl looked confused. "I hadn't thought of that. I guess you're right. I'll take off the shower picture, even though it's my favorite. Have you met Josh? He's what my grandma would call dreamy. I've told my husband if Josh ever comes calling I am so outta here."

So every other woman on the planet also reacted to Josh the way Charity had. Fabulous. Nothing was as thrilling as being part of an adoring crowd, she thought as she made her way into her office.

But it wasn't a problem. She would simply avoid the man until she figured out how to control her reaction to him. She wanted a nice, normal, safe man. Her mother had always been attracted to the Joshes of the world: too handsome and adored by women everywhere. She'd gotten her heart broken regularly and painfully. Charity had been determined to learn from her mother's mistakes.

After putting her dead laptop next to her box of personal

things she had yet to unpack, Charity glanced through the open door toward Sheryl.

"Would you call the mayor and ask if I can stop by and see her this morning?"

Sheryl shook her head. "This isn't the big city, Charity. You can pop in to see Marsha anytime."

"All right. Thank you."

Charity took the folder with the signed letter of intent with her as she walked to the end of the hallway. Mayor Marsha Tilson's office was behind huge carved double doors, both of which stood open.

There was a big desk, two flags—U.S. and State of California—and a small conference table that seated six by the window.

Marsha sat in the small conversation group in the corner. As Charity entered, she saw that Josh was already there, lounging on a sofa, looking breathtakingly handsome and completely at home.

Marsha, an attractive, well-dressed woman in her sixties, smiled and rose to her feet. "We were just talking about you, Charity. You've had a busy morning. Congratulations. Josh here tells me you convinced Bernie to sign the letter of intent."

Charity moved toward them, doing her best to appear friendly without actually looking at Josh. When she made the mistake of meeting his hazel-green eyes, she could have sworn she heard the theme from Gone with the Wind playing softly in the background.

Josh stood and gave her a lazy grin. One that made her toes curl inside her pumps. "We haven't been formally introduced," he said, holding out his hand. "I'm Josh Golden."

She so did not want to shake his hand, given the symptoms she'd already experienced. Actual physical contact might lead to heart failure, or something even more embarrassing. She swallowed, sucked in a breath, then braced herself for it.

His large hand engulfed hers. Sparks even bigger than those that had killed her computer jumped between them. Her stomach flipped, her privates cheered and she half-expected to see fireworks shooting up by the ceiling.

"Mr. Golden," she murmured, withdrawing quickly, then sinking into the seat behind her. She did her best not to think about the fact that, thanks to Sheryl's screen saver, she had now seen his bare butt.

"Josh, please."

And how many women screamed that on a regular basis? she wondered, turning her attention to the much safer mayor.

"Josh is exaggerating my role in the meeting," she said, pleased to find out she could speak in a complete sentence. "He knew about the other offer of land, which was the problem with getting the university to sign. Once that was dealt with, the other problems were easily solved."

"I see." Marsha looked at Josh, who shrugged modestly.

Given the fact that Josh was obviously a famous athlete and comfortable flashing his butt for the camera, she would have expected him to jump at the chance to make himself the star of the moment. Oddly enough, he didn't.

"We have the letter of intent," Charity continued. "I'll have Sheryl set up a meeting to move forward. With the construction bids already in place, we can streamline the process and get the research facility built quickly."

"Excellent." Marsha smiled at her. "Why don't you go get settled? You've had a busy first hour. We'll have lunch tomorrow so you can tell me how it's going."

"Thanks." Charity rose. "Nice to meet you, Josh," she

said, backing away so there was no chance for him to offer to shake hands again.

Once she was safely back in her office, her first order of business would be to give herself a stern talking-to. She had never once, in her whole life, reacted to a man this way. It was beyond embarrassing—it had the potential to interfere with her ability to do her job. She could accept that some flaw in her genetic makeup made her always pick exactly the wrong guy. She didn't like it, and she wouldn't allow herself to act like a freaked-out groupie or sex-starved crazy person when she was around Josh. Fool's Gold was small. They were bound to run into each other. She had to get a grip on herself and her hormones.

There had to be a reasonable explanation, she told herself firmly. She hadn't been sleeping that well. Or she could be missing a B vitamin or not eating enough broccoli. Whatever the cause, she would figure it out and fix it. She refused to live her life all quivery and weak. She was strong. She was self-actualized. She was not going to let a little thing like a gorgeous man with a butt like a Greek god mess up her day.

"WELL?" MARSHA ASKED when Charity had left.

A single word with a thousand meanings, Josh thought grimly. What was it about women and language? They could make a man squirm without putting much effort into the task. A skill he both admired and feared.

"She's smart and fair," he said.

Marsha raised her eyebrows. "You don't think she's pretty?"

He slumped back in the chair and closed his eyes. "Here we go. Why do you feel a compulsion to pair up everyone you meet? I've been married, Marsha. Remember? It didn't go well."

"Not your fault. She was a bitch."

He opened one eye. "I thought you liked Angelique."

"I was concerned that if she stood in the sun, the heat would melt all the plastic she'd had put into her body."

He laughed. "Very much a possibility." His ex-wife had been born beautiful, but hadn't rested until she was extraordinary.

"So you like her," Marsha asked.

He had a feeling they weren't talking about his ex anymore. "Why does my opinion matter?"

"Because it does."

"Fine. I like her. Are you happy?"

"No, but it's a start."

He was used to the matchmaking. It went with the not very subtle invitations. He supposed if a man had to live under a curse, his was easy to live with. Too many women all offering whatever he wanted. Too bad being with them didn't fix what was really wrong with him.

He stood. "I said I'd watch out for her and I will. I don't know what you're worried about. This is Fool's Gold. Nothing bad happens here." Which was why he'd come home. This was a great place to escape. Or it had been. Lately it felt as if his past was catching up with him.

"I want Charity to be happy," Marsha said. "I want her to fit in."

"The longer you don't tell her the truth, the more pissed she's going to be."

Marsha's mouth twisted into a frown. "I know. I'm waiting for the right time."

He crossed to her, bent down and kissed her soft, wrinkled cheek. "There's never a good time, kid. You taught me that."

He straightened and headed to the door.

"You could take her out to dinner," Marsha called after him.

"I could," he agreed as he left.

He could ask out Charity, but then what? In a matter of days she would have heard enough about him to think she knew everything. After that, she would either be eager to find out if all the talk was true, or she would think he was scum on the pond of life. Judging by her sensible shoes and conservative dress, he would guess she would put him on the side of scum.

He crossed through the lobby, ignoring the glass case off to the side, the one containing the yellow jersey he'd won during his third Tour de France race. He stepped out into the sunny morning, then wished he hadn't when he saw Ethan Hendrix getting out of his car. Ethan who had once been his best friend in the world.

Ethan moved with ease. After all this time, the limp was nearly gone. For anyone else, it wouldn't even be worth noting. But Ethan wasn't like everyone else. He'd once been a ranked cyclist. He and Josh were supposed to take on the Tour de France together while they were still in college. They'd spent hours training together, shouting insults back and forth, each claiming he would be the one who would win. After the accident, only Josh had entered, becoming the second youngest winner in the history of the race. Henri Cornet had been younger, by all of twenty-one days, back in 1904.

Ethan looked across the street and their eyes met. Josh wanted to go to his former friend, to tell him that enough time had passed and they both needed to get over it. But despite the phone messages Josh had left, Ethan had never once called him back. Never forgiven him. Not for the accident— Ethan had been at fault. But for what had happened after.

In a way, Josh couldn't blame him. After all, Josh hadn't forgiven himself.

THE NEXT DAY, Charity unpacked her small box of personal items, then dove into her morning. She had brainstormed several ideas to bring businesses to Fool's Gold, and wanted to run them past the mayor. After printing out her preliminary reports, she familiarized herself with the city's cranky e-mail system and was surprised to look up and see the mayor standing in her doorway.

"Is it eleven-thirty already?" Charity asked, not able to believe how quickly the time had flown by.

"You look intense," Marsha said. "Should we delay our lunch?"

"Of course not." Charity pulled her handbag from the bottom drawer of her desk, then stood and straightened her tailored jacket. "I'm ready."

They walked down the wide staircase and out onto the sunny street.

City Hall was in the middle of downtown, with old-fashioned street lights lining the wide sidewalk. There were mature trees, a barber shop and a soda fountain advertising old-fashioned milkshakes. Tulips and crocuses grew in window boxes in front of the various businesses.

"The town is beautiful," Charity said as they crossed the street and headed for the restaurant on the corner. They walked around an open manhole cover where two female city workers set up equipment.

"Quiet," Marsha murmured. "Too quiet."

"Part of the reason you hired me." Charity smiled. "To bring in businesses and with them employment."

"Exactly."

"I've brainstormed some ideas," Charity told her, not sure if this was a working lunch or a get-to-know-you lunch.

"How many of them are run by and employ mostly men?"

Charity paused in front of the restaurant, sure she'd misunderstood the mayor's question. "Excuse me?"

Marsha's dark blue eyes danced with amusement. "I asked about men. Oh, don't get frightened. Not for me. For the town. You haven't noticed?"

Charity slowly shook her head, wondering if the otherwise together mayor had hit her head or taken some questionable medication. "Noticed what?"

"Look around," the mayor told her. "Show me where the men are."

Charity had no idea what she was talking about. Men, as in men?

She slowly scanned the street around them. There were two female city workers, a woman in a postal service uniform delivering mail, a young woman painting a store window.

"I don't see any."

"Exactly. Fool's Gold has a serious man shortage. It's part of the reason I hired you. To bring more men to our town."

CHAPTER TWO

THE FOX AND HOUND RESTAURANT was decorated the an American version of a classic English pub. Deep booths, a long wooden bar and English hunting prints on the wall. Charity was sure it was lovely, and later, when she was able to focus better, she would take it all in. Now all she could do was trail after the mayor as they were led to a quiet table by the window.

Charity took her seat across from the older woman and pressed her lips together. She wasn't going to say a word until Marsha had explained herself.

Marsha began right away. "The problem started years ago. Men left to find better jobs and never came back. That was in my day and for some reason, it's not getting better. The preliminary census numbers are a disaster. When the actual 2010 census comes out, it's going to be a disaster— both in the press and in how the town sees itself. If we don't get some men here for our young women to marry, they'll start leaving, too, and then the town will die. That's not going to happen on my watch."

The mayor sounded fierce as she spoke. And determined.

Charity had reached for her water, mostly to buy time. A man shortage? Was this a joke? Part of a small-town initiation ritual?

"There are plenty of businesses that traditionally employ men," she began slowly. "If you're serious about this."

"I am." Marsha leaned toward her. "Fool's Gold was a gold rush town, founded in the 1870s. It grew and prospered, and when the gold ran out, just after the turn of the century, it started to have problems."

A waitress appeared with menus. She took their drink orders and left.

"Geographically, we're blessed," Marsha continued. "That kept us from disappearing completely. The original ski resort was built in the fifties, the vineyards west of here are at least sixty years old. So far we're holding our own. There are plenty of service industries, some small businesses. Ethan Hendrix owns a construction company that has branched out into windmills, so he brings in a few men, but it's not enough."

Marsha shrugged. "I tell myself I should be thrilled by the women he employs. Equality and all that, but I can't. Men leave here and we don't know why. Topography? A Native curse? It's getting out of hand. The young women in town are having trouble finding husbands. Worse, the few men we do have tend to find their wives elsewhere."

Charity did her best to look both intelligent and interested. "I can see where that would be a difficult situation." Intellectually she understood a growing population was essential for any town to survive. But a lack of men? Seriously? "You've investigated the Native curse issue?" she asked, when she couldn't think of anything else.

Marsha laughed. "The only Natives who lived in the hills weren't the curse type. My thought was if we're bringing in business anyway, how could it hurt to focus on those with traditionally male jobs? Engineering, high tech, a second hospital. Of course hospitals do employ more women, but it would give us a great job base."

Right. Because Charity could simply go online and order

a hospital. She drew in a breath. She needed a little more time to process the information. A man shortage? She'd never heard of anything like that in her life. Not that she could blame the mayor for failing to mention it during the interview process. Talk about an easy way to terrify candidates.

"Over the next couple of days, as you get to know your way around town, I want you to do a mental head count. You'll see for yourself that men are in desperately short supply. My biggest fear is that word will get out somehow. That a reporter somewhere will find out and start doing stories on the town."

"Wouldn't the attention help?"

"This town is special to all of us. We're not interested in being considered an oddity. We just need to balance our population."

Charity thought of Josh Golden. He was shiny enough for three men. Mayor Marsha should marry him off to one of the lonely single women.

"There is a bright spot in all this," Marsha told her with a wink. "As you're the one meeting with the business owners, you'll get first pick of any of the men."

"Lucky me," Charity murmured, grateful the waitress reappeared and interrupted them. Charity wasn't going to share the details of her social life, or lack thereof, with her new boss. And there was no reason to explain that she had been totally unsuccessful in the man department.

While avoiding her mother's penchant for men who were too pretty by far was a good start, it didn't guarantee a happy ending. So far Charity was practically the poster girl for romance disasters.

When they'd finished placing their orders, a curly-haired

well-dressed woman walked up to the table. She was a little taller than Charity, and exuded style and sex appeal.

"So you're the new girl," the twenty-something woman said cheerfully. "Hi. I'm Pia O'Brian, Fool's Gold's own party planner."

Marsha shook her head. "Event coordinator. It sounds better."

"Maybe to you. I like the party aspect of my job." Pia grinned at Charity. "It's nice to meet you."

"You, too."

"I don't actually plan parties," Pia admitted. "I organize the Spring Festival, the Summer Festival, the Fourth of July fireworks."

"And the Fall Festival?" Charity asked.

Pia laughed. "Yes, but that comes after the End of Summer Festival and focuses on books. We're a party crowd here."

"Apparently." The closest Charity had ever come to a town festival had been a craft show back in college. "I look forward to going to the events."

"If only that were all that was involved," Pia said dramatically. "You and I are going to have to talk. I'll call and set up an appointment."

"Should I be nervous?" Charity asked with a laugh.

"No. It'll be fine. Enjoy your lunch," she called over her shoulder as she sailed toward the door.

"She's nice," Charity said. And close to her age. Maybe Pia was a potential friend.

"Just so you know, Pia's a lot more talk than action, at least when it comes to being bad." Marsha shook her head. "Oh, Charity, you're being thrown in the deep end. I hope that's all right."

"I was looking for a challenge," Charity told her. Not to mention a job that was far away from her old one. She'd wanted a fresh start and the job in Fool's Gold had offered exactly that.

"Good. I don't want to scare you away on your first day. Maybe on your second."

Charity laughed. "I don't scare so easy. In fact, this weekend I'm going to drive around and get to know the different neighborhoods in town."

"Thinking of buying a house?"

"Not right away, but in a couple of months. I want to settle down." Having a permanent address and ties to a community had always been her fantasy.

"There are some lovely homes. Although with all the men who will be moving to town, you might want to wait a bit. You did mention you were single. Maybe you'll meet Mr. Right."

"Uh-huh," Charity said and sipped her coffee. Mayor Marsha was very nice, but not the most subtle person.

As for Mr. Right—Charity wasn't looking for perfect. She just wanted a nice guy who loved her as much as she loved him. Oh, and a man who was single, honest and faithful. Characteristics depressingly hard to find on the dating scene—at least in her experience.

"If anyone around town catches your eye," Marsha said as their food was delivered. "Just ask me. I know everyone."

Once again Charity's brain flashed to Josh. Fifteen kinds of physically amazing and a thousand kinds of trouble, she thought grimly. She might not be able to ignore the weird way her body reacted when he was in the room, but she could do her best to ignore him. And she would. Even in a town as small as Fool's Gold, it couldn't be hard.

"You make me crazy. You know that, right?"

Josh continued to study his computer screen and ignore

his assistant. Something he was good at. It came from years of practice.

Unfortunately Eddie wasn't the type to take the hint. "I'm talking to you, Josh."

"I knew that." He turned his attention from the e-mail to his seventy-something assistant who stood with her hands on her hips.

Eddie Carberry wore her white hair in short curls. She liked heavy makeup and velour track suits. She had one for every day of the week. If it was Monday, she was wearing violet.

"They're getting on my nerves," she announced. "What the hell were you thinking? I know you're not sleeping with them, so it's not about sex. Don't tell me you're being nice, either. You know how I hate that." Eddie glared at him as she spoke.

He knew better than to take her temper seriously, just as he knew the "they" in question were the three college-aged girls that were supposed to be helping her in the office.

"You said you wanted to cut back on your responsibilities," he hedged. "You said you wanted a staff."

Eddie rolled her eyes. "I said I wanted to look like Demi Moore, too, but I don't see you doing anything about that. They're not staff, they're blonde and every cliché that goes with the hair color. All they want to talk about is you." She raised her voice. "Josh is just so handsome," she said in a mocking squeak. "Do you think he's going to ask me out?"

She lowered her voice to its normal gravelly tone. "I thought you'd explained everything when you hired them."

He winced. "I did. In detail."

"Then you're going to have to do it again."

Apparently.

Young women had done everything from showing up

in his bed naked and uninvited to claiming to be pregnant with his baby—all in a bid to get his attention. He understood the theory. If they belonged to someone the public perceived as special then they were special, as well. Telling them he wasn't worth their time didn't seem to get through. This summer he'd tried offering jobs instead, thinking the reality of working around him would allow them to see the man behind the myth. So far the plan wasn't working.

"I could get more help out of a couple of cats," Eddie grumbled. "And you know how I feel about cats."

He did. She resented any creature who dared to shed on one of her track suits.

"I'll talk to them," he said.

"You'd better." She lowered her arms to her sides, then walked toward his desk. "The storefront on Third leased out."

He leaned back in his chair as she sat down. "Good." It had been vacant nearly three months.

"The lease is at the attorney's. I'll pick it up later today for you to read." She cleared her throat. "You have a request to ride in a charity race."

"No."

"It's for sick kids."

"It usually is."

"You should do this one."

She was trying to provoke him. For some reason Eddie believed if she could get him to yell, he would give in.

"It's in Florida," she said. "You could go to Disney World."

"I've been to Disney World."

"You need to get out, Josh. Ride again. You can't—"

"Next?" he asked cutting her off.

She stared at him, her eyes narrowed. He stared back. She blinked first. "Fine. Be that way." She sighed heavily, as if her life was nothing but pain. "I keep getting calls about a charity golf tournament. The sponsor has a connection with the ski resort and they're thinking of holding it in town."

Golf he could do. It wasn't his sport, so excellence wasn't expected or required. He could simply be charming for the cameras, raise some money and call it a day.

"Okay on the golf."

"At least that's something," she grumbled. "I'll have the sales figures for the sporting goods store later today. Preliminary numbers are good. The flyers did a nice job of bringing in business. Internet sales are up, too. Now if we could get a picture of you on some of the bikes we carry..."

He ignored her. Which meant looking away. One of the blondes walked by just then and assumed he was glancing at her rather than away from Eddie. The young woman smiled and slowed.

Damn.

Eddie turned and saw the girl. "Get back to work," she snapped. "This isn't about you."

The girl pouted, but did as she was told.

"Did I say they make me crazy?" Eddie asked.

"More than once."

"You need a girlfriend. If they think you're with someone else, they'll back off."

"No, they won't."

"Probably not," she agreed. "I swear, Josh, there's something about you. Women everywhere are just dying to be in your bed."

He winced, not wanting to have this conversation with his septuagenarian assistant.

"I guess the good news is if you'd done it as much as they said, you'd be dead now."

"A cheerful thought," he said dryly.

Eddie stood. "I'll be back later with those numbers."

"I'll count the hours."

She barked a laugh as she left. Josh returned his gaze to the computer screen, but not his attention. The girls in his office were the least of his problems. What kept him up nights wasn't the young women so convinced he was the answer to every prayer they'd ever had. It was the reality of knowing he was a total fraud and no one had seemed to figure that out.

OVER THE NEXT few days Charity continued to learn about her job and meet the rest of the staff. She noticed that every one of them was female, with the exception of Robert Anderson, the treasurer.

"Robert's been with us five years," Marsha said after a meeting on Wednesday, then excused herself to make a call to the county commissioner.

Robert was a nice-looking man in his early thirties. His dark eyes sparkled with amusement as he shook Charity's hand. "You look a little surprised to see me. Is it because I'm a guy? Did the Mayor tell you about our little problem?"

"Yes, which must make you really popular."

He grinned and motioned for her to follow him into his office, where they sat on opposite sides of his desk. "I do okay."

"Did you know about the odds being in your favor when you took the job?"

He chuckled. "No, and I never noticed during my interviews. I was focused on the job, not the surroundings. Not very observant, I guess. About the second week after I moved here, I realized that a lot of women were dropping in to welcome me."

Charity was still having trouble grasping the whole "man shortage" concept. "It's real then—the demographic issue?"

"A very delicate way of putting things. Yes, it's real. I haven't figured out why, not that I put a lot of thought into it. Men don't stay. Or move here. Statistically in an average population, more male babies are born than female babies. It's around one hundred and ten male babies for every one hundred female babies. But more males die before the age of eighteen, and by middle age there are more women in any given population. Except here. There are more females of every age group."

Charity had thought the fried computer and seeing Josh Golden's butt on her assistant's screen saver would be the strangest parts of her week.

"I'm speechless," she admitted. "I don't say that often."

Robert laughed. "It's not that big a deal."

"Not for you. Not only are you one of the precious few, you haven't been instructed to bring in more male-based businesses."

His laugh turned into a wince. "Marsha said that?"

"It was a clear directive." She glanced at Robert's left hand. "Hmm, I don't see a wedding ring there. Why aren't you doing your part for the town by being married?"

He held up both hands, palms facing her. "I tried. I got engaged. We broke things off when we realized we had different ideas about family. I wanted kids, she didn't. She moved to Sacramento."

"One less single female to worry about," Charity murmured, wondering if some TV personality was going to jump out of a closet and tell her she'd been part of an elaborate hoax. As much as she wouldn't enjoy the humiliation, it would be kind of nice to find out the mayor had been kidding about the man thing. Not that she thought her luck was that good.

Then she realized her response to Robert had been slightly less than sensitive. "Oh, wait. I didn't mean to say that. I'm sorry your engagement didn't work out."

He shrugged. "It was a while ago. I'm dating again."

"Are they rejoicing in the streets?"

"There was a parade last week."

"Sorry I missed that. I met Pia O'Brian a couple of days ago. It seems there are a lot of parades in Fool's Gold."

"Festivals," he corrected. "It's our thing. There's one nearly every month. It brings in tourists and the locals seem to love them. Is this your first small town?"

She nodded. "I've mostly grown up in large suburbs, which isn't the same thing. I'm looking forward to the change."

"Just be aware that everyone knows everything about everyone. There aren't any secrets. But I grew up in a place like this. I wouldn't want to be in the big city." He leaned toward her. "We should grab lunch sometime. I could fill you in on small town eccentricities."

Robert was nice, she thought, looking into his dark eyes. Smart, with a good sense of humor. "I'd like that."

She paused, hoping for a slight whisper of anticipation, a quiver or a hint of physical reaction. Something. Anything.

Nothing, she thought with a sigh, refusing to think about her amazing reaction to Josh Golden. It had been a blood sugar thing. Or too much coffee and not enough sleep. Robert was a better choice by far.

She was about to excuse herself when her gaze fell on a plastic toy on Robert's desk. It was a bobblehead and the oversized head looked oddly familiar.

"Is that…"

"Josh Golden," Robert told her. "Have you met him?"

"Um, yes." The man had his own bobbleheads?

"What did you think?" Robert's voice was casual but she thought she saw a flash of something intense in his gaze.

"I didn't have time to think anything," she said, telling herself it was nearly the truth. Not being able to breathe meant fewer functioning brain cells.

"He's pretty famous. A cyclist. Tour de France, and all that."

"I'm not much of a sports fan," she admitted. "Why is he here and not out racing?"

"He retired a while ago. All the women here go crazy for him. He has a reputation for being something of a ladies man. You'll probably fall for him."

Charity stared at Robert. "Excuse me?"

"It's inevitable. No woman is able to resist him."

Talk about a challenge, she thought, a little annoyed. "There must be at least one who's said no."

"I haven't heard of her. But Josh isn't in it for anything but the thrill of the chase."

Some of her pleasure at the conversation faded. "Is that a warning?"

"No. I'd, ah…" He glanced at her. "I'd really like you to be different, Charity."

His gaze was warm, which was nice. She smiled.

"I'll do my best," she said. "I'm not really the groupie type."

"Good."

She stood. "I need to get back to work. It was nice to meet you."

He rose as well. "The pleasure is all mine."

A nice man, she thought as she left. On the surface, everything she was looking for. Of course the handful of other men who had been in her life could have fit that description, as well. But they had all been disasters.

She hadn't come to Fool's Gold to fall in love, she reminded herself. She'd come for a job and to put down roots. Although falling in love with the right guy and getting married would be really nice. Having a family had always been part of her dream.

There was time, she thought as she made her way back to her office. Robert might not make her heart go into arrhythmia, but that could be for the best. She'd learned her lesson several times over. She was going to be completely sensible when it came to her personal life. Sensible and calm and rational. Anything else would just blow up in her face—she was sure of it.

THE REST OF Charity's work week passed quickly. She met more of the city council members—all women—and familiarized herself with ongoing development projects. Sheryl left at four-thirty nearly every day, but Charity worked later. On Thursday, she stayed until nearly seven, when her stomach growled loudly enough to break her concentration. She glanced out her window and was surprised to see that it was dark.

After shutting down her shiny new computer, she collected her handbag, a briefcase filled with files she would review after she had dinner, and left.

The building was quiet and a little spooky. She walked quickly out onto the street where a cool breeze made her wish for a slightly thicker coat. The coldest day of winter in Henderson, a suburb of Las Vegas, had been warmer than this early-spring evening in the foothills of the Sierra Nevada.

Fortunately, the hotel was only a couple of blocks away.

Charity hurried along the sidewalk. When she reached the corner, she saw an old man sweeping the front steps of the bookshop she'd already visited at lunch. He nodded at her, then paused.

"Now, I don't know you," he said, squinting at her in the light from the streetlamp. "Do I?"

His tone was friendly. She smiled.

"I'm Charity Jones, the new city planner."

"Are you now? You're a pretty little thing, aren't you? All young ladies are pretty, even the ones that aren't." He chuckled then gave a wheezy cough. "I'm Morgan. Just Morgan. This is my bookstore."

"Oh. It's wonderful. I've already shopped here twice."

"I must have missed you. Next time we'll talk. You tell me what you like to read and I'll make sure it's in stock."

Talk about small-town service, she thought, delighted. "Thank you. That's very nice."

"My pleasure. You know your way home?"

"I'm staying at Ronan's Lodge."

"That's just down two blocks. I'll stand here and make sure you make it. You turn back and give me a wave when you reach the steps."

His offer was unexpected. She wasn't worried about anything happening between here and the hotel, but it was nice to know that someone would notice if it did.

"Thank you," she said. "You're very kind."

He winked at her. "I've been called a lot of different things, Charity, but I'll accept kind. You have yourself a nice night."

"I will."

She walked the rest of the way to the hotel. Once she reached the steps leading to the lobby, she turned back.

Morgan was watching. She gave a wave and he raised his hand in return. Then he went back to sweeping.

She was going to like it here, she decided. While every place had its quirks, there was a lot to appreciate in Fool's Gold.

She paused before pushing through the double doors leading to the inside of the hotel. They were large and heavily carved, the workmanship from another era.

Ronan's Lodge, also known as Ronan's Folly, was a huge hotel on the edge of the lake. It had been built when gold flowed like the rivers the men panned it from. Ronan McGee, an Irish immigrant, had come west to make his fortune, then he'd spent much of what he'd earned to create the hotel.

Charity had read its history the last time she'd been in town. She'd been unable to sleep the night before her interview and had read all the tourist brochures in her room.

Now, as she walked into the large lobby, with the carved wood panels on the walls and the massive imported chandelier made of Irish crystal, she felt a sense of homecoming. Eventually she would buy a house and settle in to life in Fool's Gold, but Ronan's Lodge was the best kind of temporary housing.

She walked past the registration desk, toward the curved staircase that would take her to the second floor. From there a smaller staircase wound up to the third floor, where she had a small suite.

She'd barely put her hand on the banister, had yet to take even that first step, when someone spoke. The voice came from behind her and spoke only a single word.

"Hello."

She didn't have to look to know who was talking. All

she had to do was stand there, feeling her heart race un-
controllably in her chest as heat and awareness flooded her.

Her week had begun with a Josh Golden invasion and it
seemed it would end that way, as well. The only question
she had as she braced herself before turning to face him
was why, of all the men in all the world, it had to be him.

CHAPTER THREE

CHARITY TURNED TO find Josh standing next to her in the lobby. He was just as tall as she remembered, his tousled hair looking more gold than blond in the flattering light. His hazel-green eyes crinkled slightly at the corners as his mouth curved up in an easy smile. He was very possibly the best-looking man she'd ever seen in person. And hey, she'd seen his naked butt again just a few hours earlier. Talk about making it difficult to concentrate.

"I'm Josh," he said. "We met in the mayor's office."

She nearly choked on a laugh. As if she would forget. "Yes," she said, hoping she sounded calm and completely unaffected by his presence. "Earlier this week. You took over my meeting, then closed the deal. I remember."

"You're not pissed about that, are you?"

She was many things—confused about why her body had to react to him the way it did. Annoyed that he'd had access to information she couldn't get and had therefore done a better job than her at the presentation. Hungry and tired. But she wasn't pissed.

"I'm fine," she assured him. "We needed to get the university to sign and that's what happened. I should probably thank you."

She paused, hoping he would excuse himself to get back to whatever...or whoever...brought him to the hotel. Instead he continued to look at her.

She tried not to feel his gaze, or react to it. A task that took way more effort than it should have.

After a few seconds of staring at him and watching him stare back, she said, "I don't want to keep you from your evening."

"You're not." He pointed to the stairs. "Shall we?"

"Shall we what?"

"Climb. We're neighbors. You're 301, and I'm 303."

He put his hand on the small of her back, as if to guide her up the stairs. Instinctively, she moved with the pressure, refusing to acknowledge the bolts of electricity zigging and zagging in every direction. There was heat radiating from each of his fingers—a heat that made her desperately long for bare skin on skin, an unused closet and fifteen minutes alone with Josh.

Blood sugar, she told herself. She had low blood sugar.

"Why do you live at a hotel?" she asked, mostly to distract herself.

"Why not? It's centrally located, there's room service and someone else makes my bed every morning."

"The ultimate in not taking responsibility for your life?" she asked, then wished she hadn't. So much for a flip answer.

Instead of getting annoyed, Josh chuckled. A low, sexy, appealing sound that made her break out in goosebumps.

"Because taking responsibility is the height of perfection?" he asked.

"It's a sign of maturity."

"A quality that's highly overrated."

For him, she thought grimly. She'd been responsible for taking care of herself since she was nine or ten years old. She'd always envied those who were carefree enough to not have to worry. Those who knew they would be looked after by others. That hadn't been an option for her. Her mother had been the free spirit in the family, leaving Charity to make sure their world ran smoothly.

Charity had always loved her mother and wished she was different in equal measures. Sure it was fun to have a parent who never said you had to go to school or do homework, but there were also times when a kid wanted structure and rules. Charity had learned to provide those for herself.

They reached the third floor. She hurried ahead, wanting to reach her room and escape inside. Somehow, though, he got in front of her and leaned against her door.

"We should have a drink sometime," he said, his hazel-green eyes gazing into hers and making every cell in her body sigh in appreciation.

"I'm not sure spending time with a man who cheerfully declares himself to be immature and irresponsible is a good thing."

The low chuckle came again. "I'm not as bad as all that."

"Aren't you?"

He turned in a slow circle. "Look. I'm completely normal. Practically boring."

He was many things, but boring wasn't one of them.

Before she could point that out, his door opened. A beautiful blonde wearing one of his shirts and nothing else looked at him.

"Hello, Josh. I thought I heard your voice."

Josh straightened. Charity took advantage of the distraction to slip into her room and carefully lock the door behind her. She leaned against the wall for a few seconds before bending over and turning on a lamp.

As light flooded the small but elegantly furnished living room, she ignored the sense of defeat knotting in her stomach and told herself she wasn't even surprised. Of course a guy like Josh would have a woman waiting in his room. They probably came in shifts. From everything she'd heard, he loved women and they loved him back.

She squared her shoulders. Even if she couldn't control her physical reaction to him, she could control what she did about it, which would be exactly nothing.

BY FRIDAY CHARITY was more comfortable in the old City Hall building and had learned the name of nearly everyone who worked there.

Her eleven o'clock meeting was with Pia O'Brian, something she'd been looking forward to ever since Sheryl had put it on her calendar.

Pia arrived right on time, her brown curly hair tumbling past her shoulders, her well-cut suit emphasizing her long legs.

"How are you settling in?" Pia asked as Charity led her to the small conference table by the window. "Ready to run screaming back to the big city?"

"I like it here. Small-town life suits me."

"You say that now," Pia said, her voice teasing. She set a stack of folders on the table. "Give it a few months, when you realize everyone in town knows your business and they're not afraid to talk."

Charity laughed. "My life isn't that interesting. Why would anyone care?"

"You're new. Fresh gossip for the ladies in town. Just remember—there aren't any secrets. Not for long."

"Thanks for the warning." She eyed the folders. "Light reading?"

"I like to think the information won't put you to sleep, but I can't guarantee that." Pia tapped the pile. "These are recaps of the last two years' worth of festivals, celebrations and general civic good times. The Fourth of July parade, the Christmas Lights Fantasy Night, that sort of thing. The ever-popular Gold Rush Days. If it needs a booth of any kind and it's happening in Fool's Gold, I'm probably involved. Or at the very least, offering advice. So if you ever need two thousand folding chairs at a great price, see me first."

"I hope I never do," Charity murmured.

"Not planning a big wedding?"

"Not dating."

"Me, either."

"I'm new in town," Charity told her. "What's your excuse?" She couldn't imagine Pia being without a man. She was so pretty and outgoing.

"A total lack of men," Pia said cheerfully. "I'm sure Marsha explained that you need to focus on male-based businesses. The last thing we need around here is a beauty college. I do my best with male-oriented events. Golf tournaments, car shows." Pia both looked and sounded serious.

Charity couldn't help laughing. "I know this is a big deal, but you have to admit, it's really strange."

"Tell me about it. There were ten percent more girls than guys in my high school graduating class. That made prom time very ugly."

"Not that you went without a date."

Pia shrugged. "No, but a couple of my friends had to import guys for the dance. Very humiliating."

"You grew up here?"

Pia hesitated, then nodded. "Born and raised. Third generation. Or is it fourth? I can never remember. My parents moved away years ago, but I stayed. The last of the O'Brians in Fool's Gold." She grinned. "It's a lot of responsibility."

"Apparently." Charity leaned toward her. "Living here

all your life must be great. I moved around constantly when I was growing up. My mom didn't like to settle, but it was all I dreamed about. Getting to know everything about a place, putting down roots. You're lucky."

Something flickered in Pia's eyes. "The disadvantage is that whole lack of secrets thing. Everyone knows everything about you. Sometimes I think it would be very nice to be able to walk down the street without anyone knowing who I was."

"It can be lonely."

"So can small-town life." Pia shook her head. "Okay, enough with the philosophy and back to business. I have this year's festival schedule for you to look over. Depending on what kind of business you're courting, you might want to invite a few executives and their families to experience small-town life. Or better yet, single male executives. We're at our best during the festivals. All friendly and spruced up."

Charity scanned the list. "When is the town not spruced up? There's something nearly every month."

"That's not even everything," Pia continued. "There are also various charity events. We were going to have a bike race, but that keeps getting pushed off."

Bike race? As in Josh Golden's territory? Charity thought about asking but was afraid Pia would think the question implied interest.

"There are the charity golf tournaments," Pia continued. "We have a great golf course. Several, actually, but the pro course is well known. Don't ask me why—I don't do the golf thing. And I'm not big on the celebrities themselves. Too high-maintenance."

"Good to know," Charity murmured. "So you won't be looking there for a husband."

Pia laughed. "I'm not sure I'm the marrying kind. I don't even know if I want kids. I'm still at the keeping-a-plant alive stage of my life. Next, I'll consider getting a pet."

"At least you have a plan."

"I'll let you know how it works out for me."

They went through the rest of the festival event schedule. Charity promised to look over the material and let Pia know if she had any questions.

Pia collected her purse and briefcase and stood. "I'm glad you took the job, Charity. I know you were Marsha's number one choice for it. Which is saying something because numbers two and three were single guys."

"I'm all the more appreciative."

"As you should be." Pia laughed. "By the way, there's a group of women who get together a couple times a month. Sort of a girls' night out. Want me to call you the next time we get together?"

"Yes. Thanks. I'd really like that."

"Then I'll be in touch." Pia gave a little wave and left.

Charity returned to her desk, where she could see the stack of folders she would be carrying home that evening for review. She'd been so busy with her job that she hadn't had time to turn on the TV in her hotel room. Probably not a bad thing. Although a case could be made that a social life would be nice.

Instead of thinking of Robert, a perfectly pleasant and normal single guy, her brain immediately flitted to Josh. The man who had been hitting on her while his nightly entertainment waited in his room. Talk about tacky.

At least a girls' night out would be fun and a chance to make friends in town. Over the weekend, she could start exploring the area, maybe find out if the local community college had interesting classes on things like cooking or knitting. She needed to get out more.

She noted on her calendar to get a catalog, then turned to her computer. But before she could read her e-mail, there was a knock on her open door.

Charity glanced up to see a forty-something woman wearing a dark blue police uniform walk into her office.

"Alice Barns," the woman said as she crossed to the desk and shook Charity's hand firmly. "Fool's Gold's Chief of Police. Thought I'd come introduce myself."

Charity motioned to the chair on the other side of her desk. "I'm glad you did. It's nice to meet you." She tilted her head and smiled. "What should I call you?"

The other woman grinned. "Chief Barns in front of the press or my men. Alice when we're off the clock."

"Good to know."

"How are you settling in?" Alice asked.

"It's been a busy week. Lots to learn. So far, I adore the town."

"It's a good place to live," Alice told her. "Not a lot of crime. A few teenagers thinking they're smarter than they are. The occasional break-in at one of the vacation rentals. Tourists speeding. Nothing my force can't handle." She shifted in her seat. "There might be a new homeless person in town."

"Why do you say that?"

"Someone's stealing from the local grocery stores. Mostly snacks and convenience foods. A few toiletries. Not to worry. We'll find out who's doing it and put a stop to the stealing."

While Charity hated the thought of someone going hungry, she understood that local businesses didn't want to be paying for shoplifters.

"You plan to go exploring around town?" Alice asked.

"Yes. I want to get to know the area."

"Good idea. Just a word of caution. The abandoned mines are dangerous. Don't go slipping past the fencing and try to hike down."

"I'm not much of a hiker," Charity admitted.

"You'd be surprised how many people try it. They think an old, dangerous mine sounds romantic. If I had my way, we'd leave 'em lost and let natural selection work things out for us. But Mayor Marsha feels we need to show the tourists a good time, regardless of how stupid they are."

Charity couldn't help laughing. Alice's lips twitched.

"Not that I would say that to the mayor," Alice murmured.

"Probably for the best."

Alice rose. "Well, that's about it. We have zero tolerance for drunk driving, but you're not the type to try, so I won't lecture you."

Charity stood and joined the chief on the other side of the desk. "How can you tell I wouldn't do that?"

"Am I wrong?"

"No, but you sound sure."

"I'm a pretty good judge of character."

They walked out together.

On the main floor of the building Chief Barns shook hands with her again.

"You have any problems, you get in touch with me or anyone in my office," Alice told her. "Mayor Marsha is very impressed with you and your work and that's good enough for me."

Charity felt herself flush a little at the compliment. "Thank you. I'll do my best to stay out of trouble."

"I know you will."

The chief put on her blue cap and walked out onto the sidewalk. Charity watched her go. She'd meant her staying out of trouble comment to be a joke, but Alice had taken it seriously. As if she knew that Charity always did the right thing. She was just that kind of person.

Which was a good thing, right? She'd never believed that bad girls had more fun.

"Alice trying to scare you?"

She turned and saw Robert coming down the stairs.

"I liked her."

"Wait until she pulls you over for speeding. She can be very intimidating. She has three sons. They play football in high school, so they tower over her. But I swear they all tremble in her presence."

Charity chuckled. "That could be more a mom thing than a police thing."

"You're probably right." He paused. "I'm heading out to San Francisco this weekend, to meet up with friends. But I wanted to know if you'll be free next weekend for dinner."

Dinner with Robert. It sounded…nice.

"I'd like that," she said.

"Great. We'll firm up the day and time during the week." He glanced at his watch. "I need to get going, if I'm going to be in San Francisco on time."

"Sure. Enjoy your time with your friends."

"I will."

He left through a side door that led to the employee parking lot.

Dinner with Robert would be a very pleasant way to spend an evening, she told herself, then winced. Pleasant? Couldn't she do better than that? So what if she didn't feel sparks when she was around him? Sparks were dangerous, not to mention highly overrated. Better substance than flash.

She returned to the second floor, but before she got all the way to her office, Sheryl came running out to meet her.

"You're going to be late," her assistant told her. "You'd better hurry."

"For what? I don't have any more meetings today."

"You have one now." Sheryl sounded delighted. "Marsha called a little bit ago and put it on your calendar. I'm beyond jealous. Not that I need a tour, but still. I wish it were me."

Charity didn't like the sound of that. "What's the meeting?"

"Josh is coming here to show you around town!" Sheryl's eyes brightened with excitement. "Just the two of you, alone. It would make all my fantasies come true. Well, not all of them, of course, but at least the ones I can talk about."

Time with Josh? "Why would Marsha set something like that up? I can find my way around town on my own."

"This is with Josh! You're so lucky. Marsha is doing you a really big favor."

Charity privately thought she didn't need those kinds of favors, but she wouldn't say that to Sheryl. Not only was the mayor her boss, but she had to assume Marsha was simply trying to be nice. It wasn't as if Charity could confess her total lack of control whenever Josh was within twenty feet of her.

Her reaction to him was bad enough, but being a cliché made everything even worse. Apparently every woman in town reacted the same way. The poor man, so overwhelmed by female interest. It was amazing he got anything done in a day. She frowned. Maybe he didn't. For all she knew, he sat around and lived on his racing proceeds and naked-butt-picture royalties.

None of which mattered, she reminded herself. She had a meeting to get through.

"When am I supposed to meet him?" she asked Sheryl.

"Now," a low male voice said from beside her.

The sudden explosion of her heart speed took her breath away. Her thighs trembled and she watched the world narrow to a single person illuminated by an almost otherworldly light.

What was it about him that got her entire body in on the conspiracy to betray her? It had to be chemistry, or a deficiency on her part. Nutritional or possibly mental. Maybe if she went to the gym more. Or at all.

"Hello," she said, going for calm and hoping she made it. "Nice to see you again. I understand we have a meeting scheduled."

"Marsha thought I should show you the town."

"Isn't she the best?" Charity asked, trying not to clench her teeth. "And while I appreciate the thought, I'm pretty good at finding my own way around Fool's Gold, so if you have something else you need to get to…"

He didn't take the hint. Instead he smiled. "You're my only priority."

He was teasing, she told herself. He had to be. Yet there was something about the way he spoke the words that made her want to moan…or purr.

"Oh, my," Sheryl breathed.

Charity looked at her. Sheryl grinned unapologetically before returning to her desk.

Charity tugged on the hem of her conservative tweed jacket. "Fine. Good. Then we'll take our tour." She hesitated. "We're not riding bikes, are we?"

His perfect mouth curved into a knowing smile. "You've been talking about me."

Charity didn't like the sound of that. It implied an interest she absolutely refused to acknowledge. "You're difficult to avoid, what with the posters, screen savers and bobbleheads."

"Which is your favorite?"

She immediately thought of the picture on Sheryl's screen saver—the one showing Josh in the shower. Naked. His back to the camera.

"I haven't given it any thought," she lied. "Can I get back to you?"

"I can't wait to hear the answer."

"I'll bet. Does your ego ever get too big to carry around?"

The grin widened. "Sure. That's why I have fans. To help with the heavy lifting."

Impossible man, she thought, trying not to laugh. She pointed to the door. "Let's get this over with."

"Don't pretend this isn't the highlight of your day."

"Are you always so sure of yourself?"

He held open the door. "It's part of my charm."

She was sure it was—which meant she was in serious trouble.

CHAPTER FOUR

JOSH LED THE way to a shiny black SUV. A really big one that required a step to make it into the passenger seat. Charity was grateful that her simple navy dress hung past her knees and wasn't very fitted. The style allowed her to make the climb without flashing any of the good citizens who might be watching.

Josh climbed in next to her, moving with the easy grace of an athlete. He rested his arm on the console between them and leaned close. Too close. With her first breath, she caught the scent of his body—a warm and masculine smell designed to melt the last barrier between her good sense and a free-for-all begging for attention.

He was exactly like the men who had drifted in and out of her mother's life, she thought, determined not to be sucked into the same pain and heartbreak she'd seen countless times. Showy men were nice to look at, but horrible bets when it came to relationships. How many times had her mother had her heart broken? Ten? Twenty? It seemed as if every few months she found someone new. Someone perfect and shallow who promised everything, then left her shattered.

Charity wanted happily-ever-after. And normal. Something Josh could never be.

"What would you like to see?" he asked, his voice low and slightly suggestive.

She forced herself to stare out the front of the SUV and told herself she was desperately bored. There were a thousand things that needed her attention back in her office. Phone calls to be made, plans to be started, lists to be reviewed. Nothing about her time with Josh was the least bit interesting.

Charity sighed. At least when she lied to herself, there was no one to call her on it. "You're the local," she said. "I'll let you pick the route."

"Fair enough, but you're going to need to put on your seatbelt."

She reached for the strap. "Because it's the law, right? We're not going up a mountain or anything."

He chuckled. "Not on a first date. I like to save the intense stuff for later. To make sure you can handle it."

She wanted to point out this wasn't a date, but that would require speaking and his verbal play had left her throat a little dry.

The man was charm personified, she thought, wondering if it was a God-given gift or something he had to work at. With her luck, he was a natural. He probably didn't even know what he was doing to the women around him. Not that she would tell him.

He pulled into the street, then rolled to a stop at the light on the corner. "You take the interstate into town?" he asked.

"Yes."

"See much of the area since you arrived?"

"Just what I've walked to. I've only been in town a couple of weeks. There hasn't been much time."

"You don't get weekends off?"

"I spent my first weekend getting ready for the meeting with the university." She grimaced as she thought of how that morning had been a disaster until Josh had breezed in, spoken a few magic words and saved the day. Not that she was upset to have the contract signed. It was just that he'd made her feel bad at her job. Or maybe she'd done that all by herself.

"Last weekend, I was getting ready for my meetings this week."

"I sense a pattern," he said. "You need to get out more."

Was he offering? She desperately wanted him to be offering. Which was silly, because she would have to say no to any kind of offer from him. The man wasn't good for her sanity. Plus, hello. There'd been a woman waiting in his room the other night. A close-to-naked woman obviously expecting her evening to take a turn for the erotic. Josh was a player and Charity had never understood the rules of the game.

Note to self, she thought. She would look Josh up on the Internet when she got back to her room that night. Any kind of crush should be destroyed by the reality of his personal life.

"I plan to be in Fool's Gold for a long time," she said. "I'll see it all eventually."

He turned two blocks before the sign for the interstate, then headed west. "There are three different wineries growing grapes in the valley," he said, pointing to the acres of vineyards sprawling to the horizon. "Mostly cabernet sauvignon, merlot and cab franc. Some other grapes for blending."

He flashed her a smile. "Which takes us to the limit of my wine knowledge. If you want to know more, they do tours every weekend, starting in a couple of weeks."

As they sped down the highway, Charity could see tiny buds on the bare branches—the promise of grapes to come.

"Most of the wineries were started years ago," he continued. "This whole valley used to grow everything from corn to apples. Gradually the vineyards are taking over. Something about the soil and the weather."

"And money," she said. "For a lot of farmers, there's more profit in grapes. Wine is very big these days."

He glanced at her. "Impressive."

She did her best not to blush. "I did my homework before I moved here." She cleared her throat. "The wineries are closer to town than I realized," she said, turning back to see the mountains rising against the blue sky. She reached into her purse and pulled out a small notepad.

"What a great resource. Any company thinking of relocating here needs to be taken on a tour of the area," she said more to herself than him. "This is a great selling point."

There had to be some kind of brochure the town used to promote itself. She made another note to review it when she got back and make sure the wineries and vineyards were prominently mentioned. Maybe look over Pia's schedule. There had to be a wine or grape festival.

"The wineries are just part of it," Josh told her. "There's also hiking and camping in the summer and skiing in the winter. The resort has a five-star restaurant and a cooking school. We get plenty of tourists coming through."

"You know a lot about the area. How long have you been here?" she asked.

"I grew up here. Moved to the area when I was ten."

"That must have been nice," she said enviously. "When I was a kid I dreamed of staying in one place, but my mom liked to travel."

Josh glanced at her. Something questioning flashed through his eyes, then was gone. "Did she say why?"

"She had a lot of reasons. She liked the thrill of a new place. The possibilities. She used to say she was born wanting to move on." Part of the motive to move had always been to escape from anything bad that had happened before, Charity thought. Which was mostly a man, and the end of a relationship.

Charity had loved her mother, but the constant moving around hadn't been easy. Especially because Sandra moved whenever the mood struck her. She didn't care if Charity was only a few weeks from finishing a semester or a school year. "I grew up being the new girl."

"Was that a problem?"

"I wasn't outgoing. By the time I'd made a few friends and settled in, we were moving again. I felt like I was always scrambling to learn the rules."

"You'll like Fool's Gold."

"I already do. Everyone is so friendly and open."

He made a couple of turns, then they were heading back toward the mountains.

Charity found herself relaxing a little. Being close to Josh wasn't so scary—not if she remembered to keep breathing and ignore the steady hum of awareness that connected them. At least from her side.

A bright red import came toward them. The car was filled with college-aged girls who rolled down the windows and hooted and waved at Josh. He nodded back.

"Fans?" she asked, watching the car zip past.

"Probably."

She risked turning toward him. "It's the bike thing, right?"

His mouth twitched as if he were trying not to smile. "Yeah. The bike thing."

"Because you're a famous bike rider?"

"Me and Lance Armstrong."

"So you've ridden in the Tour de France?"

He glanced at her, his humor obvious. "Do you even know what that is?"

"It's, ah, a famous bike race. In France. It's done in parts or stages or legs or something. And there's a yellow jersey."

"Good start." His voice was teasing. "It's stages, by the way."

"I'm not really that into sports. But from what I've heard, you're very impressive."

He raised his eyebrows, but didn't say anything.

"Do you make a good living at that? The bike riding?"

"You can. Prize money can be substantial. A top rider can pull in over a million."

"Dollars?"

"Tour de France pays in Euros."

"Right." She was feeling a little sick to her stomach.

"Endorsements bring in the big money. Multimillion dollar deals." He glanced at her. "They pay in dollars. Or yen."

A million here, a million there. Did currency really matter? "So you were successful?"

"A case could be made."

"And worth millions?"

"On a good day."

Because the sexual appeal, incredible body and handsome face weren't enough.

"What are you doing here?" she asked.

"In the SUV or in Fool's Gold?"

"Either. Both."

"I'm showing you the area because Marsha asked me and I'm in Fool's Gold because I live here. I've retired from racing."

She shifted to face him. "Retired? You're barely in your thirties."

"It's a young man's sport."

How young? Retired? That didn't seem possible. She wondered if he'd been injured. Not that she would ask. It seemed too personal.

"What do you do now?"

"This and that. I keep busy. I have a few things going on in the area."

They were back in town. Josh drove around the lake. There were small hotels, a couple of B&Bs, restaurants and vacation homes. Across the street were the boutiques, a bakery and an open, grassy park.

"Angelo's has great Italian food," he said, pointing to the entrance to a large restaurant. "Margaritaville has the best Mexican food."

"Named after the Jimmy Buffet song?"

"Unfortunately, yes. Avoid the extra shot with the margaritas unless you're a professional. It'll knock you on your butt."

"Thanks for the tip. I'm more a single glass of wine kind of girl."

He mentioned several other restaurants, a couple of bars and the drive-in with the best fries and shakes anywhere. All of which made her happy she'd taken the job in Fool's Gold. If only she'd been able to grow up in a place like this, she thought wistfully. But her mother would have hated everything about the town. Especially the close ties.

Her mother liked to come and go as she pleased, always looking for new adventures—especially where men were concerned. Charity had learned early not to expect any one guy to stick around for long. They were always moving through, too.

She'd vowed her life would be different. That she would find someone special, get married and be with that person forever. So far, she hadn't been very successful in that department but she was determined to keep trying.

Rather than dwell on her sucky love life, she asked, "Did you ever have any bike races in town?"

"No. There was some talk, but nothing was arranged." He glanced out the window.

"What about a charity event? To raise money for kids?"

"I don't ride anymore."

"At all?"

He shook his head.

She thought he would continue to circle the large lake, but instead he made a few turns and before she realized where they were, he'd pulled up in front of City Hall. Their time together had ended abruptly, as if she'd done something wrong.

When he didn't turn off the engine, she got the hint.

"Thanks for the tour," she said, feeling awkward. "I appreciate you taking the time."

"No problem."

She hesitated, wanting to say something else, then got out of the SUV. He drove off without a word.

She stood on the sidewalk, staring after him. What had just happened? What had she said? She felt oddly guilty and wasn't sure why.

"Because the hormones weren't enough of a complication," she murmured with a sigh.

THE NIGHT WAS COOL, the sky clear. There wasn't any moonlight to illuminate the road, but that didn't bother Josh. He knew every bump, every curve. There was no danger from other riders because he rode alone. He had to. It was the only way to work through his issues.

As he headed up the incline, he pedaled harder, faster,

wanting to increase his heart rate, wanting to feel the blood pumping through his body, wanting to exhaust himself so maybe, just maybe, he would sleep.

The darkness surrounded him. At this speed the only sound was the wind in his ears and the tires on the pavement. His skin was cold, his shirt wet with sweat. Goggles protected his eyes, the helmet was snug on his head. He sped over the top of the hill and onto the straight five-mile stretch that led back to town.

This was the only part of his ride he didn't like. There was nothing to distract him, nothing to keep his mind busy, so he had time to think. To remember.

Without wanting to, he was back in Italy, at the Milan–San Remo, or as the Italians referred to it, la Classica di Primavera. The Spring Classic.

A sprinter's dream race, but deadly for the sprinter who wasn't prepared for the hills. It was one of the longest single-day races. Two hundred and ninety-eight kilometers, or one hundred and eighty-five miles. That year Josh had been in the best shape of his life. He couldn't lose.

Maybe that's what had gone wrong, he thought grimly as he rode faster and faster. The gods had decided such arrogance had to be punished. Only he hadn't been the one struck down.

A bike race was all about sensation. The sound of the crowd, of the peloton—the pack of racers—and of the bike. The feel of the road. The burn of muscles, the ache of a chest sucking in air. A racer was either ready or not. It came down to talent, skill, determination and luck.

He'd always been lucky. In life, in love—or at least in lust—and in racing. That day he'd been luckiest of all.

That's what the photographs showed. As fate, or luck, would have it, someone had been taking a series of pictures of the race just as the crash had occurred. There, in single-frame clarity, was the sequence. The first bike to go down, the second.

Josh hadn't been in the lead. He'd been holding back deliberately, letting the others exhaust themselves.

Frank had been young, early twenties, his first year racing professionally. Josh had done his best to mentor the kid, to help him out. Their coach had told Frank to do whatever Josh did and he wouldn't get into trouble.

Their coach had been wrong.

The still photographs didn't capture the sound of the moments, he thought as he rode faster. The first guy to go down had been on Josh's right. Josh had felt more than heard what had happened. He'd sensed the uneasiness in the pack and had reacted instinctively, going left then right in an effort to break away. He'd only thought about himself. In that second, he'd forgotten about Frank. About the inexperienced kid who would do what he did. Or die trying.

They'd been going around forty-two miles an hour. At that speed, any mistake was a disaster. The pictures showed the bike next to Frank's slamming into him. Frank had lost control and gone flying into the air. He'd hit the pavement, going forty miles an hour. His spine severed, his heart still pumping blood through ripped arteries, and he'd died in seconds.

Josh didn't remember what had made him look back, breaking one of the firmest rules of racing. Never look back. He'd seen Frank go flying with an unexpected grace, had—for a single second—seen the fear in his eyes. Then the body of his friend had hit the ground.

There had been silence then. Josh was sure the crowd had screamed, that the other riders had made noise, but all he'd heard was the sound of his own heartbeat in his ears.

He'd turned back, breaking the second rule of racing. He'd jumped off his bike and run to that kid lying so very still. But it was already too late.

Josh hadn't raced since. He couldn't. He'd been unable to train with his team members. Not because of what they'd said, but because being in the peloton made him nearly explode with fear.

Every time he got on his bike, he saw Frank's body lying there. Every time he started to pedal, he knew he would be next, that the crash was coming any second. He'd been forced to take a leave of absence, then retire. He gave the excuse that he was making way for the younger team members, but he suspected everyone knew the truth. That he didn't have the balls for it anymore.

Even now, he only rode alone, in the dark. Where no one could see. Where no one would be hurt but him. He faced his demons privately, taking the coward's way out.

Now, as the lights of town grew closer and brighter, he slowed. Bit by bit, the ghosts of the past faded until he was able to draw in breath again. The workout was complete.

Tomorrow night he would do it all again: ride in the gloom, wait for the final stretch, then relive what had happened. Tomorrow night he would once again hate himself, knowing that if he'd only been in front that day, Frank would still be alive.

He pulled off the main road to a shed behind the sporting goods store he owned. He went inside and drank deeply from the bottle of water he'd brought. Then he removed his helmet and pulled on jeans and a shirt, replacing his cycling shoes with boots.

He was sweaty and flushed as he made his way back to the hotel. If anyone saw him, he or she would assume he was returning from an evening rendezvous, which was fine with him.

As for being with a woman...he hadn't. Not in nearly a year. After his divorce, he'd slept around some, but there'd been no pleasure in it. Not for him. It was as if he wasn't allowed to experience anything good. Penance for what had happened to Frank.

He walked back to the hotel. He would order room service, take a shower and hope that tonight he could sleep.

Once in the lobby, he avoided making eye contact as he made his way to the stairs.

"Hey, Josh. Anyone I know?"

Josh glanced toward the speaker and waved, but kept on walking. He didn't want to have a conversation with anyone right now.

He sensed someone coming down the stairs as he went up. He glanced to his left and saw Charity. For once she wasn't in one of her old lady dresses and boxy jackets. She'd topped jeans with a pink sweater. He had a brief impression of long legs, a narrow waist and impressive breasts before his gaze moved higher to meet her frosty stare.

He liked Charity—found her attractive, smart and funny. Under other circumstances, if he were someone else, he would want her.

No—that wasn't right. He did want her. If things were different, he would do something about it, but he couldn't. She deserved better.

He knew what she was thinking, what everyone thought. Better that than the truth, he told himself as he flashed her a smile and kept on moving.

CHARITY HATED FEELING STUPID, especially when she had no one to blame but herself. She'd spent the weekend buried in work because it was the only way to stop thinking about Josh. Every time she wasn't distracted, she faced a brainful of questions, all designed to make her spiral into girl craziness.

She was fascinated by him in a way that was unexpected, unfamiliar and a teeny bit obsessive. That was fine. It happened. Eventually she would get over it. During their tour of the city the previous Friday, she'd found herself actually enjoying spending time with him. She'd found him funny and charming, which was good. Having a person inside of her crush was helpful.

But something had happened on their drive. He'd changed and she was frustrated by the feeling that she'd done something wrong. She hadn't. She knew that in her head. But try telling her active hormones that. They'd spent the entire weekend sighing dramatically, longing for just a glimpse of the man in question. Worse, Friday night he'd strolled back into the hotel looking all hot, sweaty and sexy. Which meant he'd been with someone else. Even going online and seeing dozens of pictures of him with other women hadn't helped at all.

She could understand feeling boy crazy if she was in high school, but she was twenty-eight years old. An age when one could reasonably expect some slight maturity. After all, she had plenty of romantic disasters in her past from nice, normal men. Men she'd thought she could trust. If she'd been so desperately wrong with them, falling for Josh would be nothing short of idiotic.

Shortly before ten o'clock on Monday morning, Charity filled her coffee cup and made her way to the large conference room on the third floor for her first city council meeting.

There were already about a dozen people sitting around

the large table, all of them women except for Robert. She greeted the mayor, smiled at Robert, then took a seat.

Marsha winked at her. "We're a little less formal than most council sessions you will have attended, Charity. Don't judge us too harshly."

"I won't. I promise."

"Good. Now who don't you know?" Marsha went around the table, introducing everyone.

Charity paid attention, doing her best to remember everyone's name. Pia rushed in a minute before ten.

"I know, I know," she said with a groan. "I'm late. So find someone else to plan the parties around here." She sank into the chair next to Charity. "Hi. How was your weekend?" she whispered.

"Good. Quiet. Yours?"

Pia started passing out slim folders with a picture of the American flag on the front. "I worked on the plans for Fourth of July. I was thinking we could mix it up this year. Have the parade and party on the eighth."

Alice, the police chief, rolled her eyes, but the woman next to her, someone Charity thought might be named Gladys, gasped.

"Pia, you can't. It's a national holiday with a tradition going back more than two hundred years."

"She's kidding, Gladys," Marsha said, then sighed. "Pia, don't try to be funny."

"I don't try. It just happens spontaneously. Like a sneeze."

"Get a tissue and hold it in," Marsha told her firmly.

"Yes, ma'am." Pia leaned toward Charity. "She's so bossy these days. Even Robert's afraid."

Charity's gaze moved to Robert who looked more amused than frightened. He glanced at her and smiled.

She smiled back, hoping for a hint of a reaction. A flicker. A whisper. A slight pressure that could be interpreted as a tingle.

There was nothing.

"We have quite a bit of business to get through this morning," Marsha said. "And a visitor."

"Visitors," another woman said. "That always makes me think of that old science fiction miniseries from years ago. The Visitors. Weren't they snakes or lizards underneath their human skin?"

"As far as I can tell, our visitor is human," Marsha said.

The mayor was obviously a woman with infinite patience, Charity thought as the meeting continued to spiral from one subject to another.

"Now about the road repaving by the lake," Marsha said. "I believe someone prepared a report."

They worked their way through several items on the agenda. Charity gave a brief rundown on the meeting with the university and the fact that the letter of intent had been signed. Pia talked about the Fourth of July celebration that would indeed be held on the appropriate date, then a five-minute break was called.

Robert rose and left. The door had barely closed behind him when Gladys leaned across the table toward Charity.

"You were out with Josh the other day."

Charity didn't know if the words were a statement or an accusation. "We, ah… He took me on a tour of the city. The mayor suggested it."

Marsha smiled serenely. "Just trying to make you feel welcome."

"You don't send Josh to see me," Gladys complained.

"You're already comfortable in town."

"How was it?" another woman asked. She was petite,

in her mid-forties and pretty. Renee, maybe? Or Michelle. Something vaguely French, Charity thought, wishing she'd actually written down the names as people said them.

"I really enjoyed seeing the area," Charity said. "The vineyards are so beautiful."

"Not the tour," Renee/Michelle said. "Josh. You're single, right? Wow, how I would love to spend some quality time with him."

"Sometimes at night I see him walking around town all hot and sweaty," Gladys said, a slight moan in her voice.

"I know," someone else added.

Renee/Michelle glanced toward the door, as if checking to see if Robert was within earshot. "Once, he came to the spa." She turned to Charity. "I run a day spa in town. You should come in for a massage sometime."

"Um, sure." She couldn't believe they were actually talking about Josh this way.

"He wanted me to wax him." Renee/Michelle turned back to Charity. "They all get waxed. It cuts down on air friction." She turned her attention back to the group. "He was on the table, wearing these tiny little briefs. Man, oh man, all I can say is that the rumors about his equipment are not exaggerated."

Renee/Michelle sagged back in her chair and sucked in a breath. "That night my husband got the best sex of his life and he never knew why." She fanned herself with her hand.

Robert walked back into the room, a can of soda in his hand. He looked around the table, then sighed. "You're talking about Josh, aren't you?"

Charity resisted the urge to squirm in her seat.

"Of course," Pia said. "We can't help it."

Charity wanted to snap that he was just one guy and not

all that, but she was afraid she would sound like she had something to hide.

"He's the man," Robert said with a shake of his head.

"Some big investor back east came here and wanted to open a bike school or training camp," Gladys said. "Josh wouldn't do it. He said he wouldn't exploit his fame that way."

Most of the women in the room sighed.

Charity privately thought he probably hadn't done it because being involved would cut into the hours he spent getting laid. If anyone here was special, it was Robert, not Josh. Robert was a regular guy, doing an honest day's work with minimal appreciation. Sure Josh was famous and a great athlete, but he wasn't a god. No matter what her hormones might try to tell her.

Marsha slipped on her reading glasses. "If we could get back to the subject at hand," she said, her quiet voice instantly silencing the other chatter. "Tiffany will be here any minute and I'd prefer we be discussing something of merit when she arrives."

"Tiffany?" Police Chief Alice asked. "Seriously?"

"Tiffany Hatcher." Marsha scanned the paper in front of her. "She's twenty-three and getting her Ph.D. in Human Geography. And before you ask, I went online and looked it up. It's the study of why people settle where they settle. In other words, she's studying why we don't have enough men in Fool's Gold."

The women all looked at each other. Robert chuckled. "You have me."

"And we're ever so grateful," Gladys told him. "But you're only one man."

"I do what I can."

Charity tried not to laugh. He caught her eye and grinned.

Marsha sighed. "As much as I wanted to keep our problem quiet, apparently that's not going to happen. Tiffany is very excited about the opportunity to publish her thesis when it's finished. So the whole world is going to know."

"Unless no one reads it," Alice said.

"I don't think we'll be that lucky," Pia said. "Men or a lack of them is sexy. The media loves sexy topics."

"How can a lack of men be sexy?" Gladys asked.

Just then there was a timid knock on the open door. Charity turned and saw a tiny, dark-haired young woman standing in the entrance to the conference room. Marsha had said Tiffany was in her twenties, but she could easily have passed for thirteen. She had big eyes, long dark hair and an earnest expression that made Charity think she was going to be a giant pain in the butt with her questions.

"Your assistant said I should come right in," Tiffany said apologetically.

"Of course, dear," Marsha said, rising. "We've been expecting you. Everyone, this is Tiffany. She's going to do her dissertation on why men are moving away from Fool's Gold."

"Actually, you're only a chapter," Tiffany said, her voice as tiny as the rest of her.

"Lucky us," Charity whispered to Pia.

CHAPTER FIVE

CHARITY STEPPED INTO Angelo's at exactly seven on Wednesday night. The Italian restaurant was within walking distance of the hotel, much like everything else in town. The outside was whitewashed, with a big patio seating area. Inside, the tables were covered with white tablecloths and the subdued lighting gave the intimate space an elegant air. A dozen different delicious smells competed for her attention, making her mouth water and her stomach growl. Her salad at lunch suddenly seemed like a long time ago.

Before she could attack a passing waiter and grab a couple of slices of rosemary bread off the tray he carried, she spotted Robert sitting at a table near the opposite wall.

"Go right in," the hostess said with a smile. "Enjoy your dinner."

"Thanks."

Robert rose as she approached.

There were several other diners already in the restaurant. Maybe she was imagining things, but Charity had the sense she was being watched by those already seated.

"Are they keeping tabs on me or you?" Robert asked quietly as he held out her chair.

She laughed. "I noticed that, too." She sat down. "I can't decide if it's because I'm the new girl or if it's because you're out on a date. What with you being a single man and therefore precious and rare."

He settled across from her. "You think the lack of men in town is funny."

"I don't think it's a great hardship for you. Poor Robert. Too many women want to be with you."

His brown eyes brightened with amusement. "Fame can be difficult. There's a lot of responsibility."

She wished he hadn't said the word fame. For some reason, it made her think of Josh, and she'd been determined he wouldn't intrude on her evening out, even in spirit.

"You can handle it," she said as she picked up her napkin and put it on her lap.

Their server, an older woman with dark hair pulled up in a bun, brought them menus.

"I thought we'd talk a bit before ordering," Robert said. "Would you like a glass of wine?"

"Thank you, yes." She grinned. "I'm walking tonight, so I can even have two."

"Wild."

"I have my moments."

They both ordered a glass of the house Chianti. A few minutes later the busboy brought over a basket of bread and a saucer of olive oil for dipping.

"The bread is excellent," Robert said, offering her the basket.

"I was afraid of that," Charity said. "I'll wait and try it later." Closer to when they would get their meal, so she wouldn't have a chance to inhale every slice. "How was your weekend with your friends?"

"Good. We went to a Giants game. They won. My friend Dan is getting married next month, so the trip was kind of a bachelor celebration."

"I'm impressed you went with baseball and not a strip club."

He chuckled. "We're getting too old for that. Now if we were still in college…"

"Front row seats?"

"In our dreams."

The server appeared with the wine. When she was gone, Robert picked up his glass. "To a great evening."

She raised her glass, as well.

"Dan and his girlfriend already have a kid," Robert continued. "A little girl. She's eighteen months old. It seems like a lot of people are doing that. Have a baby, then figuring out if they want to stay together. I guess I'm old-fashioned. I thought it was supposed to go the other way."

"I agree," she said. "But pregnancy happens. I guess a generation ago, people got married when they found out. Now they aren't in such a big hurry."

He leaned toward her. "It's been a couple of weeks. How are you settling in? Enjoying small-town life?"

"I love it. I'm meeting lots of people. I like that I can walk pretty much everywhere. You're right. There aren't any secrets, but then I don't have anything to hide."

"Then you'll be fine. Have you started looking for a house?"

"Not really. I'm still getting to know the different areas."

"I live on the golf course. Great views. The houses are well-built and a nice size. You should come see my place sometime."

"Sure." She wondered how he afforded one of those homes. She'd seen them on her drive around town and had even picked up a flyer for one. But unless the mayor had a secret plan to double her salary in the next week, Charity couldn't begin to pay for something like that. Prices were great in Fool's Gold, but even here a home on the golf course was pricey.

"You said you grew up in small towns," she said. "In California?"

"Oregon. I went to school in Eugene, which is a good-sized town. Got my degree in accounting and went to work for a midsized accounting firm. Then I went into the government side of the business. After about five years, I transferred to the private sector. One of my first jobs was auditing one of Josh Golden's companies. That brought me here."

"Josh has companies?"

Robert raised his eyebrows. "You didn't know?"

"No. It's not as if we've spent much time together." The tour of the city had barely been an hour. "I know he used to be some famous bike rider guy."

Robert laughed. "There's a description to make him proud."

"You know what I mean. I don't follow many sports. I'd heard about him, but nothing specific."

"He owns several companies. The sporting goods store. He's a partner at the ski resort, the hotel."

She reached for her wine and nearly knocked it over. "He owns the hotel where I'm staying?"

Robert nodded.

No wonder he chose to live there, she thought, feeling embarrassed for implying he was irresponsible. "I had no idea."

"He hired the firm I worked for and I came out to do an audit. I liked the town. When I mentioned that to Josh, he said they were looking for a treasurer. I applied and got the job."

"It's a long way from Oregon," she said, still trying to take in the fact that Josh was a business mogul.

"I don't have a lot of family. I'm an only child and my

parents were a lot older when they had me." He smiled sheepishly. "Mom always said I was a miracle." The smile faded. "They died a few years ago. I have a cousin, but that's about it. I figured I'd make my own family."

"I know the feeling," she said, surprised they had so much in common. "I was raised by my mom. I never knew my dad. My mom took off when she was pregnant, and never told me where she was from. I always wondered if I had relatives out there, somewhere. If anyone knew about us. When I lost her, I felt really alone. I wanted a place to belong."

"So you came to Fool's Gold?"

She nodded. "A recruiter got in touch with me. I was looking to make a change." Mostly due to a bad breakup, but why mention that?

"I'm glad you moved here," Robert said, his dark eyes gazing steadily into hers.

He was nice, she thought as she smiled at him. Warm and caring and he shared a lot of her goals. He was the kind of guy she was looking for. At least on the surface. If only there was some kind of physical connection between them. Something that…

The hair on the back of her neck stood up. An unexpected warmth spread through her. For one brief shining moment she thought the chemistry had finally kicked in. The second of relief was followed by a mental groan when she saw Josh walking past their table and being seated on the other side of the room. He was with Mayor Marsha and apparently here for dinner.

"Speak of the devil," Robert said lightly, nodding at the newcomers. Marsha waved.

"The downside of small-town life?" she asked.

"I told you. No secrets. Now everyone knows we're out together."

She was aware of Josh sitting within her line of sight and it took every ounce of control not to stare at him.

"I don't mind everyone knowing," she said, forcing herself to look at Robert as if he were the most interesting man in the world. The truth was she wanted to run over to Marsha's table, push the older woman aside and snuggle up next to Josh. The fact that he had a steady stream of women ready and willing to be on call was the only thing that kept her in her seat.

"Good," Robert said, looking pleased. "Are you ready to order?"

"Um, sure." She glanced at her menu, wondering how she was going to be able to eat. Acting something close to normal was going to take all her energy and attention. Honestly, when she got back to the hotel, she was going to have to figure out a way to get over this Josh thing.

She randomly picked a chicken and pasta dish, then closed the menu and reached for her wine. Inadvertently, her gaze slipped a little to the right. Josh was looking at her, his eyes bright with humor. She found herself wanting to laugh.

Reluctantly she turned her attention back to Robert, who was a very nice man. A far better bet than Josh. Apparently she was going to have to keep reminding herself of that over and over again. Eventually it would sink in. It had to.

JOSH LEANED BACK in his chair. "You did this on purpose."

Marsha didn't look up from her menu. "I have no idea what you're talking about."

"Sure you do. You're one of the smartest people I know."

She set down the menu. "And let me say how much I appreciate you saying people and not women."

"You're welcome, but not the point. You knew Robert and Charity were coming here for dinner."

"Did I?" Marsha managed to look both innocent and smug at the same time. "Are they here? I didn't notice."

Josh knew better. "You asked for this table. You wanted me facing her."

Marsha smoothed her white hair. "I am a very busy woman, Josh. I don't have time to worry about your latest conquest, however interesting she might be."

"Don't play matchmaker."

"Afraid it might work?"

The real problem was he didn't want to hurt his friend. Marsha had been good to him and he owed her. "Setting up people never goes well. Don't you watch reality television?"

"No," she said. "And neither do you. Why don't you like Charity?"

He studied the woman in question. Despite the fact that she was on a date, she was still dressed like a conservative schoolteacher. A plain dress, buttoned all the way to the collar. The loose fit and boxy jacket revealed nothing. Did she lack confidence or feel she had something to hide?

He found himself wanting to know which, nearly as much as he wanted to slowly unfasten each and every button and reveal the smooth, warm skin underneath. Just as troubling, he found himself wanting to talk to her. Just talk.

Not gonna happen, he reminded himself. At least sex was safe. But getting involved? No way.

"I like her fine," he said.

"But?"

"She's not my type."

"You don't have a type. That would require being picky."

He raised his eyebrows.

Marsha sighed. "I didn't mean that the way it came out. It's just you haven't gotten serious about anyone since Angelique. The divorce was over two years ago. It's time to move on."

His lack of dating or interest in dating had nothing to do with Angelique, but he wasn't going to tell Marsha that.

"I appreciate your concern, but I'm fine."

"No, you're not. You're lonely. And don't pretend otherwise. I'm old and you have to respect me."

"Even when you're wrong?"

She stared at him, her blue eyes unyielding. "Then tell me I'm wrong. Lie to me, if you can."

He couldn't and she knew it. "Charity's looking for something I can't give her."

"Such as?"

He shrugged. "She's not the one."

"You can't know that until you've spent some time with her."

"Can you be bought off?"

"How much are you offering?" She shook her head. "I'll stop pushing. At least for now. You know I care about you, right?"

"I do." He reached across the table and squeezed her hand. "You've always supported me."

"I just want you to be happy. Men don't do well alone. You need someone in your life. I think Charity needs someone, too. She hasn't said anything, but if I had to guess, I would say she's coming off a bad breakup. So she would understand."

"About the divorce?"

Marsha nodded.

What his friend didn't get was that the problem wasn't

his divorce. That was just a symptom of everything that had gone wrong.

The truth was, he'd enjoyed a lot about the theory of being married. He was basically a homebody. Angelique had wanted to go out more nights than not, but his best times with her had been spent with just the two of them. He wanted that again—a connection, the familiarity of knowing everything about someone. He'd always thought he would be just like everyone else, with a wife and a couple of kids.

But until he fixed what was wrong inside of him, until he was whole again, he couldn't be with anyone. He wasn't asking to rule the world, just be the man he'd been before.

"I'll be quiet now," Marsha told him.

"If only that were true."

She laughed.

Josh felt his gaze slipping over Marsha's shoulder, where he could see Charity speaking intently with Robert.

They looked like they belonged together, like they could be a couple. Charity would be better off with someone like Robert. A regular guy without a lot of baggage. Without the ghosts that kept him always searching for an answer he could never find.

THE REST OF Charity's week flew by in a blur of meetings and planning. She'd managed to set up an initial conversation with a large hospital that was thinking of expanding. She was determined to convince them that Fool's Gold was the best possible location for them.

By late Friday she was tired and oddly restless. She tried to watch television and when that didn't work, she went downstairs where the hotel kept a small library of DVDs.

None of them appealed. On a whim, Charity went back to her room, grabbed a green hoodie and headed outside.

It was a little after nine, dark and cool, but warmer than it had been. Spring had finally arrived, chasing away the last of the below-freezing temperatures. Streetlights flooded the sidewalks and made her feel safe, as did the women she saw who were out and about. There weren't a lot but she knew several of them by sight, if not by name.

She walked by the bookstore but Morgan was long gone. She usually saw him sweeping his front porch and stopped to talk at least a couple of times a week. Knowing he was a part of the landscape of Fool's Gold made her feel as if she'd made the right decision to move here.

She crossed the street to walk by the park. Even in the dark she could see the shapes of the spring flowers waving slightly in the light breeze.

Tomorrow night she had a date with Robert. They were going to Margaritaville, and while she appreciated the invitation, when he'd mentioned the restaurant, all she'd been able to think about was Josh warning her about the margaritas with extra shots.

It wasn't Robert's fault, she reminded herself. Josh was practically larger than life, a force of nature. Someone normal and nice could easily get overlooked. She was determined to make sure that didn't happen.

She continued to walk by the park. Across the street was the sporting goods store. A flash of movement caught her eye and she stopped when she saw someone riding a bike up the paved driveway beside the store and circle around back. The rider looked amazingly like Josh, except he'd told her he never rode anymore.

Charity crossed the street. She had to be mistaken. Why

would he tell her he didn't ride if he did? What was the big deal? So it was someone else. She just wanted to make sure.

As she rounded the back of the building, she saw a small shed tucked in the trees. The door stood open. As she watched, a man finished pulling on jeans. He drew a sweatshirt on over his head and stepped into boots.

The overhead bulb wasn't very bright but it gave off enough light for her to identify the man. Josh looked up and saw her.

"You said you didn't ride," she told him, blurting out the first thing that came to her.

"I didn't know you were going to spy on me." He stepped out of the shed. After closing the door, he locked it behind him, then walked toward her.

He was flushed and sweating, his breathing a little fast, as if he'd just finishing a grueling workout. Nothing about this made sense, but the far more interesting fact was that her curiosity seemed to be enough of a distraction that she could control her reaction to him. Or at least keep it more manageable. The tingles were still there, as was the awareness. But she wanted to know what was going on nearly as much as she wanted to rub against him and purr.

Progress, she thought happily. Maybe in time she would be able to have an entire conversation without hearing her hormones chanting.

"I wasn't spying," she said, still confused by his actions. "I saw you go riding by. At least I thought it was you." The pieces all fell together. "Is this what you do every night? Ride? Are you coming back to the hotel tired and sweaty from exercise? You know, everyone thinks you're off having sex."

"Including you?"

"I'm not the one who had a girl waiting in my room."

He flashed her that killer smile and her knees went weak.

"People would talk if you did," he said. "In a different way than how they talk about me."

"I'm sure that's true." She studied him in the lamplight. He looked good. Not that she thought there was a time when Josh didn't. "Everyone said there weren't any secrets in Fool's Gold."

"Then this is the only one."

"Why do you ride at night?"

He stared at her, as if judging…no, not judging. Gauging. But what? If she could be trusted? If she was really interested? She found herself wanting to urge him to believe in her. She wanted to say she would never let him down.

That was the hormones talking, she told herself, even as she continued to hope he would explain himself.

"I ride at night because riding during the day isn't an option."

JOSH HADN'T BEEN sure he would tell her, but now he'd started and there was no going back.

Maybe he wanted someone to know his guilty secret. Maybe it was how she looked in her jeans and hoodie, with her hair pulled back in a ponytail. Less proper, more approachable. Not that he'd ever been intimidated by a woman. Maybe it was the way she stared at him as if she really wanted to understand.

She already didn't think very much of him. Telling her wouldn't change anything.

"How much do you know about me?" he asked.

She groaned. "Tell me this isn't about your ego, because if it is…"

"That's not what I meant. How much do you know about the riding, and why I stopped?"

"You retired. You said so. It's a young man's game."

"Nothing else?"

"Is there more?"

"There's always more."

He moved toward the sidewalk. She kept pace with him.

"I ride at night because I don't want anyone to know I'm still riding. If people see me, they'll ask questions. They'll want me to be in charity races or consider going back to it and I can't."

"Why not? Are you injured?"

"A kid crashed during my last race. He was a teammate. I was supposed to look out for him. He crashed and he died."

"Do you blame yourself for that?"

"In part."

"Was it your fault?"

He stopped walking and shoved his hands into the front pockets of his jeans. "You ever see a pack go down? One guy wobbles, bumps another and it's all over for everyone. The only thing you can do is save yourself. I got out and Frank didn't."

Once again he saw his friend flying through the air. He heard the sickening sound of Frank's body hitting the road.

She stared up at him, her brown eyes dark and questioning in the night. "But you didn't have anything to do with the crash, right?"

"No."

"And you didn't cause him to go down."

He shook his head.

"Then it's not that you killed him."

She made a statement rather than asking a question.

Impressive, he thought, surprised she'd already figured it out. A few of his buddies had come to talk to him, trying to get him to join them again. They'd told him it wasn't his fault, that no one blamed him. They all thought it was about guilt.

In a way they were right—the guilt was there. Strong. Powerful. It chased him, doing its best to suck him down. But it wasn't the real problem.

"I can't ride with anyone else," he said quietly, staring over her head, at the black sky. "I can't be next to another rider without losing it. I panic, like a little girl. I can't breathe, I shake."

"Isn't that just anxiety? Can't you talk to someone or take something?"

"Probably, but you can't ride professionally if you're weak or drugged."

"This isn't about being weak."

"Sure it is." It was about being weak and broken and humiliated. It was about failing. "From what you see and know, this is a sport of individuals, right? But it's not really that way. There are teams. We ride in groups, in a pack. I can't do any of that. I couldn't go riding with you without falling apart. The need, the fire, is still inside of me, but I can't reach it or touch it. Whatever was there is buried in a pile of shit so deep, I'll never be able to dig it out."

He thought she would step back then. Turn away in disgust. That's what Angelique had done. Curled her perfect lip at him and said she wasn't interested in a coward for a husband. She wanted a real man. Then she'd walked out.

He'd bared his deepest flaw, had exposed his soul and she'd left. That's what people did. They left when you were broken. His mother had taught him that.

Charity surprised him. She continued to stare at him, then she shook her head. "I don't believe you. If that fire is there, it'll find a way."

If only, he thought grimly. "Want to tell me when? I have a life to get back to."

"You mean you're not content living as a small-town god?"

"Deity status aside, I don't want to end my career like this." A loser. Afraid.

"Not to get too metaphysical on you, but maybe there's a reason this happened."

"If that's true, then so is that old saying. Payback's a bitch." He shrugged. "It's okay, Charity. This isn't your problem. Go ahead and tell me that I'll figure it out and be fine."

"That won't solve anything."

"But you'll feel better."

"I felt fine before."

She started toward the hotel. He walked with her.

"You like that they think you're out having sex with fifty different women a night," she said.

"It beats the truth." He jerked his head toward the buildings next to them. "I grew up here. The good people of Fool's Gold have a lot invested in me. I don't want them to know the truth."

"There's nothing bad here. You had a very natural reaction to a horrible circumstance."

"I got spooked during a race. It's not like I faced sniper fire in a war."

"You're too hard on yourself."

"Not possible."

"Oh, please. Don't be such a guy."

"If I wasn't, my reputation would be even more interesting."

She laughed. The sweet sound carried on the night.

She was easy to be with, he thought. Nice. Down to

earth. She hadn't bolted, which he appreciated and he believed she wouldn't tell anyone what he'd told her.

When they were within sight of the hotel, he stopped. "You go on ahead."

"Why?"

"Do you want people to think we were together?"

"We were just walking."

"Come on, Charity. You've been in town what—three weeks? You really believe that's what they'll tell each other?"

"Probably not."

He raised his eyebrows.

She smiled. "Definitely not. Okay. Point taken. I'll go first."

She took a step, then turned back. "They love you. They would understand."

"They love the guy on the poster."

"They might surprise you."

"Not in a good way."

"I didn't know you were a cynic."

"I'm a realist," he told her. "And so are you."

"I think you're underestimating their affection."

"It's not a risk I'm willing to take."

She started to say something, then shook her head and walked across the street.

He watched her go. The sway of her hips drew his gaze to her butt. She was pretty in a quiet kind of way. Hers was a beauty that would age well. Before, when he'd really been Josh Golden, he could have had her in a heartbeat. The irony was back then he wouldn't have slowed down long enough to notice her.

Life sure had a sense of humor.

CHAPTER SIX

CHARITY DID EVERYTHING she could think of to prep for her meeting with the hospital committee. This was her first real chance to prove herself and she wanted everything to go perfectly.

She'd loaded her presentation on her new laptop and then had backed it up on Robert's, just in case. She'd researched the competing locations, checked for large, recent donations and walked the proposed site herself. She felt comfortable with the information and ready to make her case.

At exactly nine-thirty on Tuesday morning, eight people walked into the conference room. Charity was ready for them.

Mayor Marsha spoke first, welcoming them to Fool's Gold and assuring everyone how much the town wanted the new hospital campus. Marsha went over a few of the more important facts—the tax breaks, the incredibly reasonable price of the land, the grants they'd already made progress on.

Marsha and Charity had spent most of the previous day going over what each of them would say, so Charity was prepared for each of Marsha's points. The mayor finished with a joke about the golf courses in the area, which was Charity's signal that it was her turn.

From her research she knew that of the eight members on the committee, the real powerhouse was Dr. Daniels. A

trauma care doctor used to dealing with impossible situations, he liked to get to the point, make a decision and move
on. He considered serving on the committee a waste of his
important time, so he wanted the business settled quickly.
Charity planned to use that to her advantage.

She passed out folders, then flipped on her computer.

"I know you're all very busy," she began. "So I want to
first thank you for taking the time to come to Fool's Gold.
My goal is to provide you with the information you need to
make the right decision for your hospital expansion." She
paused to smile. "And explain to each of you why Fool's
Gold is the right place at the right time. Not only do we
offer excellent housing for your staff, superior schools for
your children and a warm and welcoming community filled
with qualified workers, we simply want you here more.
We're determined to do whatever is necessary to convince
you that this is exactly where your hospital needs to be."

She began her PowerPoint presentation, clicking through
several glossy photos of the area. The real meat of the meeting came next, with plenty of statistics on skilled labor, potential patients and quality-of-life issues. For Dr. Daniels,
she threw in a mini sales pitch.

"We're in desperate need of trauma care," she said as
she clicked to display another graph. "We might not get the
gunshot wounds of a gang-infested city, but we have other
issues. Skiing and hiking accidents on the mountains, car
accidents, especially during winter and tourist seasons.
Last year three rock climbers fell. Two died before they
could reach the trauma center in San Francisco. If we'd
had our own trauma center, those two young men would
still be alive today."

She moved on to the number of births per year, illus-
trating the need for a new maternity center. By noon she'd

gone through all the details she and Marsha had decided were necessary.

"If you'll come with me, we have lunch set up downstairs," she said, motioning to the door. "At one o'clock, we'll take you on a tour of the area and have you on the road by two, as you requested."

Everyone rose and started out of the room. Dr. Daniels, a handsome man in his mid forties, paused. "You listened. We told each of the towns we wanted to be done by two. One of the other places kept us until five, the other got us out at four-thirty."

Charity shrugged. "A partnership has to go both ways. Of course there's more I want you to see and hear, but I respect your time. We have a lot to offer, Dr. Daniels. I hope you'll give us the opportunity to show you that."

"I see that. An excellent presentation. I'm impressed."

"Then I did my job."

JOSH LEFT THE hotel a little after seven in the evening. It was early for him to go riding, what with the days getting longer, but he was restless. Normally he enjoyed his quarters at the hotel, but lately they'd felt confining. He could always move into one of the houses he owned. At any given time one of the rentals was usually available. But what would he do in a house all on his own?

He walked through the center of town, then stopped across the street from Jo's Bar. The place had been there for years. There had been a dozen or so owners in the past decade. The location worked but the owners never seemed to make a go of it. Then three years ago Josephine Torrelli had shown up and bought the place. She'd hired a crew of construction guys, demolished the place down to the beams and built it up to look like a quiet, welcoming neighborhood bar that catered primarily to women. There were a couple of big TVs showing reality TV and home shopping for the largely female crowd. All the guys got were a couple of TVs over the long bar and well-priced beer.

There were a lot of rumors about Jo. Some said she was a former child star with money to burn. She'd certainly had plenty to sink into the remodel. Others said she was running from an abusive husband and using an assumed name. A few believed she was a mafia princess determined to make it far away from her east-coast family.

Josh suspected the latter was the most likely story. Jo, a pretty woman in her mid-thirties, seemed to know a little too much about life to have been raised in the 'burbs. He knew she kept a loaded gun behind the bar, and when a fight had broken out last year, she'd looked more than ready to use it. Which also gave credence to the abusive husband story, he thought as he crossed the street and walked into the bar.

The place was well lit without breaking the mood. Baseball played on the small TVs. Giants on one, Oakland on the other. A few die-hard Dodger fans huddled around one of the smaller screens. The larger flat screen showed skinny models walking down a runway. There were several groups of women around round tables and balloons proclaiming it was someone's birthday. A few guys played pool at the lone table in the back.

Several of the customers greeted him. He waved and made his way to the bar.

"Beer," he told Jo before turning to watch the Giants. A commercial filled the screen. He looked away, glancing at the women at tables, about to face the bar again, when he saw someone he knew in a corner.

Ethan Hendrix sat with one of his brothers and a third

guy. Josh stiffened. This seemed his week for dealing with the past, he thought grimly.

In a perfect world he would walk over to Ethan and they would talk. The past had been over for years. It was time to get over it. He'd phoned Ethan a few times over the past couple of years, but his old friend had never returned the calls. Now he couldn't seem to move and Ethan never glanced in his direction. Then Jo was putting a beer in front of him.

He took a sip.

"Good," he said. "Where's it from?"

"A microbrewery in Oregon. South of Portland. The guy came through with samples. You have to respect that. Apparently he travels up and down the west coast, trying to get places to take his beer."

"Does that make you a sucker for a sad story?"

She grinned. "Maybe. What of it? You ready to take me on, Golden?"

"And get beaten by a girl? No, thanks."

"You know it. I'm tough to the bone. Ethan's here," she added, speaking low enough that only he could hear.

"I saw that."

"You could talk to him."

"I could."

He didn't question how Jo, who had only been in town three years, knew about his past with Ethan. Jo had a way of finding out things.

"You're both idiots," she said. "In case you were wondering. He's as bad as you, acting all pouty."

Josh chuckled. "There's ten bucks in it for you if you say that to his face."

"I don't need the money. You're wallowing in guilt and

he's playing the martyr. It's like living in the middle of Hamlet."

He frowned. "How do you figure?"

"I don't know. It's the only Shakespearean play I could think of. Well, there's always Romeo and Juliet, but that doesn't fit. You know what I mean. Just go talk to him."

She was right, he told himself, as he put down his beer. He would walk over and...

He turned on the stool, but Ethan and his friends were gone, the table empty.

"Next time," Jo said when he faced her again.

"Sure. Next time."

She moved on to another customer. Josh sipped his beer, thinking about Ethan, wondering how things would have been different if he'd been the one injured instead of his friend. He had a feeling Ethan wouldn't have lost his nerve. He would still be racing.

The pool game finished up. One of the guys walked toward Josh and sat next to him at the bar.

"Hey, Josh."

"Mark."

"You still thinking of heading to France this summer? We could use another win."

Sure. Because that's how it happened. A person woke up one morning and thought "I'm going to enter the Tour de France" and that was it.

"Not this year. I'm still retired."

Mark, a plumber in town, punched him in the arm. "You're too young to retire, but not too rich. Am I right?"

Josh nodded and smiled, then wondered why he'd bothered to come into the bar.

He wasn't interested in winning another race. At this

point, he simply wanted the ability to compete. To do what he did before. What he took for granted.

"My kid's pretty good," Mark said when Jo handed him a beer. "Fast on his bike. He wants to race. You know, like you did. We're thinking of sending him to one of those schools. He's begging me every day."

"There are a couple of good places. How old is he?"

"Fourteen."

"That's kind of young."

"That's what his mom and I say. He's too young to be on his own. But he won't leave it alone. Weren't you going to open a racing school here, in town?"

That had been the plan—back before the accident. Josh had several bids on construction, most of the money and his eye on a piece of property. But to do that, to commit himself to being a part of the school, meant riding again. Not a humiliation he was willing to take on right now.

"I've thought about it," he admitted, then wished he hadn't.

"You should do it. Solve our problem. You're famous, man. Lots of people would come to ride with you. I bet they'd do a story about you on CNN."

That's what he was afraid of, Josh thought grimly.

"Something to think about," he said and drained his beer. He dropped a few bills on the counter, then stood. "See you, Mark."

"Yeah. Think about it. The racing school. It could be great."

It could, Josh thought as he left the bar and headed back to the hotel. It could be a damned miracle. Because that's what it would take.

WEDNESDAY NIGHT CHARITY followed the directions Pia had given her, walking to the west part of town where the houses were older and larger, seated majestically on huge lots with mature trees. She saw the well-lit two story on the corner and walked up to the front door.

Pia opened it before she could knock. "You came. Welcome." Pia giggled. "Okay, I brought tequila and margarita mix and I've been sampling. What the hell. We're all walking, so let's have fun."

Tequila? "I just brought a couple of bottles of wine," Charity said, wondering what she'd gotten herself into. Girls' night out had sounded like fun, but she couldn't afford to get really drunk. She had meetings in the morning.

"Wine is great," Pia said, swaying slightly, then grabbing the door frame for support. "Maybe I'll have some."

A tall, pretty brunette appeared behind Pia and wrapped an arm around her waist. "You need to lie down, kid."

"I'm fine," Pia said. "Don't I look fine to you? I feel fine."

The woman smiled at Charity. "Don't be frightened. Every now and then Pia feels the need to live up to the party image. It's not a big deal."

"I can respect that," Charity said.

"Me, too. I'm Jo, your hostess for this month's girls' night. Come on in."

"I'm Charity."

"I figured that. We're glad to have you." Jo maneuvered Pia away from the door.

Charity followed the two of them into the house.

It was one of those great old places, with hardwood floors and plenty of built-ins. She suspected what had once been a lot of little rooms had been remodeled into several larger rooms. A fireplace large enough to hold an entire cow dominated the far wall. There were several sofas, comfy-looking chairs and a group of women looking at her curiously.

A thin blonde stood and reached for Pia. "You sit by me," she said. "I'll take care of you."

"Just for tonight," Pia said, slumping down on a sofa. "Tomorrow I take care of you."

"Tomorrow you'll be puking your guts out." The woman smiled at Charity. "Hi. I'm Crystal."

"Nice to meet you."

Charity was introduced to the other women and did her best to remember their names. Renee/Michelle was there and Charity was surprised to learn her name was actually Desiree. When the introductions were finished, Jo led Charity into the kitchen.

"You can see what's open, what's in the blender and what you can create on your own."

The kitchen had been partially updated. The counters and sink appeared new, but the stove was from the forties and the cabinets looked like they might have been original.

"Great place," Charity said.

"I like it. I know it's big for just me, but I enjoy the space." She pointed to the array of bottles on the counter. "Wine, both colors, margaritas in the blender, unless Pia drank them all. Mixers, vodka, Bailey's. You name it, we have it."

"I'll go with a glass of wine," Charity said.

"Playing it safe on your first night. Probably wise. Pick a color."

"White."

Jo got a glass and poured. After she handed it to Charity, she leaned against the counter. "So you're our new city planner. How are you liking Fool's Gold?"

"I love it here. All my small-town fantasies are coming true."

Jo laughed. "I moved here about three years ago. From

the east coast. It was quite a change, but a good one. The people are friendly. Pia invited me to join her and her friends. They made me feel very welcome."

Charity glanced toward the living room. "I appreciate the invitation. I want to get to know people."

"You will."

A pretty blonde walked into the kitchen and sighed. "I need more. Pia's drunker than me and I was supposed to be the drunkest one at the party." She smiled at Charity. "Hi, I'm Katie and please don't think badly of me."

"I won't."

"I don't usually drink very much."

"Or at all," Jo muttered. "Speaking as someone who owns a bar, you're a real disappointment in that department."

"I know." Katie leaned against the counter. "But tonight's different. My sister's getting married."

Charity felt confused. "And that's a bad thing?"

"The groom and I were dating when they met. For nearly a year. He'd bought me an engagement ring. But before he gave it to me, he met my sister and they kicked me to the curb."

"Ouch," Charity said. "I'm sorry."

"Don't be. He was a jerk," Katie told her.

Charity had a feeling that was the alcohol talking more than her heart.

"The worst part is that the wedding is a four-day party up at the Lodge," Jo added.

"I need a date and I don't have one." Katie hiccupped softly.

"There's always Josh," Jo offered.

Katie rolled her eyes. "I need a date with a guy people will believe I'm actually seeing. There's no one. And now my mother is offering to set me up with her best friend's son. Howie."

Charity tried to muffle a laugh. "Okay, it's not a traditionally romantic name, but he could be great."

"I met him back when we were kids. He's a total nerd, and not in a good way. We hated each other, and I get to spend four days with him. Someone just shoot me now."

"How about another margarita?" Jo asked.

"That works, too." Katie looked at Charity. "Are you happily married or dating? Because I'll warn you—in this crowd, you'd be the only one."

"Sorry, no. I have a string of bad breakups, as well."

"Bummer," Katie mumbled. "What's wrong with us?"

"Nothing," Jo said firmly. "You don't need a man to be happy."

"Try telling that to my whoo-whoo. It hasn't seen action in nearly a year."

Now Charity did laugh. Fortunately Katie didn't seem to notice.

"There's Crystal," she said. "At least she was happy before."

Jo poured another drink. "Crystal's husband was killed in Iraq." She glanced toward the doorway, then lowered her voice. "She's sick. Cancer. So she doesn't drink. Just so you don't offer her anything."

Charity thought about Pia's friend. "She looks fine."

"Right now things are good. We're hoping the treatment can kill the cancer without taking her, too."

"How awful. Does she have children?" Bad enough for them to lose their father, but now to be worried about their mother.

"Not exactly."

Charity would have blamed her confusion on the wine, only she hadn't yet taken a sip. "What do you mean?"

"They froze some embryos before her husband went off to Iraq. Just in case. She was planning to have them implanted, but the lymphoma was discovered during the routine physical. She wants to get better so she can have her babies." Jo poured herself a glass of red. "Sometimes, life's a bitch."

Charity didn't know what to say. "I'm sorry."

"We all are and there's nothing any of us can do. That's the worst part. Well, not for Crystal, obviously." Jo shook her head. "I think I've had too much to drink. I don't usually go on like this. Come on. Let's get back to the girls."

Charity followed Jo and Katie into the living room where she did her best not to stare at Crystal. Talk about sad.

"Are you enjoying Fool's Gold?" one of the women asked.

"No one cares about that," Desiree said with a laugh. "I want to know what she thinks of Josh."

The room went silent as every pair of eyes focused on Charity. She froze, her glass of wine halfway to her lips.

"Excuse me?"

"You're living at that hotel with him," Desiree said with a laugh. "Tell us everything."

Charity put down the wine. "I, ah, don't live with him. I have a room at the hotel." There was no way she was going to mention they were in rooms right next to each other. Talk about trouble. "I've met him a few times and he seems nice."

"Have you gone out on a date?" one woman asked.

"No. Of course not."

Jo rolled her eyes. "Charity's new to our evil ways. Don't scare her off the first night. There hasn't been much news on the Josh front lately, so they're hungry for gossip about their favorite topic."

"He's a favorite topic?"

Nearly everyone laughed. Even Crystal chuckled.

"He's gorgeous," Desiree said with a sigh. "That face, that body."

"That butt," Pia muttered from the couch.

"She lives," Jo said. "Hang in there, honey. It'll get worse before it gets better, but you'll survive."

"There are other good-looking men in town," Charity said.

"Maybe. But no one is like Josh," Desiree told her. "It seems like he hasn't had a real fling in a while."

"There was that ski instructor," Crystal said.

"That was last year. I can't think of anyone." Desiree looked hopefully at Charity. "Unless you want to confess something."

"I'm sorry to disappoint you, but we've barely had any contact." No way she was going to rat him out, she thought. This was a tough crowd. "Besides, I don't think I'm his type."

"If you're female, you're his type," a woman across the room said.

Everyone laughed.

Not true, Charity thought, remembering the pain in Josh's eyes. He'd been right—the town did have high expectations. A case could be made that they were completely unrealistic. No wonder he didn't want to expose any weakness.

"She's really not," Pia said, pushing herself into a more stable seated position. "You could be, but you're not."

Charity didn't know how to take that. "Meaning?"

"You dress, like, so plain. Those boxy dresses and jackets. I know you need to look professional for work, but dear God. Show a little skin."

Crystal put her arm around Pia and whispered something in her ear. She smiled apologetically at Charity. "She's not herself."

Charity smiled back, but on the inside, she was squirming. What was wrong with her clothes? Of course she dressed conservatively. She was representing the town.

She told herself Pia was drunk and that her comments didn't mean anything, but that didn't stop Charity from blushing and wishing she could bolt for freedom. No one was looking at her, but the lack of attention was so pointed, it was as if everyone was staring at her.

Jo made a comment about a movie opening on Friday and conversation shifted. After a few minutes, Charity excused herself to use the restroom.

Once inside, she locked the door, then leaned against it, as if she had to catch her breath. After a moment, she walked toward the mirror and studied her reflection.

She could only see herself from the waist up. Although she'd gone back to the hotel before coming here, she hadn't bothered to change, so she was still in the long-sleeved dress she'd worn all day.

The fabric was a cotton blend, in solid navy. A case could be made that it was a little too big, but she preferred her clothing loose. The jacket she'd worn with it was a tad boxy, but well-tailored.

As usual, she'd blown out her brown wavy hair until it was straight, then pulled it back into a braid. She wore small gold hoops, minimal makeup and a plain inexpensive watch. As she continued to study herself, she realized the best she could come up with was that she was clean.

"When did I start dressing like someone in her eighties?" she demanded, then realized she was doing seniors a disservice.

She sat on the edge of the tub and rubbed her temples. After graduating from college, she'd found a great job in Seattle. She'd been the youngest person on the mayor's staff and had found herself being dismissed whenever she made a suggestion. When she dressed older and went for a more conservative look, she'd been taken more seriously.

When she'd moved to Henderson, a suburb of Las Vegas, she'd continued to wear clothes more suited to someone a couple of decades older. That had worked for her. But somewhere along the way, she'd lost herself in the look. She'd stopped paying attention to herself. Maybe she'd stopped caring.

There was a knock on the bathroom door. Charity stood and smoothed the front of her dress.

She opened the door and was surprised to see Crystal standing there.

"I don't mean to pry or anything," the other woman said. "But are you okay?"

"I'm fine."

"Pia is actually really nice. I'm sure she didn't mean anything by what she said."

Charity stepped into the hallway and tried to smile. "I know. It's the heartache and margaritas talking. Not that she wasn't speaking the truth. I'm frumpy and I can't figure out exactly how I let that happen. Or when!"

"They say acknowledging the problem is the first step in healing." Crystal's blue eyes danced with humor as she spoke. "You're really pretty. You just need to play up your assets."

"I need a new wardrobe." She brushed the front of her dress again, feeling self-conscious about the old-fashioned fit.

"Easily done. That's why we all have credit cards."

"I've been letting mine get dusty for far too long."

"Then you should go shopping this weekend."

"Believe me, I will."

"Good for you," Crystal told her. "Retail therapy is the best kind."

They walked toward the kitchen. Charity found herself not wanting to go back to the group. The need to run and hide was fairly powerful and not very comfortable. But before she could think of an excuse, Crystal spoke.

"Can I ask you something?"

"Sure."

"We have a fundraiser every year called Race for the Cure. We support childhood diseases, mostly cancer. I'm on the committee and we're heading into our busy time. I can't…" She glanced away and cleared her throat. "I'm really busy and don't have the time I need. Anyway, I was wondering if I could talk you into taking my place."

Charity was grateful Jo had told her about Crystal's illness. With that information, she knew how to avoid misstepping.

"I'd love to be a part of that," she said.

Crystal looked surprised. "I was prepared to twist your arm and everything."

"I want to get involved with the community," she said. "This gives me a perfect way to do something good while meeting people."

"Then we both win," Crystal said. "Thank you."

A burst of laughter came from the living room.

"Looks like we're missing the party," Crystal said. "Shall we?"

Charity nodded and followed her back into the crowded room. She was determined to ignore her feelings of frumpiness, all of which could be healed fairly easily. Better to spend her time getting to know the women here. She wanted to fit in, and friends would make the transition easier.

Jo handed her the glass of white wine. "You're way behind us on the drinking, young lady."

"Then I'd better catch up."

THREE HOURS LATER, Charity made her way back to the hotel. She was in a much more mellow mood, the result of plenty of laughter and maybe a bit too much wine. The women had been a lot of fun, she thought. Jo was great, as was Crystal. Katie had kept them laughing with stories about the potential disaster that was Howie. And Charity had let go her sense of living as a fashion don't. She would go shopping over the weekend and see what people her age wore when they weren't trying out for a religious order.

She reached the hotel and thought briefly about taking the elevator to the third floor. But she was determined to walk off the nacho calories she'd eaten at Jo's.

On the second floor, she walked to the smaller staircase that would take her to the third. She'd barely taken two steps, when the lights went out.

The darkness was as absolute as it was unexpected. Charity heard doors open on the floor below and above, and people talking. There was more laughter than panic in their voices.

She kept hold of the railing and carefully continued to climb to her floor. Once there, she would probably be able to find her way to her room. Not that she was sure she could get in. Did a card key lock work off a battery or electricity?

When she neared what she thought was the top of the stairs, she went more slowly. She felt carefully with her foot, took another step and bumped into something warm and solid and male.

It took her brain less than a second to register the heat, size and scent of the man. Her belly flipped over, her thighs began to hum softly as her fingers curled tighter around the banister.

"You all right, Charity?" Josh asked.

Surprise joined the other sensations. "How did you know it was me?"

"Your perfume."

Actually it was her hair conditioner, but saying that made her sound as conservative as her clothes, so she kept quiet.

"Don't worry. The power will be on in a few minutes," he said as he put his hand on hers. "You're right by the top. Just one more step."

She eased upward, propelled by desire as much as by muscle. When she was close to Josh, even floating seemed possible. Which meant she was in worse shape than she'd thought.

It was the wine, she told herself. She wasn't herself. But maybe being herself was the problem. After all, every guy she'd ever cared about had treated her badly. They'd cheated or stolen and Ted had beaten her up. Just once, she reminded herself sternly. She'd left as soon as she'd picked herself up off the floor. Grabbed her purse and walked out, never once considering that she would go back.

"Charity?" Josh sounded puzzled. "You okay?"

"Yes. Sorry. Just thinking. I was at Jo's and…"

He laughed. "Girls' night out. Or in. Never mind. I know what happened. Margaritas?"

"White wine. Although Pia was doing the tequila thing."

He put his arm around her as they moved into the hall. "Can you walk?"

"I'm not drunk."

"Just happy?"

She was now, standing so close to him, feeling the strength of his body. He was the kind of guy who could sweep a woman up in his arms without breaking a sweat.

"I'm happy," she whispered.

She sensed movement. In the darkness, it was hard to tell. But it felt like Josh wasn't next to her anymore. That he was in front of her, and standing very, very close.

Fingertips lightly touched her cheek. The contact was delicious and she couldn't help the little sigh that escaped her lips.

"You have no idea," he murmured.

"About what?"

Instead of answering, he pressed his mouth to hers.

The contact was warm and firm and soft and just demanding enough. He kissed with an ease she couldn't explain but knew meant he really liked the kissing thing. It wasn't just a required step on the road to what he really wanted.

She probably should have been shocked, but she wasn't. Maybe it was the wine, or maybe it was simply time to let the hormones do their thing. They'd sure been bugging her enough. So she relaxed against Josh, wrapped her arms around his neck and gave herself over to every erotic sensation pouring through her.

He dropped his hands to her waist and pulled her closer. She went willingly, closing those last few inches separating them. She parted her lips and he swept inside, touching her tongue with his.

Desire raced through her. She could barely keep herself from begging. He tasted like the chocolate mints that were left on her pillow every night and something a little stronger. Maybe Scotch.

She burned inside, the need bigger than she'd imagined possible. Her breasts ached. That place between her thighs was swollen with need. Even as she kissed him back, stroking, learning, yielding, she wanted to ease him closer to her room. She wanted him naked, inside of her, taking her just as hard as she took him.

The image was so clear, it was if they were already together. Muscles tensed in anticipation of her release. Her reaction was so powerful, it frightened her and she drew back. A heartbeat later, the lights went on.

They were in the third floor hallway. A few people stood in their doorways, and they applauded the return of modern life. Charity could only stare into Josh's hazel-green eyes, wondering if hers were as bright, as filled with passion.

She knew what he was going to say. Or ask. Both their rooms were only a few feet away. But as much as she wanted him, she knew she couldn't be one of the millions. Not and still have a little pride in the morning. Turning him down seemed impossible, so she did the only thing that made sense. She ran to her room and hurried inside. Then she stood with her back to the door and waited for her heart beat to finally slow to normal.

CHAPTER SEVEN

MARSHA WALKED INTO Charity's office shaking her head. "I know, I know. I'm late. I was meeting with Tiffany." Marsha sank into the chair opposite Charity's desk and groaned. "I swear, that girl." She waved a piece of paper. "All the people she wants to meet with, and she would love for me to make the introductions."

Charity did her best not to laugh. "I know it's difficult."

"It's beyond difficult. It's humiliating to have our town's problems featured in her thesis."

"At least we're only a chapter."

"I know and I should be grateful, but there's a part of me that wants to ask why we're not good enough to be an entire book. Which is crazy. I must need medication." She drew in a breath. "All right. Enough about Tiffany. How are you?"

"Better than you. I was going to get a bottle of water from the vending machine. Do you want something?"

"A martini. Which I happen to know we don't stock. I'll take an iced tea." She raised her hand, then set it back on her lap. "I don't have my purse with me."

"My treat. I'll be right back."

"Thank you. I'll sit here and practice my breathing in attempt to get my blood pressure below a thousand."

Charity left her office and walked toward the vending machine. She hadn't personally spent any time with Tiffany but she'd heard the grad student's questions could be probing at best and a little annoying at worst.

She put the money into the vending machine and collected the drinks, then returned to her office.

"Thank you," Marsha said gratefully as she took the bottle. "Is that outfit new? I really like the skirt."

Charity told herself to simply accept the compliment without an explanation. Or at least not a detailed one. Her boss didn't need to know about her realization that she'd spent the past couple of years totally ignoring her appearance.

"I drove to Sacramento and did some shopping over the weekend."

The black pencil skirt was still professional, but it ended a couple of inches above her knees rather than five inches below. The pumps had a thinner heel and were about an inch higher than what she had been wearing. She'd had the white blouse for about a year, but it was fairly classic. Hanging on the back of her chair was the new cropped black-and-white pinstripe jacket. The tailored style emphasized her waist and made her feel both feminine and powerful.

"You look great. I've always had a fondness for clothing. I had a thing for leather for years, but I'm too old now. I would simply frighten people if I showed up in leather pants or, God forbid, fringe."

Charity laughed as she sat down at her desk. "You could start a trend."

"I'll leave that to those of you still under thirty. Anyway, tell me how things are going. Do we have any new businesses moving here so I can tell Tiffany we're no longer thesis worthy?"

"Not yet, but I'm working on it. I've been in touch with the hospital committee and they were very impressed.

They've dropped one site completely, so now it's down to us and one other contender. They'll want to send a few different people to explore the town and see what we have to offer. I'm already putting together different tours."

"A hospital. That would be impressive."

"It was on your to-do list."

Marsha sipped her tea. "I love it when people listen to me."

"I'm sure everyone does. From what I can tell, the biggest concern the hospital committee has is about community support, so I'll be dealing with that directly."

"Excellent."

Charity passed over a second file. "I've been meeting with a software company. They're in San Jose and while they'd keep their headquarters there, they need to expand. A lot of the staff have expressed a desire for small-town life. They want to stay in California and be relatively close to the main office. So I have high hopes we can convince them to come here."

"Software, huh?"

"Most computer geeks are guys."

"True and I've always liked that type of man. Computer guys, engineers. They're usually stable and dependable. Important qualities when it comes to marriage."

Charity glanced at the other woman's left hand. There wasn't a ring. She started to ask, then thought it might be a little too personal. But Marsha must have noticed.

"Like many women in my generation, I married young," Marsha said. "John was a sweet man. Probably too good for me, but he loved me unconditionally. We were so happy together. We had a daughter." She paused, as if remembering a moment in the past. "How that man loved his little girl. We had plans for a big family, but he was killed in a car accident when our little girl was only three. I was pregnant at the time and the shock of losing him caused me to miscarry." Marsha pressed her lips together. "It was a difficult time."

Charity was shocked to hear about the tragedy. "I'm so sorry."

"It was a long time ago. Now I just have good memories, but for a while I didn't think I could survive the double loss. My baby girl helped pull me through, just by needing me. And I had the town."

Marsha smiled at her. "John and I had both been born here, so when I lost him, so did the community. They rallied. About a year later, someone put me on the ballot for the city council. I think it was to shock me out of my depression. I never campaigned, but somehow I won. I went to my first meeting with the idea that I would resign, but somehow I got sucked into it all. Here I am, some forty years later, still working in city government."

"I'm glad you are. You do a terrific job."

"You're kind to say that."

Charity wanted to ask about Marsha's daughter, but as she'd never heard her mentioned, she didn't. She was a little afraid something bad had happened to her, too.

"I have a lot of friends," Marsha continued. "This has always been my home. So even with John gone, I belonged. I hope you're getting a sense of that belonging yourself."

"I'm really enjoying myself, getting to know people."

"Making friends?"

"I am. I went over to Jo's the other night to hang out with Pia and her friends. I met Crystal."

Marsha shook her head. "A lovely girl. So desperately sad. When she lost her husband, I completely understood what she was going through. We were all so excited when she decided to have their embryos implanted. But then they discovered she was sick. It's just not fair."

"I know. I was thinking that when Jo told me about her situation. That it would help Crystal to have a child, but if she's sick…"

"I know what you mean. Losing both parents would be so difficult. I sometimes wonder what God was thinking when He put all this in motion. We all hope she makes a full recovery. It's just the doctors seem to think that's unlikely."

Marsha smiled at her. "And this is the part of small-town life that is difficult. We know each other's joys, but we also know each other's sorrows." She shook her head. "And now let's talk about something more cheerful. I couldn't help but notice you had dinner with Robert the other night. Was that fun?"

Charity wasn't used to discussing her personal life with her boss. She knew that Marsha was just being friendly, but she honestly didn't know what to say, what with Robert being the town treasurer and all.

"He's a great guy."

"Very eligible."

"It's a little early to be marrying me off."

"True, but I can't help it. I have a matchmaker's heart. I love watching people fall in love. Robert seems very steady." She laughed. "Which sounds awful, but you know what I mean. It's the dependable thing. He's not flashy."

Not like Josh, Charity thought, doing her best not to remember the brief but incredible kiss she and Josh had shared. No point in belaboring the impossible, not to mention improbable.

Marsha sipped her tea again. "Although something could be said for a man who will always surprise you."

Charity blinked. "Excuse me? What happened to steady?"

"I suppose I'm biased. I've known Josh a long time. He's like a son to me. I'd like to see him settle down with someone special."

Charity would like to see him naked, but she wasn't going to mention that. "Wasn't he married before?"

"Yes, but she was all wrong for him. Talk about flashy. I tried to tell him, but he wouldn't listen. He was thinking with the wrong part of his anatomy, if you get my meaning."

Charity grinned. "I do."

"He's so much more than people give him credit for. I still remember the first time I saw him. He and his mother had moved here from Arizona. Josh had been in a horrible accident. He'd been hiking with his mother and fallen down the side of a mountain. He was battered and still healing. He could barely walk—his poor legs were so twisted."

Charity tried to compare that image with the man she knew. It was impossible. "He's so perfect."

"Oh, he's many things, but perfect isn't one of them. But I know what you mean. He has that face and that body. But when he was a boy, it was a different story. She left him."

"His mother?"

"Yes. She abandoned him about four months after they moved here. Just walked out one afternoon. Got in her car and drove away. I found Josh standing outside their motel room, waiting for her. At first we all assumed she would come back. But she didn't. We looked for her, of course, but if a person doesn't want to be found, hiding isn't that hard."

Charity had grown up moving from place to place. She'd hated always having to be the new girl, but she'd never been abandoned. Sandra had been flakey and selfish, but she'd never considered leaving Charity behind. It was one thing to lose a parent through an accident or illness, but to be discarded.... How did anyone recover from that?

"What happened?" she asked.

"No one knew what to do. There was the foster care system, which we weren't enthused about, but it wasn't as if the town could adopt a boy. He needed stability. The city council met to make a decision when Denise Hendrix walked in. She already had six children of her own, including triplet girls, if you can imagine. Her oldest, Ethan, was Josh's age. She said one more child wouldn't matter. So Josh moved in with them. He and Ethan became good friends. Best friends. They used to ride bikes together."

"I've heard the name. Doesn't Ethan own a windmill manufacturing company? He's on my list of people to visit."

"Yes, that's him. He also has the construction firm he inherited from his father. You'll like Ethan." Marsha's eyes twinkled. "He's single, too. A widower."

Charity laughed. "You've got to stop trying to fix me up. I'll figure it out on my own. My first order of business is to get settled and get Fool's Gold new businesses. My love life can wait."

"It seems to me you could do both. You're still thinking of buying a house?"

"Yes. I'm going to some open houses this weekend."

"You'll have a good time. There's a lot to choose from in town. You should talk to Josh. He always knows when a new property is coming on the market."

Charity raised her eyebrows.

Marsha shook her head. "I mean that in the real estate sense, I'm not trying to fix you up."

"I don't think I believe you."

Marsha winked. "You probably shouldn't. I can be wily."

Once again Charity was delighted she'd taken this job. Working for Marsha was a pleasure and she hoped she and the mayor could become good friends. Marsha was easy to be with.

There was a knock on her open door. She looked up and saw Robert walking toward them.

"I'm sorry to interrupt," he said, handing Marsha a legal-looking letter. "This couldn't wait."

Marsha scanned the letter. "It's from the State of California."

"They're following up on money they sent. It was earmarked for road repair. They want confirmation that it was used correctly."

"Road repair. I don't know anything about this."

"None of us do," Robert said. "The money was never received by my office. It's missing."

Charity shifted her gaze to Marsha, who looked stunned.

"How much are we talking about?" the mayor asked.

"Seven hundred and fifty thousand dollars."

"THANKS FOR TAKING Crystal's place on the committee," Pia said as she and Charity walked to the recreation center by the park.

"I'm looking forward to it," Charity said. "I want to get involved with town activities."

"Uh-huh. You say that now. But let me be clear—you've agreed so there's no backing out. Don't come whining to me later."

Charity laughed. "How bad could it be?"

"Ask me that again in three months when you're signing in fifteen hundred racers."

"There's an actual race?" Charity said, pretending surprise.

"Very funny."

"I'll be fine."

"You'd better be. You're new and have energy. I plan to use you shamelessly." Pia shifted her tote to her other shoulder. "Love the jacket, by the way. Red is so your color."

"Thanks. I did some shopping." The black pants were new, too. Boot cut and long, which worked as she was in high-heeled boots. The black short-sleeved sweater provided a simple backdrop for the deep Red Riding-inspired jacket.

Pia slowed, then stopped. "Oh, God. I'm having a weird out-of-body experience. The other night, at Jo's, did I say something about your clothes?"

"You mentioned they were a little out of date."

Pia winced. "I was so drunk. I'm sorry. At Jo's place—I was hideous, wasn't I? Can you forgive me?"

Charity touched her arm. "There's nothing to forgive. You weren't wrong. I was dressing too conservatively. Hiding from my life. It's not like I need therapy or anything. You were a good wake-up call."

"I'm sorry."

"No. Stop apologizing. I needed to hear the truth about my clothes. You were right—I was dressing like someone a lot older."

Pia winced. "Note to self. Never have alcohol again."

"How long will that last?"

Pia grinned. "At least a week."

They walked into the recreation center. There was a small snack bar with a few dozen tables, then a long, wide hallway with classrooms on either side. As they walked, Charity saw a group of older women scrapbooking, while across the way, grade school kids did some kind of martial arts.

"You can learn just about anything here," Pia said. "Last year, someone flew up from L.A. and did a class on Feng

Shui. It was interesting. I shifted my entire bedroom to draw in love and power. It didn't work. Maybe I should have worked on my money center instead."

"Um, probably not in your bedroom," Charity told her.

Pia grinned. "You're right. That would be illegal."

They walked into the large auditorium at the far end of the building. There were already about twenty people standing around talking.

"I know we don't need a space this big now," Pia said, "but we will later, and I've learned to grab the big space early or someone else will claim it. Do you know everyone here?"

"I think so."

Charity saw several familiar faces, including Morgan, who waved at her. There was one of the women on the city council and a—

The hair on the back of her neck stood up. She felt a ripple of awareness tiptoe down her spine and without turning she knew Josh was in the room.

Ever since the kiss, she'd done her best to avoid him, and so far it had worked. Looked like her luck had run out.

She turned slowly and saw him talking to several people. Even in the crummy fluorescent lighting, he looked amazing. His gold-blond hair needed cutting, but that only added to his appeal. He was tall, built and had a face that would make an angel want to sin. Worse, he kissed with a fiery passion that left her past weak and nearly to begging. How was anything about the situation fair?

Just then he glanced up and saw her. Although he didn't greet her in any way, she saw something very close to a twinkle in his eyes. As if they shared a private joke. She turned away.

Pia glanced between them. "Wow. You really hate him."

"What? Why would you say that?"

"You were glaring. I can't believe the old charm isn't working on you."

Yikes. The last thing Charity needed was for Pia to start asking questions. "No. It's not like that. I barely know him. I was thinking about something else. There's, um, there's a problem with some stuff at work."

"Oh." Pia lowered her voice. "The missing three-quarters of a million dollars. Marsha told me about that. Don't worry. I haven't mentioned it to anyone. Sorry. I shouldn't have assumed you were pissed at Josh. I'm just so used to everyone adoring him that it was really strange."

"Not a problem."

"Are you looking for fun? Because Josh is available. At least I think he is. He has so many women, it's hard to tell."

"I'm not into crowd control."

"He'd be worth it. Trust me. I went to high school with him. I was a few years behind, but we all totally adored him. Even back then he was special."

"Did you ever…" Charity paused, not sure how to ask the question. "Were you ever involved?"

"No, but I wanted to be. In a generic, he's-a-god sort of way. I didn't actually know him that well." She glanced at her watch. "I should probably call this meeting to order."

Pia raised her voice. "All right, people. Let's take a seat and get going. The sooner we start, the sooner we can all get home to watch American Idol."

Charity moved toward the table. In an effort to keep anyone from thinking there was a problem, she did her best not to notice Josh at all. Which turned out to be a mistake when she ended up standing by an empty chair next to him.

"Shall we?" he asked, holding out the chair.

Not knowing what else to do, she sank into it, then wished she hadn't when he settled next to her.

Not that she objected to the proximity or the view. He was, as always, totally gorgeous. But she was tired and therefore less able to fight her attraction. Maybe she should try an energy drink before her next encounter with Josh.

"How'd you get roped into this?" he asked, leaning toward her.

Her gaze seemed to focus on his mouth—the mouth that had kissed hers so deliberately just a few days before. It was a kiss she'd been trying to forget, only to realize that spending all her time not thinking about it was the same as spending all her time thinking about it.

"Crystal asked me to take her place."

His expression tightened. "Poor kid. She's had it hard."

"I don't know her very well, but she seems really sweet. She said she wasn't feeling well enough to continue."

Charity returned her attention to Pia and tried not to notice when Josh leaned back in his chair. The movement brought his forearm perilously close to her own, which made her wonder if she should simply leave things as they were or casually shift away from him.

Talk about having it bad, she thought with a sigh.

"The race is a one-day event," Pia was saying. "Which means minimal heads in bed. You all know how I hate that. We need the heads in beds, people."

"We could make the race longer," one guy yelled.

"Not helpful." But Pia was smiling as she spoke.

"What's heads in beds?" Josh asked Charity.

"People spending the night in town or nearby. An overnight event. Like a weekend festival. The race is just part of a day."

"Aah. Thanks."

Pia went through her list. Charity found herself agreeing to work on the advertising committee, as well.

"I'm on advertising, too," Josh told her when the meeting wrapped up. "It's easy. Just get a few businesses to sponsor."

"Don't you own several businesses in town?" she asked.

"Uh huh, and I promise to be generous."

"Lucky me."

"I'd say so." He walked out with her. "You started looking for your own place yet?" he asked.

"I'm going to a few open houses this weekend to get a feel for the real estate market. I'm not sure exactly what I'm looking for."

"More of a 'I'll know it when I find it' shopper?"

"Something like that. I've never actually owned my own home before," she admitted. "When I got out of college, I was focused on paying off my student loans and saving money. I moved to Henderson right at the peak of the real estate bubble, so I couldn't afford anything I wanted. Then the market started to flatten and I wanted to wait until it was closer to the bottom. By then…"

Why had she started this detailed discussion of real estate?

Josh stood, waiting, looking at her. She could feel the intensity of his gaze and while she was sure he didn't mean it to be smoldering, it felt hot to her.

"By then I was involved with someone," she admitted, hoping she didn't blush, despite feeling foolish.

"You wanted to wait and see if the two of you would be buying a place together," he finished. "Makes sense. I'll guess that you being here means it wasn't a slam dunk?"

Despite the faint warmth on her cheeks, she laughed. "You men do love a good sports metaphor."

"It's in our blood."

"No, it wasn't a slam dunk. We broke up a few months ago. I found out about the job here and made the move. So this will be the first house I buy myself."

"You were born to own a home."

"Why do you say that?"

"You're responsible, you want to be settled and you'd look great on a porch swing." His gaze wandered down her body before returning to her eyes. "In shorts."

The warmth in her cheeks deepened. "If that was a compliment, then thank you."

"You're welcome. Not that you don't look great tonight. I like the red."

He put his hand on the small of her back and led her out of the room. She tried not to notice the contact, even when it burned through to her skin.

"By the way, I know of a house coming on the market. It's in a great part of town. Built around 1910, but fully remodeled. The electrical and plumbing have been brought up to code. It's not huge, but I think you'd like it. I, ah, know the owner and could get the key. Want me to show it to you?"

"Sure."

She told herself she was only interested in the house, but she knew she was lying. What she was hoping was that in the quiet of an empty house, Josh would try to have his way with her. Not that she would give in, but she was sure looking forward to the discussion.

SATURDAY MORNING CHARITY met Josh at the Starbucks on the corner. She ordered her nonfat latte, then splurged with a couple of pumps of mocha flavoring. Josh stood talking to a couple of women who were obviously trying to convince him of something. She waited until the other women walked off before joining him.

"That was intense," she said as she followed him outside.

"They want me to open a training camp here in town. A place for kids to take their riding to the next level. There are a few of them in the country."

She thought about what she knew about his past. "And?"

"It's an idea."

"Not one you want to take on?"

"Not today."

They started down the sidewalk.

"We're walking?" she asked.

"It's about a mile. Want to drive?"

"No. I like to walk. Living here will cut down on tire wear and tear."

They passed a couple of women jogging. They waved at them. Charity saw the woman on the left whisper something to her friend and point. She grimaced.

"We're a couple, aren't we?" she asked with a sigh. "I totally forgot about the consequences of people seeing us together."

"Do you mind the gossip?"

"Not if no one asks for details."

"They'll expect you to tell them I'm a god in bed."

Probably, she thought, grinning. "Are you?"

He raised his eyebrows. "Want references?"

"So you have them?"

"I could get a couple."

"Thanks, but I'll wing it if anyone asks."

"It's no trouble."

"I'm sure it isn't," she murmured, then sipped her coffee.

A god in bed. If anyone could meet that criterion, she had a feeling it would be Josh. He was a complete and total temptation, but one she planned to resist. He was practically worshipped everywhere he went and she was just a regular person. She'd studied mythology in school. She knew what happened to mere mortals who dared to stray into the realm of gods.

Of course, a couple of days ago, she was hoping he would make a pass at her. When it came to Josh, she simply couldn't decide if it was better to be good or be bad. Although she knew which option would be more fun.

They crossed the street and walked into a residential neighborhood filled with beautiful old houses. A few had been completely updated, thereby losing their charm, but most retained elements of the original architecture. There were big trees that stretched across the street, touching branches and providing shade. Intricately carved fences surrounded lush gardens. He pointed to a white house with blue-gray trim.

"That's it."

She stared at the two-story structure, the wide front porch and big windows. Everything about the house welcomed her.

"I already love it," she said.

"Wait until you see the inside."

He pulled a key out of his jeans pocket and unlocked the front door. They stepped into the stillness.

Light spilled in the windows, illuminating the polished hardwood floors. The living room was large, with a fireplace and Craftsman style built-ins. There was a dining room, also with built-in storage and a small library with bookshelves that went up to the ceiling.

Everywhere she looked she spotted amazing details. The baseboards were at least eight inches high and crown molding emphasized the plaster ceiling. In the kitchen, the appliances were refurbished fifties style and blended perfectly with sleek new cabinets and a slate floor. There was an eat-in nook and French doors that led out into the garden.

A lot like Jo's house, she thought with a happy sigh. Only better.

"I love it," she said wistfully. "I don't even have to see the upstairs. It's beautiful, but I have a feeling it's out of my price range."

"I know the owner and he'll deal."

"Is there anyone in town you don't know?"

"There might be a couple of babies I haven't met yet."

"Life in a small town," she said.

"It works."

She turned in the center of the kitchen, admiring the light fixtures, the original doors, the feeling of home and space.

"You're not the least bit tempted to buy something like this for yourself?" she asked.

"I like where I live."

"But it's a hotel."

"Exactly. No maintenance, cleaning service is provided and I get a break on pay-per-view movies."

Because he owned the hotel, she thought, trying to keep her attention on the house rather than the man. She was alone with Josh in a quiet, empty space. If she didn't keep her mind focused, she was in danger of throwing herself at him and begging to find out if he really was a god in bed.

"Don't you get tired of the room service menu?"

"They take requests."

"From you." She shook her head. "A rock star in a small town. I can't imagine."

"It has its benefits."

"And the downsides?"

His gaze locked with hers. "There are those, too."

Something stirred deep in her belly. Determined to stay strong, she deliberately switched the conversation. "Still riding alone at night?"

He nodded.

"Have you talked to anyone about what happened? A sports psychologist?"

He glanced away. "When it first happened. I've seen the pictures, the TV coverage. I know there was nothing I could have done. But knowing and believing aren't the same thing."

There was something in his voice, a hopelessness. As if something important had been lost.

"You want to go back," she said quietly.

"Every damn day. I miss being who I was. Not the fame, but the competition. Winning. The training. I ride here, but it's not the same. I miss my teammates, the anticipation of the race."

She suspected he missed the fame, as well. Who wouldn't?

"You've tried riding with other people?" she asked.

He stiffened. "More than once." He glanced at his watch in obvious dismissal. "We should see the upstairs."

Without thinking, she crossed to him, then lightly touched his arm. "I'm sorry. I shouldn't have brought it up. The past, I mean. It's not my business."

One corner of his mouth twisted into a smile. "I'm not delicate, Charity. You can say what you want."

She seemed unable to look away from his mouth. The shape of his upper lip, the unexpected fullness of the bottom one. She remembered the feel of his kiss, how she'd wanted to surrender. He was a man with way too much power.

"I'm seeing someone."

The words fell out of her without warning.

Josh looked more amused than put off. "Robert?"

"Uh-huh. We've been out to dinner."

"I remember hearing something about that. He's a good guy."

Now she felt stupid. What had she expected? That Josh would get jealous and tell her to stop seeing Robert? That he would make a move on her?

"Yes, he is," she said primly. "A very nice man."

"I hope the two of you will be very happy together. The upstairs is that way."

She moved toward the stairs, when in truth she felt like both crying and stomping her foot. She did neither. Instead she followed him to the second floor and tried to tell herself it was for the best. Wanting Josh was a one-way ticket to disasterville. A place where she'd already spent way too much time.

CHAPTER EIGHT

CHARITY WAS LOOKING forward to her meeting with Ethan Hendrix. He was a tall, good-looking guy. He and Josh used to be best friends and ride together. Then Ethan had gotten hurt ten or twelve years ago. The details on the whole thing were vague at best and she hadn't been able to figure out a way to ask without appearing too interested in either man.

Ethan owned a construction company in town and a wind turbine manufacturing facility about ten miles out. As they were meeting at the latter location, it gave her a chance to actually drive her car for once. At least she wasn't spending a lot on gas these days. Or wasting time sitting in traffic.

She followed the directions Ethan had given her, turning off at the big driveway leading to Hendrix Turbine. The site was massive, with large warehouse-like buildings and huge towers being loaded onto long trucks.

She followed arrows pointing to the office, then parked and walked inside. A small foyer led into a reception area. Beyond that were offices, desks and computers, with lots of pictures of wind turbines.

She'd done some research in anticipation of the meeting and knew that Hendrix Turbine was a fast-growing company. Wind power was popular, as were windmills. After the initial start-up costs, ongoing expenses were minimal. While wind turbine "farms" hadn't become the norm, wind power was a great potential source of green power, especially in rural communities.

An attractive woman in her twenties looked up. She was wearing jeans and a long-sleeved T-shirt, and had short blond hair.

"Hi," she said with a smile. "You must be Charity Jones. You're Ethan's eleven o'clock. He'll be back any second. There was a delivery issue." She wrinkled her nose as she walked toward Charity. "There's always a delivery issue."

When Charity shook hands with her, the woman continued, "I'm Nevada Hendrix, Ethan's sister. I'm one of the engineers here."

"Nice to meet you. A female engineer. The mayor will be so disappointed."

Nevada laughed. "When I graduated from college Marsha told me to bring as many of my male classmates as I could to town. So far none of them have followed me, but I keep asking."

"I'm sure we all appreciate the effort."

A door slammed in the back. "That's Ethan." Nevada lowered her voice. "He's single, by the way. One of the few in town, if you're interested."

"Ah, thank you," she said, not sure of the correct and polite response. Fool's Gold might not be swimming in men, but Charity had had more single guys tossed her way in the past month than in the past three years. Okay—only three, but still.

Ethan strode around the corner. "Am I late?" he asked.

"Right on time," Charity told him.

Ethan was tall, with dark hair and eyes, and very nice looking. Not up there with Josh, but few mortals were.

Nevada introduced them, then went back to her computer. When she was behind Ethan, she gave Charity a thumb's up.

"You have your sister working for you," she said. "So this is a family business?"

"Three out of six," he told her, motioning for her to lead the way out of the office. "My brother handles the sales end of things. I oversee manufacturing. Nevada is our resident engineer. I tell her she's not all that, just because she's in on the technical end of things, but she doesn't believe me."

"There are six of you?" she asked, thinking it would have been great to have a brother or sister. And a whole lot less lonely when she'd been growing up.

"Sometimes it felt like twenty, but it was good. We're a close family."

"Everyone still in Fool's Gold?"

"One of my brothers moved away, but the girls are here." He pointed to one of the big warehouses. "That's where we store the components. They're not here long. We have a whole lot more demand than we can fill. Wind turbines are popular."

"That's what I hear," Charity told him. "As I said in my call, I'm the new city planner. I'm coming around and meeting all the business owners in the area." She was also interested in his relationship with Josh, but doubted she would figure out a way to bring that up.

"What do you know about wind turbines?"

She thought for a second. "They're really tall?"

He grinned. "Good start. Come on. I'll take you to the sales office and give you a quick course in what we do here."

The sales office was another building. Inside there was a model of a wind farm, with working wind turbines, pictures of different kinds of wind turbines, cutaways of the machinery and several blank TV screens.

"I won't show you the entire DVD collection. Not until you have a few million you'd like to invest."

"Not this week. I'm thinking of buying a house."

"Maybe when the budget's not so tight?"

She laughed. "You'll be first on my list."

He pointed to the models of turbines. "This is what we build. They come in various sizes, the largest of which produces six megawatts of power. Assume it's going at full speed twenty-four-seven, we're talking about enough electricity generated to power fifteen hundred households a year."

"You're kidding? From one of those? We all should have one in our yard."

"Don't get too excited, that's under extremely optimal conditions. Reality is a little less easy to calculate. The wind doesn't always blow, and the turbines are fairly loud."

He hit a switch and one of the TV screens came on. The picture scanned across a seemingly isolated patch of desert scrub. The background noise increased until it was uncomfortably loud.

"That's close to what they're like at fifty feet."

Charity wanted to cover her ears. "Okay, maybe not in the front yard."

He hit another button and the picture shifted to a large display of wind turbines.

"There are other considerations," he said. "Some areas are windier than others. We use something called Wind Power Density to determine the best placement for the turbines. There are also problems with delivery. The towers are usually between two and three hundred feet tall. The blades are between sixty-five and a hundred and thirty feet long."

She tried to picture that, but couldn't. Ethan must have been used to those unfamiliar with his industry. He immediately hit a button and the TV screen changed to a drawing of a blade next to a six foot man.

"The blade wins," she murmured.

"It's going about a hundred and sixty miles an hour. It always wins. So we want a relatively isolated location that we can deliver to and provide service to. Not too close to the community but not too far away. Lots of wind, but not so much wildlife."

"Right," she said. "Birds get clipped by the blades and die."

"We actually have a bigger problem with bats."

She blinked. "Bats, as in bats? Don't they have sonar that allows them to see anything that's moving in the sky?"

"Yes, but the spinning blades create a change in pressure." He paused. "You don't want to know. Let's just say turbines can have a negative impact on bat migration. To change that, we recommend owners shut down the turbines during slow wind nights."

"A computer does that, right?"

"It can. The biggest concerns are during late summer and early fall, when bats migrate."

She had the weird feeling there was something crawling in her hair. "Um, bats migrate?"

He nodded.

"I could have gone my whole life without knowing that."

"They don't want to hang with you any more than you want to hang with them."

"Uh-huh. That sounds nice, but I don't actually believe that. I think bats get a good laugh out of making girls scream."

"Maybe. I hadn't thought about it, but you could be right."

He showed her part of a DVD and a few more pictures, then handed her a map of the area.

"Here's the closest wind farm," he said, pointing to the map. "You can take a drive out there if you want to see them in person. The area is fenced off, but you can drive up close enough to get an idea of the size and the noise." He grinned. "Go during the day and you'll avoid the bats."

"Note to self," she said, taking the paper. "Thanks. I appreciate all the info."

They started back toward the main building.

"How are you liking small-town life?" he asked.

"It's great. I'm still learning everyone's name."

"That will take a while. I've seen you and Josh Golden together a few times."

His voice was casual, but she had an idea that the statement was anything but.

"We're not together," she said quickly. "He showed me a house that's coming on the market and we're on a committee. Nothing more."

Ethan laughed. "Women aren't usually so quick to separate themselves from any association with him."

She winced. "I don't mean to say I don't like him." She paused. "Just not, you know, in that way."

Almost the truth, she reminded herself. Wanting to have sex with someone was not the same as liking the person. Erratic hormones had a will of their own, while her mind was more concerned with the inner qualities of a man.

"Apparently," Ethan said, his dark eyes twinkling with humor.

She sighed. "The local celebrity thing is a challenge. I don't know what to say."

"You're doing fine. Truthfully, Josh is a whole lot more interesting than the guy who carves jewelry out of cattle dung."

"At least he probably smells better."

Ethan glanced at her. "He's not a bad guy."

"I thought you two didn't get along," she said, then clamped her fingers over her mouth. "Sorry," she mumbled, dropping her hand. "People talk and sometimes I listen."

"I understand. Don't worry about it." He kept walking. "Whatever happened between Josh and me was a long time ago. Have you ever been to a race?"

She shook her head.

"There's always a crowd. The riders are in packs, so close together that the slightest mistake can take nearly anyone down. The speeds are incredible. On the downhill part of a course, fifty or sixty miles an hour isn't impossible. What happened to me wasn't Josh's fault. I actually hit him, but I'm the one who went down."

"Then why aren't you two speaking?"

Ethan flashed her a grin. "You'll have to ask Josh that." They reached her car.

"I appreciate the time," she told him. "Thanks for the tour and the lesson on bats."

"Anytime."

He waved and walked back to the office.

His stride was long and easy, with only the faintest hint of a limp. He was single, good-looking and charming. And she felt absolutely nothing when she was around him. Somebody somewhere sure had a sense of humor.

JOSH LOOKED UP as both Marsha and Pia walked into his office. Eddie waved at him from her desk, then turned her back on him, as if silently claiming this wasn't her business. A sentiment that didn't leave Josh with an especially good feeling.

"Have you heard?" Pia asked, plopping into one of the chairs on the other side of his desk. "A big bike race got canceled and they're shopping for a new location. I just got a call. It's fantastic."

"Yes. A company pulling out of an event because they're losing money is a reason to celebrate," Marsha said dryly. "Maybe later we'll find out there are layoffs and we can really party."

Pia rolled her eyes. "You know what I mean. Of course I don't want anyone to lose their job. But this doesn't have to be a bad thing for the charity. Not if someone else picks up the slack, which we're going to do." She handed Josh a sheet of paper. "I know what you're thinking. We're doing Race for the Cure, but that's a race for runners. And only one day. This is so much more. Major event on the tour, dozens of sexy guys on bikes. Heads in beds. They're desperate— which is where we come in."

"We who?" he asked, already having a good idea of where this conversation was going.

"The town," Pia told him triumphantly. "I've done some checking on the costs and expectations and I know we can pull this off. We'll move the entire bike race to Fool's Gold. It's a quiet weekend for us, so there are plenty of hotel rooms. I've already put a tentative hold on every empty room between here and Sacramento. Heads in beds. You know how we love that."

Marsha studied him. He read the concern in her gaze and knew she was worried about him.

"The town can't cover all the costs," he began.

"I know, but I'm already talking to a few companies," Pia told him, slapping a folder on his desk. "If they'll cough up the prize money, we're good to go. The rest of the work can be done by volunteers. You know how this town loves a good project. Especially when that project supports you."

Here it comes, he thought grimly. "How does it support me?"

"It's bike racing, Josh," Pia told him. "Your thing. I was thinking we'd have a little parade and you can be the grand marshal. Then you can give the prizes at the finish. You know, the old guard, the new guard."

Right. Because the highlight of his day would be handing out prize money to guys he used to race with. Guys who could still compete.

"Or you could even race," she added with a wink. "Announce your comeback. It would mean a huge boost in publicity. The charity is for sick kids, Josh."

"It always is."

Marsha leaned toward Pia. "I think you've hit him with the highlights. Why don't you give him a couple of days to think about all of this?"

"Okay, but we don't have long. I would hate to see some other town snap up this opportunity."

"That would be bad," Josh said as Pia stood and left. He turned his attention to Marsha. "What do you think?"

"Pia's a smart girl. This would be good for the town. Put us on the map."

"I thought we already were."

"It would bring a lot of attention to Fool's Gold. Positive attention. Something other than a chapter in a thesis where the reality of who we are is reduced to statistics."

He leaned back in his chair. "You want the race."

Marsha studied him. "I want you to be comfortable with the decision we make. It's a great opportunity, but there will be others."

When he'd been a kid and his mother had dumped him in town and taken off, he'd been more alone and scared than any ten-year-old should be. Denise Hendrix had taken him in. Ethan had become his best friend. He'd been one of seven kids in a loud, happy, loving family. But there had been times when he'd never felt as if he truly fit in.

Whenever life at the Hendrix house had overwhelmed him, Marsha seemed to know. She would drop by during the late afternoon and take him out for dinner. In the quiet of a local restaurant, he felt comfortable talking about whatever was bothering him. She listened more than offered advice and most of the time, that was enough.

They'd never talked about what had happened during that last race. When he'd returned to Fool's Gold, she'd told him that she was feeling old and frail and had insisted he spend the first week in her guestroom. He hadn't been fooled. There was nothing frail about Marsha. She hadn't wanted him to be alone and he'd been willing to pretend it was about her.

They'd never talked about Frank's death or his fear, but he suspected she'd figured it all out. A theory she confirmed when she said, "You have a choice. Face the demons or keep running from them."

"It's not that easy."

"Why not? Ethan was hurt and you moved on."

"I felt guilty." But she was right. He'd moved on. But that had been different. Ethan's accident had been one of those things. Frank's death seemed more like his fault. "There's no way to face them without everyone knowing."

"What do you think will happen if everyone finds out the truth about you?"

A thousand things he didn't want to consider.

"You should trust us more," she said, rising. "Trust those

of us who love you. You're more than your fame, Josh. You always have been."

Maybe, but was he enough without it?

"Running hasn't worked so far," she said as she walked to the door. "Maybe it's time for a new plan."

ROBERT INVITED CHARITY over to his place for dinner. He promised a grilled steak and the best salads the corner deli had to offer. Charity hoped that if they could hang out together, talking without any pressure or her being able to see Josh across the restaurant, that she would become more interested in Robert.

His house was within walking distance of the hotel, hardly a surprise, in a quiet residential neighborhood on a golf course. The homes were mostly two stories tall with big windows and well-groomed front yards. Robert's was no exception, although it looked a little newer and better kept than the others on the block.

"Hi," she said when Robert opened the front door. "I brought wine."

"Something I really like in a woman," he said, taking her hand and drawing her in, then lightly kissing her cheek. "You look great."

"Thanks."

She'd worn a short denim skirt with high-heeled sandals and a pale peach silky wrap shirt. Another new purchase designed to show the world, and herself, that she wasn't always conservative. Buying the clothes had started an interesting ripple effect. When she'd started paying attention to what she wore, she'd found herself thinking about things like highlights and pedicures. She had an appointment for the former next week and would find out if the salon had a nail person while she was there.

She'd visited a large discount store and bought a bunch of new makeup to try, including a honey-jasmine body scrub she'd been using in the shower. It was fun being a girl, she thought, wondering how she could have allowed herself to forget.

"Shall I give you the tour?" he asked.

"I would like that."

The main floor had high ceilings. The living room flowed into a formal dining room. Both had beautiful furniture that looked expensive. The big TV and high-tech sound system could have been at home in a movie theater. There was a wet bar tucked into an alcove by the hallway, then the eat-in kitchen was in back. The patio beyond held a lush potted garden and a man-sized grill with lots of knobs and storage.

"I can't help it," Robert said. "Fire good."

"Those caveman roots are hard to cut." She handed over the bottle of wine.

He opened it and poured them each a glass. Once they'd toasted and sipped, they went out onto the patio.

"Impressive garden," she said. "I don't know much about growing plants."

"My mom liked to dig in the dirt," he told her. "I started helping out when I was a kid. I can make nearly anything grow, which is both a blessing and a curse." He pointed to a dozen or so small pots suspended on the fence. Each overflowed with some kind of a plant. "Herbs."

"You grow your own?"

"My ex-fiancée and I did that together. Planted the seeds. Then, when things didn't work out, I couldn't bring myself to take them down. They keep growing. I don't cook much, so I have no use for them. Every few weeks I bring in bags of them to the office. Once you get your place, you can take them home and use them if you'd like."

"The assumption being I'll know what they are and what to do with them?"

"They have books for that."

"Apparently I'll need to find a couple."

Was it just her, or was keeping an herb garden born in a previous relationship a little odd? Especially when Robert didn't use them himself?

Maybe not, she told herself. He was obviously a great gardener. That was nice. She shouldn't be critical. This was a guy she wanted to get to know better.

"Did your mom have a big garden?" she asked.

"About a quarter acre. My parents were older when I was born. They'd given up on having a kid. Living in a small town, they didn't have access to a fertility specialist. I'm not sure why they never adopted."

He motioned for her to take a seat in one of the wicker chairs on the patio, then he sat next to her.

"They were excited to have me, but a little old-fashioned. They didn't want me to go away to college, so I went locally. Then after I graduated and got my first job, I lived at home for a while. By then Dad was gone and Mom was having trouble getting around."

"That was nice of you."

He shrugged. "They were my parents. I had to take care of them. When Mom passed, I decided to leave town."

"You didn't have anyone special to keep you there?"

"No. I didn't date a lot. Mom preferred me to spend my time with her."

Creepy music played softly in the back of her mind. Charity told herself that Robert was simply that rare breed of good guy, but she wasn't sure she completely believed it. She'd had enough disasters in her past to look for warning signs. Was there one here or was she simply comparing Robert to Josh?

Figuring out the truth was made all the more challenging by her physical reaction to Josh every time she was around him. No man could compete with that, either, she though sadly. Were the Roberts of the world destined to be outshone by those who were special?

"I like life here," he said. "No complications. At least there weren't until we found there was money missing."

That's right. The missing seven hundred and fifty thousand dollars. "I assume there's going to be an investigation," she said.

"It's already started. The city council is bringing in someone to audit the books." He grimaced. "It's a lot of money to be accounted for."

"Do you have any ideas about what happened?"

"Not a clue. Normally I know exactly when money is coming in from the state. But this time…" He sipped his wine. "Something's wrong."

"The police chief mentioned something to me about somebody stealing. We're having quite the crime spree in town."

"I doubt they're related." He glanced at her. "Those thefts were small amounts. Stuff you get at a grocery store. This is major. Somebody's going to jail." He smiled. "Shall I start the steaks?"

"Sure. How can I help?"

"Just watch and pretend to admire my prowess with the grill."

She laughed. "I can do that."

THREE HOURS LATER Charity walked back to the hotel, fighting the feeling of finally escaping a long duty dinner. As much as she'd tried to enjoy herself and connect with Robert, they had absolutely no chemistry together and very little in common. The herb garden growing on the fence had turned out to be the highlight of the evening.

Robert was a man of many interests. He had an entire bedroom devoted to Civil War battle reenactments. The models were all to scale, with tiny trees and houses dotting the mossy landscape. He'd shown her the mistakes of the Battle of Bull Run, including both sound effects and falling men. She would guess he had a fair amount of money invested in that hobby.

He also had a large collection of action figures, all in their original boxes. It was like a low-budget version of The Forty Year Old Virgin, but without the laugh track. She'd had such hopes for Robert, she thought. Hopes that were not going to be realized. Even without thoughts of Josh tugging at her subconscious, she wouldn't have been able to fall for a guy who seemed way more interested in his soldier models than in the woman standing next to him.

She walked into the hotel and told herself not to feel defeated. She would find the right guy for her...eventually. If she kept putting herself out there, eventually she had to find the one, didn't she? Statistically, at least, if not in real life.

She took the stairs to her floor, then turned toward her room. Her mystery guy was out there. She just had to be patient.

JOSH STEPPED OUT into the hallway and nearly bumped into Charity.

They both came to a stop. He was aware he was standing too close, he could feel her warm breath on his face. His gaze settled on her mouth, which made him remember what it had been like to kiss her.

"How was your evening?" he asked.

"Fine. Great. I had dinner with Robert."

Of course she had, Josh thought humorously, but didn't react in any way. "He's a good guy."

"Yes, he is."

She spoke defiantly, raising her chin as if daring him to disagree with her. Not that he would. From what he knew about Robert, the man was solid. A little weird, but who was he to be critical of anyone? If Charity had found someone, that was great.

Only it wasn't, and knowing she'd been out with Robert seriously pissed him off.

It wasn't just Robert, he admitted. It was everything else. The race, how he was stuck, unable to do what he loved. He knew he should just get on the damn bike and ride through the fear, but whenever he tried, he broke out in a sweat and thought he was going to pass out. Then he had to step away to throw up. Not a pretty picture. Or one to be proud of.

"My going out with him isn't about you," she told him.

"Never thought it was."

"I'm just saying."

"Right." Now he was pissed. "Have you kissed Robert? Because you sure as hell kissed me."

She stiffened, then looked around as if she didn't want anyone to hear.

"That was an accident," she said, her voice low and tense.

"Right. You fell into my arms and our mouths bumped."

Irritation flashed in her brown eyes. "You're not all that."

Truer words had never been spoken, he thought, then he grabbed her upper arms and drew her in those last few inches.

"Want to bet?" he asked, right before his mouth settled on hers.

For a second, there was nothing. Charity didn't react, which left him feeling like a complete jerk. What was he thinking? This wasn't his style. That would imply caring— something he didn't do anymore.

He was about to pull back, to apologize, when she wrapped her arms around his neck, parted her mouth and kissed him as if he was her last, best hope to survive.

Where there had been only irritation and a vague desire to prove something, now there was need and wanting. His blood heated to boiling. He placed his hands on either side of her face as he kissed her deeply, taking and giving, wanting her to lose herself in him.

She gave as good as he offered, her tongue dueling with his. She squirmed to get closer, which took him from hard to aching. He might not have had sex in a really long time, but he hadn't forgotten what all the fuss was about. He wanted Charity and he wanted her now.

CHAPTER NINE

CHARITY HADN'T MEANT to kiss Josh back. He was obviously annoyed about something and as much as she would like to think it had to do with her spending time with Robert, she wasn't to the point of being willing to fool herself. So resisting his pushy kiss was the smartest reaction.

If only, she thought, straining to get closer, to deepen the kiss. Passion erupted with a fury that left her shaken and weak in every sense of the word. There was something about this man—all it took was the promise of a touch and she lost control. She needed his body with an intensity that frightened her. Now, with his mouth on hers, his hands roaming down her back to her hips, she found herself perilously close to begging. More. She needed more.

She angled her head and met him stroke for stroke. His tongue ignited need, fueling the melting. Her skin seemed ultrasensitive, making her aware of every stroke, each caress as he rubbed her arms, then settled his hands on her waist. Her breasts were heavy and aching. Between her legs, she was already wet and swollen. Ready. Desperately ready.

In case he hadn't figured that out, she closed the millimeter or two separating them, pressing her body against his. He was strong and broad, but what interested her the most was the thick ridge that settled against her belly. The physical proof he wanted her, too.

He drew back enough to kiss along her jaw before dropping to her neck. Open-mouthed kisses sent shivers of delight racing through her.

Maybe he'd had as many women as people claimed. Maybe this was a hideous mistake. Either way, she knew she'd never felt such heat before. Such surging hunger. To make sure he got the message, she drew his hands to her breasts.

As his palms cupped her curves and his skilled fingers teased her tight and sensitive nipples, their eyes locked. She saw an answering fire in his, a desire that eased any concern she had about whether he was just being polite.

As if answering the unspoken question, he grabbed her hand and drew her toward his hotel room door. His key was out, then they were inside before she had time to think. A good thing, she told herself. Thinking was highly overrated.

The second the door closed behind him, he had her up against the wall. He leaned in close and claimed her mouth again. At the same time, he tugged at the knot holding her wrapped shirt, then jerked it open. He half pulled off the fabric, then reached for her bra. It took mere seconds for him to bare her breasts.

Then his hands were on her skin, touching, teasing, rubbing his fingers against her nipples. Pleasure shot through her. She clamped down on his tongue and sucked. He groaned. When she released him, he nipped her bottom lip before dropping his head to her breasts and drawing deeply on her left nipple.

She felt the pull all the way to her belly. Every inch of her burned. Her muscles tensed. She touched everywhere she could reach—his broad back, his arms, then lower, pressing her palm against his erection. He retaliated by slipping a hand between her thighs. Now it was her turn to groan.

His searching fingers found her very center. He pushed her bikini panties aside and moved his fingers over that part of her—the bundle of nerves already quivering in anticipation. She was so ready, so swollen, that it only took a few quick strokes to steal her breath and make her cling to him. Then he shifted, pressing his fingers inside her and using his thumb to rub her to near ecstasy.

She couldn't catch her breath, she thought, torn between the way his mouth moved on her breasts and the way his fingers moved between her legs. Couldn't think, couldn't do anything but feel the waves of pleasure building inside of her.

She had to hang on to him to stay upright, to concentrate on her balance. He straightened and kissed her mouth, claiming her with a passion that pushed her closer to the edge.

Then she felt it. The telltale hum that began deep inside her, the warning clenching that her orgasm was nearly there, practically a sure thing. And just as she braced herself for the release she knew was going to be incredible, Josh stopped.

She stared at him, unable to believe what was happening. His hands reached between them and she realized he was unfastening his jeans. Before she could join in and help, he'd freed his thick erection. She quickly pushed her panties to the ground and stepped out of them. He grabbed her around the hips and boosted her up, so she was pressed against the wall, her body settling onto his arousal.

This was impossible, she thought frantically. She'd never done anything like this. She couldn't touch the ground, she was completely dependent on him supporting her. There was no way she could relax enough to—

He moved inside of her. He pushed in hard, thrusting up

and back, filling her. His body rubbed against her, teasing her swollen parts even as he pleasured her from the inside. She wrapped her legs around his hips, her arms around his neck and hung on for the ride.

It didn't take long. She'd been so close that in a dozen or so thrusts, she wasn't thinking anymore. She was feeling how he stretched her, savoring every aroused nerve ending quiver, giving herself over to the promise that any second now she would explode.

She came with a cry, her body shuddering, drawing him in deeper. She lost herself in the pleasure. He pushed in faster and deeper, taking everything she offered, drawing out her release until she was too weak to do much more than lean into him. Then he was shuddering, as well, going still, his hot breath fanning her cheek.

They stayed like that far longer than she would have thought possible. When she was sure he had to be ready to collapse from holding her, he slowly slipped back, gently lowering her legs to the floor. When she'd regained her footing, Charity did her best to straighten only to find she was still a little wobbly. Josh grabbed her around the waist.

"You okay?" he asked.

Okay? How could she be okay? She'd just had incredible up-against-the-wall sex with a man she barely knew. Something she never did. She'd run a background check on the last guy she'd slept with, and that had been after three months of serious dating. What did she really know about Josh except he was probably going to break her heart?

"The question wasn't supposed to be that hard."

"Sorry." She glanced into his eyes, then away. "I was thinking."

"Dangerous, especially now."

She tried standing on her own again and managed to

stay upright. The shoes weren't helping, so she stepped out of them, which lowered her about three inches. Her right sandal landed on top of her panties.

Physical balance wasn't her only issue, she thought. Her head was spinning. What the hell had just happened? Not that she needed that question answered. Maybe the better issue was why. Why hadn't she stopped to think?

He gently touched her cheek. "Are you okay?" he asked again.

She nodded, figuring he wouldn't want to know the truth. Second thoughts didn't begin to cover her emotional freefall. Thirty-eighth thoughts were more like it. She'd had sex with Josh. Willingly. Wildly. In those moments, in his arms, she'd been someone else.

Or the person she was always meant to be, a little voice in her head whispered.

No way, she told herself. No. That wasn't it.

She shook her head to clear her thoughts. Her shirt was still tucked into her skirt, but was hanging back down over her butt. Her bra was somewhere on the floor. It only took him a few seconds to look decent again, but she had a tougher road. Rather than risk struggling, she pulled up her shirt and reknotted it, figuring she would deal with the bra and panties later. When she was leaving.

Unless she was supposed to leave now.

She'd never been one for casual sex and honestly, she didn't know the rules.

"I know what you're thinking," he said, his hazel-green eyes staring deeply into her own.

"I doubt that." He would have to be beyond psychic to make it through the maze that was her mind.

"I don't do this every day," he told her. "The rumors, the things people say, they're not true."

"They're mostly true," she said. "The first week I was here, I saw that woman waiting in your room. I haven't seen her around town, so I figure you imported her."

"No. I didn't ask her to be there. Hell, I didn't know her. She got someone in housekeeping to let her in."

Information she was sure he thought she would find comforting. "Now you're going to tell me you told her to get dressed and sent her on her way."

"I did." When she would have looked away, he touched her chin. "I mean it, Charity."

The funny thing was, she wanted to believe him. Talk about confusing.

He took her hand and drew her into the room. A single lamp in the corner provided a little light. He flipped on a couple more.

"Can I get you something?" he asked. "Wine? Coffee? Dessert?"

She hesitated. Wine sounded good, but she couldn't face the thought of one of the room-service people seeing her in Josh's room, then telling the entire town about it.

He motioned to his left. "I have a private stash."

She followed the movement.

What he had was a mini-fridge and a small under-the-counter wine refrigerator.

"Something red?"

He grinned. "My favorite color."

While he picked a wine, she collected her bra and panties, then ducked into the half bath in the corner. By the time she was done straightening and had returned to the living room of his suite, he'd poured them each a glass and turned on the gas fireplace.

"Now you're going for the romance thing?" she asked. "Isn't it a little late?"

"You mean because I already got the girl?" He led her to the sofa and settled next to her.

"You got the girl in a bright and shiny new way. You have a lot of upper body strength."

"I should accept the compliment with a knowing smile," he said as he put his arm around her. "Instead I'll tell the truth, which is that it's all about leverage."

She winced. "Not sure I wanted to know that."

"Why?"

She stared at the fire, trying not to enjoy the moment too much. "Not the mechanics. The fact that you have so much experience that you can talk about them. It's scary."

He angled toward her, which meant his warm arm wasn't around her, but he left his hand on her shoulder. "I won't lie to you. I had a great time when I was in my early twenties. I was a well-known athlete and women were everywhere. I took advantage of that." He gave her a slow, sexy smile. "It was fun."

And he was telling her this why? Because it wasn't making her feel any better.

"I'm not that guy anymore," he said. "I grew up a long time ago. But people don't want to believe that. They like the legend and stories that go with that. If I'm still the guy on the poster, then they get glory by association."

She could almost understand that. "The opposite of the old saying that you can't be a hero in your hometown?"

"Yeah. I can't stop being a hero." He grimaced. "That sounds arrogant. I'm not trying to be a jerk. I'm just saying that's how it's been with me for years. This town took care of me. They looked out for me and they feel they've earned a piece of me. They like thinking I have a different woman in my room every night because it feeds the story and they like how that story plays."

She thought about him riding his bike, coming back sweaty and everyone assuming it was because he was out getting lucky.

"It's not like you want to correct the assumption," she pointed out. "You don't tell them differently."

"I don't want them to know the truth."

That he couldn't ride, she thought. He didn't want to spoil the fantasy.

"I got divorced about two years ago," he told her. "I dated a little after that, but nothing came of it. I moved back here, and since then..." Now it was his turn to glance away. "Let's just say it's been a hell of a dry spell."

"Thank you. That makes me feel better. I've never been good at being one in a crowd."

"Me, either."

"What? There's no crowd."

He raised his eyebrows.

"Oh, please. Do not even pretend I'm sleeping with Robert," she told him. "We've had all of three dates. Besides, he's not my type."

"That's not what you were saying earlier."

"You annoyed me," she told him. "On purpose. What was I supposed to say?"

"You annoyed me, too."

"How?"

"You went out with him."

Oh.

Talk about unexpected. Charity glanced at Josh, then away. She sipped her wine, more for something to do than because she was thirsty. Her confusion faded and she found herself feeling a little gooey inside. Maybe the wild wall sex wasn't the smartest decision she'd ever made, but maybe it hadn't been a total mistake.

"I won't be going out with him again," she murmured.

"Good."

She glanced at Josh from under her lashes. "He, ah, has a fondness for the Civil War. One of the bedrooms is devoted to miniature displays of various battles. There are buildings and roads and little tiny trees."

His mouth twitched. "I'm sure a lot of research goes into making those."

"I'm sure it does."

She shifted so she was facing him, tucking her right leg under her. "Don't take this the wrong way, because I'm not really a sports person." She paused. "So how good were you?"

He laughed. "I was the best. Ranked number one, and for a couple of years that was against Lance Armstrong. You name a race and I've probably won it. I had multimillion-dollar endorsement deals. I still have a couple. I was on the cover of every racing magazine and most sports-related publications. I've been in People's sexiest issues a couple of times."

"I read People," she murmured, knowing she would have looked at his picture as just one of the pretty people who weren't real. "Now I'm getting scared again."

"Why?"

"It's the rock star thing. I never had that fantasy."

"I can't play guitar."

"You know what I mean. The fame. I never wanted any association with someone well known. My life is quiet and I prefer it that way."

"I'm not famous now."

"You are, but it's different here. I told you my mom and I moved around a lot when I was young. All I ever wanted was a place to belong. Roots. Connection. Family. Mostly family. I don't need to be important to the world. In fact I don't want that—too much responsibility. But I do want someone to care, if that makes sense."

"It does."

THE LAMP BEHIND them caught the lighter tones of Charity's soft brown hair. It played with the side of her face, making her eyes seem larger and more mysterious. She had a look about her, a combination of satisfaction and "what the hell was I thinking?"

Not that Josh had any answers. The sex hadn't been planned, but it sure had been good. One second he'd been pissed about her date with Robert and how unexpectedly good she'd looked, the next he'd been hell bent for taking anything she offered. He wanted her again, but slower this time. He wanted her in his bed, naked, with all the time in the world to explore her body, touch her soft skin. He wanted to taste her everywhere. He wanted to make her come in a thousand different ways. He wanted to lose himself in her over and over again. So much for being a guy who didn't ever get involved.

"You have the Hendrixes," she said. "They're your family."

It took him a second to remember what they were talking about. "They've always been good to me. Denise wanted a daughter. After three boys she was desperate to try one more time. She really wanted a girl. She got three."

Charity's eyes widened. "Must have been a shock."

"Uh-huh. By the time I moved in, the girls were about three. They were a handful. Still are. Denise was pretty sick after they were born. For a while, the doctors were afraid she wasn't going to pull through. The boys were scared and there were three babies to worry about. To make the kids feel better, their dad said they could name the trip-lets." He grinned.

"That sounds like trouble."

"Not so bad. They're Nevada, Montana and Dakota."

"It could be worse."

"I heard Oceania was in the running."

She winced. "Okay, then Montana is a whole lot more mainstream than that." She looked at him. "You enjoyed living with them."

"I did."

"Everyone here has ties," she said, sounding wistful. "A history."

Josh swore silently. At times like this, he really hated the position Marsha had put him in. The secret was hers to keep or tell, but the longer she was quiet, the worse it was going to be.

"I think it's better if no one knows what happened to-night," he said quickly, to distract her.

Charity's head snapped up. "What?"

"People will talk, what with you being new and all in town." He shrugged. "I don't want anyone to know you're using me."

Her mouth dropped open. "Using you?"

"You took advantage of me. Tempted me with your femi-nine wiles so you could trick me into having sex with you."

She put her glass of wine on the coffee table and launched herself at him. Fortunately his drink was also safely on the table, so he was able to catch her.

She wiggled and twisted, shrieking, not quite hitting him, but coming close. He wrapped his arms around her and held her still.

"What are you doing?" he asked.

"I'm not sure."

"Because if you were trying to hurt me, you failed."

"I know." She shifted so she could glare at him. "I'm not using you for sex."

"You didn't even buy me dinner first."

She shrieked. "You're the guy."

"Great. So you not only took advantage of me, you're sexist, too."

"Dammit, Josh." She shoved at his chest, then dropped her head on his shoulder. "You make me crazy."

"I do what I can."

She chuckled. "I've never known anyone like you."

"I get that a lot."

"I didn't mean it as a compliment." She looked up at him again, her expression serious. "About what we did… It would probably be better if we didn't talk about it. You're right. I am new in town and while I do believe you're not the wild man everyone thinks, no one else does."

"I know." He cupped her face, then kissed her. "You're not the type to enjoy being another notch on my bike."

"I've never heard it put quite like that, but it gets the point across."

As she stared at him, looking both worried and hopeful, he knew she wasn't trying to be cruel. That in her world, privacy mattered and her reputation was everything. A reputation he could destroy with a casual comment or two.

He'd been living in the public eye for so long, he'd forgotten what anything else was like.

She smiled slowly. "Is there a fan club? I should probably join."

"I'll get you an application. The dues are reasonable and you get an autographed picture of me, suitable for framing."

She laughed. "Really? Is it that bare-butt shower shot?"

"How do you know about that?"

"Sheryl, my assistant, had it as part of her screen saver. I had to ask her to remove it." She lowered her voice. "It's not exactly appropriate for a work setting."

"Probably not. You don't have to worry. The fan club doesn't send out the butt shot."

"Too bad. It was impressive."

"Yeah?"

"Uh-huh."

"Good."

She was stretched out across him, her body nestling against his. Despite his recent release, he could feel the need building up inside of him. Once again, the image of taking things slow, of learning every inch of her body, filled his mind.

But this wasn't the time. What had happened earlier had been spontaneous. Taking her to his bed would imply more than he was willing to offer right now. He might not know everything about Charity, but he knew she was the type who got involved first. Who gave her heart along with her body. He wasn't anyone to be trusted with a good woman's heart.

So as much as he wanted to lower his head and kiss her again, he instead shifted out from under her. He rose, and then pulled her to her feet.

"I'm going to walk you home."

"I know the way."

"Maybe, but the streets are dangerous. I don't want anything to happen to you."

"My door is about five feet from yours. What could happen?"

"You never know."

She smiled, then picked up her sandals and her purse. He followed her to the door.

She reached for the handle, then turned back to him. "You're nothing like I thought."

"Don't be telling people that. If anyone asks, I'm a god in bed, remember."

"Oh, you're that. It's just…" She placed her fingers on his cheek. "Someone who's as famous as you, as successful, as good-looking, could easily be a real jerk. You're not. You care about people. You understand. I know my opinion doesn't mean anything, but your ex-wife was really stupid to let you go."

He'd been given thousands of compliments over the years. Maybe more. Women had praised everything from his looks to his equipment. Most of the time, he'd known they were simply trying to get what they wanted.

Now, as he stared into Charity's pretty eyes and saw the earnest truth there, he knew she meant what she said.

"Thank you," he said.

She gave him a quick smile, then opened the door. Seconds later, she was safely in her own room, and he was alone in the hallway. As he walked the few feet back to his room, he realized it had been a very long time since anyone had believed in him. No, that wasn't true. He'd always had supporters. The only person who mattered who didn't believe in him was himself.

Josh slept like a rock, woke early and got to his office a little before seven. Eddie arrived at seven-thirty, dressed in her yellow velour track suit, and glared at him.

"This is my quiet time," she announced. "What are you doing here?"

"Working." He didn't bother mentioning it was his office and he employed her. Eddie wouldn't see the point of the statement.

"You're never here before eight. You better not make a habit of coming in early."

He winked at her. "I'll do my best."

"Did you at least make coffee?"

He pointed to the pot.

She sighed. "Sometimes, you're not half bad."

She poured herself a cup, then returned to her desk. He could still hear her grumbling, probably at him, but ignored the sound. He had needed to focus on the proposal his attorney had sent over. A potential investment in the form of a shopping mall in Las Vegas. When the real estate market bottomed out, a lot of commercial properties went into foreclosure. Now they were available for pennies on the dollar, especially for an investor willing to pay cash.

He reviewed the demographics of the immediate neighborhood, the list of current renters and the retail competition. The corner lot of two busy streets was prime, and if he didn't like the tenant mix, he could always change it.

"It's Steve," Eddie called.

Josh looked up. She was waving her phone at him.

"Steve, your former coach. Tall guy, balding."

"Thanks. I got it."

He and Steve hadn't talked in months. Maybe over a year. Josh hadn't needed a coach after he retired.

"Morning," he said when he'd grabbed the phone. "You're up early."

"I'm in Florida. It's practically noon here. How's it going?"

"Good. And with you?"

Steve grunted. "I'm working with a bunch of kids. A lot of potential but no discipline. They're like puppies, too easily distracted. A pretty girl in a bikini walks by and they go crashing into each other. It makes me tired."

Josh leaned back in his chair. "Anyone special?" He meant the riders, not the girl, but knew Steve would figure that out.

"There's this one guy. Jorge. Poor family, didn't start riding seriously until high school. He has a lot of catching up to do, but I think he has it."

"Looking for sponsorship?" Josh had been approached before. So far he hadn't been willing, but if Steve thought the guy was worth it, he could consider the investment.

"I wasn't, but let me think about it. You'd want to come see him ride before you decide."

Josh hadn't thought that far ahead, although his former coach was right. He would have to fly to Florida before making a decision. Which meant stepping foot back in the world where he'd once been king. Something he'd been avoiding for the past two years.

"But Jorge isn't why I called," Steve told him. "It's about the charity bike race. You heard we lost our corporate sponsor."

"That's what happens when the CEO steals the pension fund and runs off with his secretary."

"Apparently." Steve sounded frustrated. "You know these races happen all over the country and normally I wouldn't bother you, but this is different. The proceeds go to support medical research for juvenile diabetes and my sister's kid has it, so it's personal. I saw your town was asking for more information, and I figured you were behind that. I wanted to talk to you personally, to do what you could to get them to say yes. Everything is in place. We have a lot of great riders lined up. You'd get to see a lot of friends. And Jorge will be racing, so it would save you a trip. Hell, we'd even let you enter if you wanted to stage a comeback. You were always the best, Josh. No reason to think that's changed."

Josh felt as if someone had slugged him in the gut. "I, ah, haven't been training," he said, knowing his night rides had kept him in decent shape but nowhere near ready to compete. Assuming he ever could. Hell, at this point, just the thought of it had him shaking like a little girl.

"There's time," Steve told him. "You know what to do. If you're interested. You retired too early, Josh. I know you were shaken by what happened to Frank, but walking away didn't bring him back."

"Always the coach."

"I try. Can you help with the race?"

Josh had been wrestling with his demons for two years now. So far they'd won every round. Maybe it was time for a little payback.

Before he could come up with an easy list of why this was a massive mistake, he said, "I know a few people in town. I can make the race happen."

"That's great. I owe you. Anything, Josh. I mean it." Steve paused. "Are you going to ride?"

No. He couldn't ride with a five-year-old on a bike with training wheels. There was no way he was ready. If he said yes, he would only humiliate himself in front of the best riders in the sport. Word would spread and everyone would know he was a frightened, broken loser. Not much of a legacy.

"Josh?"

Dammit it all to hell, he thought and held the phone so tightly, he was surprised it didn't snap. "Sure," he said, hoping he sounded casual instead of terrified. "I'll ride."

CHAPTER TEN

"OBVIOUSLY THE MISSING money is our primary concern," Marsha said from her place at the head of the table. "I had an unpleasant call from the governor this morning. It's not an experience I want to repeat." She sighed. "I'm not blaming you, Robert, I'm just frustrated."

"So am I," he said. "You've hired an auditor. She'll be here next week. In the meantime, we've already begun our own investigation. Three quarters of a million dollars is a lot of money to lose."

Charity heard the worry in his voice and understood the cause. He was the treasurer and the money had gone missing on his watch. He had to be frantic. She wished she could help, but her accounting expertise was limited to a single class she'd taken in college and barely passed. Math wasn't exactly her thing.

The morning meeting had started right on time, with several items on the agenda. Charity enjoyed the review of everything going on in the world that was Fool's Gold. Normally the items were discussed in order, but for the past thirty minutes, Pia had been squirming in her seat.

Charity tried not to stare, but it was difficult to ignore Pia's eager expression and tapping foot.

Marsha made a few notes on the pad in front of her, then glanced at Pia. "I assume you're not trying to tell me you have to go to the bathroom?"

"No."

"Then why don't you tell us what is obviously the most exciting news ever."

Pia grinned. "I can wait my turn."

"Perhaps, but then you'll so annoy one of the city council members that she'll snap and kill you. What is it, Pia?"

Pia cleared her throat. "Remember that bike race that lost its sponsors and had nowhere to go? We're getting it! I've spoken with the committee leaders and they're very excited about the opportunity to bring their event to our town. The bike race is only one day, but there's a celebrity golf tournament, as well. We're talking three, maybe four nights of people staying."

She paused as the council members started murmuring to each other.

"That's huge," Gladys said. "Four nights? We're talking some major revenue."

"It's going to be a logistical nightmare," Alice said. "I'll need overtime approval and money to hire a few temporary people to help with crowd control."

"Get me an estimate," Marsha told her. "Pia, do you have a full report prepared?"

"I just found out this morning. I'll have it to you tomorrow. Most of the preliminary work is done. We did that golf tournament last year, so I'll use that for a blueprint. I'm talking to Josh later, to get a feel for the race."

Gladys raised her eyebrows. "Is that all you'll be getting a feel for?"

"Not everyone has your thing for Josh," Pia told the older woman.

"Name one woman who doesn't."

Most of the women chuckled. Charity did her best to

look as if she was enjoying the joke without drawing attention to herself.

Last night was burned into her brain. She couldn't believe what had happened, what she'd done. She'd never been that wild or uninhibited in her life and she'd certainly never made love with a guy she barely knew.

And yet…she couldn't seem to find even a hint of a regret. Not only because the physical experience had been incredible, but because the more time she spent with Josh, the more she actually liked him.

Now, as Pia went into more detail about the race, Charity wondered how he would handle the news. It would probably upset him, she thought, feeling sympathy. His past would be discussed, the press might even want interviews. Plus, having all those racers in town would remind him of everything he'd been forced to walk away from.

If he were anyone else, she would suggest that he head out of town for the weekend and avoid the circus. But Josh wouldn't. He would stay and be available and not let anyone know how it was eating him up inside.

"There's more," Pia said, her eyes bright with excitement. "I saved the best for last."

"I'm not sure how there can be more," Marsha told her.

"There is. Josh is going to be riding in the race. He's making his comeback right here in Fool's Gold."

Conversation exploded. Everyone was talking over everyone else. Even Alice looked happy about the news. Charity did her best to join in the moment, but it was difficult for her to get her mind around the information. Josh racing? How could he?

She'd heard the pain in his voice when he talked about the accident and his inability to ride with anyone. Wouldn't racing mean training and exposure? Wouldn't the whole town see what he was doing?

Even as she asked herself the questions, she wondered if that was the point. If he'd decided to face the problem head-on. If he was successful, it would be an impressive moment. But if he failed, the world would know. Talk about jumping in the deep end. She didn't know if she should admire him or tell him to think about therapy.

Marsha called for order and the meeting resumed. When it was finished, Charity made sure she walked out with Robert. They had some unfinished business.

"I had a great time last night," he said as they headed down the hall. "What are you doing this weekend?"

She winced silently. She waited until they'd stepped into her office to speak.

"Thanks for inviting me over," she began. "Your home is lovely. Especially the garden. The thing is, while I would love for us to be friends, I don't see us having a romantic relationship."

He frowned at her. "I don't understand. Last night I thought you had a good time."

"I did." A polite lie, she told herself.

"Is there someone else?"

"No."

Not a lie. Yes, she and Josh had done the wild thing, but that did not a relationship make. After all, it wasn't as if she was in love with him.

"When we first went out, I thought I was ready to get involved," she said. "But I'm not. I'm busy with working and getting settled. You're great, Robert. I know you'll find someone."

"In this town, finding someone is the easy part," he said, sounding more confused than annoyed. "I guess I understand. I thought you were special, Charity. That's why I wanted to get to know you better."

"I appreciate that."

"If you're sure?"

"I am."

"Okay."

He left. She returned to her desk, relieved there hadn't been anything remotely uncomfortable about their conversation. A cheap lesson, she told herself. Workplace romances were innately difficult. She should avoid them.

Josh didn't work in City Hall, a little voice in her whispered. Interesting, but not significant, she told herself firmly. Josh was a fantasy. She was looking for someone real. Although the way she'd felt in his arms last night had been about as real as it could get.

"MY LIFE IS INSANE," Pia said, two days later, as she sat across from Charity at the Fox and Hound. "I'm loving the idea of the bike race, but talk about extra work. I may come after you for help when it gets closer."

"Absolutely," Charity told her.

"I'm lining up a team, then figuring out what volunteers can do. Crystal's really excited about the whole thing, especially Josh coming out of retirement." Pia grinned. "Like the rest of us, she once had a thing for him. Before she met her husband."

"It does seem to be a universal condition," Charity said, hoping she sounded both friendly and neutral.

"Crystal's great at organizing, but with her being sick, she can't always be available. Still, I'll take what I can get." She scanned the menu. "The Josh angle is the best part. It'll give us a lot more press than we would have gotten otherwise. I never understood why he retired when he did. He was at the top of his game. That last season, he couldn't lose. It was amazing to watch."

Until the race where Frank died, Charity thought, knowing the loss had devastated Josh and stolen a piece of him.

The server came and they placed their orders. When she'd left, Pia leaned toward Charity. "You look great. That jacket is adorable. Am I allowed to say that?"

Charity laughed. "Yes. Pia, it's fine. I told you before, I appreciate your blunt, albeit drunk, honesty about how I looked. I'm having fun remembering how to do the girly stuff. I'm even getting highlights."

"They'd look good on you." Pia sipped her diet soda. "The problem is where to go. The two best places in town are owned by two sisters who have a serious rivalry. Not only for clients, but for gossip. Each of them has to be the first to know anything. If you're loyal to one, you're the enemy of the other. I get around the problem by alternating back and forth. They try to pin me down, but I won't let them."

"That sounds like a lot of work."

"It is, but worth it to keep the peace. You're still living at the hotel, aren't you? There used to be a salon there, but it closed. How is it living like the rich and famous?"

"Not so rich and certainly not famous. It's fine until I can find a place of my own. I get a special rate through the city." Compliments of Josh, she thought. Marsha had told her about the discount when she'd hired Charity.

"I've started looking for a house to buy," she continued. "There was one place I saw that was terrific. It's a restored craftsman-style house. I love everything about it except the price. I heard the owner would be willing to bargain, but even then I'm not sure I can swing it."

Pia frowned. "Which house is that?"

Charity told her the street. "There's a wide porch and a beautiful backyard. I love the mature trees on the street."

"Who told you the owner was willing to deal?"

Charity tried not to feel trapped. "Um, Josh mentioned it."

"Did he?" Pia's mouth turned into a knowing smile. "He must really like you. He put a lot of money into that property and was expecting top dollar for it."

"What do you mean?"

"He owns the house. He bought it a few years ago and fixed it up. Actually he was still racing then, so he had the work done. He used it as a rental, then decided to sell it. I know a few people are interested and he's not lowering the price for them."

Pia's expression turned speculative. "He's always put business before the ladies, but that seems to be changing."

Charity did her best not to blush. "I have no idea what you're talking about. I didn't know Josh owned the house."

"You do now."

"But he didn't tell me."

He hadn't even hinted when he'd shown her the house. Although looking back, she should have guessed something was up when he'd had a key.

"Why would he do that?"

Pia raised her eyebrows. "You tell me."

"We're not together."

"Maybe he wants to be."

"No. Guys like him don't…" She shook her head. "He's too…"

"Rich, successful, hot?"

"I'm not his type."

"How do you know?"

"Then I'll pose it as a question. Am I his type?"

"Until today, I would have said no. But maybe times are changing."

CHARITY LEFT HER lunch with Pia nearly as hungry as when she'd arrived. She'd only been able to pick at her salad, mostly because she was thinking about Josh and the house and what Pia had said.

It made no sense for him to give her a break on the price when other people would be offering him more. It implied a relationship they didn't have. The fact that he'd done it before the "incident"—as she was now thinking of it—should have helped, but only made the situation more confusing.

Just as mind-bending was Pia's implication that Josh might be interested in her. He wasn't. His ex-wife had been some gorgeous actress. Charity was going to have to go online and find out who, exactly. But the point was, he was not someone orbiting in her universe. Interested? On what planet?

Yes, they'd had sex, but only because they'd both been carried away by the moment. Her more literally, but still. She refused to read too much into a single evening of hot lovemaking. That's how hearts got broken.

She did her best to push any thoughts of Josh out of her mind, only to have them resurface when she saw his offices up ahead. Maybe she should simply ask the question outright. Why was he giving her a deal on a house when he didn't have to? Asking him was the adult, mature thing to do. She squared her shoulders and walked into the building.

"THERE'S SOMEONE HERE to see you," Eddie told Josh. "She doesn't have an appointment. She being the operative word here. Although I'll give her credit. She's not like the usual groupies who come looking for you. She's out of her teens, for one thing, and dressed like a regular person."

Josh wasn't in the mood to dash anyone's hopes this afternoon. He had a lot to deal with, including figuring out

how he was going to start training—a relatively easy problem to solve—while dealing with an irrational inability to
ride with other people. A problem with a less clear solution.

"You can handle her," he told Eddie.

"I can, but I don't want to. She claims you know her.
Charity Jones."

He was out of his seat before she'd finished speaking.
"Why didn't you say so?"

"I just did. Are you giving me attitude?"

He ignored her outrage and went out to the reception
area. Charity stood in the center, looking nervous and determined. She managed a faint smile, which made him want
to promise to fix whatever problem she had.

"I didn't have an appointment," she told him. "Do you
have a minute?"

"Sure. You don't need an appointment."

"It would be nice if someone made one," Eddie said
with a sniff.

Josh pointed to her desk. Eddie sighed heavily before
returning to it. He put his hand on the small of Charity's
back, leading her to his office and then closing the door
behind them.

"Your assistant has a lot of personality," Charity said.

"She's efficient and takes care of me."

"I like her."

"Me, too. Not that I want her to know."

Charity's smile turned genuine. "She'd use it against
you forever."

"Tell me about it."

He motioned to the sofa and chairs in the corner. "Can
I get you anything? Coffee? Iced tea?"

"I'm fine. I just had lunch with Pia." She sat in a chair.

He took the center of the sofa. "What's going on?"

She clasped her hands together. "I'm not sure where to start."

She didn't sound worried, which was good. As he didn't have a clue as to what she wanted to talk about, he simply waited. Checking out the view filled the seconds. She wore a short jacket over a lacy shirt and black pants. Very "woman in charge," a look he enjoyed. It made him think about taming that power, and making the lady in question weak with longing.

"That house we went to," she began, forcing him to ignore the fantasy of a naked Charity writhing under him.

"You want to make an offer?"

"Not exactly. You own that house."

He wasn't sure how she found out, but he wasn't surprised, either.

"Does it matter who's selling it?"

She drew in a breath. "You've had other offers. People who can pay more than me."

"I put a lot into that house. I want it to go to the right person."

"You're giving me a break on the price that you're not giving them."

Normally he would have been happy to take credit for being a great guy, but there was something in her tone, in the way she stared so intently.

"And that's bad why?" he asked.

"How much of the town do you own?" she asked. "I know about the hotel. Do you own this building? More houses?"

"Want to see a profit and loss statement? My accountant prepares one every quarter."

"No. Of course not. But you're rich."

"By some definitions."

She shook her head. "Don't play games. You're successful and rich and gorgeous and great in bed." She sucked in a breath. "Well, I can't say about the 'in bed' part, but you obviously know what you're doing and you do it well. And you're nice."

Her tone told him she wasn't trying to compliment him. The last statement had come out like an accusation.

"Okay," he said neutrally.

She stood, so he rose. She faced him.

"It's so not fair. Why can't this be easier?" she asked.

He shoved his hands in his pockets. Answering the question would be less of a problem if he knew what they were talking about. "I, ah…"

"Sure. For you," she grumbled. "You get whoever you want. You practically have women being delivered by room service."

"I don't do that."

"I know. I didn't mean that, exactly. It's just you could if you wanted. And you don't, which means more points for you."

"Charity? What are we talking about?"

She glared at him. "My life. My sucky love life. I don't get it. Is it genetic? Karma? Did I do something bad in a previous life?"

He stood there, feeling helpless. "There's nothing wrong with you." She was pretty and smart and funny and when she smiled at him, he had the feeling that he could do just about anything.

"Isn't there? Look at Robert. Isn't he nice? Calm and pleasant and looking to settle down. But there's not a scrap of chemistry. I couldn't do it. I tried, but I couldn't do it. And he would fall in the column of my more successful relationships. My first boyfriend hit me. Just once, but he did it."

Josh's hands curled into fists. "Where is he now?" he asked, his voice low and angry.

"It was ten years ago," she said. "I walked out and never saw him again. But still. It made me wonder. My second serious boyfriend cleaned out my savings account. Talk about feeling stupid. The last one…" She sighed. "I'm not even going there. It's too humiliating. And now there's you. I like you. I like you a lot. Which means all I can think is if I like you then what on earth is wrong with you?"

With that, she turned and left.

Josh stood in the center of his office, trying not to grin like a fool. She liked him? Hot damn!

CHARITY STALKED OUT of Josh's office, feeling foolish and exposed and a thousand other things that weren't very pleasant. Her head was spinning, her chest felt tight and if she were the type to give in to tears, she would be having a breakdown right here on the sidewalk.

Instead she kept moving, head held high, smiling at people on the street. She saw Morgan in his bookstore and waved at the old man. He grinned back.

Now that was a simple relationship, she thought, trying to grit her teeth. She understood all the elements of it. She and Morgan were friends. They said hello, talked about the weather and went on with their lives. No complications. No handsome, hunky guy messing with her head.

What had she been thinking, telling Josh she liked him? Were they in high school? "Tell Bobby I like him, but only if he says he likes me first."

She was confused, upset and unsettled.

Despite the fact that her mother hadn't been the most

maternal of women, Charity found herself wishing she was still alive so that she could ask for her advice. As silly as it sounded, right now she could use a hug from her mother. Or an aunt. Even a long-lost cousin would be good.

She walked into City Hall and started up the stairs. At the top, she passed Marsha, walking out of the break room with a cup of coffee.

"How was your lunch?" the mayor asked.

"Good. Pia's always fun."

"She is. She was a bit of a terror when she was younger." Marsha frowned. "What's that expression? She was a mean girl."

"Pia?" Charity couldn't imagine it.

"She was pretty and popular and wanted her way. Not a good combination in a teenager. But she turned out well." Marsha sipped her coffee. "Is everything all right? I don't mean to pry, but you look… I'm not sure. If I had to pick, I would say you look sad."

Charity forced herself to smile. "I'm fine. Missing my mom, a little. She died several years ago. I guess that's something you never get over."

Marsha stiffened and the color drained from her face.

Charity moved toward her. "Are you all right?"

"Yes. Of course. The loss of a mother is always tragic. I still miss mine and she's been gone over thirty years." Marsha squared her shoulders. "Charity, would you please come with me into my office."

"Sure."

Charity followed her. Something was wrong, she could feel it, but she had no idea what it was. Had she done something wrong? Had she crossed a line talking about something personal?

When they reached Marsha's office, the mayor did

something Charity had never experienced before. Not in Fool's Gold. She closed her doors. Then she led the way to the small conversation area by the wall.

"There's something I have to tell you," Marsha said when they were both seated. "I've been waiting for the right time. Which is the coward's way of saying I didn't know how to tell you. I suppose the best way is to simply blurt out the words."

Charity did her best not to go to the bad place. Possibilities flashed through her mind. Marsha was sick and/or dying. Charity was about to be fired. The town was going to disappear into a giant sinkhole. But no scenario prepared her for what came next.

Marsha leaned forward, lightly touching Charity's arm as she gave her a gentle smile. "I'm your grandmother."

CHAPTER ELEVEN

CHARITY WAS GLAD she was seated. There was no way she could have stayed standing after hearing Marsha's announcement.

"My..."

"Grandmother. Sandra Tilson, or as you knew her, Sandra Jones, was my daughter. Do you need some water?"

Charity shook her head. The words made sense, but she couldn't accept their meaning. Grandmother, as in family? Sandra had always told Charity they were alone in the world, that they only had each other. Although Charity was sure her mother would have easily withheld that kind of truth if she wanted to. Sandra wasn't a bad person, but she'd been determined to live by her own rules.

Now, in the quiet office of the mayor of Fool's Gold, Charity stared at the sixty-something woman sitting across from her and looked for the truth in her eyes.

She thought it might be there in the shape of the jaw, the particular shade of her eyes. Just like her mother's. But a grandmother?

"I don't understand," she whispered.

Marsha rose and crossed to her desk. She opened a side drawer and pulled out a slim photo album then walked back and handed it to Charity.

Charity ran her fingers across the red leather cover, almost afraid to open it.

"My husband died when I was very young and our daughter was still a toddler," the older woman began. "Having her helped me survive the grief. We were so close. She was a lovely, friendly child. So smart in school. But when she became a teenager, everything fell apart. She began to rebel."

Marsha clasped her hands together on her lap. "I didn't know what to do," she admitted. "I tried loving her more. I negotiated with her. Then, when things only got worse, I grounded her. Made the rules tougher. I became a controlling, dictatorial parent."

Charity continued to hold the album. "She wouldn't have done well with a lot of rules."

"You're right. The tighter I held on, the more she tried to slip away. I'd always been strict, but I became impossible. She responded by skipping school, going to parties, drinking and using drugs. She and a few friends were arrested for stealing a car. I was humiliated and at my wit's end. I didn't know how to get through to her. Then she told me she was pregnant. She was barely seventeen."

Marsha drew in a breath. "It was too much. I completely lost it and screamed at her like no mother should. I accused her of ruining my life, of planning ways to embarrass me. I think at that second, I hated her."

She dropped her head a little. "I'm so ashamed now. I would give anything to have that moment, those words, back. Sandra glared at me with all the loathing a seventeen-year-old is capable of and said she would make my life easier. She would go away. I remember I laughed and told her that my luck wasn't that good."

Marsha swallowed and met Charity's gaze. "She was gone the next morning. I couldn't believe it. That she would really leave. I was convinced she loved her creature comforts too much to give them up. But I was wrong." Tears filled her eyes.

Charity leaned toward her. "You didn't do anything wrong. You had a fight. Mothers and daughters fight. My mother and I—" She paused. Her mother might possibly be Marsha's daughter. Could they really be talking about the same person?

"I appreciate you taking my side, but I know what I did and where the blame lies. With me." A single tear slipped down her cheek. She brushed it away. "She disappeared. I don't know how she did it, but she was gone. Totally and completely gone. I couldn't find her. I looked and looked, hired professionals, begged God, sent flyers across the country. There wasn't a trace. Finally, nearly three years later, we got a break. One of the detectives I'd hired sent me an address in Georgia. I was on the next plane."

Hearing the story was like listening to a recap of a made-for-TV movie, Charity thought. She was compelled, but not involved. This wasn't about her. In theory, she was part of it, but she couldn't feel the connection to events.

"You were so beautiful," Marsha said, her smile trembling. "I saw you first, playing in the yard. You were pushing a little plastic baby carriage around the lawn. You were about two and a half. Sandra was sitting on the step, watching you. The house was small, the neighborhood terrible. All I wanted to do was gather you both up and bring you home. Back here, to live with me."

Which didn't happen, Charity thought, not daring to wonder how her life would have been different if she'd grown up in a place like Fool's Gold. A small town where people cared about each other. A place where she could finally have roots.

"She was still angry," Marsha whispered. The smile

faded. "So angry. She wouldn't let me say anything, wouldn't listen to my apology. There was such rage in her voice and her eyes. She told me to go away. That she never wanted to see me again. She said if I tried to see her or you, she would make sure you both disappeared again, and that I would never find you. I was devastated."

Marsha drew in a breath. "Sorry. It's been a long time, but it feels so recent. So raw. I explained I had changed, learned from my mistakes. I said I wanted her back in my life. Both of you. She didn't care. She said she was done with me, with the rules and expectations. She was doing fine on her own and repeated that if she ever saw me again, she would disappear and I would never find either of you."

Charity's chest tightened as she saw the other woman's pain. "I'm sorry," she whispered. There was a part of her that said Sandra wouldn't have done that, except she knew it was more than possible. When Sandra made up her mind, she couldn't be budged. There was no going back. More than one of Sandra's men had discovered that too late to keep her.

"I came back home," Marsha said. "I was broken inside. I knew it was all my fault."

"It wasn't," Charity told her firmly. "You made a mistake, but you wanted to make it right. No one is perfect. We all make mistakes. It was Sandra's decision not to listen. Not to give you a second chance."

"Perhaps. I tried telling myself that. The truth is I tried to control every aspect of Sandra's life. Most children would have had trouble with that, but for Sandra, it was impossible to stand. Knowing that it was because I'd lost my husband, and was terrified that if I didn't handle everything, yet another tragedy would invade my life didn't seem to help."

She pressed her lips together, then spoke. "I left the

two of you. I didn't know what else to do. I thought about keeping tabs on her, but I was afraid she would find out. Years passed. The memories faded, but not the longing, the wondering. I thought about the two of you all the time. Ten years later, I hired another detective, to see if she could be found. He located her easily. The boy who had been your father…" Marsha's voice trailed off. "I'm saying too much."

Charity reached across the space separating them and touched Marsha's arm. "I know he died. She told me. I'd been asking a lot of questions. While I could believe my mom didn't have any family, I knew I had to have a father. Once he was gone, I stopped asking questions."

She'd been twelve, Charity remembered. Sandra had come in her room. They'd been living in a rented mobile home, in a park at the edge of Phoenix. Charity recalled everything about the room, the view out of her small window, the sound of the dripping faucet as Sandra told her that the boy who had gotten her pregnant had gone into the military and he'd been killed. A helicopter crash.

Marsha squeezed her hand. "I'm sorry. I thought it would make a difference, but it didn't. She never answered my letter and when I sent the detective to check on her, she was gone. Just like she'd promised. I'd lost her all over again."

She shrugged. "So I gave up. I stopped looking. Stopped hoping. I accepted that I'd chased away my only child and moved on with my life. Then a few months ago, I decided to try again."

Charity's chest tightened. "You hired another detective?"

Marsha nodded, her eyes filling with tears. "It didn't take him long to find out my baby girl had died. Cancer. He said it took her quickly."

Charity nodded. She'd had time to get used to the loss of her mother, but for Marsha, that news was fresh. Still painful. "I'm sorry," she whispered, realizing that when it came to Sandra everyone had been sorry except Sandra herself.

"It was a shock," Marsha admitted. "She was my only child. Shouldn't I have known? Guessed? Felt it in my heart? But there was nothing. No warning. I mourned her. I mourned what could have been. What I had thrown away."

"No," Charity said firmly. "You aren't completely responsible. Yes, you made mistakes, but so did she. The whole time I was growing up, I begged her to tell me about my family and she wouldn't. She refused, because what she felt was more important than what I wanted. She died, leaving me alone in the world, and never bothered to tell me the truth. I had you all this time and she never told me."

Now Charity was the one fighting tears. "I hated moving around. I would beg her to stay, but she wouldn't. When I was a junior in high school, I told her I was done. I was going to graduate from that high school. She promised to stay as long as she could. It was six months, and then she took off. I stayed. She sent me money when she could and I worked part-time. The rental was cheap enough. She wasn't even worried about me. She said I would be fine. She didn't even come back for graduation."

She turned to face Marsha. "Tell me you would have been there."

"Yes, but that's not—"

"The point? It's exactly the point."

Feelings Charity didn't normally allow surged up inside her. She'd learned that it was better not to think about some things too much. Better to always be in control. Now, as she felt that control starting to slip, she knew she had to get away.

"I'm sorry," she whispered. "I need to go. I'll… We'll talk later."

She grabbed her handbag and hurried from the room. After racing down the stairs and out of the building, she glanced in both directions, not sure where she should go. In the distance, to the left, she saw one of the three parks in town and headed there.

She wouldn't think about it, she told herself. And there was no way she was going to cry. She never cried. It accomplished nothing and left her feeling weak.

She walked briskly along the sidewalk, remembering to smile at people she passed. She reached the lush green park in a couple of minutes and ducked down one of the tree-lined paths until she found an empty bench. Once there, she collapsed and tried to sort out everything spinning in her head.

Her reaction to her mother keeping the information about Marsha to herself was obviously an emotional misdirect. Better to be pissed at Sandra than think about all she'd lost. All she'd missed out on.

She had family. A grandmother. And if it wasn't for her own mother's stubborn ways, she could have spent the past twenty-eight years knowing her.

Marsha Tilson. Which meant Charity's last name was probably Tilson and not Jones. Jeez, had Sandra even bothered to change her name legally before slapping "Jones" on Charity's birth certificate?

She heard footsteps and angled away from the path. At least there weren't any tears to wipe away. She braced herself to have to make polite chitchat, then nearly fell off her seat when she saw Josh moving toward her.

He looked concerned and uneasy, not to mention his usual stunningly handsome self.

"Hey," he said.

"Hey, yourself."

He paused in front of her. "I'm here to make sure you're all right."

How could he possibly know what was going on? There hadn't been enough time for him to hear the story from Marsha. Unless he already knew.

"When did she tell you she was my grandmother?" she asked, not sure if she was pissed or not.

"The day before the first interview."

The interview. The job. "Oh, God," she whispered. "Marsha hired me because I'm her granddaughter."

He sat next to her and put his arm around her. "She hired you because you were the best one for the job. She didn't make the decision by herself and you weren't the only candidate. It was a group decision. Don't you have enough on your plate without going there?"

"Maybe," she admitted, relaxing against him. She didn't want to. She wanted to be strong all on her own. But it felt so good to lean into his strength. As if he could hold all of her problems at bay.

"Who else knows?" she asked.

"Just me. She needed someone to talk to. Then after you got here, she wanted me to keep an eye on you."

Charity sat straight up. "What? Is that why you've been so nice to me? Did you sleep with me because my grandmother told you to?"

He grinned. "Want to run that last sentence by your common sense? What grandmother asks a guy to sleep with her only granddaughter?"

"Oh. You're probably right."

"Probably?"

Some of her outrage faded. She sagged back against him. "My head hurts."

"It'll get better. You need a little time to take everything in. But if you're going to have some surprise family, she's the one to have. Marsha's one of the good guys."

"I know, but it's so strange to think about. She's known about me all my life. She wanted to be a part of things. She wanted us to be together." Her eyes began to burn. She blinked away the sensation.

"My mother was the most stubborn person in the world," Charity whispered. "She was totally unconventional. She didn't care if I ate cake for breakfast, or what time I went to bed. She said she'd grown up with too many rules, that she didn't believe in them."

She glanced at him. "It sounds great in theory, but the truth was, I would have liked a few rules. I had to take responsibility for everything myself. I knew she wouldn't. I was making sure there was food in the house by the time I was nine and handling the bills by the time I was twelve. I wanted to be a kid, but I was too scared of what would happen if no one was in charge."

"I'm sorry," he said, stroking her hair. "You should have had better."

"I had better than a lot of people. I never went hungry. I had clothes and a roof over my head."

A pretty low bar, Josh thought, seriously pissed, but determined not to show it. The last thing Charity needed was to deal with his feelings. This was about her.

"She wasn't a bad person," Charity said. "Sandra loved me."

Another point he wouldn't argue, but he didn't believe Sandra was all that good a person. He doubted Marsha had been a perfect mother—no one was—but she'd always led with her heart. She was tough, but fair. No one changed that much and the woman he'd known since he was ten years old was giving and loving, and if she'd been strict, there would have been a reason. He would know—she'd looked after him, offering advice and support.

He knew she'd supplemented dozens of kids' college educations, gave both money and time to several charities and ached for the one thing she'd lost—a family.

To his way of thinking, the fault was Sandra's. Not for running away, but for insisting that Charity not have anything to do with her grandmother. It was one thing for Sandra to hold a grudge, but she'd had no right to impose those rules on her daughter.

"I don't know what to think," Charity admitted.

"Give it time. Things have a way of getting clearer."

"I ran out on Marsha. I have to say something to her. Explain."

"She knows you were overwhelmed. That's why she called me."

"The neutral third party?"

"The brilliant and hunky guy who will distract you."

Charity managed a smile. "Oh, right. Silly me." She straightened. "You're right. I need to give it time. This has been a huge shock and I don't have to do anything about it right now. I can live with the information, then decide what it means to me."

"An excellent plan."

The smile faded. "The worst of it is, I can't get closure. Not totally. Sandra's gone and I can't go back and ask why she never told me about my grandmother."

"She had her reasons," he said carefully, not wanting to step into anything unpleasant.

"Stupid ones." She stood. "Okay. I need to get back to work. That will distract me." She lightly kissed him. "Thank you."

"You're welcome."

"You didn't have to come after me. I would have been fine."

"I enjoy a good rescue."

Her dark eyes stared into his. "You're a really nice guy."

He pressed his index finger to his mouth. "It's a secret. Don't tell anyone."

That earned him another smile. "I think word has already gotten out."

DEMONS CAME IN all shapes and sizes. Josh's were in the form of twelve guys from the local high school. They ranged in age from fifteen to eighteen, mostly skinny and awkward-looking on the ground, but they could fly like the wind on bikes.

Coach Green, a tall, skinny guy about Josh's age, practically danced in place. "This is the best," he said, grinning. "I raced in college. Nothing like you did, of course. I didn't have the raw ability. But man, I wanted to be just like you. I can't tell you how excited we all are to have you working out with us."

Josh swallowed against the tightness in his chest. It didn't help. The worship in Coach Green's voice was only making a crappy situation even more potentially disastrous. What the hell had he been thinking when he'd agreed to participate in the race? It wasn't that he was going to get his ass kicked—it was that he was going to humiliate himself in front of the world. Everyone was going to know he was a sniveling, frightened coward. Talk about a shitty legacy.

"It's been a long time since I've been on a bike," Josh lied. His last ride had been the previous night. But it had been what felt like fifteen lifetimes since he'd ridden with anyone else. Stood next to other riders. Heard the sounds, exchanged conversation, then focused on the race.

Even looking at the kids who kept glancing at him, he felt the bands lock around his chest. He couldn't breathe, but that was the least of it. What killed him was the mind-numbing terror. Anywhere but here, he told himself. He'd rather stand in fire than go through this.

"The guys will go easy on you," the coach joked.

Only it wasn't a joke and no one knew, Josh though grimly.

Green called the guys over. They walked their bikes toward him, their young faces bright with anticipation. They introduced themselves. A couple shook hands with him.

He'd seen most of them around town. He recognized their faces. Now he was supposed to ride with them.

"Josh is coming out of retirement for a charity race in a few weeks," Coach Green said. "He's going to be training with us until then."

"Sweet!" one of the guys said.

"I'm old and out of shape," Josh said. "Be gentle."

The guys laughed.

Coach Green yelled for them to line up and start the warm up.

Josh moved behind the kids. He'd go in the back, he thought. Keep the other riders where he could see them. A few miles at an easy pace would be good.

A whistle blew. The riders pushed off and cycled away. Josh waited until they were at least a hundred yards ahead before starting himself. He focused on moving the bike forward, of warming up his muscles, of the familiar feel of what he did.

It had been two years since he'd ridden during the day. He'd forgotten how bright everything was, the colors of trees and buildings as they passed in a blur. There was a light wind and the temperature was in the sixties. Perfect, he thought.

The kids in front of him had picked up the pace, so he did, as well. Inside of him, something woke, stirring to life. A burning need to reach them and pass them. The desire to win.

The sensation surprised him. He would have thought humiliation would have crushed any competitive spirit he had left, but obviously not.

Without any kind of a plan, he pedaled harder and faster, easily closing the distance between him and the students. One of the guys noticed and yelled something. The pack sped up. Josh continued to gain, feeling the blood moving through his body, the rush when he realized all he was capable of, knew that he hadn't lost everything.

"No way, Golden," one of the kids yelled as he reached them. "You're not beating us."

They crowded together, around him. Moving close to trap him between them.

Their tactic was obvious and not especially skillful. He knew the maneuvers to outflank them. He didn't even have to think about it—the movements were instinctive.

Only he couldn't do it. The instructions flowed from his brain to his muscles, but somehow never arrived. Maybe it was the coldness seeping into his body. The chill that told him he was afraid. Maybe it was the memories flashing so quickly that he couldn't see anything but Frank soaring through the air before falling to his death. Suddenly Josh couldn't breathe. Cold sweat broke out everywhere. His muscles cramped painfully, forcing him to stop.

He didn't remember moving, but suddenly he was beside his bike, hunched over, waiting for his heart rate to return to something close to normal. Nausea rose inside of him. He shook like a frightened, dripping dog.

When the kids started to turn, to come back and check on him, he waved them off. After he pointed to his bike, they nodded and waved, then continued their ride. They would assume he had a flat or something mechanical had gone wrong. With luck, they would never guess the truth.

As much as he wanted to compete, as strong and powerful as the drive was within him, he couldn't do it. That part of him, the pieces that made him whole, were shattered beyond repair. None of the trophies sitting in boxes mattered. There wasn't enough money in the world to make this right. He was a loser and a coward, and the hell of it was, he didn't know how to make any of it better.

SATURDAY AFTERNOON, CHARITY walked the short distance between the hotel and Marsha's house. Despite the weeks she'd been in town, she'd never been to her boss's house before. Not that she was visiting as Marsha's employee. Instead, Charity was going to see her grandmother for the first time in her life.

Grandmother. The word felt strange. She couldn't seem to grasp the whole meaning of what she'd been told. For the past couple of days she'd alternated between happiness and confusion. She'd wanted to be a part of a family for so long, she couldn't believe it had finally happened.

She was also wrestling with anger, mostly at her mother. Maybe Sandra hadn't wanted anything to do with Marsha, but she'd had no right to keep Charity from that relationship. Especially after her death. Why hadn't she told her own daughter that she had other family? Sandra had known how much Charity had wanted to belong somewhere. Yet she hadn't bothered to leave a note, or even a hint.

As Charity approached the house, she did her best to push away the annoyance she felt. She didn't want to start her afternoon with Marsha in a bad mood.

She turned the corner and saw the white house Marsha had described. It was two stories, in a craftsman style typical of the area, probably built in the 1920s. There were elements that were similar to the house Charity had fallen in love with. The house Josh wanted to sell her at a discount. Something else she'd yet to come to terms with, she thought humorously. Who could have known her life would go from fairly boring to wildly confusing in a matter of a few days?

She walked up the three steps to the wide porch and knocked. Marsha opened the door almost immediately.

"I'm so glad you're here," the older woman said. "Come in."

Charity stepped into a bright, open living room. Something about the combination of colors, furniture placement and windows made her want to sink into one of the overstuffed seats and never leave.

"Thanks for having me," she said, feeling a tiny bit awkward.

Marsha had replaced her usual well-tailored suits with jeans and a long-sleeved blouse. Her white hair was more casual, soft waves rather than a bun. She linked arms with Charity.

"Instead of dancing around the topic, I thought we'd face it head-on," she said, leading the way to the stairs. "Let's go look at Sandra's room. I'm hoping you can get a sense of what her life was like before you were born."

"I'd like that," Charity told her.

They climbed the wide staircase and turned left at the landing.

"The last door on the right," Marsha said, releasing

Charity. "Nothing has been changed, I'm afraid. Despite my best intentions, I turned my daughter's room into a shrine. I'm sure any number of psychologists would have plenty to say about that."

Her tone was easy, but Charity saw the flash of pain in her eyes.

Not knowing what to say, she walked toward the open door. When she reached it, she turned and looked at the bedroom that had belonged to her mother.

The whole room had been done in shades of lavender, her mother's favorite color. A full-sized bed was covered in a purple and lavender quilt. Built-in bookcases flanked the bed. The shelves were crowded with books, knick-knacks and pictures. There were posters on the wall. A very young Michael Jackson and a group Charity wouldn't have known except for the word "Blondie" in script at the bottom.

She stepped inside the bedroom and walked to the desk. School books were still stacked. A half-written essay on Julius Caesar was next to them. A gold flower necklace on a thin chain lay carelessly across the paper.

She moved to the shelves and studied the pictures. Sandra was in nearly all of them. Her mother with her friends, at a school dance. The familiar smile made her chest ache, but other than that, she felt no connection with the room or the former occupant.

"All she took were some clothes and money," Marsha said from the doorway. "Nothing else. There wasn't a note. She never said goodbye."

"I'm sorry," Charity said, not sure how to ease Marsha's pain. "For what it's worth, I don't think her constant moving on was about you. She loved new places. We'd settle somewhere for a few months and then she'd start talking about the next place and the next. Where we were going was always more exciting than where we were."

Charity looked around at the room. The pretty curtains, the small collection of worn stuffed animals shoved carelessly in a corner. Something like this was exactly what she'd dreamed about when she'd been younger. A place to call her own. Nothing fancy—just a regular kind of home. Yet her mother had walked away from it and had never looked back.

"I wish she'd told me about you," she said.

"Me, too." Marsha's eyes were sad again. "I wish I'd been more understanding of who she was. She desperately wanted to go away to college, but I always said she had to stay here. I was such a fool. Controlling and unyielding. I had to be right. In the end, being right cost me my only child. If I'd—"

"No," Charity said, cutting her off. "She would have left anyway. It's what she wanted. I don't think there's anything you could have done to change her."

"You can't be sure about that."

"Yes, I can," Charity said, trying not to sound bitter. "I knew her."

"Perhaps," Marsha said. "I still have that album for you. It's downstairs."

Charity nodded and followed her back to the living room. Together they looked through pictures of Sandra. There were laughing photos of a toddler, then more familiar poses and smiles as she got older.

Marsha gazed lovingly at each photo. She told stories about when they were taken and what happened next. Charity shifted uncomfortably on the sofa.

"Is this why you hired me?" she asked abruptly. "Because I'm your granddaughter?"

Marsha smiled at her. "While I did want the chance to get to know you, I have devoted most of my life to this town. I wouldn't have risked the future of so many just to have you around. When we hired the recruiter to fill your job, I gave her your name. I said I'd heard good things about you, but that was all. She wouldn't have put you on the slate if you hadn't been an excellent candidate."

That made Charity feel better. "Will people be upset when they find out? Won't they think you tricked the city council into hiring me?"

"You've been in meetings. You know how stubborn everyone can be. Do you really think I could have convinced them to hire an unqualified candidate?"

"No," she admitted. "They would rebel."

"Exactly." Marsha touched her arm. "You're very good at what you do. You're honest, caring and you have a fresh perspective. You have the experience necessary and the energy to get the job done. You're the one we wanted. I would have hired you even if you hadn't been my granddaughter. I hope you believe me." She hesitated. "I know that coming to meet you directly would have been more straightforward, but I was terrified. I thought by bringing you here, we could get to know each other."

Charity nodded. "It's okay. I understand why you'd be cautious. I want to get to know you. I want us to be family."

"We already are," Marsha told her. She smiled again, but the sadness had returned to her eyes. "You're probably still trying to figure this all out. Do you want to pick this up another time?"

"If you don't mind," Charity said, grateful Marsha understood. "It's a lot to take in."

"We have time," Marsha told her, rising. "I'm not going anywhere."

Charity stood and started for the door. When she reached it, she turned and hugged Marsha. The older woman hugged her back. The brief embrace made her feel both better and worse. The nagging sense of having lost nearly twenty-eight years tugged at her.

As she stepped out into the afternoon, she wondered what she could have done to make the outcome different, but knew there was no answer. She'd been a kid, dependent on what her mother told her. Even if she'd wanted to go looking for family, she hadn't known Sandra's real last name. After her mother's death, she'd gone through her things and hadn't found even a hint about her life before Charity had been born.

If only, she thought sadly. But there was no way to change the past. There was only the future and what she chose to do with her life.

CHAPTER TWELVE

CHARITY RETURNED TO the hotel and climbed the stairs toward her room. She wrestled with dozens of emotions, most of which she couldn't identify. Without thinking, she stopped in front of Josh's door and knocked.

It was a Saturday afternoon, she reminded herself. He wasn't likely to be there. But seconds later he opened the door, looking as gorgeous as ever in a T-shirt and jeans. He needed a haircut, she thought, taking in the slightly shaggy hair. And a shave. She had to admit the scruff looked good on him.

"Hey," he said, motioning for her to come in. "What's wrong?"

"Nothing bad. I went to see Marsha."

He shut the door behind her, then took her hand and led her toward the sofa. But when they got there, she couldn't sit. She felt restless and uneasy.

"Why?" she asked, facing Josh. "She was my mother. I know she cared about me. She knew I wanted to be part of a family. She knew that mattered to me more than anything. But she didn't tell me, not even when she was dying. Not even after she was dead. That's all it would have taken. A little note with a name and an address. But she didn't bother."

Charity couldn't reconcile the information. "So where does that leave me? Was she just incredibly selfish or am I fooling myself, thinking she gave a damn about me?"

He reached for her.

She shook her head. "No. Don't. I need to say this."

He shoved his hands into his jeans pockets. "Then I'll stand here and listen."

She drew in a breath. "When I was a junior in high school, we moved again. I told her this was the last time. That I wanted to graduate from a school I'd attended for at least a year. I made her promise." She struggled against the memory but it was everywhere, surrounding her with how things had been.

"Did she keep it?"

"No. She left and I stayed. I had a job and the rent on our mobile home was cheap. She sent money every now and then. I got by and I graduated with my class. I had friends. I was able to send out college applications and know I would still be at the same address when they sent the answers. But she wasn't."

Charity felt the burn of tears and willed them away. She didn't cry. Giving in accomplished nothing.

"She didn't come to my graduation. It was too far and she didn't have the money. I told myself I was fine, but I wasn't. I wanted someone there, someone to see me take this momentous step. She didn't bother and she didn't tell me there was someone who would care, who would take the time to be with me. She kept that from me, and there's no good reason. How am I supposed to tell her how pissed I am? She's dead."

He reached for her again and this time she went into his arms. He might not have the answers, but he was warm and strong and for a few minutes she could pretend that everything was going to be all right.

He stroked her hair, then ran his hand down her back.

She rested her head on his shoulder and breathed in the scent of him.

"My mom left, too," he said. "I was ten."

Charity remembered Marsha telling her the story. She pulled back enough to look into his eyes. "I'm sorry. I shouldn't be whining."

"You're not whining." He cupped her face in his hands. "I'm saying I understand what it's like to be abandoned by the person who's supposed to love you best in the world. By the time I was old enough to go look for her, it was too late. She'd died. I was angry. Beyond angry. I wanted her punished. I wanted her to pay, but mostly I wanted her to tell me why. Why did other moms give up everything for their children and she couldn't even stay? Was it me? Or was it her?"

She saw the pain in his eyes. The questions that would never be answered.

"Eventually you make peace with it," he told her. "You make peace and you move on."

Maybe, she thought. But there was a scar from the wound and sometimes that scar ached.

She raised herself on tiptoe and pressed her mouth to his. Her kiss was gentle, sharing. He responded in kind. She closed her eyes and lost herself in the heat that flooded her body. There was something to be said for a dependable chemical reaction.

His hands dropped to her waist, then her hips. He urged her closer and she went willingly, her body nestling against his. She parted her lips and he deepened the kiss. She met him willingly, enjoying the stroking of his tongue against hers, giving herself over to the blood rushing through her body.

Wanting began low in her belly and spiraled out in all directions. Her breasts began to ache. Between her legs, she felt that telltale combination of tension and dampness. Anticipation sharpened.

He cupped her rear, causing her to arch against him. She felt his arousal against her belly and the memory of how he'd felt inside her, of what he'd done to her body, made her moan. He moved his hands up and under her thin short-sleeved sweater. His fingers were warm against her bare skin, moving deliberately across her ribs, then cupping her breasts through her bra.

Everything about his touch was perfect, she thought as he caressed the curves and brushed his thumbs against her tight, sensitive nipples. She closed her lips around his tongue and sucked.

Now it was his turn to moan. But instead of starting to remove clothing, he pulled back, then took her hand and led her into the bedroom.

The king-sized bed dominated the space. The layout was similar to hers, with an armoire, a desk and a view of lush gardens. None of which interested her, she thought as he reached for the hem of her sweater and tugged it over her head.

Her bra followed, leaving her bare to the waist. He stood in front of her, gazing at her breasts, anticipation darkening his eyes.

"You're so beautiful," he whispered, before bending down and taking her left nipple in his mouth.

He licked the tight tip several times before sucking in deeply. The tugging drew waves of pleasure from deep inside of her. She felt a rush of heat and dampness between her legs. A heightening of her arousal. His day-old beard teased her skin. He bit down gently, taking pleasure to the level of exquisite, then sucked again.

She had to hang on to him to keep from sinking onto

the thick carpet. When he moved to her other breast and repeated the process, she found it difficult to breathe.

More, she thought, wanting them both naked and on the bed. It was time for more.

She tugged at his T-shirt, giving him a not-so-subtle hint. He straightened and pulled it off in one easy, fluid move. She stepped out of her sandals. As he unfastened her jeans, she ran her hands across his smooth, bare chest. Defined muscles felt like stone. He was sculpted male beauty, she thought, pressing her mouth to the center of his chest before moving to his flat nipples.

She licked until he caught her face in his hands, tilted her upwards and kissed her on the mouth. Then they were each pulling off the last of their clothes. When they were naked, he grabbed her around the waist and they tumbled onto the bed.

She landed on her back, him on his side, facing her. He lowered himself so he could kiss her breasts again. This time as he drew her nipples in deeply, he put a hand on her belly.

Her legs stirred restlessly. Her attention was equally divided between what he was doing with his mouth and the slow, steady journey his fingers took down, down, down.

At last he reached between her legs. She parted her thighs for him, then sucked in a breath as he slipped between the folds of skin and found her swollen and damp center.

The man had a fabulous sense of direction, she thought hazily as he began to explore that tight bundle of nerves. First he circled, teasingly close, but not actually touching. Around and around, moving slow enough to make her impatient. Then he lightly brushed across it with a single finger. She shuddered. When he did it again, she knew he was going to bring her to the kind of release that shook the world.

But instead of settling into a steady rhythm, he shifted so that he was between her legs. He pressed his mouth against her in an intimate kiss. The feel of his lips, the sweep of his tongue, the light abrasion of his stubble all conspired against any self-control she might have left.

Electricity shot through her at that first second of contact. Delicious need burned away shyness or pride. She opened her legs wider and arched her hips in a very clear invitation. One he accepted.

He ran his tongue over every inch of her. He dipped into her swollen and ready center, then returned to that single point of exquisite pleasure. He rubbed it with the flat of his tongue, teased it with the point. Then he closed his lips around the engorged flesh and sucked.

Charity felt the tension build. It grew until she had no control, no choice but to lose herself in the trembling release that shuddered through her. She grabbed onto the blankets, tossed her head from side to side and clenched her teeth to keep from screaming.

Josh continued to caress her gently, drawing out every drop of bliss until she was weak and breathless.

When the last wave had ebbed, he shifted so that he was on his knees. He opened the nightstand, grabbed a condom and quickly put it on. Then he was in her, filling her, taking her deeply, thoroughly. She hung on for the second half of the ride.

Later, when they were both breathing normally, lying facing each other, his hazel-green eyes bright with contentment, she traced the outline of his perfect mouth.

"You didn't have to do that," she murmured.

"Yeah, I did."

She smiled. "You know what I mean. Thank you for…"
What? Distracting her? Making her realize that she hadn't
really known what good sex was supposed to be before
now?

"Charity," he said, staring into her eyes. "I want you. I'm
a guy. It doesn't get more complicated than that."

The words were oddly comforting. "Do you get every
woman you want?"

"No." He shrugged. "It's different with you. Better."

"I aim to please."

"You do good work."

She laughed. "So do you. All that practice has really
paid off."

"Knowing what to do is the easy part. Finding the right
person to do it with is a whole lot harder."

Sweet words that made her chest ache a little.

Not him, she reminded herself. He fell in the category
of "too much." Too good looking, too charming, too famous. She wanted regular. She'd seen what happened when
a woman fell for the wrong kind of guy. It had happened to
her mother enough times.

Thinking about Sandra destroyed her good mood, so
she focused on something else.

"I haven't seen you around in the past few days. What's
been going on?"

He rolled onto his back, pulling her with him. She snug-
gled close, loving the feel of his naked body next to hers.

"I rode with the high school team yesterday."

She half sat up. "Really? How did it go?"

He lightly circled her nipple, then drew her against him
again. "Badly. I couldn't do it. I pretended there was something wrong with my bike." He swore. "Talk about a loser."

He wasn't that, but telling him wouldn't make a difference, she thought sadly. He needed to believe in himself. But was that possible?

"Have you thought about talking to someone?" she asked. "A professional?"

"A shrink? No. Sitting around and talking about my feelings isn't going to help."

"You don't actually know that."

"Yeah, I do. I tried it after the accident and it didn't help."

She sighed. "You tried it what? One time, then gave up? You're such a guy."

"That makes the sex less awkward." He looked at her. "Want to stay? We could order in, watch dirty movies on pay-per-view, take a bath. I have a spa tub."

Make love, she thought, losing herself in his mesmerizing gaze. "You know how to tempt a girl."

He rolled toward her, stopping when he was above her. She wrapped her arms around his neck.

"Is that a yes?" he asked, the corners of his mouth turning up.

"That's a yes and a please and a let's do it again."

SUNDAY CHARITY DRAGGED herself from Josh's bed. She was having lunch with Pia, and Josh had to go work out. As she showered and dressed, she found it difficult to keep from smiling all the time. Every part of her body seemed satisfied and the little aches were a delicious reminder of how they'd spent their night.

By noon she was walking toward Pia's place. She had the top floor in an older building. The large single-family home had been divided into three apartments. Charity climbed the stairs and knocked on her friend's door.

"Hi," Pia said with a grin. "Are you winded by the climb?"

"I'm on the third floor in the hotel and I take the stairs there."

"Built-in exercise," Pia said, closing the door behind her. "I'm so not the gym type. I have a great deck. I thought we'd eat there."

"Sounds good."

Pia's place was bright and airy, with lots of windows and large rooms. The sloping ceiling added character and everywhere Charity looked was a splash of color. The sofa was lipstick red microfiber with patterned pillows. There was a purple and yellow throw on the back of an old wooden rocking chair and travel stickers pasted on an old steamer trunk that served as an end table.

"This is great," Charity said, following Pia into a bright green kitchen. "I love the colors."

"I'm not a beige kind of girl. I've done most of my decorating at garage sales and flea markets. I have a thing about finding a bargain." She pointed at the flowered plates sitting on a rack on a shelf. "Eight plates for two dollars. It was a proud moment for me."

"Impressive."

"Thank you."

Pia picked up a tray of sandwiches and salads, then motioned to another tray with iced tea in a pitcher and two glasses. Charity collected it and they went out onto the large balcony.

The day was sunny and warm. They could see most of the town, a bit of the lake and the mountains beyond.

"A view of the kingdom," Charity teased.

"Exactly. I look at the little people and wonder about their lives."

They settled into lunch and talked about what was going on in Fool's Gold.

"Does Alice have any information on the thefts?" Charity asked. "I haven't heard if the person stealing has been caught."

"Last time we talked, she was still searching for the culprit. I hope whoever it is stops before Alice finds them. She can be scary. Of course the loss of a few packages of Easy Mac is a whole lot less interesting than the missing money from the state." She curled her feet under herself and sipped her tea. "Three quarters of a million dollars. Wouldn't that be nice?"

"It's a life changer," Charity said. "I just don't understand how that kind of money goes missing."

"Me, either, but accounting isn't my thing. I guess that's why the city is bringing in an auditor. Poor Robert. I wouldn't want the responsibility or anyone thinking it was me."

"It's not Robert. Does anyone think it is?"

"Not really. That would require a level of creativity he doesn't have." Pia covered her mouth. "Sorry. That sounded mean. I just meant…"

"He's not that guy," Charity said with a grin.

"Exactly." Pia reached for a half a sandwich. "So what did you do yesterday?"

Charity blinked, not sure which of her many activities she should choose from. Remembering her afternoon and night with Josh made her think she might blush, so she blurted the only other thing she could think of.

"I spent some time with Marsha. I just found out she's my grandmother."

Pia's eyes widened with shock. "What? You're Sandra's daughter?"

"Yes." Charity briefly explained everything she'd learned about in this last seventy-two hours.

"That's amazing," Pia said, still looking stunned. "You are so lucky. I would love to have Marsha for my grandmother. She's always taking care of everybody. If someone needs help, she's right there. Sandra was an idiot to run off." She winced. "Okay, I'm putting my foot in my mouth more than usual today. Sorry."

Charity assumed Pia thought she would be insulted about the comment aimed at her mother. "I agree. I don't know why she was always running. Some of it was the men in her life. She chased after gorgeous, hunky guys, all of whom were lousy bets. When they moved on, she followed. I swore I would never be like that."

"So you're not interested in Josh."

The statement was unexpected. Charity didn't mean to react, but she had just taken a sip of her tea and nearly choked on it. As she coughed and sputtered, Pia looked on knowingly.

"Uh-huh. Just as I thought. You're a little too cool around him. Something's up. Tell Auntie Pia everything."

"There's nothing to tell."

"Do I look like I believe that? Because I don't."

Now it was Charity's turn to feel uncomfortable. "I know better," she began. "Men like Josh are a disaster."

"But you've fallen for him."

Charity covered her face with her hands. "Sort of. But he's a really nice guy."

"Don't tell him you said that."

"I won't. He'd be wounded."

"You and Josh." Pia looked speculative. "Okay, I have to know. Is he the god everyone claims?"

Charity sighed. "The rumors are not wrong."

"That's what I need in my life. Hunky hot sex. Like that's going to happen." She glanced at Charity. "Josh really is a sweetie and I totally adore him, but you need to be careful. He's famous and everything that goes with that. His ex is an actress. Very beautiful. He's been linked with some amazing women."

"You mean he's not for us lesser mortals?"

"I'm saying don't get your heart broken."

"Speaking from the voice of experience?" Charity asked.

"I've had my share of cracks, but so far nothing fatal."

"I appreciate the concern, but you don't have to worry. I'm not in love with him."

"Good. Because loving Josh would be a hard road for anyone."

"ARE YOU TRYING to get me drunk?" Charity asked when the server left the table.

Josh leaned back in his chair. "I have no idea what you're talking about."

"Oh, please. You're the one who warned me about the margaritas here." She angled toward him. "Alcohol is not required to have your way with me."

"I know. It's one of your best qualities."

They were having dinner at Margaritaville. The place wasn't too busy on a Sunday night, so they'd gotten a booth in the back. Somewhere they wouldn't be disturbed.

The soft light added a golden glow to Charity's brown hair. She wore it loose and a little curly—a sexy look he enjoyed. Her mouth curved into a smile and there was a look of complete satisfaction in her eyes. He liked knowing he'd been the one to do the satisfying.

"How was your afternoon?" she asked. "You rode through town?"

"Uh-huh. I got a lot of support from the locals."

"They know about the race. They want you to do well."

At this point he just wanted to get through it without humiliating himself further. Why couldn't he have something normal wrong with him? A bad back. A disease of some kind. Something that could be fixed with a pill or rest and an ice pack.

"How was Pia?" he asked.

"Good. We had fun." She shook her head. "She knows we're, um, that we've..." She cleared her throat. "You know."

"That we're seeing each other?" He wasn't sure what was so hard about saying that.

She looked slightly relieved. "That. I wasn't sure about... So that's what we're doing?"

"Isn't it?"

She shifted on the seat. "I didn't know. You're not like anyone I've ever gone out with. You're famous."

"Oh, please."

"Your ex-wife is a big star."

"She's a b-list star at best."

"But beautiful and famous. I'm a regular person."

He reached across the table and took her hand. "The whole famous thing is highly overrated, and you are definitely beautiful."

She rolled her eyes.

"You don't believe me?" he asked.

"No, but thanks for the compliment."

"I'm not that guy you see on the poster. Not anymore. Even if I got it all back, I wouldn't want to be him."

She didn't look as if she believed him. "There had to be things about that life you enjoyed."

"Sure, but been there, done that." He squeezed her fingers. "I like you, Charity. I want to keep seeing you."

"I want that, too."

"Then we have a plan." He pretended worry. "It includes sex, right?"

She smiled. "If you're lucky."

"I'm always lucky. Didn't they tell you?"

CHAPTER THIRTEEN

"THIS IS BERNICE JACKSON," Robert said at the next city council meeting.

The tall, pretty redhead grimaced as she stood. "Bernie, please. Bad enough to be an accountant, but an accountant named Bernice? I don't think so."

Charity smiled. Gladys leaned toward her.

"Figures," the older woman muttered. "How many forensic accountants out there in the world are men? I'd say most of them. But do we hire a good-looking guy? Of course not."

"If you think that then you shouldn't care that there isn't another man moving to town," Charity said, doing her best not to smile. "However temporarily."

"You're pretty smart," Gladys conceded.

"Thank you."

Bernie pulled out a folder and opened it. "According to my preliminary investigation, cross-referencing the information the state sent, there are multiple checks missing." She looked up. "The total we're talking about is close to one and a half million dollars."

Charity sat up straighter. "That much?" she breathed.

Marsha paled. "How did this happen? How can there be that much missing?"

"I'm going to find that out," Bernie promised. "I have some paperwork to discuss first. You'll want to look over my non-disclosure agreement. It says that I won't talk about this case unless subpoenaed. My goal is to protect my clients. I suggest you have the city attorney look at it before anyone signs it."

Charity watched Marsha nod, as if she approved of what Bernie was saying. Charity found herself liking the attractive accountant, even as Gladys scowled at her for not being a man.

When the meeting broke up, Charity lingered to check the schedule for the room. She had a few meetings coming up and preferred to use this conference room for her presentations. When she had confirmed the times were open, she turned and was surprised to see Robert waiting for her.

"Bernie seems great," she said. "Very efficient."

"She has a good reputation. She'll find out what's going on." He frowned. "The sooner the better for me."

There was something in his tone. She moved toward him. "You don't think people are assuming it's you, do you?"

"I'm the treasurer. I have access to all the money coming in. My office processes the checks. If not me, then one of my staff. I don't like how it looks. I would never do anything like that, but not everyone will believe that."

"The important people will," she told him.

Robert shrugged, then looked at her. "It's Josh, isn't it?"

The unexpected question made her stiffen. She hoped she wasn't blushing.

"I saw the two of you at dinner," he continued. "You looked...cozy."

"We're, ah, friends," she began.

"I'm not surprised. Him being who he is. The rest of us don't really stand a chance."

There was something about the way he spoke, as if her falling for Josh was inevitable.

"It's not because he's famous," she said sharply. "Josh is a really nice guy. He cares about people. He's a lot more than his reputation."

Robert's mouth twisted. "Sure. Keep telling yourself that."

"It's true."

"Right. I still think you're great, Charity. When he dumps you, if you want, we can try again."

He walked out of the room. She stared after him, her mouth hanging open.

She didn't know which of Robert's assumptions stunned her more. The belief that Josh would dump her—not an "if" statement, but a when. Or the assumption that the only reason she wasn't going out with Robert was because she'd been blinded by Josh's brilliance.

She'd already made her decision about Robert before she got involved with Josh. She'd done her best to prefer Robert.

"Pinhead," she muttered. "Stupid, egocentric pinhead."

Funny how Josh had all the flash, but Robert turned out to be the man lacking in substance.

Yet as she left the conference room, she found herself wondering if she was blinded by Josh. She was her mother's daughter, after all, and Sandra had always been interested in handsome, superficial men.

Charity told herself she knew what she was doing. That Josh was more than he seemed. Still, it would be up to her to make sure she really was falling for the man rather than the persona.

"WE HAVEN'T SEEN you here in a long time," Bella said as she combed Josh's hair.

"Uh huh," he said, ignoring the not-so-subtle complaint inherent in her words.

"Your last haircut was terrible."

He smiled. "You say that every time."

Bella, a middle-aged woman with beautiful eyes and a will of iron, glared at him in the mirror. "I suppose she says the same thing when you go to her."

"I'm not going to discuss that with you."

Bella snorted. "You know I'm better."

"Are those new earrings?" he asked. "They're pretty."

She fingered the gold hoops at her ears. "You're trying to distract me."

"Yes, and you're going to pretend I've succeeded."

Her mouth twitched, as if she were trying not to smile.

Bella Gionni and her sister Julia were the two best hair stylists in town. Unfortunately, they'd been involved in a running feud for the past twenty-five years. They had competing shops on opposite sides of town. To pick one over the other was to get involved in the fight. The problem was no one but the sisters knew the cause of the argument.

The surest way to keep the peace, and the one Josh had chosen, was to alternate his business. Each of them complained about his time with the other.

Not going to either of them would be easier, he knew, but that wasn't an option. He owed the sisters. While he'd had most of his college paid for by scholarships, there hadn't been quite enough to cover everything. The town had come through with funding for both him and Ethan. He happened to know that Marsha had contributed the most, but the second-largest donors had been the Gionni sisters.

"I heard you're dating Charity," Bella said as she began to cut his hair.

He winced. "I'm not going to talk about that."

"Of course you are. She's nice. I heard she's thinking of getting highlights." She smiled. "They're for you, I think.

I know when a woman wants to look pretty for a man."
She winked.

He shifted uncomfortably in the padded chair. "Charity
and I are, um, dating."

"More than dating, eh? I hear things, Joshua. What the
ladies say."

He so didn't want to be having this conversation with a
woman nearly old enough to be his mother. "There's a lot
of talk. Most of it is just that."

"Maybe, maybe not." Bella continued cutting. "It's been
a long time since you went on a date."

"A couple of years," he admitted.

"Then it's time to get back on the horse."

Just the visual that Josh needed.

PIA WALKED INTO Charity's office and flopped down on a
seat. "Have a minute?" she asked.

"Sure." Charity studied her friend's sad expression.
"What's wrong?"

"It's Crystal. The last round of chemo didn't do anything. They've run out of treatment options." Pia sucked in
a breath and seemed to fight tears. "She's deciding if she
wants to stay home or go into a facility. Hospice care," she
added. "She said the doctor gave her two months. Maybe
three."

Charity swallowed. "I'm sorry. How awful." She didn't
know Crystal very well, but felt badly for all she'd gone
through.

"It's been horrible. We'd really hoped that last round
of chemo would do something. Anything. She's gotten so
weak. I don't think she can be at home by herself. And she
says she likes the idea of a hospice. She says they're actually really nice places."

"Is it in town?" Charity asked.

"Uh-huh. I'll get to go see her and stuff, but I don't want her to die." Pia wiped the tears off her cheek. "I hate this. There's nothing I can do to make a difference. I'm taking her cat, which is the only thing I can think of to do."

"People worry about their pets. Taking her cat will be a big help."

"I'm not really a pet person," Pia admitted. "I don't know anything about cats. Crystal says he's quiet and clean. I guess I'll get a book or something. It's just so unfair."

Charity nodded. There didn't seem to be any words.

"She's already lost her husband," Pia continued. "All she ever wanted was to get married and be a mom. Now that's never going to happen. And I know she's worried about those embryos. There's no way she's going to donate them to research, but they can't stay frozen forever. Can you imagine being in her position—dying, and having to decide the fate of children you'll never have?"

"No," Charity said truthfully. It was an impossible decision. One no woman should ever have to make. "Does she have any family? A sister or cousin who might want the embryos?"

"No. It's just her." Pia looked at her. "Sorry. You were probably having a good day before I showed up."

"I'm happy to listen."

"Thanks." She drew in a deep breath. "I'd better get back to work. I'm going to see Crystal tonight so I can get to know her cat a little better."

"You'll be a good pet mom," Charity told her. "You'll care and that's what matters."

"I hope so." She stood. "Thanks again for letting me vent."

"Anytime. I mean that."

Pia nodded and left.

Charity stared after her. Crystal's situation did seem bitterly unfair. The dilemma of the embryos was potentially heartbreaking. To have to lose everything like that.

She thought about her own life, about the second chance she'd been given to be a part of a family. It was more than a lucky break—it was a gift.

She rose and walked down the hall to Marsha's office. Her grandmother sat at her desk. She smiled when she saw Charity.

"How's it going?" Marsha asked.

Charity tried to smile, but couldn't. Tears she could usually hold back with ease filled her eyes.

Marsha stood. "What's wrong?"

"Nothing," Charity said, going to her and holding her close. "I'm so grateful you're my grandmother. I don't think I said that before, but I wanted you to know."

Marsha hugged her back. A fierce hug full of love and promise. "I'm happy, too," she said. "It's been a long time coming."

Charity straightened. "I won't go away. I'm not like my mother."

Marsha touched her cheek and smiled. "I know that. We'll both stay right here. Together."

CHAPTER FOURTEEN

THE ANNOUNCEMENT FOR the special session city council meeting didn't come with an agenda, which Charity thought was odd. Usually there was an entire list of subjects to be covered. She didn't like not being able to prepare and as the announcement showed up in her e-mail a mere thirty minutes before the meeting itself, she didn't have time to ask around. So she was stunned to walk into the conference and find Josh sitting at the table. Why would he be at a city council meeting?

Gladys sat next to him, batting her false eyelashes. Charity sat across and down a couple of seats, concerned about being too close and giving away her body's predictable reaction whenever he was near. He gave her a quick grin as she took her seat. She smiled back, trying not to let anyone see she was baffled and a little annoyed. They were involved—shouldn't he have said something?

When everyone had arrived, Marsha called the special session to order. Then she motioned to Josh.

"Thanks for coming today," he began, then passed out a blue folder to everyone. "I want to talk about starting a bike racing school in town."

Charity stared at him. Since when?

"I've been approached by a few people in town over the years," he continued. "I never considered the idea until a few weeks ago. Then I started doing some research. Not only is there a need in the area, but a successful school brings in big money to the local community. Not just the taxes paid by the business itself, but through visitors and races."

"Gotta have those heads in beds," Pia said. "We need the tax revenue."

"I've also been talking to some potential corporate sponsors. They're very interested."

Marsha didn't look surprised by any of this, so Charity had the feeling Josh had discussed it with her.

"What would you want?" Gladys asked.

"Land. I have a few sites picked out. I have a couple of acres I could donate and Marsha owns two more that neighbor mine. The last plot is owned by the city."

He got up and dimmed the lights, then flicked on a projector that lit up the screen on the far wall.

An aerial view of the town showed the land in question. With the exception of the bit owned by the city, it was just outside the limits of Fool's Gold.

"We'd want to be annexed," he said. "The taxes will be higher for us, but that will be offset by city services." He clicked and another picture appeared. This was a rendering of a large building.

"We're thinking indoor and outdoor tracks. Weight rooms, simulators. There would be two or three small houses where students could live while they trained. Kids still in high school would be a problem. Tutors are an option but then there's a lack of socialization. If we could work something out with the board of education, they could attend local classes while they're training."

He continued to talk, explaining his well-thought-out plan. Charity listened, impressed but still a little hurt for being left out of the loop. Apparently she thought they had more of a relationship than they actually did. But she didn't let that get in the way of her vote. She gave the idea a yes vote, as did everyone else.

When the meeting was over, she returned to her office. Josh walked in a few minutes later. He was grinning and obviously pleased with how things had gone.

"What did you think?" he asked.

"I was surprised. How are you going to have a training facility here and not ride?"

"I can't," he admitted. "I'll have to be a part of things. One way or the other, I'll beat this."

"By boxing yourself into a corner?"

"Whatever works." He moved toward her desk. "Did you think the presentation was well done?"

She didn't understand the question. If he was anyone else, she would assume her opinion mattered. That he wanted to hear she'd been blown away. But this was Josh. Everyone loved him. Why would her praise matter?

"I didn't want to say anything to you," he continued. "Actually I did. I could have used your help. But I didn't want to take advantage of our relationship and put you in an awkward position. If you hated the idea, I didn't want you to feel you had to support it."

He'd been thinking of her? Being considerate?

Her irritation faded, replaced by a reminder that it was always better to get all the facts before jumping to conclusions.

"You did fine on your own," she told him, grateful she hadn't been snarky about any of it. "It's a great idea. And hey, it should bring in a lot of men, right? Gladys will be thrilled."

"Pleasing her is what I live for."

Charity laughed. "She'll be delighted to know that." Her

humor faded. "I'm not sure throwing yourself in the deep end is the best way to fix the problem, though."

"Nothing else has worked. That's who I am. That guy who races to win. I don't intend to do it for the rest of my life, but I want to go out on my terms. If I'd been injured, then it would be one of those things. I could accept that. But there's nothing wrong with me. At least not on the outside."

She could see his determination. "Okay. Apparently Fool's Gold is getting a riding school. Are we naming it after you?"

He grinned. "Of course. I was thinking of something like 'The Golden Institute.'"

"Sounds like a place you go to get a tan."

"Show a little respect or I'll tell Gladys you're not treating me right."

"You're threatening me with a woman in her sixties?"

"She could take you."

"I'm afraid she could."

He walked around the desk, gave her a quick kiss on the mouth, then stepped back. "You have to work. Want to go out to dinner tonight?"

"Very much."

"Seven?"

"I'll come to your place," she said, anticipating the time they would spend together.

"I'll be the handsome guy. In case there's someone else in the room."

"Thanks for the heads-up."

Charity watched him leave, then sat down behind her desk. While she appreciated that Josh felt he had to fix the problem, she was worried there was more at stake. Were his actions about leaving the sport on his terms, as he claimed, or was this about becoming that famous guy again? The star.

Because a world-class athlete wouldn't be staying in Fool's Gold. He would be out in the world. Far, far away from her.

CHARITY DRESSED FOR DINNER, then left her room to walk the few steps to Josh's. But as she closed her door, she saw a pretty teenager knocking on his. The girl was eighteen or nineteen, wearing a frilly sundress, looking more defiant than happy.

He opened the door. "You're right on—" His look of pleasure faded. He glanced past the teen to Charity, who raised her eyebrows.

"Haven't got a clue," he said, then returned his attention to the girl. "Yes?"

The girl made an attempt to smile. "It's me. Emily."

"Okay."

"Emily. We met a couple of months ago at Jo's Bar. You bought me a drink. Well, more than one. Then we came back here…" Emily glanced at Charity. "Who are you?"

"His date."

Emily looked startled for a second, then squared her shoulders. "Whatever. This is private. Maybe you should come back later."

"Not a chance," Josh said, sounding certain.

Charity did her best to keep from racing to the worst conclusion.

"Why don't you both come in?" Josh said.

Emily pushed past him and entered the suite. Charity hesitated.

He held out his hand, his gaze steady. "It's not what you think."

She was remembering him telling her how long it had been since he'd been intimate with anyone. At the time, she'd believed him. Did she now? Did she go with the evidence, or trust her gut? Because right now her gut was saying that Josh was someone special. Someone she wanted to get to know better.

She put her hand in his. He pulled her close.

"Thank you," he murmured in her ear, then led her into the suite.

Emily stood behind the sofa. She looked less certain and a whole lot younger. Her hair fell in dark curls. Her eyes were wide and carefully made-up.

"Are you sure you want her here?" Emily asked, looking only at Josh.

"Yes."

"You'll be sorry."

"A risk I'm willing to take."

Emily drew in a breath and tossed her head. "I'm pregnant."

Charity pulled back her hand. Josh didn't let it go.

Her mind whirled and spun. Pregnant? Meaning she really had had sex with Josh?

"I've never slept with you," Josh said calmly.

"You were drunk but I didn't think you were that drunk." Emily's large eyes filled with tears. "I can't believe you don't remember. You do it with everyone. I know that. But that night meant something to me and now I'm pregnant."

The tears began to fall in earnest. "I was supposed to go to college in the fall. How can that happen now? This is your baby. You need to take responsibility for it."

Charity felt sick to her stomach. She jerked her hand free and was grateful Emily had shown up before dinner. If she'd eaten a big meal, she would be throwing up right about now.

"How far along are you?" he asked.

"S-seven weeks."

"Do you remember the date we had our special night together?"

There was a hint of annoyance in his voice. Not concern or worry. He obviously didn't believe Emily. Josh was a lot of things, but he wasn't irresponsible. She knew that much. So if he was certain the baby wasn't his, then she would guess he hadn't been with Emily at all.

She drew in a breath and reminded herself she was going to give him the benefit of the doubt.

"It was a Tuesday," Emily said, still crying.

Josh folded his arms across his chest. "Here's what we're going to do. The three of us will walk downstairs to the gift shop where we'll buy a pregnancy test. Then you and Charity are going to come back here where you'll pee on the stick." He narrowed his gaze. "With Charity watching."

"What?" Emily demanded.

"I want confirmation that you're the one doing the peeing." He glanced at Charity. "To make sure she's the one who's pregnant. I had a woman do this a few years ago. She came back with a positive pregnancy test, but it turned out she'd brought her friend's urine in a container. The friend was pregnant."

"You've been through this before?"

Weariness invaded his eyes. "You have no idea."

Any lingering doubt faded. She moved next to him and put her hand on his back. "Let's go get the test."

"I'm not peeing in front of her," Emily said.

"Would you rather pee in front of me?" Josh asked.

"Fine." Emily marched past them and out the door.

They all walked to the elevator and rode down. The three of them entered the gift store where the clerk, a woman in her thirties, took one look at Emily and rolled her eyes.

"Hi, Josh," she said.

"Lisa. We need a pregnancy test. Please put it on my bill."

"Sure thing."

Lisa turned around and studied the collection of sundries. She grabbed a box and passed it to Josh.

They made the return trip to the third floor and walked back into Josh's suite. He handed the pregnancy test to Charity. "Do I know how to show you a good time or what?"

She took the test.

Emily glared at them both. "I'm not doing this."

He shrugged. "Then I have nothing to say to you. Come back when the baby's born and we'll do a DNA test."

Emily's determined expression crumbled. Tears filled her eyes, then began to pour down her cheeks. She dropped to the sofa and covered her face with her hands.

"I'm sorry," she said with a sob. "I'm sorry." She looked up. Her makeup stained her skin, making her look like a little girl. "You win. I didn't sleep with you. I'm not pregnant."

While Charity wasn't exactly surprised, everything about the moment was still surreal.

"What do you need the money for?" Josh asked.

Emily sniffed. "College. My dad took off years ago and I have two younger brothers. Mom does the best she can, but there's nothing left over. I have a partial scholarship. Enough to pay for tuition, but I need living expenses, too."

"You thought I'd be an easy mark?" Josh asked, sounding more conversational than angry.

"Everybody says you've, you know, been with a lot of girls. I figured I could pretend and you'd pay me off." She glanced down at her hands. "It was pretty stupid, huh?"

"It's not a moment you're going to remember with pride," he said. "What's your major?"

Emily glanced up, frowning. "What do you mean?"

"What were you going to study in college?"

"Oh. Nursing. I want to be an RN. Pediatrics." She smiled. "I like kids."

"Have you looked at grants?" he asked.

"A couple. It's confusing. I really don't want to get a bunch of loans, if I don't have to."

"You take the SATs yet?"

"Uh-huh." She smiled again. "625 on English and 630 on Math."

"Impressive." He was silent for a minute. "After school on Monday, I want you to go to my office. You know where it is?"

"Sure."

"You're going to talk to a lady named Eddie. She's my assistant." He hesitated. "She sounds a lot meaner than she is, so don't let her scare you off. She'll help you with the grants. As for the rest of it, you can work for me this summer. Part-time. I'll pay you minimum wage, if you want. Or I won't pay you anything, but I'll put away twenty dollars for every hour you work. At the end of the summer, I'll send that money to the college of your choice. But if you start and then quit, you get nothing."

Emily's eyes widened. "You're really going to help me, even though I lied to you?"

"You have to do the work. If you'll see it through, I'll know you've learned your lesson."

Charity felt as surprised as Emily looked. She'd figured Josh would lecture the girl, then let her go. Instead he'd offered her a way to get everything she wanted, while still having to be responsible and show initiative.

Emily stood, rushed to Josh and hugged him. Then she stepped back. "I'll be there," she promised. "I'll do whatever you say. I swear. I'm so sorry." She turned to Charity. "I am sorry. I was desperate and that's not an excuse. Please don't be mad at him."

"I'm not," Charity told her.

"Thank you," Emily said again. She hurried to the door and let herself out.

Josh walked over to a small cabinet by the wall, pulled out a bottle of Scotch.

"Want some?" he asked.

"I'll wait and have wine with dinner."

He poured himself a glass, then set down the bottle and took a long drink. "Welcome to my world."

"Does that happen a lot?"

"Every now and then, in different forms. People get desperate, I'm an easy target." He looked at her over the glass. "You know I didn't sleep with her, right?"

"Of course. I knew it before she confessed everything."

He put down the glass. "How?"

"You told me there hadn't been anyone for a while and I believed you. Plus, she's not really your type."

He crossed to her and put his hands on her waist. "What's my type?"

"I'm not sure exactly, but I'm confident you're not into girls still in high school."

"You know me well."

He kissed her.

As his mouth claimed hers, she realized that tonight she knew him a little better than she had before. He could have simply thrown Emily out after her confession. There was no reason for him to help a girl he didn't know who'd tried to blackmail him. Josh was a complicated man. He was also someone she liked. A lot.

The thought terrified her. Not only did she have to worry about the stupidity of falling for a man like him, she had her own hideous track record looming. Still, it was too late to run for cover now.

He drew back and smiled at her. "How hungry are you?"

She wrapped her arms around his neck and leaned into him. "Dinner can wait."

"That's my girl."

JOSH WARMED UP with the high school team. They rode slowly for a couple of miles, mostly talking and laughing without paying attention to anything beyond getting ready for the real workout.

Josh didn't listen to the conversation. He couldn't. Every bit of his attention, every ounce of self-control, was focused on not freaking out like a kid at a monster movie.

The students rode in a pack, which wasn't unusual. What made the event incredibly different for Josh was the fact that he was part of the pack. Not in it, exactly, more on the outside, but still riding with the others. At least he was doing it.

Maybe the slow pace helped. There was no sense of being out of control. He knew nothing bad was going to happen. At this speed, the worst result of a fall would be a skinned knee or elbow.

One of the students maneuvered his bike closer to Josh's. The boy, tall but skinny with that awkward, lanky look of an adolescent who hasn't figured out what to do with his new body, smiled tentatively.

Josh smiled back. "Brandon, right?"

The kid nodded. "I can't believe you're riding with us.

I'm on a loop with some other guys who ride around the country. They think I'm lying."

"Then you should bring your camera next time and we'll take pictures to prove it."

"You'd do that?"

"Sure. For a hundred bucks a pop."

Brandon's mouth dropped open.

Josh laughed. "I'm kidding. Yes, I'll take pictures with you and the other guys. You can load them on your Facebook page."

"Sweet." Brandon glanced at him, then away.

Josh wondered if he had more he wanted to say.

The pace picked up a little. Josh easily kept up with everyone.

"You, um, work out, right?" Brandon asked.

"Sure."

"Coach has me doing some weight lifting, but I'm not…" He looked around at the other guys, as if judging how many of them could hear. "I need to put on some muscle."

"How old are you?" Josh asked.

"I'll be seventeen in three months." Brandon sounded excited by the fact.

Josh tried to remember the last time he'd been thrilled to be getting older. It had been a while.

"In the next couple of years, you'll start to put on some serious muscle," he told the teen. "Don't push too hard on the weight training until you're done growing. A lot of guys do that, but what they don't realize is all that muscle keeps the bones from growing as much as they should. They can lose a couple of inches of height that way."

"I'm already six feet," Brandon told him. "But my dad says the men in our family stop growing early."

"When you've stabilized your height, you'll start picking

up muscle. Don't forget there are more ways to get strong than just lifting weights. Off-season riding is all about conditioning. This winter you should ride inside a few times a week. Alternate between high rpm workouts and low rpm workouts. High-cadence workouts help you learn to contract and relax your muscles quickly. You'll move in the pack better and be able to dig deep for a sprint. Low-cadence workouts on a high gear build muscle."

Josh grabbed his water bottle and took a drink. "You also need to work on your whole body. Use the winter months for different kinds of sports. Skiing is great. Take a yoga class once a week. You'll stretch your muscles, improve your balance and it's a great way to meet girls."

Brandon laughed. "Yoga?"

"I'm serious. It will help with your riding and girls love a cyclist's ass."

Brandon's cheeks turned red. "Good to know," he mumbled.

Josh held in a chuckle.

One of the other guys dropped back to join Brandon and asked Josh his opinion on a bike he was thinking of buying. They discussed equipment until Coach Green drove up and blew his whistle.

Conversation immediately stopped as the guys rode faster. The pack spread out a little as they turned onto a mountain road and headed straight up. Josh stayed on the left rear, watching the other riders. But this time, instead of feeling the panic, he noted their technique. One guy jerked his bike back and forth, wasting energy and adding distance. Brandon was an intense rider, but he was late with his gears, taxing himself more than necessary. Most of the other riders did the same.

Without thinking he yelled, "Everybody stop. Stop where you are."

The guys looked at each other before slowing to a stop. They straddled their bikes and looked at him. He pointed at the teens one by one and gave each of them a critique. When necessary, he demonstrated the wrong way, then the right way.

"Now we're going to ride up the hill together," he said. He explained the gear sequence and why he made the choices he did. Then they started riding together.

Josh found himself in the center of the pack. He called out instructions and the other riders crowded around him. One kid nearly ran into him.

His heart seemed to stop in his chest. The tightness began in his gut, spreading out in every direction. Breathing was impossible as the panic claimed him.

Not now, he thought grimly, swearing silently. Not like this.

"Squirrel," one of the guys yelled as a squirrel darted across the road in front of them.

"Watch each other," Josh yelled instinctively. "You don't want to hit the squirrel, but you don't want to go down, either. Be aware of where you are."

They were nearing the top of the road. He knew in another mile it would turn and provide a gradual descent back to town.

"When we start down, I want you to keep your speed under thirty miles an hour."

"What?"

"No way."

"Going fast is the best part."

Josh ignored them. "You're going to practice breaking out of the pack. Call out numbers."

Brandon yelled one, a second guy yelled two, until they'd counted through the team.

"That's the order," Josh said. "Start in the middle of the pack and work your way to the front. You get a minute of glory, then move over and drop to the back. Is that clear?"

Everyone nodded.

They reached the crest and the road started down. Brandon moved to the center of the pack.

Josh was aware of everyone's placement. The kids didn't ride close enough to really get in the way, but this would still be good practice. When Brandon—

He kept pedaling even as his mind did a double take. Wait a minute. He'd been in the middle of a panic attack. He'd been seconds away from losing it completely. What the hell had happened?

He replayed the events, realizing the squirrel had distracted him so completely, he'd forgotten about his symptoms. Apparently without his tension feeding them, they faded of their own accord.

It was the first glimmer of hope he'd had in two years. It meant there was a chance he could conquer this. That he could go back and be everything he'd been before. He didn't have to be afraid.

He sat up on his bike and started to laugh. The sound echoed off the sides of the mountains around them. One of the kids looked at his friend.

"Old people are weird," he muttered.

Josh grinned. "We sure are."

CHAPTER FIFTEEN

CHARITY CLICKED TO the next screen on her computer. "Now we move into the lifestyle part of the show," she said. "I've uploaded an assortment of real estate listings. Everything from starter homes and condos to doctor-priced beauties on the lake or the golf course."

She clicked again. "Here's a few pictures of the wineries, looking pretty. The ski lodge, the award-winning restaurant. For local flavor we have the farmer's market, the Fourth of July parade and the obligatory sunset picture."

The latter showed a family walking by the lake. Dad held a little girl, Mom held the hand of a little boy. The figures were silhouetted against a beautiful orange and red sunset.

"Very nice," Marsha said, from her seat next to Charity. They were in the mayor's office, reviewing Charity's presentation. "What about the financial package?"

Charity went over the information for the hospital itself—tax breaks, potential grants, how much the state, county and city would kick in.

Marsha smiled. "You've done your homework," she said approvingly.

"I'm determined. Fool's Gold is absolutely the best place for the new hospital campus to be. I'm going to make them see that." She grinned. "In a very polite, professional way, of course."

"I have no doubt."

"The good news is there's only one other site that's competitive. So we have a really good chance. At least this time there's no rich family who wants their name over the door. I'm still annoyed I didn't know that."

"You'd been here all of five minutes. How could you?"

"You're right," Charity said, but she couldn't help feeling she should have been able to figure it out. It was her job, after all. "This time is different. There aren't going to be any surprises."

"You sound resolute."

"An immoveable force."

"Then I have every confidence you'll succeed." Marsha picked up her coffee and sipped. "I noticed Josh training with the high school team."

Her voice was casual, but Charity wasn't fooled. While she and her grandmother were getting to know each other, they hadn't spent a whole lot of time talking about Charity's personal life. As everyone in town knew Charity was seeing Josh, it wasn't hard to assume Marsha knew, as well. But she'd never brought it up before.

"He has a race coming up," Charity said, hoping today's session went better than the last one.

"He's also determined. Even when he was younger, he was incredibly focused. Talent is never enough. Drive is just as important. He's a good man."

Charity leaned back against the sofa. "Is there a 'but' in that sentence?"

"No. I think Josh is very special. He needs someone in his life, and I'm going to risk our new relationship by saying you do, as well."

"I want that," she admitted. "But I'm not sure about Josh."

"Because the rumors about his talents are overrated?" Marsha's lips twitched as she asked the question.

"Are you trying to find out about my love life?"

"Only in the broadest sense. I think too many details would make us both uncomfortable."

Charity laughed. "You're right. No, the rumors aren't exaggerated. Josh is great and I really like being with him. He's funny and caring and smart. Not to mention gorgeous."

"Now I'm sensing a 'but' in the conversation."

"But he's dangerous. The whole fame thing is uncomfortable. I don't want to be a bright star in the world. I want my life to be anchored here. I want normal."

"Josh is very normal and this is his home."

"For now. But what happens when he competes again? What happens if he makes his comeback? He becomes successful racer-guy again. I'm not saying I don't want that. If it makes him happy, if it heals him, then he should go for it. But I'm not interested in someone who needs the approval of the world to feel good about himself."

"Is that what you think he wants?"

"I'm not sure," Charity admitted. "But I'm worried about it. I want to be in a relationship where I'm the most important person in someone's life. I want to feel the same way about him. I can't compete with an adoring crowd."

"Maybe you wouldn't have to."

"Maybe." Charity was less sure. "For now, it's not an issue. We're getting to know each other."

Marsha smiled. "Be careful. That's how every great love begins."

AFTER JOSH FINISHED working out with the team, he went back to the hotel and showered. When he was dressed, he glanced at the clock. Charity wouldn't leave work for another couple of hours. He could go into his office, but he wasn't in the mood. Restlessness drove him out of the hotel. He walked along the sidewalk, no destination in mind. Then he turned a corner and saw a sign for a familiar business.

Hendrix Construction had been around for about forty years. Ethan's grandfather had started the company, and his father had taken it over a decade later. When they'd been kids, Ethan had sworn he wasn't going to follow anyone into the family business. A few weeks after Ethan had graduated from college, his father had died unexpectedly. As the oldest son, it fell to him to take over the company and keep it going.

Maybe Ethan had planned for one of his brothers to join him or buy him out, but that hadn't happened. Nearly ten years later, Ethan ran both the construction and the windmill businesses.

Josh stared at the building. He could see several people inside and wondered if Ethan was one of them. For all he knew his former friend could be at a job site or out at the windmill building plant. Still, he could walk over and find out.

He took a step, then stopped. Not counting the phone messages he'd left, it had been a long time since he'd talked to Ethan. Over ten years. He wasn't sure what to say. The truth was he hadn't done anything wrong. Ethan's injury wasn't his responsibility or his fault. So why did he feel so damned bad about it?

Knowing there was only one way to get the answer, he crossed the street and walked into the office.

Nevada Hendrix, one of Ethan's sisters, sat on the reception desk, her feet dangling. Her jeans and T-shirt were smudged with plaster dust, her boots worn and practical, rather than a fashion statement. She gestured intensely as she spoke.

"You couldn't be more wrong," she was saying. "About all of it. If you would just shut up and—" She raised her head and saw Josh. "Dear God!"

She jumped off the desk and stared at him. "You're here."

"In the flesh. Is he here?"

He didn't have to tell Nevada who he meant.

"Ah, sure. In his office." She gestured toward the rear of the building.

"I can find it," he told her, then pointed to the receiver she held. "You're still on a call."

"What? Oh." She returned her attention to the call.

He walked between the desks, which were mostly empty. The engineers and sales staff would be out calling on customers or at job sites.

At the rear of the building was a large lunch room, an alcove with office supplies and several big printers, and a single door with Ethan's name on it. Josh knocked once, then pushed it open.

Ethan sat behind his desk, working on his computer. His expression was intense as he used his mouse.

"Not my problem," he said, his attention still on the screen. "I don't care about your engineering degree. You're wrong about the bridge and I'm going to prove it to you."

"Huh. And here I thought I had a business degree."

Ethan looked up. He raised his eyebrows. "I thought you were Nevada."

"Apparently."

Ethan motioned to the seat across from his desk, saved his work, then faced Josh. "This is a surprise."

"For me, too," Josh admitted before sitting. "I came to talk to you."

Ethan stared at him, his expression unreadable. "So talk."

Now that he was here, Josh didn't know what to say. He'd had ten years to plan for this conversation and the hell of it was, he couldn't remember half of what had happened between them.

"I've left you phone messages," he said. "First every few months and then every couple of years, I tried to get in touch with you."

Ethan's left eyebrow raised. "The effort was very meaningful."

"You didn't call me back."

"I was waiting for you to man up and come see me in person."

"Here I am."

"I can see that." Ethan shook his head. "You were gone, Josh. You'd been a part of my life, a part of my family's life and then you just disappeared. Do you know how that made my mom feel?"

Josh felt his gut roll. "No, but I know it was bad."

"Worse than bad. Mom loved you like you were one of her own. She kept a goddamn scrapbook of your racing career."

Josh wished there was a nearby rock. Crawling under it would feel better than this.

"I fucked up," he admitted.

"You sure did."

They stared at each other.

"The accident wasn't my fault," Josh said at last. "You ran into me. I'm lucky I didn't go down, too."

Ethan leaned back in his chair, but didn't speak.

"You got hurt," Josh continued. "It happens. You moved on, you've got a great life. Look at this place. It's what, double the size it was when your dad ran it? And the windmill company. You're a success."

"I know."

Ethan wasn't giving anything away, which really pissed Josh off. He stood.

"I'm done feeling guilty. It's not my fault that you had to give up racing. I'm done paying for it. I was wrong to stay away and I've apologized for that. So you need to get off my ass."

Ethan waited a couple of seconds. "You about done?"

"Yeah." Josh sat back down.

Ethan leaned toward him. "I was never on your ass."

"What are you talking about?"

"I never blamed you for what happened." A smile flashed. "I had that race locked." The smile faded and his expression hardened. "After the accident, you didn't come to see me in the hospital. You were like a brother to me and you didn't want to get close, in case getting injured was something you could catch."

Josh shifted on his seat, feeling ashamed and stupid. "It wasn't that," he began, then shook his head. "No. It was that. You were great, Ethan, and I knew if it could happen to you, it could happen to anyone. So I stayed away. I'm sorry."

"We were like brothers."

Josh nodded.

"You kept staying away."

"I didn't know what to say," Josh admitted.

"I figured."

"What? Then why didn't you come talk to me?"

"I knew you'd be back one day." Ethan looked smug. "I just didn't think it would take ten years. Of course I've always been the one with the brains. And the good looks."

"In your dreams."

There was more to say. More to explain and apologize for, but that would come later. Right now, the first step had been taken. All he could think was how much time he'd wasted—they'd both wasted. Gladys was right—men were idiots.

Josh stood. "Want to go to Jo's and get a drink?"

"Sure."

They headed out. Nevada was still on the phone. She stopped talking and stared at them as they left.

"You're going to be getting some calls later," Josh said, as they headed for Jo's.

"From the girls and Mom. Should make for an interesting day."

They walked into the bar and grabbed a table against the wall. A few of the women already there looked twice, then went back to watching some dating reality show. Jo walked over.

"The usual?" she asked.

Josh nodded. Ethan did the same.

She glanced between them. "You two kiss and make up?"

"There wasn't any kissing," Ethan said. "Unless you're offering."

She rolled her eyes. "You so couldn't handle me." She walked back to the bar.

Josh glanced at his friend. "Jo?"

He shook his head. "No. We flirt, but it doesn't mean anything. She's not my type."

"Since when do you have a type?" Josh asked, then wished he hadn't. Ethan had been married. He'd loved and lost in the worst way possible. "Sorry."

"It's okay. So I hear you're competing again."

"It's one race."

"That's all it takes to get back in the game."

Josh wasn't sure he wanted to be in the game. Right now he was mostly interested in proving something to himself.

"It's been a long time," he said. "I've been riding, but not seriously."

"That has to change."

"I know."

"It's all about fundamentals," Ethan said. "Get back to the basics. Training and focus. There's an element of luck when you win and being prepared is the best luck you can bring to the game."

Ethan grabbed a couple of napkins and together they sketched out a training schedule. Grueling, Josh thought as he stared at the breakdown, but worth it. He didn't tell Ethan that winning was the least of it. Right now competing would be enough of a win.

Josh finished the last of his beer. After tonight there wouldn't be any more drinking. His diet would be as strict as his training schedule. He didn't have much time to get in the best shape of his life.

He turned his attention back to his friend. "If you weren't pissed at me, why have you been in a bad mood for the past few years?"

Ethan shrugged. "Why else? A woman."

"No one wants me there," Charity said, as she sat in the passenger seat of Josh's car.

"I want you there," he said.

They were in the parking lot of a local television studio where a reporter from one of the sports networks was going to interview Josh.

While she appreciated the invitation and all, she wasn't sure how to tell him everything about this situation made her uncomfortable. She knew she and Josh were involved, but this felt too much like being a celebrity girlfriend. Like she was hanging on to get noticed by the media. It reminded her that once Josh started racing again, his world would be totally different from hers.

She angled toward him, intent on explaining. But before she could speak, he said, "I had a fling with her. Years ago. Right after the divorce."

It took Charity a second to put the pieces together. "The reporter?"

"Uh-huh."

"You had sex with her?"

He nodded, looking chagrined. "Kind of."

She didn't know if she should be hurt or annoyed. "Why did you agree to the interview?"

"It was set up by the race committee. They sent me an e-mail and asked me, so I said yes. We need the publicity. I hoped it wouldn't be Melrose doing the interview, but it is." He stared at Charity. "I'm not interested in her. What happened before was a mistake. A really stupid one."

She could accept that, but she was still confused. "You had to know this could get you in big trouble with me. So why did you risk that and bring me?"

He cleared his throat and shifted his gaze to the window. "She, ah, called to talk to me a couple of days ago. She sounded really happy that we were going to be spending some time together. Too happy."

If Charity didn't know better, she would swear there was a hint of fear in Josh's eyes.

"And?" she prompted.

"I knew it would be awkward. Having you around makes things more clear."

The annoyance and hurt faded. "You're scared of her."

He stiffened. "I'm not scared."

"You're terrified."

"It's not like that."

She grinned. "You expect me to protect you."

"I thought it would be nice if people knew we were together."

Did he really expect her to believe that? "Josh, you've been this famous guy for years. You must have a lot of experience at telling women no."

"I do, but it's different now. I don't go to parties and hang out with Hollywood types."

"You were great with Emily."

"That was different." He stared out the front window. "If you'd rather wait in the car, I understand."

She could almost hear the pout in his voice. "I'll come with you," she said as she opened her door. "And do my best to protect you from the big, bad reporter."

They walked into the studio and were greeted by a production assistant. She introduced herself as Brittany, looked as if she couldn't be more than twelve, but showed absolutely no interest in Josh. Refreshing, Charity thought. Unusual, but refreshing.

They walked past the sets used for the local news and the various cable access shows. Brittany pointed to a small area with a green-screen background and two upholstered chairs facing each other.

"You'll do the interview there. Melrose asked for the green screen so she can load in graphics later." She glanced at Josh. "You've done this sort of thing before, right?"

He nodded.

"Great. The makeup girl wants to pat you down with some powder, but we're doing a sports interview. No one expects you to be pretty."

"Oh, but you already are," Charity whispered.

Josh shot her a glare. She did her best not to laugh.

"She's in there," the assistant said, pointing to a door and moving down the hall. "Yell if you need me."

Josh paused in front of the closed door, but before he could knock, it burst open.

"Finally," a throaty but feminine voice purred. "If you knew how I'd been counting the hours."

Josh dropped his hand to Charity's waist and pushed her in the room first. Charity felt like the sacrificial goat in some pagan ceremony. She stepped into a plain room with a large, well-lit mirror, a few chairs, a sofa and a long counter. But what really caught her attention was the woman standing by the mirror.

She was tall, maybe five-ten or eleven, with flaming red hair that tumbled in loose curls down to the middle of her back. Her body was lean, yet curved in all the right places and breasts the size of melons spilled out of a low-cut blouse.

Melrose wasn't just beautiful, Charity thought, feeling as if there wasn't enough air in the room. She was perfect. The boobs didn't look real, but they suited her. Melrose was a walking, breathing male fantasy. Charity went from sacrificial goat to invisible.

"Josh," Melrose breathed, crossing the room in two long strides, wrapping her arms around his neck and pressing her mouth to his.

Charity blinked in astonishment, then touched her own arm to make sure she really was there.

"Melrose," Josh said, grabbing her wrists and holding her in place while he stepped back. "This is Charity Jones. My girlfriend."

Girlfriend. Charity hadn't been expecting that, and tried

to figure out if he'd said it because he meant it or if it was a form of self-protection.

"Hello," Melrose said, never taking her eyes off Josh. "You're racing again. That's good. The sport needs someone like you. God knows, I do. I'm staying in town tonight. I have a luscious room at a little B&B by the lake. Big tub, big bed, big fireplace. The interview will air tonight. We can watch it together. Naked. Say yes?"

Charity went from feeling less-than to pissed in a nanosecond. She stepped between Josh and the piranha, held out her right hand and forced a smile.

"Hi," she said loudly. "I'm Charity."

"We've met," Melrose said coolly, still staring hungrily at Josh.

"Apparently not," Charity told her firmly. "Hey." She poked Melrose in the chest, right above her left breast. "Look at me."

Melrose slowly lowered her cool, green gaze. "You didn't just touch me."

"I did and I'll do it again, if I have to. Yes, Josh is very crushworthy. And the sex, and as I'm sure you'll remember, is fantastic. But there's a line between wanting and being a complete cliché. No offense, Melrose, but you're not in a prime-time soap. This is real life. And Josh is with me."

JOSH HAD KNOWN there was a risk involved when he'd asked Charity to join him today. But he'd been willing to deal with her being pissed—mostly because Melrose wasn't the kind of woman who accepted rejection easily. He'd thought having Charity along would make things easier. And he'd have a witness to anything that happened…or didn't happen. He hadn't expected her to unleash her inner tiger.

She stood glaring at Melrose, fearless, beautiful and

determined. Not many women were willing to take on a powerhouse reporter. Damn, Charity was good.

Melrose looked from Charity to him, then back. "I haven't heard Josh tell me no."

"Josh, would you please respond to Melrose's very graphic invitation?" Charity said.

She didn't bother to turn around. He liked that she didn't worry that she had to look at him or give hints as to what he should say.

"No, thanks," he said. "I'm with Charity."

"Fine," Melrose snapped. "Whatever." She glanced at her watch. "Let's get this over with. If we hurry, I can still catch a flight out of Sacramento and get the hell out of this pissant town."

Ten minutes later he was powdered and miked, sitting across from a still annoyed Melrose. But the second the red light went on above the camera, her face relaxed and she smiled.

"I'm here with Josh Golden, who dazzled us for years, winning every major race, including back-to-back victories at the Tour de France." She turned her gaze to him. "Rumor has it you're back in the game."

"I've entered a race to be held here, in Fool's Gold. We'll see how I do there."

"Not ready to formally announce you're returning to the sport you love?"

"No." He wasn't ready to do much of anything but get through another practice session without freaking out.

"You were the best," Melrose reminded him. "Don't you want a piece of the glory?"

"There's more to competing than winning."

"Yes, but none of that really matters, does it?" She

smiled knowingly. "I know how you like to come out on top."

Josh thought about Charity, watching just beyond the bright lights and held in a groan. Melrose was nothing if not persistent. At one time he might have found that intriguing, but not anymore. Now he wanted something different. Someone different. And as soon as the interview was over, he planned to tell her.

CHAPTER SIXTEEN

"DID I THANK you for coming with me today?" Josh asked.

Charity rested her head on his shoulder. "About fifteen times."

"Want to make it sixteen?"

They were in his bed, propped up on pillows, watching the sports show. Josh's interview was next.

"If it makes you happy," she said. "I'm okay with what happened and I understand why you felt you needed protection."

"I didn't need protection."

She smiled, then kissed his shoulder. "You sure did. Melrose was scary. What were you thinking?"

A stupid question, she told herself. No doubt he'd been thinking that Melrose was beautiful and sexually aggressive and exactly what he needed after a difficult divorce. If she just thought about the ridiculous exchange they'd all had at the studio, she was fine, but if she allowed herself to actually dwell on the idea of Melrose and Josh in bed together, she started to freak.

She didn't need ongoing proof that they were from different worlds and possibly headed in different directions.

She didn't want that, she thought. But if Josh did, then that's what he should do.

The show host announced the interview, doing a quick

introduction, then the screen switched to the recording of Josh with Melrose.

"I'm here with Josh Golden, who dazzled us for years, winning every major race, including back-to-back victories at the Tour de France."

Charity had seen the whole thing happening live, but it was worse on the flat-screen TV. "Oh my God! She wants to have sex with you. I knew it before, but you can see it in her eyes. The way she looks at you."

Josh reached for the remote. "I can't watch this." He clicked off the TV. "I'll get feedback tomorrow. Steve, my former coach, will let me know how it went."

"He'll probably want to know if you're current on your shots."

Josh rolled toward her and grinned. "Someone's being defensive."

"Apparently someone needs to stand between you and every single woman on the planet. I'm not sure if I should find this funny or have a total freakout."

"Do I get a vote?"

She stared into his hazel-green eyes, then lightly touched his cheek. "I'm laughing on the inside. Did stuff like this really happen all the time?"

He hesitated. "Some. Before I was married. I was young and willing and so were they."

She wondered if he could give an approximate count on the "they." A hundred? A thousand? Did she want to know?

"Once I got into a relationship, the rules changed. I'm always faithful."

She raised her eyebrows. "Seriously?"

"Never cheated once. I wasn't tempted. I always figured if I was interested in someone enough to want to sleep with her, then there were problems with my current relationship.

So I either fixed those or ended things. I was faithful during my marriage, and even during the divorce. I waited until the paperwork was signed." He grimaced. "Angelique didn't share my reticence."

"She screwed up big time letting you go."

He smiled. "Thanks for saying that, but she wouldn't believe you. It worked out for the best. We never would have lasted. She wanted what I was. The guy on the cereal box with a bestselling poster. She wanted our names in the tabloids, photographers following us. I wanted something different."

"You were followed by photographers?"

"Sometimes," he admitted, putting his hand on her waist. She felt the warmth of his fingers through the oversized T-shirt she wore. "There are ways around that sort of thing. Live a normal life and for the most part they ignore you."

"So what was the best part of your former life?"

He thought for a second. "Being on a team. Working hard, then kicking ass in a race. Waiting for the ranking, wanting to be number one and knowing if I wasn't I would have to work harder. Sometimes I miss the screaming fans, but not as much as everything else. Mostly I miss being that guy."

"You're still that guy." She thought about what he'd said. "What about all the travel? Not having a home?"

"Fool's Gold is home."

"You weren't here much."

"I didn't have to be here to know I belonged."

Probably because he'd grown up here. He could take the relationship, so to speak, for granted. But it wasn't like that for her. She wanted permanent roots, ones she could see. She wanted to wake up in the same bed every day knowing that she would continue to wake up there year after year. The only changes she wanted were paint colors and carpeting.

"Will you go back?" she asked. "After the race, if it goes well?"

"I don't know." He smiled at her. "Whatever happens, this will be my home, Charity. I'm not running from you."

"I didn't think you were. You're the type to run to something, not from it. Do you think about what it would be like now?"

"Some. I'd be different. Not take any of it for granted. There's something to be said for wisdom, but I'm not sure it can completely make up for being older. A comeback would require a huge commitment."

He continued talking about the "what ifs" of racing. If he was able to compete and if he did well. He didn't mention winning because that was to challenge the gods.

Charity listened and did her best to be supportive, but in her heart, she felt the first whisper of a chill. The coldness surprised her. Didn't she care enough about Josh to want him to be happy?

She already knew the answer to that, and wondered if it was something else. Something far more frightening than being selfish. As she turned over the possibilities, one of them became more clear than the others. A truth she couldn't avoid.

She was in love with Josh.

Life was nothing if not ironic. She was in love with a man who made his living moving at top speed, when she only wanted to stay in one place. She'd done her best to avoid her mother's trap, and here she was, completely caught.

"You okay?" he asked.

"I'm fine. Just thinking about your future."

"Not a very interesting topic."

"It could be. Imagine if you do well during the race. You'll have it all."

He shrugged, as if it didn't matter, but she knew otherwise. Josh would never be happy just being a regular guy. He was someone who needed the roar of the crowd, and she was just one person.

BERNIE JACKSON HELD a meeting on Monday, to bring everyone up to speed on the investigation. Charity spent the first few minutes doing her best not to let her newly discovered dislike of attractive redheads get in the way of paying attention. She reminded herself it wasn't Bernie's fault she had a more than passing resemblance to a barracuda-like reporter.

"We've tracked the money from the state to here," Bernie explained. "We have copies of the cleared checks. They show the city stamp and apparently passed through the city account. However, there are no records of a deposit and even more troubling, no records of a withdrawal."

"Do you think someone went back and removed the items from the computer?" Marsha asked. "The deposit and the withdrawal?"

"Possibly," Bernie said. "But what about the bank? It doesn't show the money going in or out, which means it went into another account."

"Do we know if it even arrived here in town?" Charity asked. "The check could have been intercepted in Sacramento or before it physically arrived here. It was a paper check, wasn't it?"

"Yes," Bernie said. "If it never arrived here, then whoever is perpetrating the fraud is going to be harder to find. But based on what I know so far, that seems a fairly likely explanation. I've contacted other communities to find out if anyone else is having the same problem."

"I don't like it," Chief Barns said. "I like criminals who do their dirty work out where someone can see."

"That would make things simpler," Bernie agreed.

She discussed the rest of her investigation, took a few more questions, then the meeting ended. Charity found herself walking with Robert back to their floor.

"How are you holding up?" she asked.

"Okay. People are still looking at me funny. I'm living with it. Bernie's told me privately that she should have me completely cleared in a couple of weeks." He grimaced. "I've given her complete access to my financial records. Checking and saving accounts, my retirement account. All of it."

"I'm sorry you're having to deal with all this," she said.

"It'll pass. Things will get back to normal." He paused by her office. "I just want her to catch the bastard who's doing this."

"So does the chief."

"I think she's happiest when she's arresting someone."

"Everyone needs a moment of joy in his or her life."

Robert shuffled his feet. "Are you… How are things going with Josh?"

Not a question she wanted to answer, she thought, wishing this were easier. "Good."

"You really like him, don't you?"

As she was sure being in love fell very close to "really liking" she had no problem nodding.

"Too bad." He turned and walked away.

Another downside of small-town life, she thought. There was no way to escape seeing Robert. Working with him didn't make matters easier. She could only hope he would find someone who could appreciate his niceness, along with his little quirks.

WEDNESDAY AFTER WORK, Charity headed out on an errand she'd been rescheduling for some time. She liked her new and improved wardrobe, which was great, but now she had to deal with her hair.

She'd been wearing it exactly the same way since she graduated from high school. Blown dry, so no hint of her natural waves showed, parted in the middle, hanging just below her shoulders. Some days she pulled it back in a French braid. Other days she wore it up. Occasionally it was loose. But there wasn't anything stylish about it and the color was a boring medium brown. It was time for a change.

She'd asked around for recommendations and had been given two names. Sisters who were in competition with each other. Pia had warned her she would have to alternate between the two unless she wanted people to think she was taking sides. When Charity had asked what the fight was about, Pia couldn't say for sure, which was part of the problem. No one really knew, which made staying out of trouble that much harder.

But they were the best hairstylists in town, so Charity had randomly chosen Julia's salon—Chez Julia—not to be confused with her sister's establishment, the House of Bella.

"You're the one who wanted to live in a small town," Charity reminded herself as she walked toward the bright blue building. There were posters of hair models in the window, a lush garden out front and a porch with a rocking chair.

She stepped into the surprisingly large salon. There were about ten stations lined up along two walls. The windows provided a lot of natural light. The main colors were a deep brown, from the wood at the stations, and turquoise. The walls were a rich blue-green up to the chair rail, then cream to the ceiling. The tile floor was done in a dozen shades of turquoise. Soft music played in the background, the place was spotless and had an air of relaxed elegance. Under any other circumstances, Charity would have been pleased with her find.

Instead she found herself feeling trapped as everyone in the salon turned to look at her, then didn't look away. It was as if they knew who she was—which they probably did.

An attractive woman in her forties hurried toward her. "Charity," she said. "You're my four-thirty. I'm Julia. So nice to meet you."

"Hi."

Julia glanced behind and made a shooing motion, then returned her attention to Charity. "Ignore them. I do."

Charity managed a smile. "Just like being the new girl in school."

"I know. But it will get better, I promise." Julia smiled. "Now, I have you down for highlights and a cut. Come have a seat and tell me what you were thinking of doing."

Charity followed her to a station in the back. She sat in the padded chair and faced herself in the mirror. Julia stood behind her, waiting.

"I want something different," Charity told her. "I've been wearing my hair at the same length, in relatively the same style, for years. The color needs help, too."

Julia ran her hands through Charity's hair. "Very thick," she murmured. "Do you have a wave?"

"Sort of. I control it with blow drying."

"About how much time are you willing to spend in the morning?"

"Not more than fifteen minutes. I don't have the patience for it."

"Good to know." Julia tilted her head. "We'll do subtle

highlights? Nothing too obvious. Just enough to give you a little depth."

"That sounds great."

"And for the cut, I'm thinking a blunt longish bob, with bangs."

Charity blinked. "Bangs?"

Julia dropped her hands to Charity's shoulders and squeezed. "Trust me."

By now conversation had resumed around them. Charity decided to simply go with the flow. Hair grew. If she didn't like the new style, eventually she could go back to what she'd been doing before.

Julia left her with a couple of magazines and went off to mix color. A few minutes later, Charity was covered in a plastic cape while Julia expertly applied color to a few strands of hair, then carefully wrapped them in foil.

"How are you settling in to living here?" Julia asked. "It's been a few months."

"I really like it. I've never lived in a small town before. The adjustment has been fun."

"What's Josh like in bed?" a woman in pink curlers yelled from across the room.

Conversation stopped. For a second there was only the sound of the soft music. Once again everyone was staring at Charity.

Julia sighed. "You don't have to answer that," she said. "Not that we're not interested," she added with a wink.

She turned to the salon. "She's new, remember. Everyone back off."

"But I want to know," another woman insisted. "I'm sixty-two. The odds of me finding out for myself are slim."

Charity laughed. "He's everything you could imagine and more."

The woman in curlers sighed. "I knew it," she said dreamily.

"I saw him riding his bike the other day," another client said. "What that man does for those bicycle shorts. It was the highlight of my day." She glanced at Charity. "No offense."

"None taken."

"You've been dating for a while now," Julia said. "How's that working out?"

The questions weren't subtle, Charity thought, more amused than offended.

"He's a great guy. I like spending time with him."

"Josh is one of the good ones. That first wife of his was a total bitch."

"I remember her," another client said with a sniff. "She came to town once. Walked around like she was afraid of getting dog poop on her shoes. She was beautiful, but what a bitch."

There was a murmur of agreement.

Charity would have loved to ask questions about Angelique but wasn't sure how. After all, she was fairly confident that anything she said would be reported to the entire town, not to mention get back to Josh.

"You came from Henderson, didn't you?" Julia asked. "I thought I heard that."

"Yes."

"Leave anyone special behind?"

Charity met Julia's interested gaze in the mirror. "No."

"I'm surprised. A pretty girl like you. There had to be someone."

Not a topic Charity wanted to discuss. Not with this crowd. "Not really."

"My first husband was a total loser," Julia said. "He

cheated, which I could live with, but then lied about it, which I couldn't. I chased him out of the house with a frying pan. He never came back. Good riddance."

"All men cheat," one of the customers said.

"Not all," another protested. "Some don't."

"Name one."

"My Arnie. He's a good man."

Julia leaned close to Charity. "And butt ugly. A sweetheart, but the lights would have to be off all the time."

Charity did her best not to respond to any part of the conversation.

"Josh ever cheated?" someone asked.

"Not that I've heard. He was faithful to that wife of his, not that she deserved it. Stupid cow."

Josh had claimed to be faithful and Charity had believed him. Which might make her a fool, but she was tired of trying to be sure. After her first two disastrous relationships, she hadn't been taking any chances with her third. She'd run a credit check and had a friend on the police force get her a DMV report. He'd been clean. Engaged to someone else living in Los Angeles, but clean.

Hurt but determined to learn from yet another mistake, Charity had accepted the job in Fool's Gold as a way to start over. Maybe having such a public history was part of Josh's appeal, she thought. She didn't have to worry about any secrets. Everyone in town knew everything important about him.

She went under the hair dryer for about twenty minutes, then enjoyed a very lovely massage with her wash. When she got back into Julia's chair, the stylist turned her away from the mirror.

"I don't want you to see anything until I'm done."

Charity felt a tiny knot of fear in her stomach. "I guess that means I'm going to have to trust you."

"You'll be happy, I promise."

"That's a big promise."

One of the older ladies had finished. With her silver hair all neatly teased and sprayed, she slipped on her jacket, but instead of leaving, she walked over to Charity.

"I remember Josh when he first came here," she said. "That mother of his was awful. He'd been in a bad fall and walked on crutches. He was about the most pitiful thing I'd ever seen. It took him nearly fifteen minutes to go a single block. How he struggled to get to school every day. That poor boy. His clothes were ragged and he was skinny as an alley cat. It about broke my heart. Then one day she was gone."

Charity knew the general story of Josh's past, but she'd never heard it told with such clarity.

"None of us knew what to do," another woman added. "We didn't want to send him to a state home, but there wasn't much choice. Then Denise Hendrix offered to take him in. The rest of us contributed to the family, helping pay for Josh's medical expenses."

The first woman nodded. "He needed surgery to repair how his legs had healed wrong, then physical therapy. That's why he started riding a bike. To strengthen his legs. Ethan rode, too." She patted Charity's arm. "So Josh is special to us. Always has been. You've got yourself a good man there."

"Thank you."

The old woman started to leave, then paused. Her expression turned sly. "He proposed yet?"

Charity felt the color flooding her face. Anywhere but here, she thought grimly. She wanted to be anywhere but here.

"We're still dating. Getting to know each other."

"I wouldn't be as concerned about him proposing. There's a bigger danger."

Several of the women laughed. Charity didn't get it until one of them added, "Feeling any cravings, hon?"

"No. I'm good. But thanks for asking."

"Leave her alone," Julia said firmly. "All of you. You'll scare her off and we'll never see her again."

The old woman waved and left. The conversation shifted to more comfortable topics. Julia got out a blow dryer. Once she turned it on, Charity couldn't hear anything that was being said—probably a good thing.

She promised herself she was never, ever getting her hair done in town, again. Or if she did anything, she would go see Morgan. She doubted he would bother her with a lot of personal questions.

Asking about Josh was one thing, but hinting she might be pregnant was way too intrusive. And annoying, she thought. Just because everyone knew Josh didn't mean they had the right to butt into his personal life. There were rules in polite society. Expectations and—

"Here you go," Julia said and turned the chair.

Charity was prepared to simply pay and run. She didn't want to deal with the teasing anymore. But when she caught sight of herself in the mirror, she couldn't move. She could only stare.

Her once boring plain brown hair was now rich and shiny. There were hints of gold and a tiny whisper of red threaded through the strands. But even more amazing was the cut.

Julia had shortened her hair to just below her jaw, then blown it under in a perfect bob. Feathered bangs made her eyes seem huge. When she moved her head, her hair swayed, then fell perfectly into place. It was the best cut she'd ever received in her life.

"It's perfect," she breathed. "I love it."

"Good. Do you have a big round brush?"

Charity nodded her head, mostly to watch her hair move.

Julia demonstrated the way to get the shape right, explained what products worked best and how to use them. Charity listened carefully, then paid her bill and left a large tip. The fact that everyone in the salon would talk about her after she was gone didn't bother her one bit. Not when her hair looked so good.

She walked back toward the hotel, catching her reflection every now and then and smiling as she saw her hair move. When she walked by Morgan's bookstore, the old man stuck his head out the open door.

"Lookin' good, pretty lady."

She laughed. "Thank you."

"Hope Josh knows he's a lucky man."

"I'll tell him in case he doesn't."

"You do that."

Now, feeling fabulous, she could think about the conversation in the salon and tell herself no one meant anything bad by their meddling. Josh was important to them, and with her dating him, she was part of what was going on. Although things had gotten out of hand with the whole pregnancy topic. That wasn't a subject to kid about. Talk about a disaster. An unplanned pregnancy would...

Charity stopped in front of the hotel and stared at the beautiful old building. But instead of seeing the impressive architecture or the gleaming windows, she stared at the mental calendar in her head and tried to do the math. Exactly how many days had it been since her last period?

She hurried inside, calling out distracted greetings when

the staff welcomed her. When she reached the third floor, she ran to her room, raced inside and closed the door behind her. Her date book was on the desk by the wall. She flipped back until she found the day with a little daisy by the date—her private notation of her period's arrival—then counted forward.

As the numbers mounted, so did her panic. She counted a second time and got the same number. She was two weeks late. Two weeks.

Her first thought was to rush to the nearest drugstore, buy a test and find out. Then she thought of all the people who would see her and how the information would be spread from one end of town to the other in a matter of minutes. Which meant what? That she had to drive to the next town?

She was halfway across the room, heading for her car keys, when she remembered the pregnancy test Josh had bought when Emily had insisted she was pregnant with his baby. He'd handed the kit to Charity who had brought it to her room and put it where?

It took two minutes of frantic drawer pulling to find it, another few seconds to get in the bathroom and pee, then three minutes of pacing until she could know one way or the other.

She stared at the two straight lines, then at the chart in the instructions.

She was pregnant.

CHAPTER SEVENTEEN

CHARITY STARED AT the stick for a long time, then carefully wrapped it in tissue and put it in her pocket. She would have to get rid of it somewhere other than her room. Because the maid would probably tell the entire town what it said.

After circling the room several times, Charity realized she couldn't stay here. Not with her mind swirling and her stomach flipping and flopping and her hands shaking. Maybe walking somewhere would help. She didn't have anywhere to go, but right now a destination seemed highly overrated.

Once she reached the street, she moved purposefully, which made her feel a little better. She started to go back to the office, but wasn't sure what she would do there. After turning down a couple of streets, she found herself in front of Marsha's house. Maybe this was the best place to start.

She walked up to the porch. The front door opened before she could knock.

"Look at your hair," Marsha said, smiling at her. "I love it."

Charity had nearly forgotten about her sassy new style. "Julia did it."

"It suits you. The highlights are great. You look even more beautiful than you did before."

"Thanks." Charity walked in.

Marsha closed the door. "This is a nice surprise. I was just thinking about what I wanted for dinner. Would you like to join me? We can go out. I'm thinking Angelo's. I do love the bread." She patted her hips. "Even though I shouldn't."

Charity drew in a breath. "I'm pregnant."

She hadn't meant to say that, exactly, but now that she had, there was no going back.

Marsha's eyes widened and her mouth dropped open. "Pregnant?" she whispered.

"Apparently. I peed on a stick and everything." She swallowed. "It's Josh, in case you were wondering. He's the only one I've... You know." While she didn't have a lot of experience with having a grandmother, she was going to go out on a limb and assume Marsha didn't want any more details about her intimate relationships.

"I don't know how this happened," Charity continued, giving in to her frustration. "Well, I know how it happened. I guess I don't know how I let it happen. Why now? I'm just settling in here. I'm finding my way and I really like it here. Being pregnant will change everything."

She sucked in a breath. "And did it have to be Josh? He's the poster child for self-absorption. I don't mean that to sound as harsh as it does, but you know what I mean. He's got his life, too. He's not interested in anything but getting back on the racing circuit. He's going to be that famous athlete again, which is great for him, but a baby? He's not going to be happy."

She wondered if he would think she was like all the other women who did their best to trick him into supporting them. She thought about Emily showing up in his room and who knows how many others. Of course he would think the worst about her, she thought grimly. What other choice would she have? Talk about a disaster.

She opened her mouth to continue her rant, then noticed

that Marsha was staring at her with a happy, almost bliss-ful expression.

"You're having a baby," the other woman said, then stepped close and hugged her.

The warm, supportive embrace melted away Charity's anxiety. Suddenly she could breathe easily.

"I guess I am," Charity said, realizing that not keeping the baby wasn't an option. Ready or not, she was going to be a mom. "I'm having a baby. Me."

Marsha drew back slightly. "I'm going to be a great-grandmother. That sounds impressive. And old."

"Not old. Experienced."

Marsha laughed. "I think experienced makes me sound like an aging hooker." She took Charity's arm and led her into the living room. "Are you still in shock?"

"Yes, and I don't see that changing anytime soon. It's not real. I just found out five minutes ago."

Marsha sat next to her and took her hand. "So you haven't told Josh?"

"No. I just found myself coming here." A million thoughts tumbled through her brain. She tried to pick just one to focus on, but she couldn't. Talk about impossible.

"Are you staying?"

At first Charity didn't understand the question, then she was hugging Marsha again, feeling the other woman's fear over losing her family for the second time.

"I'm staying," Charity told her firmly. "Being pregnant and single isn't how I wanted to be known around town, but if you can live with it, then I can, too."

"Of course I can live with it. I'm delighted."

Charity straightened, then leaned back against the sofa. She pressed a hand to her belly. "Pregnant. There's a con-versation starter." She glanced at Marsha. "Don't worry.

I know I have to tell him. And considering where I live, I need to do it soon. This is not a good place to keep secrets."

"Have the two of you talked about any kind of future together?" Marsha asked delicately.

"We don't plan much past the weekend. Josh is focused on the race and what that means to him. He wants to go back to his old life. I know that. I know he misses the excitement of racing." The thrill of being famous. "He's not going to like this."

"He might surprise you. Josh has always wanted a family."

"He strikes me as a 'one day' kind of guy. The man who always says that he would like to settle down, one day." She looked at Marsha. "I'm not hoping for a miracle. He's not going to fall to his knees and beg me to marry him."

"Would you like him to?"

Charity looked away. She loved Josh—that was the easy part. But having a future with him? Not possible. "We want different things. We have different visions for our lives."

"Marriage is all about compromise."

"He wants to be in the limelight. I want normal, in every sense of the word. A really normal guy would be great."

"But you're not pregnant with a really normal guy's baby. You're pregnant with Josh's."

"A technicality," Charity said with a smile. "But I do love him."

Marsha patted her arm. "You're a smart girl. You'll figure it out. Josh will need a little time to get used to the fact that you're pregnant, but I think it's going to all work out. You'll see."

Charity hoped she was right. "If he doesn't want to be a part of our lives, we'll be fine. I was raised by a single mom. I know the good and the bad of the situation." She took Marsha's hand in her own. "It's not like I'll be completely by myself."

"No, you won't. You'll have me, no matter what."

The words gave her comfort.

"And the town," Marsha added.

Charity groaned. "I didn't think that part through. Everyone is going to go crazy when they find out I'm carrying Josh's baby. What am I supposed to do about that?"

"Honestly?" Marsha asked. "Keep it a secret as long as possible."

Charity laughed. "That's not very helpful."

"It's the best I can do."

Two NIGHTS LATER, Charity sat on her bed as she and Josh watched a movie together. In the past forty-eight hours, she'd had dozens of opportunities to tell him she was pregnant and had chickened out each and every time.

She told herself she was looking for the perfect moment, which was a complete lie. She simply didn't want him to know. Once he knew, everything would change and she wasn't ready to lose him. Still, each day that went by created a problem. Withholding the information made her uncomfortable with herself. So she was going to have to suck it up and say the words.

The action on the television shifted. They were watching some kind of an international spy movie with the fate of the world resting on the shoulders of a handsome leading man. Sort of like James Bond, but without the yummy accent. The leading lady was supposed to be Russian and the bad guy was from a nameless European country.

When the bad guy's girlfriend moved onto the screen, Josh pointed. "That's Angelique. She made this movie right before we split up. I visited her on the set a few times."

He spoke casually, as if sharing an interesting fact that had no consequence. Which would be the case, for anyone else. Not so much for her.

Charity had known Josh had been married to Angelique. She had a vague memory of a beautiful brunette with large eyes and huge breasts. But that mental image wasn't anything like the very real, very beautiful woman she watched now.

Angelique wore little more than a short nightshirt. Her legs were endlessly long and perfect. Her breasts thrust toward the camera, her tight nipples clearly visible beneath the thin layer of silk.

There was something about her, some indefinable element that made her watchable and appealing. Charisma, Charity thought grimly. The same as Josh.

She'd never seen a picture of the two of them together, but she had a feeling they would look as if they completely belonged with each other. No one would question what either saw in the other. It made sense.

"You were married to her?" Her words came out as a question, even though she already knew the answer.

"I told you about her."

Oh, sure. But there was a big difference between mentioning a former wife and admitting that one had been married to a goddess-like creature.

Not that she was going to say that to him. "She's very beautiful," she murmured.

"I guess." Josh stared at the screen, then shrugged. "The nose job didn't go well. She had to get a second surgery to fix it."

Charity raised her eyebrows. "I'm not sure you should be telling me that."

He turned to her, his hazel-green eyes dark with concern. "I know what you think when you look at her."

"I doubt that."

"I know what I think. It was a long time ago. I'm not sorry it's over."

Wasn't he? After all, Angelique had left him. He wanted to get back into racing, to return to his former glory. How much of that was about showing his ex-wife exactly what she'd lost? Once he was on top again, it would be his turn to do the rejecting. Or maybe he planned to get back together with her and make perfect babies together. A completely irrational thought, she told herself. No doubt brought to life by worry and surging hormones.

"Don't go there," he told her.

"Go where?"

"Wherever it is you are right now. I'm not interested in her. Been there, done that."

"Bought the T-shirt?"

He grinned at her. "Uh-huh."

She looked at him, as if seeing him for the first time. The perfect features, the easy smile, the giant ego and warm, caring heart. He was a good guy, and under other circumstances, she would be almost comfortable having fallen in love with him. Unfortunately, she was dealing with these circumstances.

"Charity?" he asked, looking concerned. "What's wrong?"

She drew in a breath, then coughed up the truth.

"I'm pregnant."

JOSH HAD BEEN prepared to hear her say she thought she was coming down with something, or the sight of Angelique was intimidating or that she had decided she hated small-town living and wanted to move to L.A.

Instead there were two words and a faint buzzing sound in his head. He felt as if all the air had been sucked from the room. He couldn't breathe, but that was the least of it. He couldn't think. Couldn't figure out what she'd meant.

She gazed at him expectantly, making him aware that he was supposed to say something in response.

Pregnant? Pregnant.

There was going to be a baby. His baby.

Josh rose from the bed and stared at Charity. A sense of urgency swept through him. He couldn't have a kid now— he wasn't ready. He didn't have enough of his shit together. He would screw up everything.

Time, he told himself quickly. He had a few months to get ready. To figure it out and be the kind of dad a kid deserved.

Charity turned away. "I don't expect anything," she said flatly. "You don't have to panic. I'm telling you as a courtesy, nothing more."

He didn't like the sound of that. "What do you mean?"

"I'm the one who's pregnant, not you. The baby is my responsibility."

"Mine, too," he said, still not able to grasp the significance of what was happening.

A child. They were going to bring a child into the world. The phrase "ready or not" had never been so significant.

"I'll figure this out," he said, more to himself than her.

"You don't have to."

"I'm a part of this," he told her. "I'll be there for you and the baby."

She didn't look as if she believed him. Knowing all she did about his past, how he'd failed, he knew why she had doubts.

"Just give me a little time," he told her, as he backed toward the door. "You'll see."

And then he was gone. Charity leaned back against the pillow and smoothed her hand over the still warm place on the bed. What she would see was how quickly he left, she thought sadly. His reaction wasn't a surprise, but it was still very much a disappointment.

"Oh my God!" Pia stood in the doorway to her apartment and stared wide-eyed at Charity. "You look incredible. I love the cut and the color. You went to Julia, didn't you? No one does highlights like her. Don't tell Bella I said that. Wow. You're all fluffy and pretty."

Charity smiled wanly at her friend. "I'm not feeling especially fluffy."

"Then come in and we'll change that."

Charity walked into the cheerful apartment. "I'm sorry for dropping in like this. I should have called. It's late."

Pia shook her head. "Don't be silly. It's not like I have a date or anything." She led the way into the living room, where the TV showed a frozen frame of a movie. Sandra Bullock stood by a mailbox next to a house made almost entirely of glass.

"The Lake House," Pia said. "I love it. I can't help myself. He waited for her for two years. What guy does that?"

Charity hadn't meant to come here. After Josh had left, she'd told herself that she would be fine. That she would get through this. Hundreds, maybe thousands of single women found out they were pregnant every day. They managed. It wasn't the idea of being a parent on her own that was ripping her up inside. It was the realization that Josh didn't love her back. She hadn't really expected him to, but now she couldn't even hope for a happy ending.

"All men are pigs," she said, then motioned to the screen. "Except Keanu Reeves."

"Exactly." Pia led her to the sofa. "Although I should probably tell you I do have a new guy in my life." She motioned to the short-haired marmalade cat curled up in a club chair. "That's Jake," she said, lowering her voice. "Crystal's cat."

"Oh. He's beautiful."

The cat looked up and stared at Charity. His eyes were large and the color of emeralds. His expression turned haughty, as if he found her wanting, then he put his head back down and closed his eyes.

"We're spending the weekend together, seeing if we can figure out if we get along." Pia wrinkled her nose. "I'm not really a pet person, but it's a way to help Crystal. And maybe having a cat around will be a good thing." She sounded doubtful.

"Is he friendly?"

"I don't know. He keeps to himself. I'm respecting his need to take things slow."

Charity stared at her friend. "He's a cat."

"I know, but aren't they supposed to be haughty and aloof? I thought if I let him make the first move, things would go better. I don't want him to think I want the relationship more than he does."

"I think you're giving him way too much credit. He doesn't have a master plan."

Pia eyed her loaner pet. "I'm thinking maybe he does. We'll see what happens. So far he's very quiet. And clean. I thought I'd be freaked out by the idea of a litterbox, but I'm not. His aim is a lot better than most guys I know."

"Maybe he's the answer."

"Maybe." Pia turned toward her. "Can I get you something? I have an assortment of ice cream selections. I'm going through a dairy phase. There's not a single cookie in the whole place, but I probably have five different kinds of ice cream."

"No, thanks." Charity touched her stomach. So far she hadn't had any cravings or queasiness, but she didn't want to push anything too far.

"What's going on?" Pia asked. "Something happened and I'm guessing it was with Josh."

Charity nodded. "I don't know why I let myself believe this would be different. Of all the guys to fall for. What was I thinking?"

"You weren't thinking. That's the problem. We don't think when it comes to men. Honestly, I don't know why Marsha is so hell-bent on getting more of them in town. They're nothing but trouble."

She reached for Charity's hand and squeezed it. "Start at the beginning and tell me the horrible thing he's done. Then we'll get drunk and call him names."

"I can't."

Pia smiled. "Don't worry. We'll find your anger. It's right under the hurt. Trust me—I have a world of experience at this. I'll have you swearing in ways you never thought possible."

Charity stared at her friend. "No, I mean I can't have anything to drink. I'm pregnant."

She had to give Pia credit. Nothing about her expression changed. Her only reaction was to calmly ask, "Are you sure?"

"I peed on a stick."

"And there's only been Josh?"

That made Charity smile. "Do I seem like someone who would sleep with more than one guy?"

"You have depths. It could happen."

"It didn't. I'm pregnant." She said the words more for herself than Pia, to help herself get used to the idea.

"How do you feel about it?" Pia asked. "Have you always dreamed of having children?"

"Sure. Haven't you?"

Pia shrugged. "Some days. But it's a lot of responsibility, and parents can really screw up a kid. I'm not sure I want to take the risk of passing on the family tradition of emotional devastation. But we're not talking about me. How do you feel?"

"I don't know. Excited, scared." She drew in a breath and mentally poked around inside. "Happy," she said slowly, then realized it was true. "I'm happy."

"Then yay you." Pia squeezed her fingers again. "You'll be a great mom."

"How do you know?"

"You have the personality. You take care of things. You care. You have Marsha for a grandmother and she's amazing."

"This isn't how I would have chosen to do things," she admitted. "But I don't have regrets."

Pia released her hand, then wrinkled her nose. "At the risk of breaking your mood, I'm guessing Josh didn't take it very well? You wouldn't be here if he did."

"He freaked," Charity said with a sigh. "He mumbled something about figuring it out, swore he would be there for me and the baby, then raced out so fast he left those clichéd skid marks on the floor. There's no way he's going to be able to handle it."

She hated to think that, let alone say it. "I didn't realize I had a whole fantasy about Josh until it all came crashing down around me. I'd hoped he would be excited, or at least open to the idea."

"At the risk of violating the girl code, you need to give him a break. You told him something huge. He should get a few minutes to absorb it all. He might surprise you."

"Not in a good way."

Pia shook her head. "Josh is a good guy. When things are tough, he comes through. Give him a little credit."

"For running?"

"Okay, then give him a chance to step up and do the right thing. He said he'd be there for you."

"What does that mean?" Charity found herself getting irritated. "Maybe he'll do promo shots with the baby for someone who makes athletic gear for infants. That's about all he's interested in. He's getting back into racing. What matters to him is being the man he was. He's told me that. He wants to return to that world, claim it all again. This is about being famous. He wants to be the guy on the poster."

Pia stared at her for a long time. "What do you want?" she asked softly.

"I want everything he doesn't. A traditional life. Husband, kids. A house and a dog." She glanced at the now sleeping Jake. "Maybe a cat. I want a certainty to my days. I want roots and neighbors and date night and the rhythm of the seasons. I want passion and loyalty."

"Did you tell him that?"

"I didn't have a chance. I barely managed to say I was pregnant and he was gone."

"He'll be back."

"It won't change anything." Charity leaned toward her friend. "You've known Josh for years. Has he ever once struck you as the domestic type?"

"He has his moments."

"The man lives in a hotel. You know that racing is everything to him. No. Not the racing. He doesn't want to compete, he wants to win. He wants to be a god again. There's no room for ordinary where he's going."

"So you're going to assume the worst about him without asking for what you want, or even hinting that there's something he can do to make you happy."

"What? No. That's not fair."

"You didn't tell him what you want?"

"I already told you. There wasn't time."

"And when he comes back to talk to you about all this? You know he will. What happens then? Is he supposed to read your mind?"

"If he cared about me at all, he'd already know what I want."

The words sounded lame, even as Charity spoke them. Pia simply raised her eyebrows.

Charity shifted on her seat. "Okay," she began. "I sort of see your point. I should probably tell Josh what I'm thinking. It's the mature thing to do."

"I know you don't want to get hurt," Pia said.

Charity nodded. "I love him. I'm in love with him, which I'm okay with. The thing is, I don't think he's interested in loving me back."

"You won't know until you talk to him."

"And when he crushes me like a bug?"

Pia gave her a warm smile. "You don't know he will."

"Can you honestly see him saying he loves me and wants to be with me for the rest of his life?"

"Yes."

Now it was Charity's turn to smile, although her feelings were more sad than hopeful. "You're not a very good liar."

"I think there's a chance."

There was always a chance, Charity thought sadly. Just not a very good one.

CHAPTER EIGHTEEN

JOSH ALWAYS ENJOYED Los Angeles. The city was big and sprawling, with an air of self-importance. New York might be the leading edge of the country and the midsection might have the heart, but L.A. was cool and everyone knew it.

He took the elevator down to the baggage-claim level at LAX, then walked toward the petite woman in a suit, holding a sign that said Golden.

"Not that I wouldn't know you anywhere," she said when he walked up to her. "How was your flight?"

"Good," he said. "Quick."

"I prefer mine to last," she said as she led the way to the town car.

She was pretty enough. Mid twenties, easy smile and a body no conservative suit could conceal. There was a time when he would have considered pursuing her not very subtle invitation. Maybe even in the back of the town car. Today…not so much.

The flight from Sacramento had been less than an hour. The drive into Century City took nearly that long. Airport traffic was tough, as always, and once they arrived at the high rise, they went underground to find parking.

Josh took the elevator to the thirty-second floor, where a tall, thin man was waiting. The offices were quietly elegant, as was typical for an upscale law firm. The carpeting was plush, the views amazing and the conference room massive.

Josh walked in and greeted the people already waiting for him. There were two lawyers, an advertising executive, three former racing coaches, a representative from a bike manufacturer and an athletic-shoe designer.

After introductions and offers of coffee, they sat down at the table. One of the lawyers, Pete Gray, went first.

"Your proposal was interesting," Pete began, nodding at the folder in front of him. "Our clients are intrigued. You've lined up excellent sponsors, you have regional and local support. The city obviously wants this to happen."

"They've offered land and tax breaks," Josh said. "It doesn't get much better than that."

Everyone nodded.

Pete continued. "We have preliminary bids for the construction itself. There was an interesting one from Hendrix Construction. The owner, an Ethan Hendrix, asked for the opportunity to undercut the lowest bid by five percent."

Josh hadn't known about that. "His firm does quality work. They would be my preferred choice."

"We're putting together a prospectus for our clients," Pete continued. "We're recommending they invest. On one condition."

Josh had had an idea about this ever since he'd been invited to L.A. for the meeting. He still didn't know how he felt about it.

"We want you to run the school."

Josh opened the folder in front of him. As he'd put together much of the package, he knew what was inside. The pictures of kids on racing bikes were familiar, as was the diagram for the facility. There would be workout space, an indoor track, classrooms and lecture halls. His idea had always been to integrate the school into the community. Over time he could see them bringing in experts to talk about everything from nutrition and aging to different sports for every season.

"I've never run anything like this," he said.

"You have several successful businesses," one of the women said. He thought she might be the advertising executive. "You understand how to make a profit."

"I'm not a coach."

"No. You'll be hiring coaches," Pete told him. "You have the skill set we're looking for and a name. Being Josh Golden helps get investors interested. My recommendation hinges on you, Josh. Unless you're thinking of getting back into racing professionally. I've heard some rumors."

"I'm in a race," he said. "I'm going to see how that goes."

Two of the coaches looked interested. The third was skeptical.

He knew that professional racing was a grueling sport and that he would be facing a hell of a challenge if he planned on competing professionally. Training would take over his life. He would have to commit with every fiber of his being. There wouldn't be room for anything else. Not even the fear.

But glory and fame weren't what drove him. Instead he wanted to find that part of himself he'd lost. Once he had it, there wouldn't be anything left to prove. If he could get that piece back in a single race, that's all it would take.

"If you were to return to professional racing, do you have any idea as to how long you would be on the circuit?"

"No more than a year or two," he said, hoping it would be a lot less than that.

Pete looked at the other people around the table. "If he committed to running the school when he retired, we could get by with a temporary administrator." He turned to Josh. "Would that interest you?"

"It might."

While he was intrigued by the idea of the school, what interested him most was that being in charge of something like the racing school meant he would have something stable to offer Charity and the baby. Something that would make her proud of him. Something that might make him enough.

He hadn't spoken to her since he'd found out she was pregnant. Probably a mistake, he told himself. They had to talk about what was happening, come up with a game plan. If he could explain that he was going to try to be worthy, maybe she would give him a chance.

A kid, he thought, still not able to take it all in. He was having a kid.

"You'll let us know?" Pete asked.

Josh nodded. "After the race. I'll let you know if I'm going to run the school and when I plan to start."

"Excellent. We want you on board. You're an integral part of this plan."

They all shook hands, then Josh went back down to the parking garage where his car and driver waited.

If he didn't agree to run the school, he would lose the funding he needed. It could probably be found elsewhere, but it might take a while. The town needed the school now. Which meant it all came down to him.

Was that the kind of job he wanted? Could he do it and did he want to?

He thought about the high school kids he rode with several times a week. How he'd gone from being terrified of being anywhere close to them on a bike, to helping them train. He enjoyed watching them get better and knowing he was a part of the improvement. He liked the idea that Brandon could go all the way—be an international contender.

The school would be a way for Brandon and other kids like him to get to the next level. Of course he wanted to be a part of that. But first he had to get back to being the man he'd been. He had to compete and win.

When he landed back in Sacramento, he drove directly to Fool's Gold. But instead of going to his place or Charity's office, he made his way out of town to the large manufacturing facility Ethan owned. He drove around several guys loading the base of a windmill on a big rig and headed for the office.

Ethan's truck was out front. He went inside and found his friend in his office.

"Got a minute?" he asked as he walked in.

Ethan waved at the chair on the opposite side of his desk. "Sure. What's up?"

"I just got back from L.A."

Ethan grinned. "I thought you looked a little frayed around the edges. What's new in La La land?"

"I met with the people who can get funding for the racing school. The school you bid on."

"Interesting."

"They want me to run it."

Ethan leaned back in his chair. "I turned them down last week. In case you were wondering."

Josh chuckled. "Sure you did."

"I'm busy with my own empire. As are you. Considering it?"

"Maybe. The other businesses—the sporting goods store, the hotel, the real estate—any good manager could handle it. But the school is different."

"They want your name."

It wasn't a question, but Josh nodded anyway. "Having me on board makes it easy to get sponsors and students."

"So why aren't you jumping at the chance?"

"I don't know if I can do it."

"You'd have coaches. Staff. Hell, you could just stand around and look pretty and they'd be happy."

Josh ignored the slam. "I don't know if I can ride."

Ethan's eyebrows drew together. "You're going to find out in a few short weeks."

True enough. The race was rapidly approaching. Sometimes Josh knew he had it in him—that he had conquered his demons. Other times he knew he was fooling himself and that he would totally lose it in the middle of a race, on international television so the entire world would know he was a useless coward. If that happened, he would have trouble finding work at a hot dog stand, let alone in the racing community.

"You can do it," Ethan told him.

"Want to bet?"

"Sure. You've never walked away from anything in your life."

"I walked away from you," Josh reminded him. "I was scared. You were a friend and you needed me and I still hid from you for years."

"That was different."

"No. It was exactly the same. After Frank died…" He rubbed his temples. "I still see the body flying, him hitting the ground. It's not like in the movies. Death doesn't come with a soundtrack."

"Beating yourself up doesn't do a damn thing for Frank," Ethan told him. "He was a pro. He knew what he was doing."

"He was a kid. I was supposed to watch out for him."

Ethan stared at him for a long time. "Is there anything you could have done to change things?"

"I don't know. Maybe I could have shown him the way out of the peloton."

"You really believe that?"

Josh didn't have an answer and that was the hell of it.

"Charity's pregnant," he said instead.

Ethan looked at him and grinned. "Seriously? She slept with you? Why?"

Despite everything, Josh chuckled. "I'm the best."

"Keep telling yourself that." The smile faded a little. "You happy about this?"

"Still stunned. We've been seeing each other for a while, but we hadn't talked about the future or getting serious."

"A baby has a way of changing that."

"Tell me about it. She said she wasn't expecting anything from me. That she was telling me as a courtesy, nothing more."

"That's cold."

"Maybe, but given my reputation, do you blame her?"

"No." Ethan leaned toward him. "What do you want? To marry her? Settle down?"

Marriage? Again? There would be no halfway with Charity. If he let himself love her, he would be all in. Angelique had bruised him when she'd left. Charity would have the ability to rip out his heart and leave him for dead. Why would anyone give away that kind of power on purpose?

But they were having a baby together. A child. A piece of each of them. It was pretty damned spectacular.

"I always wanted kids," he said slowly. "In the future. More abstract than real. This is different. What if I can't do it?" He studied his friend. "I never knew my dad. What if I'm like him? What if I screw up everything? I don't know if I'm in the right place."

"Every new dad is scared," Ethan told him. "My dad had six kids and he was terrified every time. But you do it anyway. You live with the fear and vow to do your best. That's what I did."

Four words. Simple, easy words. Josh wanted to bang his head against the desk.

"I'm sorry," he said quietly.

"Don't worry about it."

"I shouldn't have brought this up."

Ethan shook his head. "You think you're the first person to talk about someone being pregnant in front of me? It was a long time ago." He stared at Josh. "What I remember most was wanting that baby more than anything. We'd just found out Rayanne was having a boy. My son. God, that felt good." He cleared his throat. "Trust me. You want that."

Josh nodded because he didn't know what to say. He tried to remember how long it had been since Rayanne had died, taking their unborn child with her. Leaving Ethan alone.

What if something happened to Charity? It was one thing for her to decide he wasn't good enough. He would eventually figure out how to recover from that. But to know she was gone seemed unimaginable.

"Have you talked to her since she told you she was pregnant?" Ethan asked.

"No."

"That would be the first step. She's had what, two or three days to imagine the worst? And believe me, women are good at imagining the worst. Go see her. Find out what she wants. Tell her what you want. Work it out. You always did have a way with the ladies, although I could never understand what they saw in you."

Josh grinned. "They're blinded by my perfection."

"I'm impressed by your ability to delude yourself."

Both men stood.

"You okay?" Ethan asked.

"Yeah." Or he would be, once he figured out how to be

whole again. Because being who he'd been before meant being worthy. Not just of the baby, but also of Charity.

"Hi."

Charity looked up and saw Josh standing in the entrance to her office.

She hadn't seen him in three days. Not a word or a glimpse. Just incredibly painful silence after she'd told him she was having his baby.

Every hour that passed made her more and more sad as she realized he wasn't the least bit interested in even pretending to want the baby. He was going to walk away. He would probably pay child support, maybe offer to take the kid for a day here or there, but that would be it.

The death of her dreams, dreams she hadn't been willing to admit, was painful. Even worse was looking up at him, and knowing that she could never be in the same room as him and not want him, not love him. It made the concept of getting over him and moving on impossible to imagine.

"Charity?"

"Come in," she said.

He stepped inside and closed her door, then moved to her desk. He took a seat and gave her a crooked smile. "How are you feeling?"

"Fine."

"No morning sickness or anything?"

"Not yet."

He gazed into her eyes. "Tell me what you want."

"Excuse me?"

"You're pregnant. We're having a child together. Tell me what you want. How do you see this playing out? Do you want me to stay away? Be involved? Do you think we should get married? What do you think would work best for you?"

What worked best for her was a man who genuinely loved her. One who couldn't picture life without her. A man who longed to have a family with her and grow old with her. She wanted passionate declarations, not rational lists of possibilities.

The semi-proposal hurt the worst, she admitted. Getting married for the sake of the baby crushed nearly every romantic dream she had.

As she looked at him, she saw caring in his eyes. A little worry—maybe for her, maybe for himself. Affection. But he was still Josh Golden, perfect, worship-worthy, not for lesser mortals such as herself.

Even as she thought she could tell him the truth, that she was completely in love with him, she dismissed the idea. Why make him feel bad? It wasn't as if he was going to love her back.

"I'm sure we can come to some kind of an agreement," she said.

"What does that mean?"

"Just what I said. Do you want to be part of the baby's life? I'm open to that. I'm staying here in Fool's Gold. While you'll probably be racing all over the world, this is your home base. So when you're in town, we'll have a schedule or something."

He frowned. "And that's what you want?"

"It seems the most rational approach."

"Nothing more?"

She tried not to flinch. What did he expect her to tell him?

"What more did you have in mind?" she asked.

"I don't know. Something."

"When you get it figured out, let me know. We'll talk about it."

He studied her. "What aren't you telling me?"

"I have no idea."

"There's something."

She gazed at him, willing her expression to stay neutral. If he guessed how she felt, he would feel sorry for her. Worse, he might try to make things better by offering a crumb or two of attention. Not exactly the road to happiness.

Finally he stood. "I guess we have time to figure it out."

She nodded.

He hesitated for a second, then left.

When she was alone, she breathed out a sigh of relief. One conversation down, who knows how many left to endure. She told herself it would get easier and hoped she was telling the truth.

But before she could turn back to her computer, Bernie hurried in. Her normally calm expression was tense.

"You won't believe it," she began. "I don't believe it."

"What are we talking about?" Charity asked.

"The money. The missing money." Bernie put her hands on her hips. "I found it."

Charity blinked at her. "You're kidding."

"No. Well, I found most of it. Some has already been spent, but most of it is sitting in an offshore account. It wasn't easy to trace, but I'm good at what I do. I'm just so pissed."

Charity almost didn't want to ask. "Who took it?"

"It's always the person you least expect. I should know that by now. But once again I was sucked in by a friendly smile and an offer to help."

"Who?" Charity repeated.

"Robert."

She stood and stared at Bernie. "No. I don't believe it." Robert? Quiet Robert who lived alone and cared way too much about the Civil War? "He's the one who figured out the money was missing and reported it."

"I know. He was angry about the money, too. Always talking about how whoever took it was stealing from the good people of Fool's Gold. I bought it. Hell, I even went to dinner with him."

"Me, too," Charity murmured, unable to take it in. Robert? Not possible. "You're sure?"

"There's a paper trail leading right back to him. I found it through dumb luck, which annoys me. There are money transfers, withdrawals. He's good, I'll give him that. Just not good enough."

"What happens now?"

Bernie rolled her eyes. "I've already called your police chief to take him into custody while I notify state authorities. She'll be here any second. I'm just so mad. He had me completely fooled."

"He had all of us fooled," Charity said, still not able to believe it. "Is he going to jail?"

"For a really long time. I have to go make those calls."

"Do you need me to do anything?" Charity asked.

"Just don't tell anyone I thought he was a nice guy."

"You and me, both."

After Bernie left, Charity tried to go back to work, but she couldn't think. Robert the thief? The information proved that once again she was a horrible judge of character. She'd been convinced his only flaws were that he was a little boring and kind of a mama's boy. Instead he'd stolen millions of dollars, spearheaded the investigation, most likely to keep attention off himself, and had fooled an entire town.

She was furious. Beyond furious. She'd actually felt bad about not wanting to go out with him. Talk about a new level of stupid!

She stood and crossed to her window, where she saw the police cars pull up. In a matter of a minute or two, Robert would be in custody.

Still pissed, she went down the hall and entered Robert's office. He glanced up and smiled.

"Hello, Charity. How's it going?"

"Not well for you. Did you really steal that money?"

His expression twisted a little. There was a second of confusion, followed by surprise, then an annoyingly smug look.

"What a question. I'm insulted."

"Are you? I don't think so." She studied him, looking for the truth. "How? No, wait. That doesn't matter. Why? That's the more important question. Why would you take money from the town? Did you really think we were all so stupid that you wouldn't get caught?"

"I didn't do anything," he told her. "But if I did, no one would find out."

"Is that what you think? That you're smarter than all of us?" She leaned against the doorframe. "Sorry, Robert. It turns out Bernie's even smarter than you."

The smugness faded. "What are you talking about?"

"She's already called the chief. Apparently she found your secret accounts and has everything she needs to put you away for a long time."

He sprang to his feet and started for the door. She stepped out of the way and watched him fly toward the stairs. Seconds later he tripped on Bernie's outstretched foot and went tumbling onto the marble floor. He lay sprawled there on his belly. Sheriff Burns climbed the stairs and calmly put her foot on the small of his back.

"I was halfway home when I got this call," the sheriff told him, not sounding happy. "I don't like it when anyone messes with my plans."

CHAPTER NINETEEN

"I FEEL SO USED," Marsha said the next morning as she and Charity sat in the mayor's office. "I liked Robert. I believed in him."

"I dated him," Charity said, shaking her head. "I felt bad that I didn't like him more. How did this happen?"

"We were too trusting," Marsha told her. "He had such excellent recommendations."

"Is this where we talk about what a nice, quiet man he was?"

News had spread quickly. Not only had Robert stolen the town's money, he'd been using a false name. Apparently the circumstances under which his elderly mother had died were suspicious and he was sitting in the city jail, waiting to be extradited back to Oregon for a possible murder charge.

"I have inherited my mother's bad taste in men," Charity said glumly. "Here's one more example."

"Robert doesn't count. You barely went out with him."

"I had no sense there was anything wrong with him. That should be a few points against me."

"Half a point," Marsha told her. "How are you feeing?"

"Fine. No obvious symptoms yet. No weird cravings or morning sickness."

"Have you talked to Josh recently?"

"Since the original announcement? He came by and asked me what I want from him. When I didn't have an answer, he said we would work it out. It was a thrilling moment for me."

"You're hurt."

"Some. And angry."

"Because he couldn't read your mind?"

Partly, but Charity wasn't going to admit that. "Why do I have to do the asking? Shouldn't he be offering? This is as much his child as mine."

"So you want him to do the right thing. Are you waiting for him to propose?"

"No." She tried to put a little force behind the word. "I want him to…" She wanted so much—it was difficult to pick just one direction. "I want him to want to be with me and the baby. I'm not interested in doing anything because he thinks he has to."

"Does he know you want to be with him?"

Charity didn't want to answer that either.

"You have a hard time asking for what you want," Marsha said. "Is it because your mother was never there for you?"

"Probably. I don't trust easily."

"What has Josh done to make you not trust him?"

"Nothing," she admitted reluctantly. "But look at his past. He wants to get back into racing. He wants everything that goes with it."

"Or maybe he just wants to know he hasn't failed."

An interesting point, Charity admitted grudgingly. But before she could figure out what to say, Sheryl stuck her head in the door.

"Charity, I'm sorry to bother you, but it's Dr. Daniels from the hospital committee. He says it's important."

"Thanks." Charity rose.

"You can take it here," Marsha told her. "I'll go get some coffee."

"Thanks." Charity waited until she was alone in the mayor's office, then picked up the phone. "Hello, Dr. Daniels."

"Ms. Jones. How are you?"

There was something about his voice. A hesitation. Her heart sank. "I'm good. What's going on?"

"You know we really enjoyed your presentation and everyone on the committee thinks the town is great."

Here came the but.

"But we have some concerns. While Fool's Gold is a great town, it's small and you already have one hospital. We're concerned we won't have enough of a workforce to support the new hospital and we didn't see much in the way of community support."

The need to scream grew, but she forced herself to breathe deeply and calmly. "Dr. Daniels, we have a very well-educated workforce and a community that is beyond eager to embrace the new hospital."

"I'm sure you think that's the case, Charity—"

"I don't think it, I know it," she said, interrupting him. "And I can prove it. Please give me one more chance with the committee."

There was a long pause. "I'll give you that because you've impressed me from the beginning. However, I'll warn you, we've already voted on the other site."

"Then I have my work cut out for me, don't I?" she said, determined to sound positive when she felt crushed inside.

"Friday," Dr. Daniels said. "Nine o'clock."

"I'll be ready."

They hung up. Charity staggered to the sofa and collapsed, then covered her face with her hands.

Three days. She had three days to find a miracle. Three days to come up with a way to convince the hospital committee that yes, there was plenty of local support, not to mention a trained workforce. She'd already provided plenty of statistics, shown them Fool's Gold, offered tax and housing incentives. What was left?

"Not good news?" Marsha asked when she returned to her office.

Charity briefly outlined what had happened. "I don't know what to do," she admitted. "We were so close. I know they liked our town better, so why are they balking?"

"Is the other city larger?"

"Yes. It's about twice the size, but it doesn't have any of our charm. The location isn't close to this nice, they don't have a better trained workforce and I know we're more enthusiastic than they are. Why won't they believe me?"

"I guess you're going to have to show them."

"How? How do I prove something they've already seen but won't believe?"

"Give them proof they can't ignore." Marsha patted her arm. "Ask, Charity. Ask for what you want."

For someone used to being in complete control, the concept was impossible to imagine, let alone do. "How?"

Marsha gave her an enigmatic, grandmotherly smile. "You're going to have to trust me," she said. "And the town."

Trust someone with her future? Her job? "What if I can't?"

"Take a leap of faith. Let us surprise you."

GERALD SATERLEE WAS an annoying sonofabitch, Josh thought as he pushed himself to ride faster. Sweat poured down his back, his legs ached, but he wasn't about to let some second-rate French racer beat him during a practice run.

Saterlee had shown up in Fool's Gold the day before, a week ahead of anyone else arriving for the race. He claimed to want to acclimate, but Josh knew better. The bastard had been sent ahead to check him out and report back. The world of racing wanted to know if Josh Golden still had it.

A smart strategy would be to let Saterlee beat him easily so no one would have any expectations. That had been Josh's plan. But as soon as they started riding, he'd felt his competitive nature kick in. He couldn't do it—couldn't let Saterlee think he was better.

They continued up the hill, most of the high school racers falling back. Brandon kept pace, but he was fading fast. Josh looked up at the few miles of hill left and knew that it would just be him and Saterlee in a few minutes.

Sure enough, a mile short of the peak, Brandon slowed. "Sorry, man," he yelled.

Josh waved at him and continued to pump his legs.

His body had been honed for this, he told himself. He'd been riding every day for the past two years. He'd worked out in the gym, strengthening every part of him. While his brain had been busy healing, his body had been preparing for a comeback. Now he would find out if he'd managed to pull it all together.

As they closed in on the highest point in the road, Josh felt that magic surge of energy. The sense that there were plenty of reserves, that he could ride forever. He glanced at Saterlee and saw exhaustion in his eyes. Josh knew he wasn't just winning. This was better—it was certainty.

He slowed suddenly and reached down to rub his calf. As if something hurt. He bent his head to hide any hint of satisfaction. Saterlee looked back, grinned like an idiot and rode on. Josh watched him go.

Word would spread quickly. They would say he wasn't what he'd once been. That the comeback was about ego rather than ability. They would speak of him sadly, with respect, but on the inside they'd be pleased.

He could live with that, he told himself. Because on the day of the race, he would kick their collective asses. And then he would walk away, having won it all. It was going to be a good day.

THE TV STUDIO was exactly as Charity remembered, only this time she was the one being interviewed, not Josh. And there was no one salivating to have sex with her. Probably a good thing, she thought. She was freaked out enough about the possibility of losing the hospital. The idea of having to deal with an aggressive suitor would probably push her over the edge.

Unless the guy in question was Josh, she thought sadly. Him she would like to see. But the last couple of days had been crazy busy, with her trying to pull together a new presentation. Josh had left her a couple of messages. She'd returned his calls only to miss him, as well. She'd seen him around town, training for the upcoming race, but hadn't been able to do much more than wave.

At some point they were going to have to have an actual conversation. Make decisions. Be grown-ups. But apparently not today.

The local reporter, a pretty woman about Charity's age, waited until Charity was seated comfortably. The sound girl had already put the mike on her and someone had put a light meter in front of her face.

"How long do you think you'll need?" the reporter asked. "We don't like the segments to go past two minutes."

"Not a problem," Charity told her. "I plan to beg quickly."

"Is this about the hospital bid? I thought they loved us."

"So did I. They have some concerns, which is why I'm here."

"Damn. My mom wants me to marry a doctor." The reporter flashed a smile. "Easier to do if there's a new hospital."

Charity laughed, then straightened in her chair when the reporter indicated they were ready to begin. A few seconds later, bright lights clicked on.

"I'm sitting here with Charity Jones, Fool's Gold's new city planner. One of Charity's current projects is convincing a California hospital to open their newest campus here in town. How's that going, Charity?"

Charity stared into the camera. She drew in a breath and told herself to go for confident and capable.

"We've had excellent negotiations," she began, then went through a few of the particulars. "Unfortunately, we seem to have hit a little bump in the road."

"How's that?"

"The planning committee has some concerns." Charity explained about the need for local support and a training program for nurses and technicians. "I'm meeting with the committee in two days. If anyone has any ideas, please e-mail me directly." She gave her e-mail address. "Or you can call City Hall and leave me a message." She gave that number, as well. "A hospital of this size would be a great benefit to the community. While our current hospital is excellent, the new hospital offers a trauma center. This town deserves the facility. I'm determined to make it happen, but I'll need your help. Thank you."

FRIDAY MORNING CHARITY couldn't eat breakfast. She'd been up most of the night, reviewing her presentation. Adding and deleting points until she could barely remember what she was supposed to be talking about.

But as she slipped on her shoes and checked herself one more time in the mirror, she felt a kind of calm. Whatever happened, the town had come through for her.

After her TV appearance, so many e-mails had flooded her inbox, the city's computer system had shut down for three hours. On Thursday, it had been overloaded and fizzled for half the day. She'd received phone calls, hand-delivered notes and dozens of ideas. Many of them had been excellent and had rounded out her presentation. Now she could only hope a small percentage of those people actually showed up, demonstrating to the committee that Fool's Gold was the right place to build.

She left the hotel shortly after eight and made her way to City Hall. The meeting was at nine. She'd reserved the large auditorium in the basement, hoping she wasn't being too optimistic. It seated about two hundred. If they could get fifty or sixty people there, that would help. A hundred would be better.

"It's a work day," she told herself as she entered the building. "That will cut down on the crowd." Still, this was important. If they could just make time…

She took the stairs down to the basement. Last night she'd gone over her presentation twice, had made sure the screen was in place and checked the sound system. She'd also arranged for a backup computer just in case. Sheryl had ordered in large pots of coffee. The Fox and Hound had donated mugs and napkins. Morgan's daughter ran a bakery that would be providing donuts.

Charity stepped off the stairs and entered a dark, quiet hall. No one was here.

She stood in the shadows, fighting disappointment. Not a single member of the community had come. There wasn't anyone. Worse, she couldn't see Sheryl or anyone else from the city. There was only silence.

Her stomach turned over as panic flooded her. What was wrong? Had she missed the meeting? Was it the wrong day? Had she woken up in an alternate universe?

"Charity?"

The warm, familiar voice made her turn. She glanced toward the auditorium and saw Josh waiting for her.

He smiled. "You turned your phone off."

"What?"

"Everyone's been trying to leave a message. Come on." He took her hand and led her to the stairs.

"What are you doing? I have a presentation."

"Tell me about it. Didn't it occur to you that on one of the most important days of your life, you should leave your cell phone on?"

She followed him up the stairs. "I don't understand. Of course it's on." She pulled it out of her purse and stared at the blank screen. Apparently the battery had died in the night. "Oh God. What did I miss?"

"So many people said they wanted to come that we had to move the meeting."

Move? "Where is it now?"

"High school gym." He glanced at his watch. "We have forty minutes. Don't worry."

Her heart thudded in her chest. "I can't be late."

"You won't be."

They raced out of City Hall and toward the SUV parked

in front. She'd barely thrown herself inside when Josh started the engine.

"My presentation," she said, remembering everything she'd left in her office.

"Sheryl took care of it. Everything's been moved. She tried to call you this morning, but Mary at the front desk knew you'd been up until three, so she wouldn't put the calls through. I was training, so I didn't get the calls either."

He raced through the oddly deserted streets of Fool's Gold. About a half mile from the high school, they ran into traffic. Josh stuck his head out the window, yelling that he had Charity with him. Instantly cars began moving out of the way.

They continued to the high school. There wasn't anywhere to park, so Josh simply pulled to the side of the road.

"Go," he said, pointing toward the gym. "The doors are standing open. Marsha's already inside. I'll be there as soon as I can." He grinned. "You're going to do great."

Charity wanted to say something, to touch him, kiss him and maybe talk about their future. But there wasn't time. She was already opening the door, then jumping down and hurrying toward the gym.

Once inside, she stopped to stare. The huge space was overflowing with people. The bleachers were full, as were the rows of chairs on the gym floor. There was a stage at one end, with a table. The hospital committee sat there, looking slightly dazed. Banners proclaiming that Fool's Gold wanted the hospital covered the walls and the cheerleaders were leading the crowd in several strange but interesting cheers about health care and becoming a nurse.

Marsha saw Charity and waved. Charity made her way to the stage.

"My phone died," she murmured to her grandmother. "I didn't know we'd moved."

"We had to. People started arriving about seven this morning. I've never seen a turnout like this." She smiled at Charity. "They heard your appeal and responded. You won't believe the offers that have been pouring in." She motioned to the folders lying on the table. "You did very well."

"We don't know if the hospital is going to build here or not yet."

"Either way, I'm proud of you."

"Thanks." Charity gave herself a moment to enjoy feeling as if she'd finally found where she belonged, then drew in a breath and walked over to the conference table. "Good morning."

"Impressive," Dr. Daniels said, motioning to the crowd. "I like the banners."

"You're going to like the information I have even more." She picked up the microphone on the table and turned it on. "Shall we get started?"

The huge gym went instantly quiet.

Charity had done a lot of presentations in the past. It was part of her job description. But she didn't remember ever having an audience this big or enthused. Although everyone stayed quiet, she could feel them willing her to do well. Their support gave her confidence.

She moved to the podium and opened the folder lying there.

"Dr. Daniels, I'd like to welcome you and your committee back to Fool's Gold and thank you for giving me one more chance to convince you this is where you should be building your new hospital. When we last spoke, you mentioned two specific concerns. A trained workforce and community support." She looked up and grinned. "Let me show you why you have nothing to worry about."

Over the next hour, she walked the committee through the detailed presentation. She explained how the California University campus at Fool's Gold had developed a nursing curriculum, including several advanced-degree specialties. That the Wilson Memorial teaching hospital would be sending different intern and resident rotations to the new hospital.

She showed them plans for a new golf course, housing projects and reviewed the excellent test scores at the local schools. Then she showed a projected schedule of fundraisers to help with special projects at the hospital.

"As for the community support," she said. "I believe the citizens of Fool's Gold have already spoken for themselves."

The crowd rose and applauded loudly. There were whistles and shouts.

Dr. Daniels looked stunned. "If you'll give us a few minutes to talk this over," he said, his eyes slightly glazed.

Charity nodded and turned off the mike. People in the gym started talking. She saw Josh hurrying toward her, weaving through the rows of chairs. After going down the stairs, she met him in front of the podium. He grabbed her hand and pulled her through a side door, into a quiet hallway.

"You did good," he told her.

"We all did. Everyone came through. The information I had was great, but having so many people show up to express their support is invaluable." She felt a growing warmth inside, a sense of being home. If the hospital moved here, she wouldn't have done it all by herself, and that made the victory even sweeter.

This town, these people, it was all that she'd been searching for her whole life. A place to call home. A place to belong.

She'd been lost for so long, she thought, staring into Josh's beautiful eyes. Doing her best to make the right choice so she wouldn't get hurt. Wouldn't be left. But living that way meant missing so much. It meant missing the best parts.

"Whatever happens," she whispered. "With the race, with the baby, with the future, I want you to know I don't regret any of it. I love you."

Josh put his hands on her shoulders, then kissed her. "I love you, too," he said when he straightened.

The floor seemed to lurch a little, then still. She felt every muscle freeze in shock. "W-what?"

He grinned. "I love you, Charity. You're everything I've ever wanted. I love being with you, how I feel when I'm around you. I want to be the man in your life. The person you can depend on. I want us to be a family. For always. I want you to marry me."

The words bounced around in her brain like a dozen pinballs. Individually they made sense but together they were impossible to believe.

"You love me?"

"Yeah." He kissed her again. "As soon as the race is over, we'll work out the details. Where we'll live, when's the wedding."

His lips continued to move, so she would guess he was still talking. But she wasn't listening.

The race. How could she have forgotten? This was all about the race. About being famous and important. About being the guy on the poster.

"I haven't said I'll marry you," she pointed out.

"I know. When I win—"

"That's what's important, isn't it? Winning. I don't want to be with someone who has to be worshiped by millions, Josh. I want to be with a guy who wants me. Just me and our kids and maybe a dog."

"I do want you. I'm not staying on the circuit. I just need to prove I'm worthy."

What crap, she thought bitterly. "That's just an excuse to be fawned over. Winning the race doesn't matter to me."

"It matters to me," he told her. His jaw was set, his expression determined. "My mother left me because I was broken. She didn't want to bother. Angelique left when I couldn't race anymore."

"I'm not either of them."

"I want you to be proud of me."

"I already am."

"I need to be proud of myself."

Which was the truth. This was about him and how he felt. She knew that. But would it end with one race? Could he hear the crowd and then walk away? No.

"I'll win and then we can be together," he said.

He was everything she'd ever wanted. The man she loved, the father of her unborn child. But he asked for the impossible.

"I won't be with you if you race," she said. "I don't want to be with someone who needs to win to feel whole."

The door next to them burst open. Pia stuck her head out. "Oh my God! They said yes. We're getting the hospital. Isn't that the best?"

"The best," Charity whispered, knowing she had won and lost in equal measures that morning.

CHAPTER TWENTY

JOSH SAT AT the bar, sipping from his glass of water. It was three days before the race and he was in the best shape of his life. His carefully choreographed workouts had honed every muscle, tightened every reflex. He'd done the work—now all he needed was a little luck.

"For a guy on the verge of being a hero, you don't look happy," Jo said. "Want to talk about it?"

He shook his head and continued to stare at the bar.

Jo glanced around, as if making sure no one could hear, then leaned close. "You'll do it, Josh. I've seen you practicing. You've been right in the middle of the pack and there hasn't been a problem. You're fine. You have to believe that."

He slowly raised his head to stare at the woman across from him. Her eyes were soft with understanding.

"What did you say?" he asked.

"I know you were scared for a long time, but you did it. You figured out how to beat the fear. I don't think I could have. To go through what you did? No way. But you're the man."

The impossible truth slammed into him. His mouth went dry. "You knew?"

"That you couldn't ride anymore? Not counting those late-night rides you took all the time. That was dangerous. But I guess it was the only way you could get through it, right?"

He felt exposed and more than a little stupid. "You knew?" he repeated.

"Um, yes."

He swallowed and straightened. "Let me guess. Everyone knew. Everyone in town."

"Not everyone. Most people. We didn't want to talk about it. You needed space to heal. It made sense."

The past two years replayed in his mind. A montage of highlights, so to speak. He remembered how carefully he'd hidden his bike, how he'd ridden in the dark, too ashamed to be out in the light. How everyone had teased him about being out having sex, when they'd known exactly what he was doing.

He didn't know if he should crawl under a rock or be grateful.

"You look confused," Jo said.

"That's one way of putting it."

She smiled. "You're one of us. We love you." Her smile widened. "I'm speaking generally, of course. I don't want Charity coming in and beating me up."

"You think she could take you?"

"Love does interesting things to a woman. Gives her strength."

Maybe, but he wasn't sure Charity loved him as much as she claimed. She certainly didn't understand him. Riding wasn't about being the guy on the poster, as she claimed. It was about being himself. He had to do this—prove that he could. Then he could walk away and get on with his life.

A couple of guys finished up a pool game and walked through the bar.

"Good luck on Saturday, Josh," they called as they left.

"Thanks."

"You okay?" Jo asked.

He nodded.

When he'd been a kid, Fool's Gold had taken him in. The town was still there for him, in ways he hadn't even known about. He wanted to say he owed them, but it wasn't like that. They were a family.

He wanted to stay here, to be here with Charity. He wanted to marry her. When the race was over, he would explain again, he promised himself. Somehow he would make her understand. He finally found the one woman he was meant to be with. No way he was letting her get away.

THE MORNING OF the race dawned bright and hot. Charity busied herself in her room until she was supposed to meet Marsha, then made her way downstairs.

Mary, the woman at the front desk, waved. "You still flying from the hospital agreeing to build here?"

"It's great news," Charity said, doing her best to sound cheerful. "For all of us."

"My little sister wants to be a nurse. She's excited."

"I'm glad."

"You off to watch the race? Josh is so going to win."

Charity smiled and kept walking. No, she wasn't going to watch the race. She would be there at the beginning, because she was part of city government and she would be expected. But then she would leave. What was the point in staying?

Josh said he needed to win. She believed that. If he lost, he would keep trying. If he won, he would be sucked back into that world. She was just a regular person—how could she compete with the immortality of fame?

She walked more quickly, wanting to get to Marsha's house before anyone else spoke to her. Nearly everyone in town was heading to line up along the race route. Thousands of visitors crowded the streets, so she didn't have to do much more than smile and slip between milling groups.

"Quite the crowd," Marsha said when Charity arrived.

"Every hotel room is booked and the restaurants are full. It's going to be a good weekend."

"I'm glad," Charity said, following her grandmother into her living room.

They'd arranged to meet and walk over to the start line together. But instead of getting her purse and pulling out keys, Marsha headed for the sofa. Charity saw several photo albums lined up on the coffee table.

"What are those?" she asked, pointing.

Marsha put her arm around Charity's waist. "Just some old pictures. Don't worry. This will only take a second."

Charity settled on the sofa. "Are they of my mom?" she asked, not sure if she wanted to spend her morning looking at Sandra.

"Not exactly." Marsha sat next to her and flipped open the first album. There were several pictures of a young boy on crutches.

Charity recognized Josh right away. He'd grown up, but his smile was still the same. Heartbreakingly appealing. Would their son or daughter have that smile?

"I remember the first time I saw him walk across the street," Marsha said. "He moved so slowly. I could tell that every step hurt him, but he never complained. He couldn't remember much about the fall and his mother didn't talk about it."

She turned the page, showing more pictures of Josh. In some he was with another boy, in a few, he was alone.

He was so physically perfect now that it was difficult to reconcile the adult with the child.

"He's come a long way," Charity said, aware of time passing.

How was Josh feeling in the hours before the race started? Tense? Confident? He'd worked the program and conquered his fears. Despite the fact that it would mean he would leave her, she found herself hoping he would win. It was what he wanted, and she loved him.

"His mother rented a room in a cheap motel. One of those horrible places with bugs and rooms by the hour. It's since been torn down." Marsha flipped another page. "He never brought a lunch to school or had any money to buy one. The principal told me how he would sit in a corner of the cafeteria, carefully not looking at any of the other students. He must have been starving."

Charity's own stomach tightened. "She didn't feed him?"

"Not enough. We arranged for him to get a hot meal every day. That helped. He was bright and friendly. He enjoyed school, all the kids liked him. I made an appointment to talk to his mother. I told her I wanted to help. But when I showed up at the motel, she was gone. Josh was standing in the parking lot. He said she'd gone out to the store, but she would be back. He'd already been waiting for three days."

Charity felt her eyes start to burn. This time she didn't fight against the tears, mostly because ten-year-old Josh deserved them.

"How could she have done that?"

Marsha shrugged. "I can't begin to understand her. You know what happened after that. The town took him in. He joined the Hendrix family and started riding a bike as part of his physical therapy." She closed the album and looked at Charity.

"He's never forgotten what happened. How his mother simply left him. He believes it's because he wasn't whole."

Broken, Charity thought. He described himself as broken. Less than. As if anyone who really knew him could find him wanting in any way. But he wouldn't believe that. And proving himself meant just what he'd said. Being worthy.

She stood and clutched her hands to her chest. "Oh no. He really does have to ride in the race, doesn't he? It's not about winning, although that would be nice. It's about healing."

"Not being broken," Marsha agreed.

Charity brushed the lingering tears from her face. "I told him I wouldn't be with him if he rode. I told him…" She covered her face. "Why was I so stupid?"

"A question people in love have been asking themselves for thousands of years."

Despite everything Charity laughed. She lowered her arms. "Is this you trying to help?"

"Do you feel better?"

"I don't know. Is it too late?"

"Do you really think an argument is enough to make Josh fall out of love with you?"

"No, but I made him feel bad. He has to race. Of course he does. He's not going anywhere afterwards. Why couldn't I see that?"

"Maybe you haven't had anyone to believe in before."

She hadn't, Charity realized. Until now. "I believe in you," she told her grandmother. "And I love you."

Marsha smiled. "I love you, too. Now I think we have a race we need to get to."

Charity nodded. They both hurried out of the house. There were throngs of people even on this quiet residential street. Marsha led the way, weaving through the crowds and slipping easily through clean, tidy alleys.

"Don't worry," her grandmother told her. "We have plenty of time. They can't start the race without me."

When they came out on the main road, they found themselves among a multitude of cycling enthusiasts.

Marsha turned and pointed. "The bike race starts over there. Put on your official ID and you can get right to the

starting line." She checked her watch. "You have five minutes before I make a few introductory remarks and Pia
starts things."

Charity hugged her. "Thank you so much."

"You delight me, child. Now hurry."

Charity pushed her way past families and couples, slipping into the tiniest openings, excusing herself when she
bumped into someone. It was bright and hot. How did anyone ride a bike in weather like this?

She pushed and wiggled and darted her way through
to the beginning of the race. Here the crowds were even
thicker and there were barricades in place to keep everyone back. Probably so the line didn't get covered with enthusiastic viewers.

Charity ran up to a deputy and smiled at the young
woman as she showed her official ID. "Hi. I'm Charity
Jones. I'm the—"

The deputy grinned. "I know who you are. You got the
hospital to come here. They're putting in a special children's wing. My cousin has cancer. Not having to drive so
far all the time is going to be great."

"That's great. Um, can you help me get through?"

"Sure."

The deputy pulled back the barricade. Charity slipped
through the opening and ran to the starting line.

There was an actual line on the street, along with TV
cameras, reporters and photographers, and the athletes.

Charity saw Josh at once. She called his name, but the
sound was lost in the crowd. She looked at all the racers,
and knew she couldn't simply walk into the middle of them
and have a personal conversation.

The loudspeakers crackled, then she heard Marsha being
introduced. There wasn't much time.

She took a step onto the street. At that moment, Josh turned and saw her.

He was wearing sunglasses, so she couldn't tell what he was thinking. Before she could decide what to do, he was already weaving his bike through the other competitors and moving toward her. She hurried toward him.

"We don't have much time," she said, speaking quickly. "I know I'm distracting you, but I had to come and tell you I was wrong. I was wrong to tell you not to race, wrong to tell you I wouldn't be with you if you did. I love you, Josh. This is who you are. If you really love me and want to be with me, then I'm the happiest, luckiest woman alive."

He took off his sunglasses and she saw the love burning in his eyes. "You mean that?"

"Of course. I'll go anywhere, just as long as we can be together." She glanced toward the start line. "You'd better get ready to race."

"What if I don't win?" he asked.

"Then you'll keep trying until you do."

He bent down and kissed her. "I do love you, Charity."

"I love you, too."

He returned to the pack. She stepped back and seconds later a gun went off. The race had begun.

PIA JOINED CHARITY as they watched as much of the race as they could. The sun rose in the sky, the day got warmer and Charity began to worry.

"Do you think he's drinking enough?" she asked her friend. "It's really hot."

"He's fine. He's a trained athlete. Come have a taco. You'll feel better."

"I can't eat while Josh is racing."

"You think going hungry will help him?"

"Maybe."

Pia sighed. "Save me from ever being in love. It makes people stupid."

Charity grinned. "It's worth it," she promised.

"Like I believe that."

When the course took the riders up the mountain, Charity and Pia went back toward the park to wait for the final leg of the race. Her ID got them in close to the finish line. She paced restlessly, wanting to know how Josh was doing, hoping he was kicking butt.

He needed this win, she thought, seeing the truth of it now. Not to have another trophy, but because he had something to prove to himself.

A gasp from the crowd told her that the lead riders had been spotted. Charity ran down to the edge of the street. She leaned as far forward as she could and watched.

A lone man on a bike rounded a corner. He was going as fast as the wind, pedaling easily, as if nothing about the race had bothered him. As if this was what he was born to do.

Even with him wearing a helmet and dark glasses, she recognized him and screamed his name.

His head came up.

She waved, laughing, waiting for him to go zooming past her. Instead he slowed, then came to stop right in front of her.

"What are you doing?" she demanded, as he put his foot on the asphalt. She pointed to the finish line, a scant hundred yards away. "Go."

People around them started screaming. Josh ignored them all.

He pulled off his glasses. "How you doing?"

"Josh! This isn't funny. Move." She glanced over his shoulder, knowing the other racers would appear at any second. "Just finish. You can win. Then we'll talk."

"We can talk now."

She shrieked. "No! I said I was wrong. I said I loved you. What more do you want?"

"You," he said. "For always."

"Yes, yes. You can have that. Now go. Cross the finish line. It's right there. Can't you see it? Hurry."

"You'll marry me?"

The man next to her turned. "For God's sake, lady. Marry him already."

"I'll marry you," she told Josh. "We'll figure it out. Your racing career."

"I don't want to race, Charity. I meant what I said. I just needed to bury a few ghosts."

She saw two riders round the corner.

"Go!" she yelled. "You have to go now."

He slipped on his sunglasses. "You told me you didn't care if I won."

"I was wrong! I've said it five billion times. Now would you please go win this race so we can get on with our lives?"

"Sure."

With that, he pushed off.

Charity didn't even breathe as he picked up speed, then crossed the finish line with seconds to spare.

The crowd exploded into cheers and laughter. Charity tried to make her way to Josh, but there were too many people between them. So she waited while someone popped bottles of champagne and the reporters asked their questions. She watched Josh be the center of the universe.

Then she heard something strange. A few feet away a woman turned and yelled, "Where's Charity? Pass it on."

The man behind her called out the same thing and it continued until the man in front of her looked over his shoulder. "You Charity?"

She nodded.

"Got her," he yelled. "Come on, honey. Get up there with Josh. He's waiting for you."

She was passed through the crowd until she found herself standing in front of Josh. He held a huge trophy in one hand and wrapped his other arm around her.

"Finally," he said. He turned back to the reporters. "Okay, guys. Ask away."

"Quite the comeback, Josh. You training for the Tour de France?"

"No. I'm done. This was a one-time race for me." He kissed the top of Charity's head, and held her closer. "My life is here."

She wrapped her arms around his waist and felt her love for him grow until she couldn't contain it. "You can race if you want. We'll work something out."

He stared into her eyes and smiled. "No. I want to run the racing school and be with you. You're my home, Charity. You're where I belong."

"I belong with you, too," she told him.

"Which is really good, because I'm not letting you go."

ETHAN HENDRIX WATCHED his best friend kiss the girl. It had taken Josh long enough, but he'd finally found what he'd always been looking for. Pleased, Ethan turned away to head back to his office.

Life was nothing if not interesting, he thought as he took a single step. Then something bright and red caught his eye. A color of hair he hadn't seen in a long time.

He turned to get a second look. To be sure. Then he swore softly.

Liz was back.

* * * * *

A FOOL'S GOLD WEDDING

CHAPTER ONE

"SO THERE'S THIS GUY."

Abby Hendrix didn't bother looking up from the tiny flower-shaped bead she was carefully gluing onto the printed place card. Her sister's wedding guest list had ballooned yet again. The increase in guests meant an increase in costs and Melissa was determined to do all she could to save money. Abby—the proud owner of a brand-new teaching certificate—was home for the summer and had offered to help with any DIY projects. She had applied tiny flower beads to forty-four place cards and was hoping to get through all three hundred and five by the end of the day. Or possibly by tomorrow.

"There's no guy," she said, before blowing on the bead to set the glue. "I know there's no guy because I know you'd never cheat on your fiancé." She looked up and smiled at her sister. "You love Davis. I have total confidence that you two will have a long, happy life together. So there."

"I do love Davis. Very much. But there *is* a guy. Joaquin."

The name was familiar. Abby set down her tweezers and leaned back in her chair. She'd definitely heard the name before. He was...

"Davis's brother," Melissa said with a sigh.

"Right. The mysterious, icky brother."

"He's not icky."

Abby grinned. "Uh-huh. Sure he's not. So why, exactly,

were you whining about him being the best man? You said, and correct me if I'm wrong, but you said he had the personality of a window frame, which was an impressive analogy, if you ask me."

"Thank you and *icky* is still the wrong word. He's..."

"Difficult? Socially awkward? Very, very tall? Allergic to shellfish?" Abby tried to remember what she'd heard about him. "Oh, wait. He's supersmart. Like scary smart and he thinks the rest of us are dumb." She laughed triumphantly. "He loathes that we are lesser mortals. That's it, right?"

Melissa, the beauty of the family, sighed again. "Not exactly how I'd phrase it—"

"That's because you're a fancy lawyer. You'd have to use the word *allegedly* like fifteen times."

"Can I talk?"

Abby batted her eyes. "I don't know. Can you?"

"When did you get annoying?"

Abby was unfazed by the question. "I'm the little sister. Just doing my job. I am, after all, a hard worker. Not as hard as you, but close."

Abby knew her place in the universe and it was a really good one. She was Liz and Ethan's adopted daughter, Melissa's full sister, Tyler's cousin and a soon-to-be third grade teacher at Ronan Elementary School. If Melissa was annoyingly beautiful and a little bit smarter, Abby was okay with that. Melissa had always looked out for her, even after they'd finally found a family. They were a team. If her sister needed a kidney or a lung, Abby was all in. If three hundred and five place cards would be happier with little flower beads on them, count on her to get that done.

Now she made an effort to control her naturally irreverent personality and address the topic seriously.

"You knew Joaquin was coming to the wedding. He's the best man. So what's the problem? He doesn't like the tux? And I can't help repeating myself by asking about the shellfish."

"Would you stop with the shellfish?" Melissa asked, obviously trying not to laugh. "This is serious."

Abby placed her hands on her jean-clad thighs, leaned forward and nodded. "I'm listening."

In theory, Abby and her sister looked alike. They were both about five-five and they wore about the same size. They were redheads with green(ish) eyes. But what sounded the same on paper was very different in real life. Melissa had thick auburn hair with a slight wave. Her eyes were dark green, her skin pale and luminous. She had all the right curves in all the right proportions. She was elegant, smart and always perfectly dressed.

Abby lived on a different appearance plane. Her hair was more carrot colored than auburn and, no matter how she curled, sprayed and sacrificed small animals to the hair gods, stick straight. She had freckles on literally every inch of her body. Her eyes were kind of a muddy green-hazel-brown, and despite wearing the same size as her sister, she had tiny boobs and what she feared would one day be a fairly good-size behind.

And yet she was okay with it. All of it. Sure, she would like bigger boobs, but barring surgery, she hadn't figured out a way to make that happen. In the name of self-confidence, she had a lovely collection of push-up bras that really did make a difference. For special occasions, she even had a pair of little gel cutlet thingies that did the trick, illusion wise. On the bright side, she could totally go without a bra if she wanted and no one even—

"Abby!" Melissa sounded exasperated.

"What?"

"You said you were listening. I've been talking for five minutes and you haven't heard a word."

"Oh. You're right. Sorry. Now I'm really listening."

Melissa didn't look convinced.

"I swear." Abby held up her left hand, then quickly switched to her right. "This is me, swearing."

"Joaquin is coming to Fool's Gold."

"Yes, for the wedding." Was the stress of the event starting to get to her sister? They'd already discussed this.

"Tomorrow."

"What? No. Tomorrow? The wedding's not for three weeks. Too-smart-for-his-own-good Joaquin is going to be in town for three weeks? That's a nightmare. What are you going to do?"

Melissa's gaze sharpened. "Yes, that is the question," she said. "He's going to need to be entertained."

"But how—" Abby fought the sudden urge to run from the room. "No. No way. Not me. I can't entertain him. I'm not smart enough. I was a solid B+ student. I'm great with kids. If he were eight or even eleven, I would be your girl, but what am I supposed to say to some sanctimonious doctor guy? Didn't he go to college when he was like five? No way. What about Mom?"

"Abby, please. There's no way he'd hang out with Mom, and even if he would, she's doing so much with the wedding and she's on deadline. I have to go back to work. In San Francisco," she added, as if Abby didn't know where she worked and lived. "Davis does, too."

"He could visit you there."

"Joaquin specifically told Davis he wants to stay in Fool's Gold. He has a room at Ronan's Lodge. I'm sure he'll keep himself busy. I just need you to, you know, help out."

"Monitor him." Abby's tone was glum. "You want me

to keep track of him and invite him out to dinner and be cheerful."

"Cheerful is a natural state for you."

"Yes, but not with a guy like him. Plus, I haven't even met him." Davis's parents had been to Fool's Gold bunches of times. Last Christmas the whole Kincaid-Hendrix clan had comingled for a gloriously massive and raucous Christmas. Everyone had been there. Everyone except the mysterious and grumpy Joaquin. He'd been working. Or dealing with his possible shellfish allergy.

Abby told herself not to judge. From all she'd heard, Joaquin was a gifted surgeon, so when he worked, he literally saved lives and stuff. But her uncle Simon was a gifted surgeon, too, and he wasn't grumpy. He was sweet and funny and he loved his family, and when she'd accidently sliced three of her fingers on a very sharp knife last summer, he'd fixed her up and now she barely had a scar.

"I know this is unexpected, but, Abby, I need you."

"Don't say that." Anything but that. If her sister needed her, she didn't have a choice. Still, she could try to get out of it. "You know I'm busy with the wedding. I have to finish these cards."

"I'll help you. We'll get them done today."

"Sure, but I have to paint all the votives and that's going to take a while."

"Joaquin can help."

"I doubt that, but there's other stuff." Surprises for her sister she didn't want to talk about. "Melissa, I really don't have time to babysit Joaquin. Please?"

Instead of relenting, Melissa only looked at her. Pointedly.

Ack! "But I don't want to."

Melissa sighed.

"Fine." Abby grumbled. "I'll do it. I won't like it, but I'll do it. You are not my favorite sister anymore."

"I'm your only sister and you love me almost as much as I love you."

"Apparently I love you more. Look what I'm doing for you. You are so going to owe me. I get to pick the name of your firstborn."

Melissa pulled her close and hugged her. "I'm not sure how Davis would feel about me promising that. He might want a vote."

"Then he should let his brother sleep on the couch."

"Fair enough. I'll let him know the price of your cooperation."

Abby turned back to the place cards. Putting on tiny bead flowers was suddenly a lot less fun. Starting tomorrow she was going to be responsible for someone she'd never met and probably wouldn't like. For three weeks! What on earth were they going to do?

Once her sister went back to San Francisco, Abby had planned to start working on her secret gift for the wedding. It was going to take a lot of time and organization. She supposed she could ask Joaquin to help. And they could walk around town. What else? She could take him to see her aunt Montana's service dogs and they could go out to the Castle Ranch and look at the horses. Or the goats. Although that might be too ordinary for a gifted surgeon. Maybe she could talk to her uncle Simon and get some ideas from him.

"I'll put together a lesson plan," she said. "Stuff for us to do every day between now and the wedding."

Melissa grinned. "I'm sure he'll love that."

"He'd better. He's messing with my summer vacation."

JOAQUIN KINCAID KNEW he was out of options. He'd done what he was supposed to and it had gotten him exactly nowhere. Faced with the choice of giving up or making an end run, he'd decided on the latter, because giving up was never an option. He didn't believe in it—not for himself or his patients. So here he was, wasting three weeks of his life in some ridiculous town on the off chance he could meet Simon Bradley and convince the man to admit Joaquin into his fellowship program.

Not an off chance, he reminded himself as he paced the length of the hotel room. He would make it happen. He had an in, after all. He was going to be spending time with a local resident who was related to Simon by marriage. Surely he could convince—he pulled the slip of paper out of his shirt pocket and glanced at it—Abby Hendrix to introduce him to her uncle. The meeting made sense— they were both surgeons specializing in trauma. Simon had gone even deeper, focusing on patients who were severely burned, a practice that had never been overly interesting to Joaquin until he'd lost one to her burns. He'd been more than capable of fixing her damaged heart and her ripped arteries, but in the end, her body had been unable to handle the burns. He'd been helpless to save her, a state of being he did not accept.

That had been a year ago and he still remembered everything about the moment when she'd died. He'd stood there, unable to intervene in any meaningful way. Two days later he'd applied for Dr. Bradley's fellowship. A month after that, he'd had a preliminary interview and had been told he wasn't a good match. Him!

He'd graduated summa cum laude from Stanford at the age of thirteen. He had three advanced degrees, wasting time until he was able to enter medical school at the age of seventeen. He was brilliant, dammit. How was it possible he hadn't made it past the first round? He hadn't even had the chance to meet Dr. Bradley. It had been an impossible situation and he didn't accept that any more than he accepted feeling helpless.

He crossed to the window and stared out at Fool's Gold. The day was sunny and warm. There were wide streets and lots of storefronts decorated with brightly colored flowers. To the east were mountains. He'd driven past a couple of vineyards on his way into town. Fool's Gold was the consummate small town. Joaquin didn't like small towns. Although he'd never been in one before, he didn't like this one. He liked large urban areas with lots going on. Not that he did much more than work, but he liked knowing there was always the opportunity for him to go to a restaurant or a club or a museum. What did people do here?

He reminded himself that for the sake of his career he would have to pretend to be enthralled by the place. After all, his brother, Davis, seemed to love it. He and Melissa were getting married here, although that probably had more to do with the fact that Melissa had grown up in the area. At least he thought she had. He'd never much paid attention when his brother had talked about his fiancée. Not that he and Davis talked much these days. Or ever. There simply wasn't that much to say. They had nothing in common— not that they ever had.

Joaquin had only met Melissa once or twice. He rarely went home for the holidays or other traditional family gatherings. He preferred to work. He told himself it was so other staff members could be with their families, but he knew in his heart he simply wasn't that altruistic. The real reason was he didn't like being around people very much. Not socially. He never knew what to say or how to act. Plus, their conversation wasn't very interesting. The things people cared about were so mundane. His was a world of life and death. Saving his patients was what mattered. Everything else was easily dismissed.

This was his life, he told himself. He was content with the choices he'd made. He was all about his work. Let others fall in love, have children, go camping. He lived on a higher plane. He didn't need ordinary pleasures. They only wasted time.

Which brought him back to why he was in town. He'd taken a three-week leave of absence from his work and was determined to meet Dr. Bradley and get him to understand that Joaquin needed to be in his program. Davis's wedding had given him an unexpected opportunity and Joaquin had seized on it, along with the offer that Melissa's sister would show him around. He planned to be charming—as much as was possible for him, given his lack of ability in that department—and friendly. As they toured the ridiculous town and did whatever it was people like her did, he would divine a way to meet her uncle. He was confident he and Simon Bradley had much in common. Once the two men met, the problem would be resolved and Joaquin could return to his life. Of that he was certain.

He glanced at his watch, then back out the window. He could see groups of what he assumed were tourists starting to fill the sidewalks. Banners advertised the Dog Days of Summer festival. He wasn't sure if there were real dogs or not, nor did he care. It was all so tiresome.

He looked at his watch again. Less than twenty seconds had passed. The next three weeks were going to be long, but worth it. The ends justified the means, he reminded himself. At least they always had for him.

CHAPTER TWO

ABBY SHIFTED IN the leather chair in her uncle's office. The
space was nice enough—big, airy, with lots of formal-
looking diploma thingies on the wall. There was a big book-
case filled with really thick medical journals, along with
citations and awards. One whole shelf had pictures of his
wife, her aunt Montana, and their kids, Skye and Henry.
She smiled at the familiar faces. Whenever she was home,
she was Simon and Montana's go-to babysitter. Abby loved
all kids, but those two in particular.

Simon ended the call and put the receiver back in place.
"Sorry about that," he said with an easy smile.

"No problem. I appreciate you meeting with me on such
short notice." She resisted the urge to moan or writhe. "I
have a problem and I need your help."

"Here I am."

Simon Bradley was an interesting guy. From what
Abby knew, he'd come to Fool's Gold on a very short-
term basis—to help out in the burn ward of the hospital.
He'd met and fallen madly in love with her aunt Montana
and had married her and settled here.

He was a tall, imposing sort of man, with piercing green
eyes. But what always caught people's attention was his
face. Half of it was perfect and the other half was terribly
scarred from burns he'd endured as a child.

"You never got surgery," she said before she could stop

herself. Abby instantly slapped her hand across her mouth. "Oh, no. I'm sorry. That was rude. I shouldn't have said anything."

Simon smiled at her. "To make the scars less noticeable? You're right. I never did."

"But something could be done."

"Yes. For a long time the scars were there to remind me of what was important."

"You mean to stay focused on your work?"

He nodded. "After a while, I realized they were reassuring for my patients. I'd been through what they're going through. The scars made it easier for my patients to trust me. Now, honestly, I just don't notice them. Do they bother you?"

The question was asked gently, as if he was trying not to upset her. "Simon, you know they don't. I don't really notice them much at all. Every now and then I see them, but it's no big deal."

"I'm glad. Now how can I help you?"

"Oh, right. That." She'd nearly forgotten. "There's this guy."

One eyebrow rose. "You've met someone?"

"What? No. I mean, I'd like to, but no. This isn't that." From what she'd heard, dating Joaquin would be a nightmare for sure. "Okay, so Melissa is marrying Davis and Davis has a brother we've never met because I don't know why. I guess he's too important or something, only he's coming to Fool's Gold like now. In fact, I'm supposed to go pick him up in a few minutes and I don't know what to do with him. He's in town for three weeks! Can you believe it? The entire three weeks before the wedding and I'm responsible for him. Only I have things to do and a couple of surprises for my sister, but Melissa said she needed my help so here I am."

Simon frowned. "How do I fit in?"

"Oh. Sorry. He's a gifted surgeon." She used air quotes and rolled her eyes as she spoke. "I doubt he's all that, but if he is, I'm not going to be able to talk to him. He's like supersmart and he went to college even younger than you did. So do you have any ideas on what I should talk about or say?"

"How old is he?"

"Um, I'm not sure. Twenty-eight-ish. Maybe thirty."

Simon leaned back in his chair. "Now I'm starting to worry about you, Abby. You're telling me that a single, age-appropriate man who happens to be a doctor needs a little attention from you and you're not sure what to do?"

"It's not romantic," she grumbled. "He sounds awful."

"He sounds lonely."

"You've never met him. He could be a jerk."

"Or he could just be a guy who wants to spend some time in Fool's Gold."

"Really?"

"You won't know until you meet him. As for what to talk about? You're an intelligent woman. You'll figure it out. Just be yourself. He won't be able to help being charmed."

If only, she thought glumly. "You're not being very helpful."

"Sorry. Tell you what. Montana and I will buy the two of you dinner one night. That will fill some time."

She smiled. "Thanks. That would be nice." She always enjoyed spending time with her aunt and uncle. And if Joaquin was too stuffy to appreciate the evening, then he was a big ol' butthead.

"So no other words of wisdom?" she asked wistfully.

"Sorry, no. Look, if he's as smart as you say, and he

went to college when he was still a kid, then he's never had a normal life. Show him what that's like. Do regular, fun things. Let him into your world. You'll do fine. If that doesn't work, flash him a smile and you'll reduce him to stammering."

"Unlikely. Need I remind you that Melissa's the pretty sister?"

"Sorry, no, she's not. And I'm a doctor so my opinion counts more than everyone else's."

She laughed as she stood. "You're very good to me."

Simon rose and held out his arms. She circled the desk and hugged him. He kissed the top of her head.

"Love you, kid," he said.

"I love you, too. Now I'm going to gird my loins and face Joaquin." She paused. "Why do people gird their loins?"

"To protect them in battle." He winked. "It's a guy thing."

"Nearly everything is. I'll be in touch to set up that dinner." Her mood brightened. "Unless he gets bored and goes back to whatever hospital he works in."

"Your luck's not that good."

"Tell me about it."

ABBY STOOD IN front of Ronan's Lodge. The hotel was beautiful—built in the 1800s and, um, there was a lot of carved wood. Sheesh! She'd lived in Fool's Gold her whole life. She really should learn something about the history of the big hotel in the center of town.

Of course she knew the basics, but the particulars, like who built what and why, had never seemed overly important. She should get a book or something and brush up on her local history. She could figure out a walking tour of the city with lots of fun facts and then give it to her students to complete over winter or spring break. That would be interesting for them and their families. Plus, it would make sure everyone was outside and doing something physical. Sometimes it was too easy to stay indoors on a computer or tablet.

She sent herself a reminder, then returned her attention to the hotel. There was no escape, she told herself. And the sooner she started, the sooner it would be over. Not that she liked wishing away three weeks of her life—especially when they were three weeks she'd been looking forward to. With Melissa working until the Thursday before her big day, Abby had volunteered to take care of anything that came up. Their mom was around to help, as well, which made it even more fun. Plus, there were the special projects Abby wanted to finish for the wedding. But instead of being excited about that, she had to worry about Joaquin— boy genius and amazing doctor.

It would have been easier if he weren't a guy, she thought, forcing herself up the few steps leading to the hotel. Not that she didn't like men—she did. One day she planned to marry one and everything. It was just sometimes she couldn't get past her disappointment. She'd had lots of boyfriends, lots of great times, but she'd never been in love. She'd never felt anything close to what people talked about in songs or the movies or even in her family. She'd never wanted anyone desperately. She'd never quivered at the thought of seeing someone. She'd never lost sleep or her appetite or even her train of thought.

She paused. Fine, she'd lost her train of thought but that happened all the time. She was twenty-two years old— shouldn't she at least have flirted with love by now? Only she hadn't and now she was going to spend three weeks with someone she didn't want to meet and it was going to be terrible.

She sighed heavily, then went inside and took the elevator to the third floor. After squaring her shoulders and telling herself that by the time the wedding arrived she would have amassed so much good karma that she wouldn't have to worry about it for decades, she knocked loudly and waited.

Seconds later the door opened and Abby was staring at a tall man. Okay, not tall-tall, but close to six feet with dark blue eyes that were kind of compelling and floppy blond hair and high cheekbones and why on earth hadn't Melissa said Joaquin was gorgeous because that would have been important information to have in advance so she could have practiced her talking and breathing.

"Abby?"

As he spoke, he smiled. O.M.G.! That smile.

"Uh-huh." She mentally slapped herself on the side of the head. "I mean, hi. Yes, I'm Abby. You must be Joaquin."

He held out his hand. She took it and she was pretty sure they shook but it was hard to focus on anything but how good-looking he was.

"Come on in."

He stepped back to let her inside. She managed to take the necessary steps without, you know, falling or anything. She had a vague impression of an oversize room with a view of the town before she turned back to holy-cow-Joaquin.

"You don't look anything like your brother," she blurted before she could censor herself. Davis was a cutie for sure, but maybe five-eight with a more muscular build. He had dark hair and eyes and could probably bicep-curl a building, but he looked nothing like lean, dreamy Joaquin. Again—the question of the day—why hadn't anyone warned her?

Later she would grill her sister and tell her to never do

anything like that again, but until then, she was going to have to get a grip and deal.

"So," she said, wishing she'd been born glib or charming. As it was, she was stuck simply being her normal, happy, slightly goofy self. "You're in Fool's Gold until the wedding."

"Through the wedding actually."

Right, because he wouldn't want to leave before the big event. And sure, brilliant surgeons probably used precise language.

"That's a long time," she murmured, thinking it was actually less long now that she'd seen him. Wait—did that make her shallow? She supposed it did. She'd been all whiny and pouty about spending time with Joaquin until she found out he was hot? That made her an awful person. Well, crap, and here she'd just gotten her karma on track.

"It is but I, ah, wanted to take a few weeks off. I've been working long hours. While I enjoy what I do, it's better for everyone if I'm rested."

His gaze slipped away as he spoke. For a second, she had the weirdest sensation that he wasn't telling her the truth about something, which was totally not possible. No doubt he was being modest because, you know, godlike creatures did that.

"I'm also very excited about the wedding."

"Really?" she asked before she could stop herself, then held in a groan. "I mean, you haven't been around much so I wondered if maybe you didn't approve or something." As she spoke she realized how ridiculous she sounded. "Not that you wouldn't approve of Melissa. How could you not? She's great. Isn't she great? She's so smart. Way smarter than me. She's a lawyer. International law. And Davis is in something with finance. But then you already know that." Her voice trailed off. Why did she have to sound like an idiot?

One corner of his mouth turned up. "Yes, I know about Davis's career in finance."

"You probably know the particulars."

"I do."

"And understand them."

"Yes."

She sighed and decided to let that topic of conversation go. "You didn't join us at Christmas. Was it because you were working?"

"Yes."

"Saving lives and stuff?"

"For the most part."

She stared into his dark blue eyes and could almost swear she heard birds singing. "So other people could be with their families?"

"It's easier for me to take those shifts."

Of course it was. She'd spent the holidays baking cookies and wrapping presents and hanging out with her friends.

"Maybe I should start volunteering somewhere," she murmured.

"Excuse me?"

"Nothing. Well, you're here now and it's nice to meet you. So do you have plans for the time you're in town?"

"Not really. I was hoping I could tag along for whatever it is you're doing. If it's not too much trouble."

And while that sounded yummy, she had to be honest. "You're more than welcome to hang out, but I have a bunch of wedding things to do. There's a special project I'm working on that my sister doesn't know about but is going to love and there are a lot of last-minute details."

"Sounds like fun."

"Are you sure? Because it's mostly family stuff. Oh, wow, you have to meet the family. You'll need to brace yourself. The Hendrix clan is massive. There is no having a small wedding if we're invited. Just the immediate family is at least forty people. Plus friends from work, college, Fool's Gold and out of town. The wedding is up to over three hundred people."

Joaquin raised his eyebrows. "I can't imagine Davis knowing that many people. Not well enough to invite to the wedding."

"Yeah, a lot of them come from Melissa's side. It's not hard. Seriously. My dad is one of six kids and they all have spouses and kids and it goes from there. Although I have to admit, I'm not a big-wedding kind of girl. I'd like something small and intimate. But again, the family kind of makes that impossible."

"What does your fiancé think about your wedding plans?"

Fiancé? She laughed. "No. There's no guy. It was a mythical, 'one day' kind of statement. I don't have a boyfriend."

She pressed her lips together and told herself to stop talking about her single state. Desperation didn't look pretty on anyone. Not that she was desperate. She wasn't. In fact, she liked being single. The whole boyfriend thing was overrated, or it had been until about fifteen minutes ago.

"What about you?" she asked. "Are you bringing someone to the wedding?"

"No. It will just be me."

Yay! She did her best to keep from bouncing in place.

"Just to double-check, you're sure, sure you're all right with the wedding stuff?"

"I'm sure-sure."

"There will be votive painting and running errands and

confirming details. In between I can show you the town and stuff…" Which all sounded really boring.

But instead of complaining, Joaquin smiled. "I have no idea what a votive is, but I am happy to learn. I will paint with gusto—or not, depending on what is required."

"You're much nicer than I expected," she said before she could stop herself, then winced. "Not that I didn't think you'd be, you know, nice. I just thought you'd be stuffier. I guess the doctor thing." She sighed. "I'm going to stop talking now."

Once again Joaquin's gaze shifted. "I have my moments, Abby. I can be as difficult and deceptive as everyone else. But for you, I will do my best to be charming."

Deceptive? That was an interesting word choice.

"I'm not sure you have to try to be charming," she murmured. "Okay, if you're ready, let's go introduce you to the town."

CHAPTER THREE

THE TOWN WAS just as strange close up as it had been from Joaquin's hotel window. There were all kinds of small stores lining the main street. Flowers hung from pots, different businesses had set out water bowls for dogs. There were banners and posters and everyone greeted everyone else. To be honest, that much friendliness was his idea of hell, but he would endure for a greater good.

Abby Hendrix was nothing like he'd imagined. She was bright and lively—radiating enough energy to light up a city block. She was unexpectedly beautiful, in an unconventional way, with freckles on pale skin and big green eyes. She wore her hair in a short, spikey cut that suited her. Her mouth was full, but what surprised him the most was the fact that he'd noticed it—and her. When it came to women, he was rarely a detail kind of man.

But there was something about her, he thought. Something about her energy. He was a big believer in people having a life force that defined who they were. A strong life force could make the difference in a touch-and-go surgery. He knew the patients who had something to live for were more likely to defy the odds. Abby was full of zest and radiated a happy, positive attitude that drew him in and, oddly enough, relaxed him.

"During the Mayan civilization, a group of women broke free and headed north. They called themselves the Máa-zib, which roughly translates to 'little man.'" She grinned at him. "Little as in few. Not small. No one's casting aspersions."

"Then I won't feel judged."

She laughed. "They headed north and settled here. Back in the day, men were brought in to, ah, get the tribe members pregnant, then sent on their way."

"Women have been using men for sex for generations," he said with a sigh. "We endure as best we can."

"Oh, please. Anyway, that went on for a few hundred years, but eventually the women started letting the men stay."

"Lucky us."

"Anyone would have been lucky to live with the Máa-zib. Anyway, something happened. No one knows if they went somewhere else, or died out or just allowed other people in, but the tribe disappeared. By the time of the gold rush, the area was unsettled. Fool's Gold was reborn a gold-mining town and it's been around ever since."

She stopped and turned back to face the hotel. "Ronan's Lodge was originally a house, built by a man for his one true love. At the time it was called Ronan's Folly." They continued walking again. "There's an old abandoned gold mine outside of town. Don't go there. It's really dangerous. Otherwise, we're very welcoming. We have mountains and vineyards and lots of interesting businesses."

She was easy to be with, he thought as she chattered on about the town. Normally he struggled with what he was supposed to say to people. Work was fine, but anything social left him feeling awkward and uncomfortable. But with Abby, he seemed to know what to say next. An unexpected phenomenon. Perhaps it wasn't her at all—perhaps it was simply the strangeness of the place or his hope for his mission. Regardless, he was grateful not to feel awkward and tongue-tied.

"A lot of the businesses in town are owned or run by women. It's kind of fun. There's a PR firm called Score. There are four owners. Three of them are former football players, but the one really in charge is Taryn Whittaker. They could all snap her like a twig, and yet she keeps them in line. We're going there."

She pointed across the street toward the fire station on the corner.

He followed her past large, gleaming fire trucks parked facing out, ready to go at a moment's notice. Abby greeted all the firefighters as she walked inside and headed for a small office.

Joaquin trailed after her, nodding as he went. He appreciated that she didn't bother introducing him to everyone. He was unlikely to see these people again, so why make the effort. Plus, small talk was always so fraught. He inevitably said the wrong thing or asked the wrong question. People were unbelievably sensitive about that sort of thing and the end result was he retreated so as not to be a bother.

The woman behind the desk was tall and broad-shouldered. Capable, Joaquin thought, relaxing in the presence of someone who knew what she was doing.

"Hey, Charlie."

Charlie smiled. "I've been waiting for you to stop by. I'm glad to get this off my desk. I've felt as if I had a homework assignment."

"You did." Abby grinned. "I was prepared to use my stern voice if you weren't done." She turned to Joaquin. "Charlie, this is Joaquin Kincaid. He's Davis's brother."

Charlie rose and shook hands. "The mysterious, missing brother. Good to meet you."

He nodded, rather than speak. He was many things but mysterious was not one of them.

"Joaquin's in town for a few weeks before the wedding. I'm going to make him help me with all sorts of last-minute projects."

Charlie looked at her. "You know if you need help, you only have to ask. We could get a work party together in a couple of hours."

"Thank you but I have it all under control." She flashed a smile. "Actually, Melissa and my mom do. I'm just filling in." She held out her hand.

Charlie reached into a desk drawer and pulled out a four-by-six index card. "Here you go."

Abby took it and scanned the writing on the front. Her eyebrows rose. "You sure you're comfortable saying this at the wedding?"

"Oh, please. You think nearly everyone there hasn't had sex before?"

Abby grinned. "The percentages are probably high." She waved the card. "Thank you for this."

They hugged briefly.

"Nice to meet you," Charlie told him.

He nodded and followed Abby out of the office and onto the sidewalk.

"You're probably wondering what all that was about," she said. "I've been talking to different couples in town—people Melissa knows. I'm asking them for advice on what makes a good marriage. I'm printing out what they tell me on big cue cards. Then during the reception, everyone will read from their cards. I think it's going to be a fun surprise."

"Very creative," he said. "What did Charlie say?"

She glanced down. "Go to bed angry. Nobody fights

well when they're tired. Make up in the morning, then have sex in the shower."

He blinked. "She's going to say that at the reception?"

"Apparently." She looked at him. "You know the best part? I have a card from her husband. His advice is to not go to bed angry." She giggled. "A lot of the couples are giving really interesting advice. It's going to be fun."

She tucked the card into her handbag. "Charlie's husband, Clay, used to be a butt model."

"Excuse me?"

"In the movies and in magazine ads and stuff, he was a butt model. Apparently he has a great naked butt. I never saw it in person, of course. Just in pictures."

She wasn't making sense. "That woman we just talked to is married to a butt model?"

"Uh-huh. Clay's retired now. While I would love the idea of having a butt that great, I think it would be really strange to have people focused on just one body part. Unless it paid really well. Then I might be able to deal with it."

"What is your actual career?"

"I'm an elementary school teacher." Her eyes brightened. "I have my certification and I've done a year of student teaching and in September I get my very first class right here in Fool's Gold. I'm excited and terrified. I want to be the best, you know? Teachers have a huge impact on kids' lives. I hope I'm good enough."

A teacher. He could see it. Her energy, her bubbly personality. "They're going to be very fond of you."

"Not just fond but very fond?"

He recognized the teasing in her voice. As a rule, people didn't tease him—he wasn't the type. He'd always wanted to be teased—in a kind way, of course. And here it was. How unexpected.

He smiled at her. "Extremely fond."

"Well, then, I feel better now."

"WHAT WERE YOU THINKING?" Abby said later that evening when she called her sister.

"What was I thinking about what?"

"Joaquin. You could have warned me that he was so gorgeous."

"You think he's good-looking?"

Abby flopped back on her bed and rolled her eyes. "And you don't? I know you're madly in love with Davis, but come on. Joaquin is seriously hot."

"If you say so." A smile entered Melissa's voice. "Is this your way of saying being with him isn't quite as awful as you'd thought?"

Abby chuckled. "It's difficult, but I'm managing." She sat up. "Actually, he's nice. Funny and easy to be with. I thought he'd be all stuffy and smart, but he's not. Okay, he's smart, but in a good way. I showed him around town and stuff."

"And stuff? What does that mean?"

"Nothing. But he's nice."

"How nice?"

Abby rolled her eyes. "It's been one day. I thought he would be a troll and he's not."

"Apparently he's quite the hunk. Who knew? Abby and Joaquin sitting in a tree."

"I'm hanging up on you now," Abby said with a laugh. "Goodbye."

"Bye."

ABBY TOLD HERSELF that the fluttery feeling in her stomach was because of the extra cinnamon roll she'd had at breakfast and not because she was looking forward to seeing Joaquin again. Yes, he'd been unexpectedly attractive and she'd liked spending time with him, but that was only because she'd been expecting something so much worse. He really hadn't been all that—he'd just been better than expected. Today she would see that he was ordinary and that she felt nothing and that she had to let the cinnamon roll thing go.

She marched up to his hotel room door and knocked briskly. He opened it and smiled at her.

"Abby!"

And there it was. A quick kick in the gut that told her he was just as wow as she remembered.

"Hi. So I have some craft projects I really need to get done in the next couple of days. You're welcome to join me, but if the thought of that makes you want to run screaming into the night, I'll totally understand."

He stepped out into the hallway and closed the bedroom door. "I've never done crafts. I'm looking forward to learning about the process."

She felt her mouth drop open. "What? Everyone's done crafts. You had to, in school or something."

"Not me. I didn't go to that kind of school."

"What kind did you go to?"

"I was tutored from the time I was about three, then I went to a private school with an accelerated program. I was in college by the time I was ten." One shoulder rose and lowered. "No crafts there. I've seen people do them in hospital waiting rooms."

Sadness gave her a little bump in the heart. While she appreciated that he was brilliant and all, what kind of life had he been living? Had there been any time for fun or friends or just being a kid? Only asking those questions seemed judgy and a little rude, so she just nodded.

"Makes sense. I promise, in the next couple of weeks, we will get you proficient in the world of crafts."

"Thank you."

They headed out of the hotel and started toward her old neighborhood.

"Did you grow up here?" he asked.

"Uh-huh. Born and raised. Right now I'm staying with my folks. I move into my own apartment on September first. It's going to be fun, but strange, you know? I've always lived at home or in a dorm or with friends. But it will just be me."

"Worried about being lonely?"

"Not really. I have a lot of friends and my parents will be three miles away." She looked at him. "You've been on your own since you were a kid."

"It was easier for everyone."

"Were *you* ever lonely?"

Something flashed in his eyes and he turned away. "Occasionally. I was always younger than the other students, and something of a freak, as you can imagine."

She wanted to tell him he was wrong, only she suspected he had a very clear view of his past.

"It must be better now that you're older," she said.

"It helps." He flashed her a smile. "At least the white coat fits."

Yes and she would guess it looked pretty darned good on him.

"Where did you go to college?" she asked.

"Stanford for undergrad. I did some advanced studies in Oxford before attending Johns Hopkins Medical School. What about you?"

"I, ah, went to UCLA, then did my student teaching in

the San Fernando Valley. Not, you know, impressive by comparison."

He stopped and smiled at her. "Abby, you are incredibly impressive just as you are."

Really? *Really?* She smiled. "Thank you."

"You're welcome. Tell me about your parents."

An easy topic, she thought happily. "They're great. Ethan, my dad, is the oldest of six kids. He runs a wind turbine company outside of town. My mom is Liz Sutton." She paused.

Joaquin looked at her blankly. "Should I know the name?"

"I wondered if you would recognize it. She's a famous mystery writer. She's supersuccessful and you can't ever mess with her because she so knows how to hide a body."

He chuckled. "I'll remember that."

"You should."

They turned into the quiet neighborhood where she and her folks had lived for the past decade.

"They're really good people. My biological mom died when I was little and my dad passed away a few years ago." He'd died of cancer, in prison. Something Abby didn't feel any need to go into. "Liz and Ethan adopted me and Melissa when I was eleven and she was fourteen. They have a son together—Tyler. He's my age. He's in Europe right now, with his friends. He'll be back for the wedding, then he's going to Washington, DC, where he'll be an intern with the senior senator from California. Now that I think about it, I'm the only one of my siblings to stay in Fool's Gold. I'm just that kind of girl."

"You went to UCLA. That's not close."

She smiled. "I went because they made me leave. Otherwise, I would have gone to college right here."

She paused in front of the familiar big house. It looked

like a happy place, she thought, with well-kept gardens and lots of windows. There were plenty of bedrooms and a huge dining room for family gatherings.

"This is it. My mom has a separate office off the garage. It meant we could invite friends over and make as much noise as we wanted, but she was always close."

Joaquin looked at her, then at the house. "Sounds idyllic."

"It was just a regular kind of childhood." Something he hadn't had, she reminded herself. "Do you ever wish you'd been different than you are, which I guess means being ordinary?"

"Not often, but I wonder what it would have been like to not be so unusual. Only I wouldn't give up what I do."

"I think if you have to be born different, being smart isn't so bad."

"I agree."

They walked into the house. Abby tried to see it as Joaquin would, but everything was too familiar. She knew what it felt like to sit on the sofa and where they put the big Christmas tree every year.

He looked around, glancing up at the high ceilings and peering at the huge dining room.

"It's nice."

"Thanks. The rec room is back here. That's where all the craft magic happens."

She led the way to the kitchen where she planned on grabbing drinks and snacks. Her mom was there, making tea.

"Hi, Mom."

"Abby." Liz smiled warmly. Her gaze moved to Joaquin. "Ah, the mysterious Dr. Kincaid, I presume. We have you in our clutches at last."

Joaquin moved toward her, his hand outstretched. "Nice to meet you."

"You, too. Welcome to Fool's Gold. How are you liking our little town?"

"It's very appealing."

"We like it." Liz checked the teapot on the counter, then replaced the lid. "The words are not flowing well today and I've run out of excuses to avoid my office. Unless you need my help with something?"

Abby ignored her hopeful tone. "Mom, go. You know you'll feel better once you start writing. Joaquin and I are going to finish the place cards and start on the birdseed holders."

"You have all the fun. I have to figure out why my serial killer wants to do in a perfectly nice botanist." She gave Abby a brief hug, then picked up her tea. "Good to meet you, Joaquin. Let me know if you need anything."

He nodded.

Liz walked out of the kitchen. Joaquin turned to Abby.

"That was about the writing, right?"

Abby laughed. "Yes. I promise you my mother isn't going to kill anyone in real life. She's very sweet. So I was thinking iced tea and cookies to keep up our energy. Or do you only eat vegan?"

"No vegan," he said with a smile.

She did her best to ignore the faint fluttering sensation in her belly. What was it about that man? she wondered. Her reaction was so confusing.

They went downstairs to what had been the playroom and was now kind of a catch-all craft-storage-junk space. There were a couple of long tables and folding chairs and a storage unit full of craft supplies.

Abby set out their snacks on one table and directed Joaquin to the other.

"There are two main projects," she told him. "The place cards. I was hoping to finish them a couple of days ago, but got distracted." By the thought of him blowing into her world, she reminded herself. If only she'd known it wasn't going to be difficult duty at all.

She showed him the stack of finished cards. "It's pretty simple, if a little tedious. Just glue on the bead flowers. You can see the design on the completed cards. You'll need tweezers. Just put a little glue on a paper plate and use a toothpick to cover the back of the beads." She hesitated. "Are you sure you want to do this?"

They were standing unexpectedly close, she thought as she stared into his dark blue eyes. She wasn't sure when that had happened, not that she was complaining. Joaquin was nice to look at and he was much less crabby and annoying than she'd first thought. In fact, he was fun to be around.

He gave her a slow smile. "I'm sure. I showed up with little warning, disrupting your schedule. The least I can do is earn my keep."

"You are nothing like I thought," she said without thinking, then groaned. "What I mean is I thought you'd be more, ah, formal."

"I can be. I usually am." He frowned. "For some reason, I'm more comfortable around you."

"You are?"

"Yes. You're easy to talk to." He gave her a sheepish smile. "I like that I can make you laugh."

"Oh." Her heart gave a little hop. "I like that, too."

They stared at each other for a couple of heartbeats, then Abby told herself she had to move things along or she would say something dumb and spoil the moment.

She motioned to the chair. "Go forth and do crafts."

He chuckled. "My first time. I'm very excited."

"Then you need to get out more."

"I probably do."

She retrieved her laptop and opened her graphics program. She needed to pick a design, then upload all the words of wisdom. She started playing with different options, not sure what would look the best on two-foot-by-three-foot pieces of cardboard.

Something easy to read, she thought, searching through her favorite fonts. Border or no border? Did she want flowers in the corners or would that be too busy?

She lost herself in her work, loading several possibilities before deleting them and starting over. She wanted the cards to look nice, but not steal attention from the words. The message was important, not the delivery system.

Eventually she decided on something simple. Just a pretty italicized font with interlocked rings at the top of the card. She printed out a sample and studied it, only to realize it had been at least an hour and what about Joaquin.

"Sorry," she said, turning to him. "I got lost in what I was doing."

"You were focused. Now that you're taking a break, is this what you were looking for?"

She walked over and glanced at the cards he'd finished. The beads were perfectly placed. As she watched, he picked up a flower bead, dabbed on some glue and set it into place.

"You have really steady hands," she said.

He looked at her. "I have some training in that."

"Oh, no!" She stared at him. "You're a fancy surgeon guy. I shouldn't be asking you to do something like this."

"Why not? It's my brother's wedding. I told you, Abby. I want to help."

"Still. What a waste."

Humor brightened his eyes. "Did you have some surgery you wanted me to perform instead of this? A patient waiting in a back room?"

"No. Of course not."

"Then let it go. This is oddly relaxing. Now what have you been working on?"

She showed him the design she'd decided on. "I want it to be clean but pretty. The message is important, not the graphics." She hesitated. "Is it too plain?"

"They're going to like it very much."

"I'm glad. I hope so. I want them to be thrilled with the surprise." She looked at the sheet of paper. "Okay, I'm going to upload all the advice and email it to the graphics place. Then I'll help you finish the place cards and then we'll start on the birdseed."

Joaquin's eyebrows drew together. "Birdseed?"

"To throw on the bride and groom."

"Not rice?"

"Rice hurts birds. They're not supposed to eat it. Birdseed is safe."

He looked at her and smiled. "Because we like birds?"

"All nature."

"Even snakes and spiders?"

"We keep our distance from them but we still like them."

"You're very fair."

"I try to be."

She returned to her computer. Joaquin was kind of a great guy. Not that it meant anything, she told herself. Spending time with him was the right thing to do. If she happened to be enjoying herself, that was simply a bonus.

CHAPTER FOUR

JOAQUIN HAD ASSUMED a morning doing crafts would be torture, but he found he'd actually enjoyed the experience. The repetitive task had quieted his mind, and seeing the growing stack of completed name cards had been oddly satisfying. Just being in the same room as Abby was an added bonus. He liked being around her. As he'd worked, he'd kept glancing at her, studying the changing expressions on her face as she completed her project.

She was beautiful, but her appeal was more than external, his mind circling around to what he'd thought before. There was something about her energy. She drew him in.

"We should go to Jo's Bar for lunch," Abby told him a little after noon. "It's unique."

"Vegan?" he asked.

She laughed. "No. You'll find meat and dairy on the menu. They have the best nachos. And margaritas, but it's a little early in the day for that. Is that okay?"

He wasn't sure if she was asking about going to Jo's Bar, the nachos or not having a margarita, and he found he didn't care. Making her laugh or smile was its own reward. Besides, food had never been that important to him. Like many things in life, it was a means to an end. He needed fuel to keep functioning. As a rule, he ate healthy food because his body preferred it.

"Sounds perfect," he told her.

"Good."

"Should we invite your mother?" Not that he had any interest in dining with Liz, but maybe there would be a way to mention Simon.

Abby shook her head. "No. When she's in her office, we leave her alone. Once she gets on a roll, any interruption breaks her concentration. She'll be fine."

They stepped out into the warm, sunny day. The neighborhood was pleasant enough, he supposed. There were houses on both sides of the streets, green lawns, bikes left on porches. He supposed this was how most people grew up—in neighborhoods of some kind. While he preferred his high-rise condo, he could see the appeal. If one had children, a yard would be nice. His parents' house had a yard—not that he'd ever been one to play outside. He hadn't seen the point. Nor did he now. He exercised because being fit made him a better surgeon but he didn't like the outdoors. It was too unpredictable.

"You're looking intense about something," Abby told him.

"Wondering what it was like to grow up in a place like this."

"Where did you grow up?"

"In schools and universities."

"So no Little League?"

"No."

"I want to say that must have been hard, but you can't miss what you didn't know. Did you have friends in school or were you too much younger?"

"I'm not a friend kind of person."

"I don't believe that for a second. Everyone needs friends." She studied him. "What about at work? There have to be people you like."

"Some more than others."

The conversation made him uncomfortable, yet he didn't try to change the subject. Mostly, he supposed, because he wanted to know what Abby was thinking. She had a unique perspective he enjoyed.

"Are people afraid of you?" she asked.

"Some."

"Do you yell or are you quietly disdainful?"

He hesitated. "Why would you ask if I'm disdainful?"

"Because you wouldn't suffer fools gladly. Is that the right expression? Plus, you obviously care about your work and your patients, so you'd be mad at anyone who wasn't perfect." She smiled. "I am jumping to many conclusions here. Feel free to stop me."

He thought about the nurses who avoided his rotations and how people quieted when he approached. More than once he'd heard a muttered "asshole" as he'd walked by.

"I am not the most popular surgeon in the hospital."

"Are you the best?"

"Sometimes, but not always."

"It must be hard when you lose someone," she said quietly.

"It is."

"I'm sorry."

He nodded, thinking that for so many people the phrase "I'm sorry" was meaningless—almost conversational punctuation. But Abby was different—he knew she genuinely was sorry.

For a second he thought about telling her about the burn patient he'd lost. How helpless he'd felt, how he hadn't known what to do to save her. Only he didn't because getting too close to the truth was dangerous. She couldn't know why he was in town.

He realized then he was deceiving her. He had been from the beginning, but suddenly he minded. She deserved better.

"I can be a jerk," he said without thinking. "I'm impatient and thoughtless when it comes to how I treat people. If someone makes a mistake, I'm rarely understanding."

He looked away, not wanting to see the smile go out of her eyes.

"Because you don't make mistakes?"

"I make them. I try not to, but they happen." Rarely. And never the same one twice.

"So you get frustrated and you react. It's not uncommon, but it's not very likable. You should change that."

He glanced at her. "Just like that?"

"Why not? If you're so very smart, it shouldn't be hard, should it?"

The corners of her mouth turned up as she spoke. She was stating a fact, not making a judgment. There was no contempt in her eyes, no scorn. He supposed that was what he'd sensed from the first. That she was one of those very rare people who accepted people for who they were.

"You are going to be an extraordinary teacher."

She smiled. "I think I could be a good teacher, but extraordinary is asking a lot. Still, I appreciate you saying that."

"I mean it."

Her smile widened.

Standing there on the sidewalk, in some ridiculous town, Joaquin had the sudden urge to lean in and kiss her. Really kiss her. He wanted to feel her lips on his and then maybe pull her close. Yes, definitely pull her close because he needed to experience what it felt like to hold Abby.

The wanting was more powerful than he'd ever felt before and the intensity shocked him.

She started walking again. He fell into step with her, not sure what had just happened.

They reached the center of town quickly.

"It's over there," Abby said, pointing to a storefront with a sign that said Jo's Bar. "It's kind of different, so brace yourself."

"I am fully braced."

They went inside.

Joaquin had expected the place to be a bar, but it wasn't. Not in the traditional sense. For one thing, the colors were all wrong. The walls were a pale lavender and there was too much light.

There was an actual bar, but there was also a play area with several small children stacking blocks together. The televisions were off and most of the clientele seemed to be female.

Nearly everyone turned to watch them walk in. Several of them called out a greeting. Joaquin had the brief thought that he should have researched Simon's wife, so he would recognize her if he saw her. As it was, he found himself being introduced as Melissa's future brother-in-law and a doctor.

They found a small table in the corner. Once they were seated, Abby looked at him. "Do you trust me?"

"Yes."

"Just like that? Aren't you going to ask me why I want to know or what I have planned?"

"I have no reason not to trust you."

"Great. Then I'll order."

Their server appeared. Abby smiled. "Chicken nachos and the lemonade of the day."

"You got it."

Abby smiled. "You will be amazed by your lunch."

"I'm not sure I've had nachos before."

"What? Aren't you from California? How is that possible?"

"I just never have."

"But nachos are a football-game-watching tradition. What about Super Bowl parties or Cinco de Mayo? What about—" Her teasing voice quieted. "Oh, no. This is another 'because you're brilliant' thing, isn't it? We should make a list and work through as much of it as we can while you're in town."

Not an offer he thought he should turn down, he told himself, wondering how he could add a few kisses onto that list.

A pair of old ladies walked over to the table. The one wearing a bright red velour tracksuit eyed him.

"Are you really a doctor?" she asked.

Abby sighed. "Joaquin, these two are Eddie and Gladys. This is Joaquin. He's new. Be nice."

"I'm perfectly nice," Eddie said, never taking her gaze off Joaquin. "So the doctor thing. It's real?"

"Yes."

"Married?"

Joaquin withdrew slightly. "No."

Eddie turned to Abby. "You could do worse, missy. It's time you had a serious boyfriend."

Gladys's gaze turned speculative. "She's right. This one could qualify for our butt show."

Joaquin had no idea what they were talking about but he knew it wasn't good. Abby waved them away.

"Stop," she said firmly. "You'll scare him. It's not nice."

"You didn't used to be so bossy," Eddie told her with a sniff.

"I am now, so you're going to have to get used to it."

"I might have to talk to your mother."

Abby grinned unrepentantly. "Mom will take my side and you know it."

The two old ladies walked away. Joaquin watched them go. "Do I want to know about the butt show?"

"Probably not, but it is a compliment." She drew in a breath. "They have a cable access show. They feature the naked butts of different men in town." She waved her hand. "It's kind of their thing. So it's flattering that you were asked."

"They're fairly old."

"Yes, but you might not want to mention that to them."

He thought about what else they'd said. "Why are they concerned you don't have a boyfriend?"

"They want to see everyone paired up and married. I want that, too. For myself, I mean, not for everyone. Eventually."

There was a wistful quality to her voice.

"You want to get married."

She held up both hands. "Let's not put it like that. Getting married isn't the goal, it's the result. I want to meet someone special and fall in love and then get married and have kids. I probably should have done it while I was in college."

"It?" She couldn't mean...

"Fall in love. There were a lot of guys on campus. You'd think I could have found one or two, but I never got beyond liking someone a fair amount. Now I'm going to suffer from a lack of appropriate guys."

"Fool's Gold doesn't have single men?"

"Oh, there are a few, but I know most of them. I'm not going to meet anyone through work." She held up one finger. "No dating where you work. It's messy if things go wrong."

"Agreed."

She held up a second finger. "Chances are the parent of a student is married, and even if he isn't, it's still wrong because his kid is in my class. I don't know where else am I going to meet a single guy, unless there's one in my apartment building."

She sounded hopeful. Joaquin wasn't sure he liked the idea of her falling for her neighbor. "It would still be a problem if you broke up. You'd run into him all the time."

"You're right. See? I should have done it in college. What about you? Did you do it in college?"

There was something suggestive about the way she asked the question. No, he told himself. He was reading it all wrong.

"You mean did I fall in love?"

"Uh-huh."

"I was twelve in college."

"Oh, right. So no." She looked at him. "Why do you and Davis look so different? He looks a lot like your parents. Is there a distant aunt who's tall and blonde?"

"You don't know?"

Abby shook her head,

"I'm adopted. My parents thought they couldn't have children and they adopted me. Two years later, Mom got pregnant." He'd often wondered if her body had done that in self-defense when she'd realized how difficult he was going to be. Not a sound biological theory but one he couldn't shake.

"I didn't know that. No one told me. We have that in

common. Only you were a baby and didn't know any different. I knew my biological parents. At least my dad. I don't remember my mom. But now I have Liz and Ethan and they're great."

"And the forty-plus other relatives."

"There is that. Did I tell you Ethan has triplet sisters? How on earth would anyone handle triplet babies? I can't begin to imagine. Oh!" She smiled. "I totally forgot. So one of my aunts is married to a surgeon. Simon Bradley. I don't know if you've heard of him or not. Anyway, he and his wife, Montana, want to take us to dinner. If you're interested. I thought you'd have a lot in common with Simon."

And there it was, Joaquin thought. With zero work on his part. For a second, he felt a flash of guilt, as if he was doing something wrong. But how could he be, he told himself. Abby was asking him to dinner with her uncle. It would be rude not to accept the invitation.

"Sounds like fun," he told her.

"Great. I'll get something set up."

Just then their server returned with two glasses and a huge plate of what he assumed were nachos.

"You're going to love this," Abby told him.

He smiled. "I'm sure I am."

I totally forgot I have a workout class this morning, so I can't pick you up until after that.

ABBY PUSHED SEND on her phone, then rolled onto her back. She'd gotten a slow start that morning—mostly because she hadn't slept well the night before. Thoughts of Joaquin had kept her awake long past her bedtime.

She wasn't usually the type to lie awake, thinking about a guy, so her reaction confused her. Yes, he was funny and really good-looking and she liked being around him, but so what? She had a wedding to deal with and a summer to enjoy and…

She liked him, she thought, admitting the truth to herself. She liked him. She wanted to spend more time with him even if they did nothing more than sit across from each other and stare into each other's eyes. She felt herself wanting to act silly and giggle and call all her friends and talk about him. It was embarrassing and more than a little scary. She was smarter than that—plus, he was just a guy.

Only he felt like more than that, she admitted. He was—

What's the class? Ladies only or can I tag along?

She sat up, trying not to grin too broadly. Guys are welcome, but it's a pretty killer workout. Aware she'd just issued a challenge, she smiled and pushed the send button.

His reply came back immediately. I'm in.

Great. I'll pick you up at quarter to nine. Hydrate and don't eat a big breakfast.

Now I'm intrigued.

Later you'll be whimpering.

Is that a challenge?

It's more of a promise.

Right on time she pulled up in front of the hotel. Joaquin was waiting in front. She tried to keep her heart from doing its stupid fluttery thing, but didn't seem to have as much control as she would have liked.

She told herself there was no earthly reason to react that way. It certainly wasn't the wardrobe. Joaquin had on workout pants and an oversize T-shirt. Nothing overtly sexy. Yet on him, it all looked good.

"You're driving," he said by way of greeting. "I thought we walked everywhere in town."

"Usually, but CDS is a little far and there's no way we'll be able to walk all the way back to the hotel when we're done." She patted her steering wheel. "If this was a manual transmission, I'd have to wait for my legs to stop shaking so I could use the clutch and drive home."

He grinned. "You're deliberately trying to scare me."

"I'm warning you—there's a difference." She turned onto the street. "But go ahead and be all smug and confident. Later, when you're whimpering, I'll resist the need to say I told you so."

"I don't whimper."

She smiled at him. "We'll see."

She drove the short distance to CDS, then parked. "So this is what we locals call the bodyguard school. The owners are all former military special forces. They provide specialty training for professional bodyguards. They also offer outdoor activities for corporate retreats. For the locals they have martial arts classes and pretty intense exercise classes. If CrossFit and your worst workout nightmare had a baby, it would be this class."

"If you say so."

Joaquin got out of the car and stretched. Abby did her best not to stare at him, instead telling herself it would be interesting to see what he was like after the workout. Total humiliation had a way of bringing out a man's character.

They walked inside. Consuelo, their petite, fit instructor, walked over to Abby.

"Who's the guy?"

"Joaquin, this is Consuelo. She's married to my uncle Kent. Consuelo, this is Joaquin. Melissa's fiancé's brother."

Consuelo held out her hand. "Every time I think I've figured out everyone in the family, they bring in someone new. Nice to meet you."

Joaquin nodded.

Consuelo raised her eyebrows. "Do we like him or should I grind him into dust?"

Joaquin looked startled at the question. Abby considered her answer. "After the wedding, he's going to be one of us, so no scars, but he was kind of dismissive when I warned him about the class."

Consuelo's eyes narrowed. "Got it."

"Why did you say that?" Joaquin asked as Consuelo headed toward the mats.

"Because it's true. You implied you'd be fine." She batted her eyes at him. "Let's find out if you were lying."

"I'm going to regret this, aren't I?"

"Yes, you are."

There were about ten students, ranging in age and fitness level. Abby had started taking the classes when she'd moved back after college. Her goal was to get to the point where she could do everything asked of her without fainting or throwing up. As it was, she was a forty-percenter. When Consuelo asked for ten, Abby gave her four. She was already better than the three she'd been able to do when she'd first started.

Consuelo blew on a whistle. "All right, people, listen up. We're going to start slow before we get into it. Ten laps at moderate speed, ten burpees, then climb the ropes and ring the bell. When you're finished, line up in front of me and we'll start class."

Joaquin's eyes widened. "That's the warm-up?"

Abby held in a smile. She pointed to the far wall. "Water's on the table. The big yellow trash can is where you throw up. Don't use one of the other trash cans. Consuelo doesn't like that."

"Good to know."

Forty-five minutes later, Abby was dripping sweat and worried that she would never walk again. Her leg muscles were twitching and she was flat on her back on a mat. What was going to happen when she tried to stand up? On the bright side, Joaquin was just as wiped out. He'd started out enthusiastically, but Consuelo had worked him until he'd collapsed. Abby had always had a soft spot for her aunt.

Now Consuelo passed out water bottles. She paused in front of Joaquin. "Not bad for a rookie. Give me a couple of months and I could really make something of you." She handed him the water. "Running is all fine and good, but you should be working out with weights. Right now you're strong because you're young and male, but that goes away. If you don't want to end up some shriveled old man, you need to have a plan. Find a trainer. Get a program going."

Joaquin managed to nod his head and take the water bottle. "Thanks," he gasped. "Good idea. How'd you know I was a runner?"

"The muscles in your legs. You have speed. Your form is crap, but you don't run enough for it to be a big deal." She handed Abby a bottle of water, then winked and walked away.

Joaquin looked after her. "Who *is* she?"

She knew he meant other than her aunt. "I'm not totally sure. She used to work for the government. She was like a spy or something. There are rumors she was an assassin. You know, getting close to a man, then killing him with a credit card. It's all very hush-hush."

He struggled to his feet, then held out his hand to pull Abby to hers.

"I was wrong," he said. "Arrogant and painfully wrong."

She smiled. "Actually, the pain is worse tomorrow. If you have a tub in your room, you'll want to take a bath and soak in it before you go to bed. Otherwise, you won't be able to move tomorrow."

"Excellent advice. I'll take it."

They limped out of the building and made it to the car. Joaquin winced as he settled in the passenger seat. "She did most of the stuff with us and she didn't even break a sweat. How is that possible?"

"I know, right? Come on. I know something that will make you feel better."

Joaquin looked at her. Something flashed in his eyes— something that made her insides clench and her nerve endings quiver.

No, she told herself. She was misreading him. There was no way he was interested in her as more than a friend. She would be foolish to think otherwise. He was a successful doctor guy and she was just some small-town teacher. They barely knew each other. Just because she was having a case of *OMG, you're amazing* didn't mean he was.

"I'm open to suggestions," he said.

She drove into town and parked in front of a newer business. He glanced at the sign.

"Juicy Joy?" he said, reading the sign. "You're going to make me feel better with juice?"

"No, a smoothie. The combination of protein powder,

antioxidants and sugar is the perfect way to replenish what was lost during the workout."

"Great, because I'm going to miss my pride if I don't get it back."

She was still laughing when they walked inside.

Once they had their drinks, they sat at one of the small tables on the sidewalk. Joaquin raised his smoothie.

"You were right. I'll never doubt you again."

"If only that were true."

"You're feeling smug."

"A little, yes."

They smiled at each other. She felt the connection clear down to her toes, but wasn't sure what he was feeling, which made her feel awkward. What was it about this guy that got to her? Knowing there was no answer, she searched for a change in topic that would give her a second to re-group.

"You said your parents adopted you, then they had your brother. I've heard that happens to quite a few couples. Do you know the biological reason?"

"No. I've never studied the reproductive system in-depth. There was some kind of assumed physical problem, but maybe it was something else. That many years ago, IVF was still rare and far too expensive for them. They got me through a friend of a friend who knew a young woman who was pregnant."

"Do you mind she gave you up?"

Joaquin looked surprised at the question. "No. I would have been too difficult for her. Not that I was a problem child, but my intelligence level made things challenging for two parents, let alone a single mom who was still a kid herself."

A very accepting attitude. She wondered how long he'd

taken to get there. Abby remembered her own shock when her father—serving several years in prison—had given his sister guardianship of his daughters. While legally it had made things easier for everyone, Abby and Melissa had both felt he'd abandoned them. He'd barely stayed in touch and then he'd died. The situation was difficult, but easier for her than most. She and Melissa had always known they had Liz and Ethan to be there for them, no matter what.

"I'm sure your mom would be proud to know how you turned out," she said, looking at Joaquin. "Even if you aren't very impressive in exercise class."

He laughed. "Thank you for reminding me of that."

"You're welcome. I think you lying on the mats, gasping for air, is going to be one of my favorite memories of this summer."

She thought he would tease her back or laugh again, but instead he did something extraordinary. He set his drink on the table, leaned forward and brushed his mouth against hers. Just like that.

The contact was brief and unexpected. There was a sense of warmth and light pressure and happy nerves dancing and then it was gone almost before she knew what was happening, which was so disappointing.

She stared at him. Their eyes locked for three or four heartbeats before she leaned in and kissed him back. She lingered just long enough to feel his lips against hers and confirm that there was definite sparkage.

"So, ah, just to confirm, there's no one waiting for you in your regular life?" she asked quietly.

"Absolutely no one."

She smiled. "Oh, good."

"My thoughts exactly."

CHAPTER FIVE

JOAQUIN FOUND IT oddly difficult to keep his mind on the task at hand. He was in Fool's Gold to meet Simon Bradley and in less than an hour he would be joining Dr. Bradley and his wife for dinner. It was the opportunity he'd been waiting for—his purpose, at least in the moment. And yet he couldn't seem to focus on how to best use the evening to his own benefit.

Instead he found himself thinking about Abby. The way she smiled, how she laughed, the feel of her mouth on his.

He'd kissed her. He hadn't meant to. There'd been no plan, no reason to do it except he'd wanted to. And when she'd kissed him back, he'd felt…happy. Not a natural state for him.

Dealing with women outside of work was always complicated for him. He never knew what to say. He knew the mechanics of casual conversation but often found it difficult to put that knowledge into practice. He felt awkward and there was so much tedious work involved. Having an actual relationship had always seemed like far too much effort for not much gain. Yes, the sex was excellent—he liked sex—but getting there was disproportionately time-consuming.

Abby was different. With her, he felt comfortable. Conversation was easy. He liked that he could make her laugh. She was open and friendly and just plain nice. He enjoyed her worldview. Being around her made him feel good. Unexpectedly, the more he got to know her, the more he wanted to take care of her, protect her even.

The physical attraction was a real plus. But unlike with other women when he was simply going through the motions to get to his ultimate goal so he could be done with it and get on with his life, he wanted to take his time. He wanted to enjoy the process.

As he drove to her house to pick her up, he thought about the possibilities. If he got the fellowship, then he would stay in town. They could continue to see each other. He would like that very much.

He parked in front of her house and walked to the front door. Abby opened it before he could knock.

"I'm superexcited," she told him. "You're going to love Simon and Montana. My aunt is just the sweetest person and Simon is a lot like you, so you'll have stuff in common. Plus, Henri's is just so fancy. I love going there. It's our special occasion place. They have the best food and the service always makes me feel special." She tilted her head. "What?"

He knew he was staring. He couldn't help it.

Abby had put on a dark green dress that brought out the color of her eyes. It was sleeveless with a scoop neck that hinted at her cleavage. She wore dangly earrings that sparkled and had put on makeup to enhance her features. Casual wanting grew into something nearly unmanageable—a state that should have annoyed him but instead made him feel incredibly normal.

"You're beautiful," he told her.

"Oh." She smiled. "Thank you. You look very nice yourself. It's the suit. Guys look great in suits."

He led the way to his car and opened the passenger door.

Once she was settled, he went around to his own side. In the confines of the vehicle, he could smell something sweet and floral.

Without much of a plan, he angled toward her and lightly kissed her. "I am very much looking forward to our dinner."

"Me, too. And not just for the Henri's part."

They smiled at each other. He started the engine and followed her directions out of town and up the mountain.

"We're going to the Gold Rush Ski Lodge and Resort," she told him. "Which is a mouthful of a name. Can you imagine having to answer the phone with that fifty times a day? There's skiing in the winter and hiking and stuff in the summer. Oh, the wedding's going to be there. It's a beautiful setting."

She talked all the way to the lodge, something Joaquin was grateful for, what with a sudden attack of nerves. This evening was important to him. Getting Dr. Bradley to recognize his talent and ability meant the possibility of getting in the program. He had to stay focused.

Surprisingly, he was grateful Abby was with him. She would be a calming presence, and he knew that if conversation slowed, she would step in to keep things moving. She was just that kind of person.

He handed his keys over to the valet, then offered his arm to Abby. They walked into the quietly elegant restaurant. She gave her uncle's name and they were shown back to a table.

Joaquin had done his research on Simon Bradley—he'd even seen pictures of the man—but nothing had prepared him for Simon's appearance. The starkness of his scars was startling. Even after all these years, they were almost raw in the sharp edges.

Abby saved him from staring by stepping forward to hug

her aunt and uncle, then turning to introduce him. Joaquin managed to say all the right things as he shook hands before they were all seated.

"Simon, Joaquin is a very gifted surgeon, so you have that in common," Abby said.

Joaquin smiled at her. "You're overselling me."

"Hardly." She smiled at her uncle. "He's supersmart, too. Please don't start talking in Latin. Montana and I will feel left out." She turned to her aunt. "Unless you've been taking lessons I don't know about."

Montana laughed. "No. Sadly I've neglected my Latin lessons. I should make more time."

Simon took his wife's hand in his. "Not to worry. There will be no work talk tonight. I promise."

Joaquin's good mood evaporated. He'd been hoping for a little shop talk to smooth the way. If they didn't discuss medicine, then how was he to mention the fellowship?

Simon's gaze settled on him. "But I would like to get to know you better, Joaquin. Perhaps we can set up a time for you to stop by my office."

"I would enjoy that, sir."

"Excellent." He pulled out his phone. "Let's get it on the calendar right now. Then we can enjoy our dinner with these beautiful women."

Joaquin entered Simon's suggested date and time into his calendar and promised he would be on time. He saw Abby looking at him with a combination of happiness and pride. He put away his phone, then slipped his hand under the table and found hers and squeezed. She squeezed back before returning her attention to Simon and Montana.

Things were working out, he told himself. When he met with Simon he would be direct about his interest in the fellowship. With his qualifications there was no reason he shouldn't be a part of the program. He would continue his training and have the added advantage of being close to Abby. As per usual, things were going exactly how he wanted them to.

THE DINNER PROGRESSED even better than Abby had hoped. She'd noticed that sometimes Joaquin seemed quiet around other people, but he seemed very comfortable with Montana and Simon. Knowing he was okay allowed her to enjoy the evening—her aunt and uncle were always fun.

Partway through their main course, Montana asked, "Are you ready for the school year to start?"

Abby laughed. "You know it's still six weeks away, don't you?"

"Yes, but I also know you. Tell me you're ready."

Abby smiled. "You're right. I am." She turned to Joaquin. "I officially start teaching the Tuesday after Labor Day, but the teachers begin a week early. And the week before that, I have a couple of meetings with my mentor."

She paused to sip her wine. "They assign new teachers a mentor to help us through the first year."

"It's not just about having more people want to be teachers," Montana told him. "It's about making sure they have a positive experience and stay in the profession."

"I have my lesson plans done and my sub-tub." Abby sighed. "It makes me so happy."

"Sub-tub?" Simon asked.

"A tub full of information for a substitute teacher. There's a lesson plan that details what the kids are doing. Suggested activities, even movies if you want to do that. I'll update it as I go. Put in notes and give ideas. That sort of thing."

"You're going to be an excellent teacher," Joaquin told her.

"I hope so. There's a difference between student teaching and actually being responsible."

His gaze was steady. "You're going to be excellent," he repeated softly.

"Tell us about yourself, Joaquin," Simon said briskly. "Where are you from? Where did you go to school?" His gaze sharpened. "Have you ever been married?"

Abby resisted the urge to roll her eyes. She knew Simon was looking out for her, and while she appreciated the gesture, she wished she'd thought to tell him she'd already vetted Joaquin. Still, a little family pressure probably wasn't a bad thing. She liked feeling loved and having a guy know she had backup was good.

Not that she and Joaquin were dating or anything. Well, they were something, but she was having a little trouble defining what they were. Friends, she thought. Friends who had kissed.

While Joaquin detailed his background, Montana leaned close and whispered, "I like your young man."

Abby glanced at Joaquin before whispering back, "I do, too."

"THANK YOU FOR setting that up," Joaquin said as he drove Abby back to her house. "They were both very interesting people."

Abby leaned back in her seat and smiled. "They're lovely. I was afraid you and Simon were going to talk shop all night and spoil my appetite, but you didn't."

"Surgical procedures are not something to be discussed over dinner."

"A man with standards. I like that."

The evening had gone really well, she thought. She'd been sure it would, but it was nice that they all got along.

"I'm glad you're going to get a chance to talk shop with Simon tomorrow. You'll enjoy that."

Joaquin glanced at her before returning his attention to the road. "I appreciate the opportunity."

"Maybe you can dissect a frog together or something."

He chuckled. "Is that what you think we do in our free time?"

"I hope not."

He parked in front of her house and turned to her. "Your uncle is very approachable. I wasn't sure he would be."

"Because of the famous surgeon stuff? He used to be all grumpy and stuffy." She unfastened her seat belt. "Back when he first got to Fool's Gold." She smiled. "Then he met Montana and fell madly in love. He was transformed."

She paused. "I thought you'd be like he was before."

"Grumpy?"

She hesitated. "Maybe *grumpy* is the wrong word, but you know, stuffy and difficult to talk to. But you're not. You're funny and easy to be with."

She almost said "handsome" but stopped herself in time. Not that he wasn't but because he might misunderstand. "You're also really good with your hands," she added without thinking, then groaned.

"I was thinking of the way you put beads on the place cards," she said quickly. "It came out way more dirty than I expected."

He leaned toward her. "I like to think I am good with my hands, but it seems a little soon. You strike me as the kind of woman who wants to get to know someone first."

Whoa! Were they talking about what she thought they were talking about? He was just so out there with it. Just saying it. Most of the guys she knew were more suggestive and less straightforward. Although she liked Joaquin's way better.

"Abby?"

"Yes, waiting is good."

His gaze locked with hers. "What about kissing?"

She shifted toward him, anticipation making her feel all tingly inside. "Kissing is nice."

"I'm glad you think so."

He pressed his mouth to hers. The feel of his lips against hers was the perfect ending to a perfect evening. She rested her hands on his shoulders. He stroked her back.

She wanted to get closer but the stupid console was in the way. Whoever designed car interiors did not take kissing into account—that was for sure.

Still, this was nice, and when she parted her lips, he swept inside, deepening the kiss and cranking up the intensity. She went from worrying about not being close enough to getting lost in how it felt to be really, really kissed by him.

Every stroke of his tongue increased her need. Heat swept through her, stealing her will and her breath. In less than five seconds she went from "sure I want to get to know the guy first" to "let's go back to your hotel."

She drew back a little and stared at him. He looked as stunned as she felt.

"Did you feel that?" she asked.

"The jolt that had me wondering if we were too old to do it in the back of a car?" he asked, his voice thick with passion.

"I was leaning toward your hotel room."

"That's an option, too."

She wanted him, that much was clear. She liked him. A lot. But… But…

"So here's the thing," she said with a quick shrug. "I've had boyfriends and we done a lot of playing around and stuff, but I've never actually gone all the way."

Joaquin stared at her. "You're a virgin?" He sounded comically surprised.

"Mostly. I've had orgasms. Like I said, I've gotten close but I've never..." She internally rolled her eyes. *Made love* was an option. *Had intercourse.* The man was a doctor—she doubted she could say anything about the human body that would shock him.

"I want it to be special," she told him. Which translated to she wanted it to be love. One without the other seemed stupid and wasteful. "Not marriage, but in an important relationship."

He looked at her for a long time before nodding. "I understand."

"I hope so." Many guys didn't. They thought she was playing a game or was too weird. A few had been fine with her limitation and had been happy to explore other options. There was a lot of fun to be had that wasn't going all the way.

He kissed her again. "So no hotel room." A statement, not a question.

"Not tonight."

He touched her face, then ran his thumb across her bottom lip. "Good for you. I'm glad you think you're worth waiting for."

He got out of the car and walked around to the passenger side and helped her out. When they were standing on the sidewalk, he pulled her close and kissed her again. The wanting flared to life, leaving her weak at the knees.

"I'll see you tomorrow after my meeting with Simon,"

he promised as they walked to her front door. "I believe the votives will be ready for their second coat."

"You're getting into the craft thing, aren't you?"

He flashed her a grin. "I have to continue to earn my reputation with my hands."

CHAPTER SIX

Joaquin had a restless night. His time with Abby had left him uncomfortably aroused, but more disturbing to his sleep had been her confession.

A virgin. She was twenty-two—not ancient, but still surprising. Knowing her the little that he did, her decision made sense. She was secure, happy and had a solid sense of herself. She wanted more than just a night with someone. He respected that and found her even more appealing because of it. He was a little surprised to find himself fighting a primal urge to claim what no man had and keep her for his own.

What did that even mean? That he wanted to marry her? He barely knew her. He liked her—how could he not—but marriage?

Fortunately the morning brought with it a different kind of distraction. He was meeting with Simon at eleven and he wanted to spend the time between now and then brushing up on Simon's work history and the fellowship opportunity.

He arrived at Simon's office right on time and was shown in to him immediately.

"Joaquin." Simon rose and shook hands. "We enjoyed dinner last night."

"As did I. Thank you for the invitation."

They sat across from each other, the large desk between them. Joaquin found himself not sure what to say. Normally in a social setting, he was uncomfortable, but this was different. He had to figure out a way to bring up the program. Maybe he should have brought Abby along with him. She made things go more easily.

Simon leaned back in his chair. "Before you arrived, Abby came to see me. She wanted advice on how to deal with you."

"I don't understand."

Simon smiled wryly. "I think she assumed because we were both surgeons, I would have some insight. She's a very sweet young woman. She babysits for us, and our kids love her. She's part of our family."

Joaquin sensed there was a message in the words but he had no idea what it was.

"I did a little research," Simon said unexpectedly. "I thought it was surprising that a man with your talents would take off three weeks to come to a place like Fool's Gold. Abby thinks it's because of your brother's wedding, but I wasn't so sure. You could have flown in the day before, attended the wedding and then gone home."

He pulled a folder out of a drawer. "You applied for the fellowship."

Joaquin sensed the conversation had taken a dangerous turn but he wasn't sure why that might be true. He'd wanted to better himself—get more training. Why was that bad? Still, he decided to be cautious.

"Yes, I did."

"You were turned down."

"Yes."

Simon flipped open the folder. "You have excellent qualifications but the director of the program thought you lacked heart. That's why you're here, isn't it? To convince me you should have been accepted? Abby and the wedding were…what? A means to an end? A lucky break?"

"The convergence of events seemed to favor making a personal connection," he said carefully. "I did want to attend my brother's wedding."

"And Abby?"

Joaquin stiffened. "She has nothing to do with this. I didn't know about Abby until I met her. I'd heard of her, but I had no idea I'd be spending time with her." He stared at Simon. "Abby is separate from this."

"You're spending a lot of time with her."

"I am. She's very enjoyable company. I'm helping with the wedding."

"I heard. You're going to paint votives today."

Joaquin knew Simon was trying to get a point across, but he had no idea what it was.

"And you still want in the program?"

"Yes."

Simon closed the folder. "Let me be clear. Abby is family. I love her as if she were my own daughter. Don't hurt her."

"I would never do that."

Simon studied him. "I recognize a bit of myself in you, Joaquin, and because of that, I'm going to give you some free advice. It's easy to overlook things when they turn up without warning. Especially when they're not part of your plan. Be careful not to dismiss something simply because it's not what you were looking for."

Joaquin had no idea what he was talking about. "Thank you for telling me that. May I reapply to the program?"

Simon sighed. "We'll discuss that after the wedding. Between now and then, tell Abby the truth. All of it. If you don't, I will, and I will not make you look like a hero if I do so."

Tell Abby what? His shoulders slumped. "You mean tell her that I came here under false pretenses."

"And that you used her to get to me."

He started to protest it hadn't been like that, only he knew it had been. He'd used her because he had assumed she wouldn't matter. But he'd been wrong about that, just like he'd been wrong about so many things.

"Everything is different now. I like her. I want to be with her and get to know her."

Simon's sharp gaze never wavered. "Tell her or I will," he repeated.

Joaquin nodded. "I'll do it."

He rose and let himself out. Once he was by his car, he looked back at the building, then around at the town. He would tell Abby. All of it. She would understand. Maybe not at first, but when he explained himself, she would get it and everything would be fine. She was the kind of person who understood, who accepted. He was counting on that and her.

FRIDAY AFTERNOON JOAQUIN left to spend the weekend with his brother in San Francisco. Abby knew it was good for them to have time together. They would go to a Giants game Saturday night and hang out in the city. Sibling bonding was important. She was superexcited that Melissa was coming home, so it was an excellent plan. Only she couldn't seem to shake the sense that she was going to miss him.

"It's just two days," she pointed out to herself as she tried to get interested in the book she was reading. Or not reading.

She glanced at her watch. He had been gone all of two hours. Why was she feeling so restless?

She had no answer. Rather than sit staring at words that didn't make sense, she went back inside and headed to her room. She'd been meaning to go through her clothes and figure out what she would need for school. She wanted a simple wardrobe of easy-to-clean outfits that allowed her to sit on the floor with the kids without flashing anyone anything. So longer, full skirts and lots of tailored pants with fun tops. She'd been collecting seasonally printed shirts and sweaters, but she would need more than that.

Three hours later, she had sorted, cataloged and made a couple of lists. She was feeling pretty smug about the whole thing when she heard her sister's voice.

"Where are you hiding, Abby?"

She raced out of her bedroom and met her sister in the kitchen. They hugged.

"You're back!" Abby said. "How was traffic?"

"Not too bad." Melissa shrugged out of her suit jacket and kicked off her heels. "I've been so busy all week," she said. "Trying to get ahead so I won't feel guilty when we're on our honeymoon."

"No feeling guilty," Abby told her, collecting her sister's small suitcase. "You're getting married. You're allowed to go away."

"I know, but work is important. I'm nearly where I wanted to be, so that's good." She smiled. "Now I have to shift gears and get into wedding mode. How have you been?"

"Great. Busy. The place cards are done, the birdseed holders are done and the votives are painted." She didn't mention her special project, but it was done, too. The graphics company had finished printing all the giant cards. Abby had picked them up that morning and was stashing them in Joaquin's hotel room so no one would see them.

Melissa led the way to her bedroom. "You *have* been busy. I'm sorry. I didn't mean for you to spend your summer working on my wedding."

"It's been fun. Joaquin helped a lot. The man can paint. And glue on beads."

Melissa put her handbag on her desk and unzipped her skirt. "Really? So you've been spending a lot of time with him?"

"Yes."

Her eyebrows rose. "And?"

Abby threw herself on the bed. "He's great. Why didn't you tell me he was so good-looking? I was unprepared."

"Is he? I don't know. I think Davis is the handsome brother."

Abby didn't point out that was probably the love talking. Davis was cute and all, but Joaquin could stop traffic. At least the female part of it.

Melissa pulled on shorts, then unfastened her blouse and dug a T-shirt out of the drawer. "So looking after him hasn't been awful?"

"Not at all. We get along great."

Melissa stared at her. "Wow. So you like him?"

"Yes. Don't be surprised. You just didn't spend enough time with him. He's not stuffy at all. He's got a good sense of humor and he's willing to do anything."

"Really?" Melissa drew out the word to several syllables. "Do tell."

Abby sat up and laughed. "There's nothing to tell. We're having fun."

"Naked fun?"

"Hardly. It's been a week."

"But you like him?"

Abby shook her head. "Don't get all speculative on me. We're not marrying brothers. I'm just saying it's been nice to get to know him." And kiss him, but she didn't say that.

"I'm glad. One less thing to feel guilty about."

"Absolutely." Abby stood up and waved for Melissa to follow her. "Come on. Let's go tell Mom you're back. She has the master wedding list. We'll figure out what we have to do over the next day and a half, then go get Mexican food tonight."

Melissa linked arms with her. "You're my favorite sister."

"I know. Isn't it great?"

JOAQUIN FOUND HIMSELF oddly excited to return to Fool's Gold. He left a couple of hours earlier than he'd planned, simply to return to the town. No, he amended as he drove east on Interstate 80, not the town. Abby.

He'd missed her. He'd been gone just over forty-eight hours and he'd missed her. He wasn't sure how that was possible or what it meant but the need to see her and talk to her urged him to drive faster so he could get there sooner.

He couldn't wait to have her smile at him and tell her about his weekend with his brother. He'd always assumed he and Davis had nothing in common, but he'd been wrong. Maybe when they'd been younger, their life experiences had been so different they couldn't relate to each other, but that wasn't true now. They were both successful in their chosen careers, they both liked baseball more than football. They'd had a great time at the game on Saturday, cheering the Giants on to their win. Conversation had rarely ebbed. Joaquin had even been interested in the talk about the wedding and where Davis was taking Melissa for their honeymoon.

The detailed description of the beachfront resort on Maui had gotten him to thinking about a vacation…with Abby. He would love to go snorkeling with her, try off-roading, ride bikes down from Haleakala at sunrise. He could imagine her laughing next to him as they explored the tropical paradise together. Or maybe they should go to Aspen. They could snowboard, then spend their evenings in front of a fire. Later, in bed, he would touch her and taste her and please her and—

He returned his attention to the highway. No more thoughts of Abby, he told himself. Not until he was safely back in Fool's Gold.

But as he saw the sign telling him he was only thirty miles from his destination, he felt a flicker of apprehension. Simon's words were ever present. He was going to have to tell Abby why he'd come here in the first place. He was going to have to convince her that those reasons weren't why he stayed and trying to do that was what had him hesitating.

He didn't want to hurt her. He didn't want to make her feel she wasn't special, because she was. She needed to know she was important to him and he didn't know how to tell her the truth without shattering whatever it was between them. But he would figure it out. He had to.

He'd tried to practice by telling Davis, only he'd never quite gotten the words out. The second time he'd tried, his brother had told him he was pleased that Joaquin was finally taking time off work. As if Joaquin had gone to Fool's Gold to rest up. Guilt had assaulted him, making him unable to speak the truth.

He wanted to have decided to visit for a different reason, only he hadn't and there was no going back. He knew there was no way he would have simply visited anywhere. He wasn't that type of person—or he hadn't been.

He arrived in town and drove directly to Abby's house. When he parked, he realized he shouldn't just show up—that he should have texted her he was on his way. What if she wasn't home? What if she had plans? What if she was with someone else?

That latter thought had him out of his car and heading for the front door. Abby opened it before he reached the porch. She grinned at him, then raced toward him and flung herself at him. He grabbed her and wrapped his arms around her, pulling her close before kissing her.

She tasted sweet and tempting and he wanted her more than he'd ever wanted a woman. This wasn't about a biological need for release—this was about Abby specifically.

But her recent confession of her virginity meant he was going to have to go more slowly, so he could earn his place in her life. He released her, then cupped her face.

"I'm back."

She smiled up at him. "I can see that. You missed Melissa by about an hour, which is too bad, but to make up for that, I'm going to take you to the Dog Days of Summer festival. It goes until sundown so we have a few hours."

"I've never been to a festival."

Her eyes widened with surprise. "Seriously?"

He'd never wanted to go, but that was hardly the point. "I know," he said, his voice teasing. "How sad is that?"

"Terribly sad. Let me put on some shoes and we can go right now."

She grabbed his hand and pulled him into the house. He followed her upstairs, not sure of their destination, then was startled when they entered what was obviously her bedroom.

The room was large, with a big window. There was a full-size bed, a dresser, a bookshelf and a desk. The walls, the bedspread and the throw rugs were all different shades of pink. There were posters on the wall, big fuzzy throw pillows in the shape of hearts and stars, and books piled everywhere. Not just textbooks, but novels and travel books.

"I'll just be a second," she said, ducking into her closet. She pulled the door half-closed behind her. "I mean, this is the Dog Days of Summer festival and your first time, so I have to look nice."

His gaze slid toward the bed. He jerked his attention away, turning so he was staring into the dresser mirror, which was a huge mistake because now he could see into the half-open door and watch Abby change her clothes.

She'd already pulled off her shorts and T-shirt. She stood in front of a rack of dresses. She was wearing a bra and panties and nothing else.

She was perfection, he thought, hunger burning inside of him. Strong and curved in all the right places. She reached for a dress and pulled it over her head, then slipped into flat sandals.

He quickly turned away, studying the bottles and brushes on the dresser itself. She stepped out of the closet and fluffed her hair, then moved next to him.

"Don't judge the pink," she said with a smile.

"I love the pink. It's very you."

"Traditionally girlie. I can't help it. I like the other colors, too, just to be fair, but pink has stolen my heart." She leaned against him. "I'm a terrible person. I convinced Melissa to have pink bridesmaid dresses just to make me happy. I was very selfish."

He kissed the top of her head. "That's not true."

"It is but I like that you won't believe it." She took his

hand again and pulled him toward the door. "Okay, so this is the festival that celebrates that it's nearly the end of summer. It's silly and fun."

"And there are dogs?"

They went outside and started for the center of town. "Not just dogs. All kinds of animals. You'll see."

They joined the huge crowds filling the blocked-off streets. There were dogs—most in costumes—along with every other kind of pet imaginable. Cats and hamsters, cages with mice, lizards and snakes. People led goats and pigs on leashes. In the shade of the large trees in the park, there was an elephant.

"That's not possible," he said, staring at the massive creature and the small pony next to it.

"Her name is Priscilla and that's her pony, Reno. They're a thing. She lives out on the Castle Ranch with the goats and horses. It's nice. At the holidays she takes part in the Christmas parade. She even has a costume."

He looked at Abby. "How do you get a costume on an elephant?"

"With a ladder and lots of hook and loop closures. The women in town made it for her. She's also in the live nativity, which is so great." Abby grinned. "One year they used a toy poodle to represent the Baby Jesus. I thought it was charming, but some people were offended so that didn't happen again."

They explored the booths selling everything from lavender soap to jewelry to local honey.

"Tell me about your weekend," Abby said as they waited in line to get lemonade.

"It was good. We went to a Giants game and they won. We walked around down by the wharf."

"So you had a good time?"

"We did." He glanced at her. "I can't remember the last time Davis and I did anything together. Even when we were kids. We weren't into the same things and I was gone a lot. I never knew what to say to him."

"You were lonely."

"Some."

"It's easy to forget how to be friends with the people you care about," she told him. "Now that you've remembered, you can stay in touch more. Melissa's not just my sister, she's my best friend, and I wouldn't—"

Without warning, she dropped his hand and took off at a run. She launched herself at a tall, dark-haired guy and laughed as he swung her around. Joaquin felt a strong kick in the gut and had no idea what to do. Beating up the other guy seemed inappropriate—nor was he sure he had the skill set. But the need was still damned powerful.

Abby pulled the man toward him, dancing and smiling the whole way. "Joaquin, you'll never guess. This is Percy and his girlfriend, GraceAnn. This is Joaquin. He's Davis's brother and the best man."

She dropped Percy's hand and returned to Joaquin's side. "Percy was Melissa's first boyfriend. They were very cute together but sadly not as cute as Percy and GraceAnn."

GraceAnn, a beautiful young woman with dark hair and skin, shook her head. "I think Melissa's cuter than me."

"She's not," Percy and Abby said together, then laughed.

"Percy has family in the area," Abby said. "It's complicated, as many relationships are. So he's home visiting but also for the wedding." She hugged GraceAnn. "Wait until you see the bridesmaid dresses."

GraceAnn leaned against Percy. "Did you talk her into pink?"

"You know I did."

The women laughed.

The four of them talked for a few more minutes, then Percy and GraceAnn excused themselves. Joaquin watched them go, still dealing with what could only be described as jealousy. He'd never felt that before, so wasn't sure, but it was the word that came to mind.

"What?" Abby asked as he handed her a lemonade. "Are you all right?"

"Yes. No." He drew her away from the crowd to a quiet area by the park. "It was hard to watch you throw yourself at another guy."

"Throw myself." Her eyes brightened with humor. "Were you jealous?"

"Yes."

"Really?" She smiled up at him. "That makes me happy." She set her lemonade on the ground and pressed her hands against his chest. "There's no one else, Joaquin. There hasn't been for a while. I don't know what exactly is happening here, but I like being with you."

He put his drink next to hers, then wrapped his arms around her. "I like you, as well. Very much."

She stared into his eyes. "Good to know."

There was more he wanted to say—more he should say—but instead of speaking he kissed her. She melted into his embrace and parted her lips. He swept his tongue inside, already anticipating how good kissing her would feel. There was something about touching her, being touched by her, that was better than being with anyone else. A combination of who she was and how comfortable he was around her, he supposed.

The kiss went on longer than it should have, given that they were out in public. Reluctantly, he drew back.

She was flushed and her gaze was unfocused.

"You're a really good kisser," she said, leaning her head against his shoulder. "It's the doctor thing, right? You're probably so sexy in your white coat that you've dated a zillion women so you're just better at kissing than most guys."

Her assessment of him was so at odds with his actual life that he started to laugh. "Abby, I'm socially awkward. There have been women, but not many."

"I'm not sure I believe you. I think there are hordes of women."

"Not even close."

"Then they're really stupid, but I'm okay with that. More for me."

She picked up their drinks and handed him his. He took it, then put his arm around her. He didn't know if Abby was teasing or not and he didn't care. Right now he felt as if he could take on the world.

CHAPTER SEVEN

"AFTER ALL THIS PLANNING, I can't believe the wedding is only a few days away," Liz said as they looked at the ballroom up at the resort.

"I know. It's happening so fast," Abby said.

Saturday Melissa and Davis would be married. Sunday morning they would drive to San Francisco for their flight to Hawaii. More significant to her, Joaquin would be heading back to Los Angeles.

Although they'd spent every day together since his return from visiting his brother, they never talked about what would happen after the wedding. Were they going to stay in touch, continue to see each other? She knew what she wanted, but was less sure about him. Obviously he liked her, liked being with her, but was she a fling or something more?

Abby didn't like feeling unsure and she certainly didn't want to be one of those women who wondered rather than asked. She'd always been fairly straightforward when it came to the guys in her life. But this time, she couldn't seem to form the words—mostly because she was afraid he would say something she didn't want to hear.

"Abby?" Liz asked.

"Sorry. Did you say something?"

Her mom smiled at her. "I think we're done here. We've delivered the votives and place cards. We've gone over everything on the checklist. Now we just have to wait for

Melissa to come home Wednesday night, and then we're going to have a wedding."

Less than a week, Abby thought glumly. She had less than a week until Joaquin went back to being a gifted surgeon and she stayed here, getting ready for the school year to start.

"Are you all right?" Liz asked as they walked back to her car for the drive to town.

"Just thinking about stuff."

"Joaquin?" Liz unlocked the car. "I couldn't help noticing how much you two have been hanging out. It's more than just being polite to a future family member."

"I know." Abby slid onto the passenger seat. "I wasn't sure what to expect with him, but he's really nice and fun and I like him."

"But?"

"But when the wedding's over, he's going back to LA and I have no idea what happens after that. I know I should ask, but I can't." She bit her lower lip. "I'm scared."

"Because you're falling in love with him?"

The gentle question caught Abby by surprise. "What? Love? No. It's too soon. I've never been in love. I probably should have been but I didn't ever feel that way and it would be ridiculous for me to fall for him."

Liz drove out of the parking lot without saying anything.

Abby sighed. "You really think I'm falling in love with him?"

"I can't answer that question, honey. You have to."

Love Joaquin? Could she? Did she? It would explain a lot. How she thought about him all the time and couldn't wait to be with him and how she was worried about him leaving.

"He lives in Los Angeles. I have a teaching job here."

"People make long-distance relationships work all the

time. It's…what? A seven-hour drive or less than an hour by plane. He's not moving to Mars."

"Mars would be more difficult," Abby said. "I should talk to him, huh? Ask him what he expects after the wedding."

"That would be a good start."

"Right. The mature decision." She looked at her mom. "What if he doesn't like me?"

Liz smiled. "You know he does. It's not a matter of if but how much. And what his expectations are. You might also want to think about what you want. He's going to ask you."

What *did* she want? "I want to keep seeing him. I want us to be exclusive. I want to see where this goes."

She wanted to let her feelings grow and then she wanted to make love with him, she thought. She wanted him to be her first one and maybe, just maybe, her only one.

"Then tell him that. Tell him you think he's special and that the two of you have potential."

"Which takes me back to what if he doesn't want that? I don't want to get my heart broken."

"It's too late for that. Whether or not he says the words, if he's not interested in you past the wedding, then you're going to find out one way or the other. You're already in too deep."

"You couldn't just say everything will be fine?"

Liz smiled. "Everything will be fine."

"Like I believe that now." She leaned her head against the seat back. "All right. I'll work on being brave and mature. I won't like it, but I'll work on it."

"That's my girl."

JOAQUIN HURRIED THROUGH Fool's Gold. He was meeting Abby at the bridal shop for the final fitting of her bridesmaid dress. He wasn't sure what that meant exactly. Why wouldn't the dress just fit because they ordered the right size? And how could a store only sell bridal stuff and stay in business? Were that many people getting married?

Not that he cared, he thought as he spotted the storefront for Paper Moon from across the street. He only wanted to spend time with Abby. He didn't mind if she was getting fitted or they were painting fences or watching cricket on BBC. As long as he was with her, he was happy.

That state of being was new to him. He was more a "content" kind of person. He wasn't given to emotions like happy or sad. The middle of the road was a much easier place to live.

But around Abby, he couldn't help himself. Just knowing he was going to see her was enough to make him practically giddy. He thought about her all the time and counted the hours until he could see her again. Looming in the background was the fact that he still had to tell her why he'd originally come to Fool's Gold, but he had time. The wedding wasn't until Saturday.

He walked into the store and immediately found himself in a foreign land. It wasn't just the displays of wedding gowns and accessories—it was the plush carpeting, the ornate furniture and the general air of being part of something he could not understand.

He came to stop just inside the door, not sure what to do. Should he go back outside and text Abby that he would join her later or should he suck it up and try to find her?

An attractive, very pregnant woman walked over to him. She smiled.

"It's all right," she said in a soothing voice. "Just breathe. The panic will fade and you'll feel better."

Her expression was teasing, her blue eyes bright with

amusement. When he managed to keep from bolting, she glanced over her shoulder.

"Abby, I'm guessing your friend is here. You need to come reassure him. The store has a chilling effect on most men and he's no exception."

Abby appeared from around a corner. She smiled and hurried toward him.

"Girlie overload?" she asked, linking arms with him. "I should have warned you what to expect."

"I'm not sure a warning would have helped," he admitted. "I've never been in a store like this before."

"And you probably never will be again." She smiled at the other woman. "Madeline, this is Joaquin Kincaid. His brother, Davis, is the groom. Joaquin, this is Madeline Blaze." She lowered her voice. "Okay, I don't usually say this, but you're going to be family, so it's okay. Madeline's married to Jonny Blaze."

Joaquin was far more interested in the feel of Abby snuggling up to him than who Madeline might be married to. He smiled politely.

"Nice to meet you."

Abby grinned. "I told you."

Madeline looked surprised. "You don't like action movies?" she asked, sounding puzzled.

Movies? What did they have to do with anything? "I don't have much free time, and when I do, I prefer to read."

Abby sighed. "This is why I'm crazy about him. I can't help it. He's perfect."

He told himself she was teasing. That she was having fun with a friend. Regardless, her words hit him with the subtlety of an eighteen-wheeler, leaving him shattered on the side of the road.

Crazy about him? Did she mean it? Was she really? And

could she possibly think he was perfect? He, who was so much more flawed than most with his awkward conversation and inability to function in normal society?

"You were right," Madeline said, smiling at Joaquin. "My husband is an action movie star. I don't usually talk about him but Abby insisted you wouldn't be impressed."

"I'm sure he's very good at his job," Joaquin said, not wanting to offend Abby's friend.

Abby leaned her head against his shoulder. "You haven't insulted her. Don't worry. You're refreshing." She took his hand and tugged him along toward the back of the store. "Come on. I need to try on my dress one more time. I told Madeline you get to sit in the comfy chair."

He found himself in a large open area with a dais and a huge mirror. There were several plush wingback chairs, small tables, magazines, boxes of tissues and a fancy tea set. Once again he had the sense of stepping into a world where he did not belong.

Abby pointed to the largest of the chairs. "I'll be right back."

Joaquin took a seat. Madeline hadn't followed them so he was saved from having to make small talk. He looked around, trying to get his bearings, then picked up one of the magazines. There was a woman in a bridal dress on the cover. He flipped through the pages and saw dozens of women in different styles of wedding gowns, along with ads for everything from invitations to dishes to rings. There were more pictures of brides, along with other women dressed like bridesmaids. In the back of the magazine were photos of honeymoon destinations.

Apparently this getting married thing was an entire industry, he thought in amazement. Given the polished nature of the magazine and the existence of the bridal dress store, it must be a large segment of the economy, worth billions of dollars. He'd had no idea.

He went through the magazine again, studying the dresses more closely. He started to see differences in the styles, although the predominant color was white. He saw a few pages devoted to a specific wedding—with details on how the tables were decorated and what flowers were in the bouquet. There—

"Ahem!"

He looked up and saw Abby walking back into the waiting area. Without thinking he let the magazine fall to the floor as he stood and stared.

She was incredible. The dress was long and beautiful, leaving her shoulders bare except for skinny straps. The top part was pleated somehow, only softer, and there was some wisp of fabric draped across her upper arms. The color was the palest of pinks, which could have clashed with her coloring but somehow didn't.

She bit her lower lip and blinked several times. "Wow. If we ever have a fight and I'm really mad at you, just look at me like that and I'll forgive you in a hot second."

"How am I looking at you?"

"Like she's the only woman in the world," Madeline said, walking toward them. "Abby, you're stunning. Now let's see if we need to do any more alterations. Although from what I can see, the dress fits perfectly."

Abby stepped up on the dais and faced the mirror. Madeline joined her, tugging and pulling, checking the fit. Joaquin couldn't look away, couldn't believe what he was seeing. Feelings swelled up inside of him. Unfamiliar feelings he couldn't name but that seemed as if they could change him forever.

He wanted this, he thought. He might have come to

Fool's Gold for the fellowship, but now that seemed secondary to his relationship with Abby. He glanced at the magazine, then back at her and realized he wanted to see her in more than a bridesmaid dress. He wanted to see her in a white wedding gown, carrying flowers, walking toward him down a long aisle. He wanted to be with her always, to do all the things they talked about—love and cherish, no matter what.

She was everything he hadn't known he was looking for. He'd come to Fool's Gold to further his career, but instead he'd found something far more important—the missing piece of his heart.

He knew it was too soon, that they'd just met and that there was no way in hell he deserved her. But in that moment, he was certain this was why he'd come to Fool's Gold. To meet her and know what was possible.

"I THINK WE'RE READY," Liz said, surveying the backyard.

Abby looked around and nodded. "We are. I'll go double-check that the downstairs bathrooms have plenty of supplies."

The big family barbecue the Thursday evening before the wedding had grown in scope, much like the wedding itself. Not anyone's fault, Abby thought as she looked in on both powder rooms along with the full bath by her dad's study.

There were plenty of towels and soap and everything was clean and tidy. She made a mental note to pop in about halfway through the evening, just to make sure all was well.

They were expecting a crowd. Melissa and Davis, of course. Abby, Joaquin, Davis's parents. All six Hendrix siblings, their spouses and kids, Grandma Denise and Grandpa Max. Rather than a fancy dinner at a restaurant, Melissa had asked for something easy and casual. Liz had arranged for tables to be set up in the backyard. She'd hired Ana Raquel to do the cooking. Instead of a bar, there was self-serve wine, a couple of kegs of beer and a metal tub filled with sodas on ice. Dessert was cupcakes stacked in the shape of a wedding cake. Ethan had set up Bluetooth speakers around the backyard and Davis had chosen the playlist.

Right at six, people started arriving. Abby hovered by the door, as much to greet her family as to wait for Joaquin. She hadn't seen him all day, which shouldn't be a big deal but it felt as if it had been weeks since she'd seen him smile at her. She also wanted to make sure she was nearby when he arrived because she knew the crowd of relatives would be a little stressful for him and she planned to run interference.

She greeted Molly and Gary Kincaid. They were both nice people—he was a dentist and she ran a daycare facility in Gardenia, California. They hugged Abby, then made their way to the backyard. Abby was just about to text Joaquin when she saw him walking up to the house.

She raced out front. He opened his arms and she threw herself against him, even as he pulled her close. When he kissed her, she felt the tingles all the way down to her toes.

"It's been forever," she complained. "How did we go the whole day without seeing each other?"

"I don't know, but let's make sure it doesn't happen again."

She thought of his practice back in Los Angeles and how her life was here. "But it's going to, isn't it?" she said before she could stop herself. "Once the wedding is over, you'll go home. This is only a vacation."

His mouth straightened. "I want to talk to you about that. I'd like it to be more. Abby, being with you has been—"

"Hey, you two," Uncle Finn said, walking toward them. "Take it inside. You'll shock the neighborhood."

Aunt Dakota followed, Hannah and Jordan Taylor at her heels. "Finn, leave them be. They're young and in love. It's nice."

In love? *In love!* What was with everyone? Abby tried to process the comment even as she hugged her relatives and introduced Joaquin.

"The mysterious but gifted doctor," Dakota teased. "Nice to meet you at last. It's good to know you have such excellent taste in women."

Joaquin grinned. "It's one of my best qualities."

They all went inside. Abby told herself to put all thoughts of the L word out of her mind for now. She had a party to get through and she didn't want to be distracted and not enjoy it. From what she could tell, Joaquin was as interested in her as she was in him. Yes, he had things he wanted to tell her, but they could figure out the logistics. They could visit on weekends and there were her long breaks at the holidays and over the summer. It could work.

Melissa and Davis arrived to cheers. Abby took Joaquin around and introduced him to everyone. When he seemed to tense up around so many people, she stayed close, linking her fingers with his. He smiled gratefully as he rubbed his thumb against the back of her hand. Over the next hour or so, he began to relax.

When her mom announced dinner would be starting in ten minutes, Abby headed toward the tables. She wanted a couple of seats near the back where they would be out of the limelight. Not only did she want the night to be all about her sister and Davis, she knew that plan would make things easier for Joaquin.

She'd just chosen their chairs when Uncle Simon walked over. He gave her a quick hug before turning to Joaquin.

"Did you tell her?"

Joaquin stiffened. "You said I had until the wedding."

Although Abby had no idea what they were talking about, she suddenly felt cold and her stomach knotted. What were they talking about?

"You had over two weeks," Simon said. "There was no reason to wait." Simon turned to her. "Abby, let me start by reminding you that I love you very much."

She didn't know what he was going to say, but there was no way she wanted to hear it. She nearly put her hands over her ears and demanded that he stop talking. Only something in her gut warned her that would be a mistake. That one of the things she knew for sure was that her uncle adored her and would never hurt her. Never do anything that wasn't in her best interest.

She glanced at Joaquin, who looked as if he wanted to speak, only he didn't. When their gazes locked, she read worry and something she couldn't define in his eyes. Guilt? Fear? Whatever it was, it wasn't good.

Simon touched her shoulder. "I'm sorry. I told Joaquin to tell you or I would. Apparently he didn't believe me."

"It's not that," Joaquin began.

Simon silenced him with a shake of his head. "You had plenty of time. Abby, Joaquin isn't here for the wedding. He came to Fool's Gold to meet me and talk to me about the fellowship I run. He applied a few months ago and didn't get past the first screening interview. He thought if we established a personal relationship, I would reconsider accepting him into the program."

Abby took a step back and stared at them both. There was no way to make her uncle's words other than what they were—a stark explanation about a situation that had never fully made sense.

She turned to Joaquin. "You used me to get to my uncle?"

"It started out that way, yes. My career is important to me, Abby. You know that. I lost a patient because of her burns. There was nothing I could do and I hated being helpless. I wanted to be a better surgeon, so I applied and was turned down. When I found out about the wedding being here, I decided to see if I could get to know Simon."

Her entire body went cold as the truth settled over her. "So it was a lie. All of it."

"No." He moved toward her, stopping a few feet in front of her. "No, it wasn't. Everything changed when I met you. Everything. You captured my attention and my feelings. I've liked everything we've done together. I've never known anyone like you, Abby. I didn't want to say anything about why I'd come here because I didn't want to destroy what we had. It's important to me. You're important to me."

She wanted to say nothing made sense, only it did. She'd been busy falling in love and he'd been taking advantage of her. He'd been playing a game. No, he'd been playing *her*.

"You used me to get to my family. You pretended to care. You tricked me." Tears burned, but she blinked them away. "Was any of it real?"

"Of course it was." He reached for her. "Abby, please. I don't want to lose you."

She pulled away. "What else are you going to say?" she asked bitterly.

She turned to run toward the house, only to remember where she was. This was a party to celebrate her sister's wedding. All their family was here. She couldn't make a scene. She couldn't scream or cry or run—not without ruining the night for her sister.

She looked at Joaquin. "Don't say a word. I don't want Melissa or Davis to know anything is wrong." She felt her mouth twist. "Not that keeping quiet will be hard for you. It's something you're really good at."

With that she walked toward her mother. When she reached Liz, she leaned in and whispered. "I think my period just got here early," she lied. "I'm going to head up to my room for a few minutes to check and maybe take something for the cramping."

Her mother smiled at her. "Of course. Should we hold dinner?"

Abby shook her head. "I won't be long. I just need a second. Go ahead with the meal service. I'll be right back."

She started for the house, careful to not run and to keep smiling. She greeted people who noticed her, doing her best to act normal. When she finally reached her room, she sat on the edge of the bed and covered her face with her hands.

She'd been a fool. For the first time in her life, she'd given her heart to a man only to discover everything about their relationship was a fraud. Just as bad, she had to get through the next two days without anyone finding out what had happened. Saturday was Melissa's special day. No matter what, Abby was going to do everything she could to make it perfect. Even if that meant lying to her entire family.

CHAPTER EIGHT

WHEN JOAQUIN HAD been eight years old, and home for the weekend from his boarding school, he'd overheard his parents talking about him. He remembered his mother speaking through her tears that while she loved her son, she was also afraid of him.

"It's like he's a different species," she'd admitted. "I never feel completely safe around him."

He hadn't known what she meant or how to fix the problem but he'd instinctively understood she didn't want him anywhere near her. In the end, he'd decided to stay away as much as he could so she wouldn't be afraid. He'd known that being alone was better for everyone.

But knowing and enduring were two different things. Even though he'd believed he'd made the right decision, he'd cried himself to sleep nearly every night for a year. He'd tried to focus on his studies, telling himself he wasn't hoping that his parents insist he come spend time with them. Not that they ever had. When he'd gone to college at such a young age, he'd seen similar looks of apprehension on some of the other students' faces. He didn't know how he could frighten them but he acknowledged that he did.

After he graduated from college, he'd gone home for a long weekend. He'd gathered the courage to ask his mother if she was still afraid of him. Her warm hugs and sobs of regret had been nice, but by then, the wound had run too deep to be healed. Joaquin had known that day nothing would ever hurt more than his parents' rejection of him.

But he'd been wrong.

Losing Abby was close, but what truly broke him was the realization that he'd hurt her. He'd taken something special and unique and precious and he'd destroyed it with his thoughtless behavior. He had found the very thing he'd been looking for his entire life and he'd destroyed it.

He spent Friday with his brother, helping with the wedding, careful not to let on that anything had changed. Friday night he went to the rehearsal.

He and Abby listened to the instructions and practiced walking out together. He was aware of everything about her—how her eyes were red and how she was so very careful not to ever brush against him.

He tried saying he was sorry, but she curtly told him this wasn't the time. That they were to get through the wedding without anyone knowing. Then she gave him an artificial smile that had crushed his already shattered heart.

Several of Melissa's family members had come by to watch the rehearsal. Joaquin saw Simon and wished he could blame the other man for what had happened. Only he knew Simon had simply done the right thing. Joaquin understood all the fault was his own. He'd been the one who had misled Abby from the start. He was the one who had been arrogant, playing with people's lives for his own end. He might be a gifted surgeon but he was a terrible human being.

As the rehearsal ended, Joaquin moved toward his brother.

"I have an unexpected consult," he lied. "There's a complex surgery. I'm going to be on the call for over an hour, so I won't make it to the dinner. I'm sorry."

His brother slapped him on the back. "We'll miss you,

but I understand. Of course you have to go save a life. I'll see you first thing in the morning." Davis grinned. "You're going to have to deal with my nerves."

Joaquin shook his head. "You've never been more sure of anything in your life. You won't be nervous." He paused. "Melissa's wonderful. You're a lucky man."

Davis looked surprised. "Thanks. I agree with you." He leaned his head to the right. "What about Abby? You think she's pretty special, don't you?"

Joaquin allowed himself to look at her. "She's the most perfect woman I've ever met." With that, he left.

There was no consult and he sure as hell didn't want to spend the evening alone, but he knew it would be easier for Abby if he wasn't around. Twenty-four hours, he told himself. Twenty-four hours and then she wouldn't have to pretend anymore. She could tell everyone what a jerk he'd been. He would leave town and do his best to avoid seeing her as much as possible.

He walked back to his hotel. He should have been the one to tell her the truth. He should have been brave. No— he shouldn't have lied in the first place.

He'd barely walked into his room when there was a knock on the door. He opened it to find Montana Bradley standing in the hallway. She smiled at him.

"May I come in?"

He stepped back without speaking. Despite her smile, he was fairly certain she was there to tell him off. He was fine with that—he deserved it.

She closed the door behind him, then drew in a breath. "So, how are you feeling?"

"Like crap."

"Interesting. Why? Because you didn't get your way?

Because now Simon will never let you in the program and you wasted all that time?"

He stared at her. How could she think that? "What? No. Of course I care about the program, but losing that isn't the problem. I hurt Abby. She is sweet and kind and sexy and all things good and I hurt her. I betrayed her. I let her believe in me when I knew I was using her. She doesn't deserve that."

As he felt an unusual burning sensation in his eyes, he instinctively turned away. He had to clear his throat before speaking.

"I don't do well around people. Not in social situations. I'm impatient and rude and dismissive. I think my work matters more than anything. With Abby, everything was different. *I* was different. It was easy to be normal, to take time to talk and get to know people." He turned back to Montana. "I'm funny with her. I can make her laugh. I like being with her. I'm in love with her."

He held up a hand. "I know it's only been a couple of weeks, but I've never felt like this with anyone before. She is magical and I destroyed her and whatever we could have been. It's never right to hurt another person, but to hurt someone like Abby is even worse. She's perfect and I have made her sad and less trusting. I have destroyed a part of her and I will never forgive myself for that."

He managed a harsh laugh. "So while I'm sorry about the program, it is really the least of it."

Montana studied him. "That's interesting. Why aren't you at the dinner?"

"I thought being that close to me would make it difficult for Abby." He still had no idea why Montana had stopped by. He drew in a breath. "Please say whatever you want to me. I deserve it." A horrible thought occurred to him. "Are you here to ask me not to come to the wedding?"

He thought about Abby in the beautiful dress. To not see

her walk down the aisle would be devastating, but if Montana thought it was best…

"Oh, I think you should be at the wedding." She pulled her phone from her handbag and began texting. When she was done, she smiled. "I told them."

He didn't understand. "Told who what?"

"I told my sisters that you get what you did and you're pretty broken up about it. That's what I wanted to know. Did you get what you'd done? Did you realize how wrong and incredibly stupid you'd been? You blew it from start to finish but that wouldn't matter if you didn't care. But you do. You're in love with her. I believe you."

He had no idea what she was talking about. "What does that mean?"

She smiled. "It means we're going to help you. Not because of you but because of Abby. You're the first guy she's fallen for. I mean ever. We were going to disembowel you and hide the body because hey, Liz is a mystery writer and she knows about stuff like that, but now that we know you care, we'll go in another direction. It's great."

He wasn't sure if she was kidding or not. "You mean there's a plan?"

"No, but there will be. We're going to talk tonight. I'll be in touch. Don't do anything stupid between now and then."

"I believe I've used up my quota for this lifetime."

"I hope so, but you're a guy, so I'm less sure. Try to get some sleep, Joaquin. I'll see you in the morning."

She left, leaving him alone with his thoughts, his guilt and the tiniest sliver of hope. If he could win back Abby, he would do anything. If only he had a clue as to what that might be.

SATURDAY MORNING ABBY stared at herself in the mirror. The sleepless nights were starting to show. She knew she was lucky she was only twenty-two so she could hide the dark circles with some concealer. If she was much older, she wouldn't be able to pretend all was well. Of course, if she was older, she liked to think she would have been smarter—able to spot liars like Joaquin and avoid them.

For the eight hundred and twenty-seventh time, she told herself she'd been a fool. She'd been trusting and dumb and had totally fallen for a guy who saw her as little more than a means to an end. She'd thought she was grandma's secret guacamole recipe when in fact she was little more than an off-brand chip. She was disposable—at least in Joaquin's life.

All of which she could handle—she might not have worked through a romantic heartbreak before, but she knew the process. There was anger and hurt and all the stages of grief, not in any particular order, plus sugar and carbs and throwing things and feeling like a failure and, eventually, moving on. She was prepared for all that—what she hadn't expected was that she would be missing Joaquin so much. Worse, she was worried about him.

Ridiculous, but there she was—actively concerned about how he was going to get through the wedding. She knew large social crowds made him uncomfortable, and that being with her made him feel better. Not that she wanted him feeling better. She should want him run over by a truck, but instead here she was, hoping he was going to be okay, which made her doubly, triply stupid. Plus the dark circles.

She threw herself back on her bed and reached for her phone. There hadn't been any phone calls and only a single text message. She opened it to read it, even though she already knew it by heart.

I apologize from the bottom of my heart. I was wrong and selfish. I should have told you the truth. I did come here to meet Simon and initially you were a means to an end. But all that changed as I got to know you. I wanted to tell you the truth, but I didn't want to ruin what was, for me, the most wonderful relationship I've ever had. I was afraid, so I acted like a coward. The results are fully justified. My greatest regret is that you are being punished, too. You are the innocent party—you don't deserve to be the least bit upset and I know you are.

I know that you are hurt and angry, and I deserve every horrible thing you're thinking and saying about me. I have no excuse for what I did. If I could take it back, I would. As I can't, I will only say that you are the most amazing person I've ever met. Being with you was a privilege and I will never forget our precious time together.

Please don't assume every guy is as much of an asshole as I am. You deserve to be happy, Abby. I'm sorry.

He'd sent the message yesterday morning. At first she'd refused to read it, but eventually she'd given in. She'd spent the rest of the day wondering if it was as good an apology as it seemed to her or if she was simply hoping it was because she couldn't stop thinking about him.

Seeing him at the rehearsal had been torture. He'd looked so good and she'd missed him so much. She'd thought maybe they could talk at dinner, but then he'd left and she'd felt stupid all over again, even though she suspected he'd left so she wouldn't have to deal with him in the first place, which made missing him so confusing.

"I'm never falling in love again," she muttered, tossing her phone onto the bed. She sat up. "Not that I'm in love with Joaquin. I'm not. He's toady and stupid and I hate him."

She looked at the clock on the nightstand. She still had

a couple of hours before she joined Melissa and their mom for mani-pedis and their hair appointments. Two hours to sulk and feel sorry for herself, knowing it was going to take a long time to get over Joaquin.

If only he hadn't been so incredibly right for her, she thought glumly. Smart, but sweet. Funny and kind, and when he kissed her...

Tears filled her eyes. She blinked them away. The man was not tear-worthy.

She got up and decided to shower. As she was gathering her clothes together, there was a knock on her bedroom door.

"Abby, do you have a minute?"

"Yes." She let in her mother.

Liz handed her a mug of coffee, then took a seat at the desk. "Did you sleep at all?"

Abby sank back on the bed. She didn't like the sound of that question. It was almost as if her mother—

Abby groaned. "Let me guess. Simon told Montana, who told the world."

Her mom smiled. "Just the sisters."

Obviously not just the triplets, Abby thought. The larger group that included Liz, Consuelo and Isabel. The Hendrix sisters and sisters-in-law.

"We should form a softball team or something," Abby told her. "I'm a decent pitcher."

"Yes, you are."

Abby sipped her coffee. "Please don't tell Melissa. I don't want to ruin her day."

"I won't say a word." Her mother's expression turned concerned. "I wish you'd said something to me, though. Abby, you shouldn't go through this alone. You had to deal with the rehearsal last night. I could have helped."

"You were busy with the wedding stuff. Mom, it was fine. Joaquin might have broken my heart, but he's well-mannered. He kept his distance and barely spoke to me. Then he made up some excuse to avoid dinner."

"Tell me what happened," her mom said.

"With Joaquin? You already know. He pretended to care about the wedding so he could figure out a way to meet Simon. He used me and the family and everything for his own gain."

"How did he get you to introduce him to Simon? That's a pretty random thing to bring up in conversation."

Abby groaned. "He didn't have to. I took care of that for him. I was afraid I wouldn't have anything to say to him, so I talked to Simon before I meet with Joaquin and arranged the dinner. It just fell in his lap."

Her mother nodded. "Fate is funny that way. I'm sorry you're hurt, but I'm glad you found out the truth before things went too far, emotionally. He sounds like a horrible person."

"He's not horrible, Mom. He's driven. And he's really smart and I think he was isolated as a kid, so social stuff is harder for him than for the rest of us. But he's kind and funny and he's a really good kisser."

"But he used you."

"I know." She set her coffee on the nightstand and shifted so she could cross her legs. "If I tell myself he made the decision to do that before he knew me, am I giving him a break or letting myself get played again? He wants into Simon's program and he was willing to do anything to get it. Only he didn't have to help with all the stuff with the wedding. Or go to the festivals or make me laugh. That's what I can't figure out. I liked him, a lot. I think I was falling in love with him. Then I found out this horrible thing about him."

"Has he apologized?"

Abby hesitated a second, then tossed her mother the phone. Liz read the text.

"As apologies go, it's not bad," her mom said.

"But is it real? How can I know if it's okay to believe him or not?"

"Only you can know that. What I do know is that loving someone means accepting all of them. Even the flaws. You don't have to like the flaws but you can't pretend they don't exist. You look at them fully and then decide if you can live with them. If the rest of him is worth it. Hopefully, he'll do the same with you."

Abby smiled. "I don't have flaws, Mom. You should know that."

Liz laughed. "How true." Her smile faded. "You should talk to him face-to-face, Abby. If this man matters, don't just walk away without having it out with him. What if he's the one and you find that out eleven years later? You will have wasted so much time."

Abby remembered the stories she'd heard about how Liz and Ethan had gotten together—theirs had not been an easy road.

"You're thinking of you and Dad," she said softly.

"I am. I can't figure out how we could have done things differently, but I also wish with my whole heart we could have found each other sooner. I'm not saying to ignore what happened, but maybe it's worth fifteen minutes of your life to listen. If your heart and mind don't believe him, then good riddance. But if you think he is truly sorry, then he might be worth a second chance."

"I'll think about it."

Liz moved to the bed and pulled her close. "I love you, Abby. I want you to be happy."

"Me, too."

"If it doesn't work out with Joaquin, let me know. I can kill him in my book. It will be painful and gruesome."

Abby smiled. "You're the best mom ever."

"I try."

CHAPTER NINE

ABBY GLANCED AT the clock on the wall in the bride's dressing room at the resort. They had nearly half an hour before the photographer was due to arrive to start taking pictures. "The Sisters" were all over Melissa, discussing the options of her stepping into her dress or them trying to pull it over her head. Once that was done, there were about eighty-seven buttons to be fastened.

Abby met her sister's gaze in the large mirror.

"Run," Melissa mouthed with a smile. "Run while you can."

Abby had put on her makeup at home. Getting her hair ready was a matter of a quick fluffing, and her dress had an easy zipper up the back. It had taken her all of two minutes to go from shorts and a T-shirt to wedding ready.

She glanced at the clock again and told herself no one would miss her for a few minutes, then stepped out into the hall.

She was fairly sure Davis and his family were somewhere in the resort, getting ready. The reception area was prepared, and Abby could smell hints of the delicious meal yet to come. The day was sunny, warm without being stifling, and Melissa was marrying the man of her dreams. It was perfect.

Abby walked to the open doors leading to the wrap-around porch at the back of the hotel. Soon, she promised herself. Soon she would stop being sad about Joaquin. Soon the wedding would be behind her and she could focus on the upcoming school year. She was going to be a teacher!

She was happy about that, she told herself. It was just—

"Abby?"

She turned and saw Joaquin had stepped out from another set of doors and was walking toward her. He had on a black tux and he looked good. Better than good.

She fought against the need to rush into his arms and be held. She wanted to feel the heat of him, inhale the scent of his body and have him tell her everything was going to be all right. Only it wasn't.

She stayed where she was, letting him come to her. She was strong and she would get through this. Later, she would ask her mom to kill him in her book, like Liz had offered.

Joaquin stopped in front of her. "You're so beautiful. I knew you would be, but you're even more so."

"Thank you." Her voice sounded stiff and strained, probably because she was so confused and hurt and mad.

He looked at her. "Montana came to see me last night. She said she believed my regret was real and that she was going to come up with a plan to help me win you back." One corner of his mouth turned up. "I haven't heard from her, just so you know."

What? "That is a very odd thing to tell me."

"I know, but I want you to know the truth. I don't want to keep anything from you, the way I did before."

His shoulders slumped. "Abby, I am sorry. I was so stupid and selfish. I thought getting into the program was more important than anything. There is such arrogance in that assumption. Just because I'm a surgeon doesn't mean my life is more important than anyone else's. Everyone has value, but somehow I forgot that. I only thought of myself. And then I met you."

She didn't want to react to what he was saying. She told herself they were just words and she didn't believe him and he was a butthead and none of this mattered, only she couldn't seem to turn and walk away.

"I was wrong. I should have been up front with you," he continued, his gaze intense. "I didn't think it mattered, that you mattered, so I didn't bother telling you the truth. And then we started hanging out together and I didn't *want* to tell you. I knew it would change everything. I was afraid you wouldn't like me anymore."

He swallowed. "I care about you, Abby. So very much. I want to say I'm in love with you, but it's only been three weeks and that would just make me a scary stalker guy. But you changed me. I like who I am when I'm with you. I like being around you and helping you with things. I want to be there for you and be someone you can depend on. I want to take care of you when you need that and stand back and let you shine the rest of the time. I have no idea what you're thinking, but if you can find it in yourself to give me another chance, I will do my best to not let you down. I'd like to keep seeing you. On weekends, and when you're on your winter and summer breaks. We could talk on the phone and over the computer." He looked away, then back at her. "If it's not too much, I was thinking I would look into a surgical practice here. There's a trauma center and I have experience."

She blinked. "You'd do that for me?"

"Of course. You're amazing and I don't want to lose you. Unless I already have."

His mouth twisted, then he cleared his throat. "That's all I have. Just my apology and who I am. I guess it's not very much." He turned away, then glanced back at her. "You will be a part of me always. I am better for having known you. I wish you could say the same about me, but you can't. I apologize for that, as well."

He started to walk away.

Abby thought about what her mom had told her and how hard the last two days had been. She didn't know if it was love, but she was sure it was more than she'd ever felt before. Yes, Joaquin had screwed up in a really awful way and she was mad at him, but maybe the fact that he got that, that he was sorry, meant something.

She didn't want to wake up in ten years and think she'd made a horrible mistake.

"Wait," she said.

Joaquin spun back to face her. The hope in his eyes blinded her. "Abby?"

"You hurt me so much. I trusted you and you betrayed me."

"I did. I have no excuse. I was wrong."

She drew in a breath. "Chances are I'm going to screw up, too. Not that badly, but some. People make mistakes. It's not the messing up, it's what you do afterward that speaks to character."

He waited.

She smiled. "It was a good speech. Thank you for telling me about Montana. I'll let her know she doesn't need to keep working on her plan." She paused. "This is where you ask if it's okay to kiss me."

"Is it?"

"Yes."

Joaquin reached for her, pulling her close. His mouth claimed her in a kiss that offered her all he was. She wrapped her arms around him and gave herself up to him.

Her broken heart began to mend as she realized that this was where she belonged.

He drew back. "I love you," he whispered, gazing into her eyes. "I know it's too soon, so I'm not going to say it again for at least two months, but I want you to know that you are all I've ever wanted. Only you, Abby. For—"

She pressed her fingers against his mouth. "Stop. You are headed in a direction that we're not ready for. Let's be honest—neither of us has been wildly successful at romantic relationships. We both have our reasons. I'm still pretty young and you're freakishly smart, so we're going to figure it out together. But if you propose right now, you'll send me screaming into the night."

One corner of his mouth turned up. "Point taken."

"Good. We'll do the L thing, like you said. In two months. And you can think about proposing in a year."

"I will note my calendar."

She put her hands on his chest and leaned in. "But just this one time, until then…" She lowered her voice to a whisper. "I love you, too."

He'd just pulled her into his arms again when she heard someone approaching. She turned and saw her uncle Simon walking toward them.

He looked between them, then settled his gaze on Abby. "Montana is still working on her plan, but it seems that won't be necessary."

Abby grinned. "Probably not." She took Joaquin's hand in hers and faced her uncle. "So here's the thing. He was very wrong. Incredibly wrong. The wrongest of wrong. He knows that now and he's apologized. He didn't try to weasel out of it. He accepted responsibility. And I really like him and we're going to keep seeing each other. So you have to be nice to him."

"I see." Simon's gaze was sharp. "Anything else?"

"Yes. He might try to get a job with the trauma center. Don't blackball him or whatever it is you could do."

Simon looked at Joaquin. "Are you going to let Abby speak for you?"

"In this case, sir, it seems like the intelligent thing to do."

"Interesting." Simon paused "Joaquin, you should get your affairs in order."

"What?" Abby glared at her uncle. "You're not having him killed. How would you even do that? Mom talks tough, but she'd never help you hurt anyone."

Simon sighed. "I meant for the move. I've decided to admit him into the fellowship program. He'll need to be in Fool's Gold for that."

"You can do that?" Abby asked. "For real?"

Simon touched her cheek. "I can, and let me be clear. I'm doing it because I like the character of the man. Not so you can date him."

He turned to Joaquin. "Your skills were never the issue. It was all about who you were. We like our doctors to have heart and understand the value of compassion. If you're still interested, of course."

Joaquin vigorously shook his hand. "I am. Thank you, Dr. Bradley."

"You're welcome."

"Seriously," Abby said. "You're going to make him call you Dr. Bradley?"

Simon smiled. "For now." He pointed toward the hotel. "Come on, you two. There's a wedding and you are both in it. Get inside. You can coo over each other later."

They all went inside. Joaquin kissed Abby one more time before heading off to meet his brother. Abby returned to the bride's room. As she stepped inside, Liz glanced at her.

"You look happy," her mother said quietly.

Abby smiled. "I am. We made up and he's moving to town. We're going to be dating."

"Just dating?"

Abby grinned. "Really, Mom? Do you want me to talk about my sex life?"

"Ah, no. Actually, I don't." Liz hugged her. "I'm glad it worked out. Despite everything, I really like Joaquin."

"Me, too."

The photographer arrived and began taking pictures. The wedding coordinator kept things moving along until it was time for the ceremony itself. Abby took her place, ready to walk down the aisle in front of her sister. As she stepped slowly, keeping time with the music, she couldn't help locking eyes with Joaquin. It almost seemed as if he was waiting for her, instead of Davis waiting for Melissa.

Abby smiled at the thought. Maybe she *was* rushing things. Now that she and Joaquin had figured it all out, they had their whole lives ahead of them. They would take it slow, getting to know each other before falling madly in love. But all things considered, they were off to a really good start.

EPILOGUE

One year later

ABBY PULLED A loose T-shirt over her damp swimsuit. As the boat headed back for the dock, she took the bottle of sunscreen Joaquin held out and dutifully applied another coat. With her fair skin, avoiding a sunburn in Hawaii was a challenge, but she was doing her best.

"That was incredible," she said, smoothing the lotion on her arms. "I can't believe how blue the water is and how many fish there were. And the coral. I love the ocean. Can we go snorkeling again?"

He smiled at her. "We can go as many times as you want. When we get back to the hotel, let's figure out everything we want to do and make a lesson plan."

She laughed. "You do know the way to my heart."

"I hope so."

She dropped the bottle of sunscreen into her tote, then shifted so she was leaning against him. Their first real vacation together was even better than she'd hoped it would be. Of course, when Joaquin was involved, everything was pretty perfect so she shouldn't be surprised.

The past year had gone by so quickly, she thought, watching the island of Maui appear to get closer and closer. Joaquin had moved to Fool's Gold for the fellowship with her uncle Simon. He'd found working with burn patients gratifying and, in May, Simon had invited him to join his practice.

While he'd been doing that, she'd been busy with her first year of teaching. She'd loved her work and the kids even more than she'd thought she would. Every day had been an adventure and she couldn't wait for the school year to start again in September.

She'd moved into her own apartment, as planned. Living on her own had been good for her, not that she was by herself all that much. Either Joaquin was at her place, or she was at his.

Three months after they'd met, he'd taken her up to Lake Tahoe for a long weekend where they'd declared their love and she'd given herself to him. She chuckled, thinking that the man really *was* good with his hands.

"What's so funny?" he asked.

"I'm amazed at how much has changed in the past year. I'm kind of impressed with us."

"You're the impressive one."

The boat docked. Joaquin collected her tote bag and their towels as they waited for the other passengers to disembark. They took the open-air shuttle bus back to their beautiful hotel and returned to their room.

"Mind if I shower first?" he asked when they were inside. "I won't take long. Then you can have the bathroom. We'll go to dinner after that."

She wrapped her arms around him. "Or we could shower together."

He kissed her, before stepping away. "Let's wait on that. I want to see if you're sunburned from today."

"Worrywart."

He grinned. "That's Dr. Worrywart to you, young lady."

While he was in the shower, she picked out a dress to

wear to dinner, then walked out onto their balcony and stared at the ocean. What an amazing vacation, she thought happily. Being here in this beautiful place with the man she loved. Life didn't get much better than moments like this.

She wandered back inside, just as he exited the bathroom.

"All yours," he told her.

She kissed him, then went to shower and get ready for dinner.

Thirty minutes later, when she'd finished dressing and putting on makeup, she walked into the bedroom and said, "There's that fish restaurant we talked about…"

The rest of the sentence trailed off as she took in the room's transformation.

There were orchids everywhere. On the bed, in vases, in a lei around Joaquin's neck and in the second lei he held in his hand. She could see a small dining table and two chairs had been placed on the balcony. A bottle of something chilled in an ice bucket, and if she had to guess, she would say it was champagne. Music played from the sound system.

She stood there, blinking, trying to understand what it all meant.

"You did this for me?" she asked as he put the lei around her neck.

"I did."

"So that's why you wouldn't shower with me?"

"It is."

She grinned. "Good surprise."

"I'm glad."

He took her hand and led her to the center of the room, then stopped and faced her.

"Melissa and Davis were married a year ago today," he said.

"I remember. I was there."

"Do you also remember what you told me?"

"At the wedding? What did I— Oh!" She swallowed as she recalled exactly what she'd said. *You can think about proposing in a year.* "Joaquin?"

He pressed her hand against his chest and stared into her eyes. "Abby, these past months with you have been the happiest of my life. You are the most incredible woman I've ever met. You are kind and funny and smart and beautiful. Every day with you is a blessing. You've shown me the value of relationships and the importance of family. You make me a better man, and I'm grateful for that, as well. And for you. I love you with all my heart. I have almost from the day we met and I will continue to love you until I breathe my last."

He released her and dropped to one knee. "Marry me, Abby. Marry me and let me be your lover, your husband, your partner, for the rest of our lives."

Tears filled her eyes as she tugged him to his feet, then threw herself at him. "I love you and yes, yes, I'll marry you."

He pulled her close and kissed her. After a few minutes of very sexy kissing, he drew back and slid a ring on her finger. They both stared at the glinting diamond.

"Was this your plan all along?" she asked softly. "You were so particular about exactly when we came to Hawaii."

"I thought it would be a good place to propose. As for asking you today, I wanted to respect your wishes."

"It was a general suggestion, not an order."

"I just want to make you happy, Abby."

She leaned against him. "You do. Always."

They walked out onto the balcony where he poured her a glass of champagne. Behind them, the sunset sent colors of fire across the sky, but Abby and Joaquin only had eyes for each other.

"You know we're going to have to have a big wedding," she told him.

"Absolutely. At least three hundred. Your family alone is close to fifty."

"Plus our friends and the people we work with. Or we could run away, if that would be better for you."

He sat down and pulled her onto his lap. "No way. When I marry you, I want the whole world watching. Let them all be amazed that I got the girl."

"And I've got you right back."

* * * * *

*Two best friends jump-start their lives in a summer
that will change them forever in a story filled with
humor, heartache, and regrettable tattoos, from*
#1 New York Times *bestselling author Susan Mallery!*

Read on for a sneak peek of
The Friendship List
by New York Times *bestselling author Susan Mallery*

CHAPTER ONE

"I SHOULD HAVE married money," Ellen Fox said glumly. "That would have solved all my problems."

Unity Leandre, her best friend, practically since birth, raised her eyebrows. "Because that was an option so many times and you kept saying no?"

"It could have been. Maybe. If I'd ever, you know, met a rich guy I liked and wanted to marry."

"Wouldn't having him want to marry you be an equally important part of the equation?"

Ellen groaned. "This is not a good time for logic. This is a good time for sympathy. Or giving me a winning lottery ticket. We've been friends for years and you've never once given me a winning lottery ticket."

Unity picked up her coffee and smiled. "True, but I did give you my pony rides when we celebrated our eighth birthdays."

A point she would have to concede, Ellen thought. With their birthdays so close together, they'd often had shared parties. The summer they'd turned eight, Unity's mom had arranged for pony rides at a nearby farm. Unity had enjoyed herself, but Ellen had fallen in love with scruffy Mr. Peepers, the crabby old pony who carried them around the paddock. At Ellen's declaration of affection for the pony, Unity had handed over the rest of her ride tickets, content to watch Ellen on Mr. Peepers's wide back.

"You were wonderful about the pony rides," Ellen said earnestly. "And I love that you were so generous. But right now I really need a small fortune. Nothing overwhelming. Just a tasteful million or so. In return, I'll give back the rides on Mr. Peepers."

Unity reached across the kitchen table and touched Ellen's arm. "He really wants to go to UCLA?"

Ellen nodded, afraid if she spoke, she would whimper. After sucking in a breath, she managed to say, "He does. Even with a partial scholarship, the price is going to kill me." She braced herself for the ugly reality. "Out-of-state costs, including room and board, are about sixty-four thousand dollars." Ellen felt her heart skip a beat and not out of excitement. "A year. A year! I don't even bring home that much after taxes. Who has that kind of money? It might as well be a million dollars."

Unity nodded. "Okay, now marrying money makes sense."

"I don't have a lot of options." Ellen pressed her hand to her chest and told herself she wasn't having a heart attack. "You know I'd do anything for Coop, and I'll figure this out, but those numbers are terrifying. I have to start buying lottery scratchers and get a second job." She looked at Unity. "How much do you think they make at Starbucks? I could work nights."

Unity, five inches taller, with long straight blond hair, grabbed her hands. "Last month it was University of Oklahoma and the month before that, he wanted to go to Notre Dame. Cooper has changed his mind a dozen times. Wait until you go look at colleges this summer and he figures out what he really wants, then see who offers the best financial aid before you panic." Her mouth curved up in a smile. "No offense, Ellen, but I've tasted your coffee. You shouldn't be working anywhere near a Starbucks."

"Very funny." Ellen squeezed her hands. "You're right. He's barely seventeen. He won't be a senior until September. I have time. And I'm saving money every month."

It was how she'd been raised, she thought. To be practical, to take responsibility. If only her parents had thought to mention marrying for money.

"After our road trip, he may decide he wants to go to the University of Washington after all, and that would solve all my problems."

Not just the money ones, but the loneliness ones, she thought wistfully. Because after eighteen years of them being a team, her nearly grown-up baby boy was going to leave her.

"Stop," Unity said. "You're getting sad. I can see it."

"I hate that you know me so well."

"No, you don't."

Ellen sighed. "No, I don't, but you're annoying."

"You're more annoying."

They smiled at each other.

Unity stood, all five feet ten of her, and stretched. "I have to get going. You have young minds to mold and I have a backed-up kitchen sink to deal with, followed by a gate repair and something with a vacuum. The message wasn't clear." She looked at Ellen. "You going to be okay?"

Ellen nodded. "I'm fine. You're right. Coop will change his mind fifteen more times. I'll wait until it's a sure thing, then have my breakdown."

"See. You always have a plan."

They walked to the front door. Ellen's mind slid back to the ridiculous cost of college.

"Any of those old people you help have money?" she asked. "For the right price, I could be a trophy wife."

Unity shook her head. "You're thirty-four. The average resident of Silver Pines is in his seventies."

"Marrying money would still solve all my problems."

Unity hugged her, hanging on tight for an extra second. "You're a freak."

"I'm a momma bear with a cub."

"Your cub is six foot three. It's time to stop worrying."

"That will never happen."

"Which is why I love you. Talk later."

Ellen smiled. "Have a good one. Avoid spiders."

"Always."

When Unity had driven away, Ellen returned to the kitchen where she quickly loaded the dishwasher, then packed her lunch. Cooper had left before six. He was doing some end-of-school-year fitness challenge. Something about running and Ellen wasn't sure what. To be honest, when he went on about his workouts, it was really hard not to tune him out. Especially when she had things like tuition to worry about.

"Not anymore today," she said out loud. She would worry again in the morning. Unity was right—Cooper was going to keep changing his mind. Their road trip to look at colleges was only a few weeks away. After that they would narrow the list and he would start to apply. Only then would she know the final number and have to figure out how to pay for it.

Until then she had plenty to keep her busy. She was giving pop quizzes in both fourth and sixth periods and she wanted to update her year-end tests for her two algebra classes. She needed to buy groceries and put gas in the car and go by the library to get all her summer reading on the reserve list.

As she finished her morning routine and drove to the high school where she taught, Ellen thought about Cooper and the college issue. While she was afraid she couldn't afford the tuition, she had to admit it was a great problem to have. Seventeen years ago, she'd been a terrified teenager, about to be a single mom, with nothing between her and living on the streets except incredibly disappointed and angry parents who had been determined to make her see the error of her ways.

Through hard work and determination, she'd managed to pull herself together—raise Cooper, go to college, get a good job, buy a duplex and save money for her kid's education. Yay her.

But it sure would have been a lot easier if she'd simply married someone with money.

"How is it possible to get a C- in Spanish?" Coach Keith Kinne asked, not bothering to keep his voice down. "Half the population in town speaks Spanish. Hell, your sister's husband is Hispanic." He glared at the strapping football player standing in front of him. "Luka, you're an idiot."

Luka hung his head. "Yes, Coach."

"Don't 'yes, Coach' me. You knew this was happening— you've known for weeks. And did you ask for help? Did you tell me?"

"No, Coach."

Keith thought about strangling the kid but he wasn't sure he could physically wrap his hands around the teen's thick neck. He swore silently, knowing they were where they were and now he had to fix things—like he always did with his students.

"You know the rules," he pointed out. "To play on any varsity team you have to get a C+ or better in every class. Did you think the rules didn't apply to you?"

Luka, nearly six-five and two hundred and fifty pounds, slumped even more. "I thought I was doing okay."

"Really? So you'd been getting better grades on your tests?"

"Not exactly." He raised his head, his expression miserable. "I thought I could pull up my grade at the last minute."

"How did that plan work out?"

"No bueno."

Keith glared at him. "You think this is funny?"

"No, Coach."

Keith shook his head. "You know there's not a Spanish summer school class. That means we're going to have to find an alternative."

Despite his dark skin, Luka went pale. "Coach, don't send me away."

"No one gets sent away." Sometimes athletes went to other districts that had a different summer curriculum. They stayed with families and focused on their studies.

"I need to stay with my family. My mom understands me."

"It would be better for all of us if she understood Spanish." Keith glared at the kid. "I'll arrange for an online class. You'll get a tutor. You will report to me twice a week, bringing me updates until you pass the class." He sharpened his gaze. "With an A."

Luka took a step back. "Coach, no! An A? I can't."

"Not with that attitude."

"But, Coach."

"You knew the rules and you broke them. You could have come to me for help early on. You know I'm always here for any of my students, but did you think about that or did you decide you were fine on your own?"

"I decided I was fine on my own," Luka mumbled.

"Exactly. And deciding on your own is not how teams work. You go it alone and you fail."

Tears filled Luka's eyes. "Yes, Coach."

Keith pointed to the door. Luka shuffled out. Keith sank into his chair. He'd been hard on the kid, but he needed to get the message across. Grades mattered. He was willing to help whenever he could, but he had to be told what was going on. He had a feeling Luka thought because he was a star athlete he was going to get special treatment. Maybe somewhere else, but not here. Forcing Luka to get an A sent a message to everyone who wanted to play varsity sports.

He'd barely turned to his computer when one of the freshman boys stuck his head in the office. "Coach Kinne! Coach Kinne! There's a girl crying in the weight room."

Keith silently groaned as he got up and jogged to the weight room, hoping he was about to deal with something simple like a broken arm or a concussion. He knew what to do for those kinds of things. Anything that was more emotional, honest to God, terrified him.

He walked into the weight room and found a group of guys huddled together. A petite, dark-haired girl he didn't know sat on a bench at the far end, her hands covering her face, her sobs audible in the uneasy silence.

He looked at the guys. "She hurt?"

They shifted their weight and shook their heads. Damn. So it wasn't physical. Why didn't things ever go his way?

"Any of you responsible for whatever it is?" he asked.

More shaken heads with a couple of guys ducking out.

Keith pointed to the door so the rest of them left, then returned his attention to the crying girl. She was small and looked young. Maybe fifteen. Not one of his daughter's friends or a school athlete—he knew all of them.

He approached the teen, trying to look friendly rather than menacing, then sat on a nearby bench.

"Hey," he said softly. "I'm Coach Kinne."

She sniffed. Her eyes were red, her skin pale. "I know who you are."

"What's going on?" *Don't be pregnant, don't be pregnant*, he chanted silently.

More tears spilled over. "I'm pregnant. The father is Dylan, only he says he's not, and I can't tell my m-mom because she'll be so mad and he said he l-loved me."

And just like that Keith watched his Monday fall directly into the crapper.

KEITH LEFT WORK exactly at three fifteen. He would be returning to his office to finish up paperwork, supervise a couple of workouts and review final grades for athletes hovering on the edge of academic problems. But first, he had pressing personal business.

He drove the two short miles to his house, walked inside and headed directly for his seventeen-year-old daughter's room.

Lissa looked up from her laptop when he entered, her smile fading as she figured out he was in a mood. Despite the attitude, she was a beauty. Long dark hair, big brown eyes. Dammit all to hell—why couldn't he have an ugly daughter who no guy would look at twice?

"Hi, Dad," she said, sounding wary. "What's up?"

"Spot check."

She rolled her eyes. "Seriously? There is something wrong with you. I heard what happened at school today. I'm not dumb enough to date a guy like Dylan who would tell a tree stump he loved it if it would have sex with him. I'm not sleeping with anyone and I'm not pregnant. I told you— I'm not ready to have sex, as in I'm still a virgin. You're obsessed. Would you feel better if I wore a chastity belt?"

"Yes, but you won't. I've asked."

"Da-ad. Why are you like this? Pregnancy isn't the worst thing that could happen. I could be sick and dying. Wouldn't that be terrible?"

"You can't win this argument with logic. I'm irrational. I accept that. But I'm also the parent, so you have to deal with me being irrational."

He pointed to her bathroom. She sighed the long-suffering sigh of those cursed with impossible fathers and got up. He followed her to the doorway and watched as she pulled the small plastic container out of the bathroom drawer and opened it.

Relief eased the tension in his body. Pills were missing. The right number of pills.

"You are a nightmare father," his daughter said, shoving the pills back in the drawer. "I can't wait until I'm eighteen and I can get the shot instead of having to take birth control pills. Then you'll only bug me every few months."

"I can't wait, either."

"It's not like I even have a boyfriend."

"You could be talking to someone online."

Her annoyance faded as she smiled at him. "Dad, only one of us in this house does the online dating thing and it's not me."

"I don't online date."

"Fine. You pick up women online, then go off and have sex with them for the weekend. It's gross. You should fall in love with someone you're not embarrassed to bring home to meet me."

"I'm not embarrassed. I just don't want complications."

"But you do want to have sex. It's yucky."

"Then why are we talking about it?" He pulled her close and hugged her, then kissed the top of her head. "Sorry, Lissa. I can't help worrying about you."

She looked up at him. "Dad, I'm taking my pills every day, not that it matters because I'm not having sex. *I'm not.* I've barely kissed a guy. Having you as my father makes it really difficult to date. Guys don't want to mess with you and risk being beat up."

"Good."

She smiled even as she hit him in the arm. "You're repressing my emotional growth."

"Just don't get pregnant."

"You need to find a more positive message. How about 'be your best self?'"

"That, too. Gotta go."

"I'm having dinner with Jessie tonight. Remember?"

"No problem. Be home by ten."

He got back in his truck but before starting the engine, he quickly texted Ellen. I need a couple of beers and a friendly ear. You around tonight?

The response came quickly. Only if you bring fried chicken. I have beer and ice cream.

You're on. See you at six.

ELLEN COULDN'T FIGURE out why a six-foot-five-inch, seventeen-year-old guy crying bothered her more than pretty much any teenage girl crying. Was it reverse sexual discrimination? Because boys cried less often, their tears had more value? Was it the sheer size of Luka juxtaposed with the implied vulnerability of tears? As she was unlikely to figure out an answer, she decided to ignore the question.

"Luka, you're going to be fine," she said, reaching up to pat the teen on his shoulder as Cooper hovered nearby. "You'll take the online Spanish class and you'll do great. You're plenty smart. You just got complacent."

"He thought because he's such a hotshot on the field, his shit didn't stink," Coop said, then groaned. "Sorry, Mom. Um, I meant to say, ah, poop."

She turned to her son and raised her eyebrows. She was pleased that, despite his age and size, he took a step back and swallowed.

"I'm really sorry," he added.

"As you should be. Luka, Coach isn't throwing you off the bus."

"You didn't see him. He was really mad. He said I was an idiot."

Not exactly the word she would have chosen, but then she didn't spend much time in the jock/jockette world.

"You're a leader, so he expects better of you."

More tears filled Luka's eyes. Next to him, Coop winced.

"What if I can't get an A?"

"You won't with that attitude."

Luka sniffed. "That's what Coach said."

Cooper leaned close. "It's a teacher thing. They think alike. Welcome to my world."

She did her best not to smile. Her boys, she thought fondly. Cooper and his friends had been running in and out of her life since he'd been old enough to invite kids back to play. Luka had been a staple in her life for nearly a decade. He and his family had moved here from Yap (a tiny island in Micronesia—she'd had to look it up). Luka and Coop had met the first day of second grade and been best friends ever since.

"Luka, I forbid you to think about this anymore today. Your mom is waiting for you. Go have a nice dinner and relax this evening. Tomorrow, get your butt in gear and get going on the Spanish studies." She hesitated. "I'll talk to Coach and make sure you're still on the college trip."

His dark eyes brightened. "You will? Thanks, Ms. F. That would be great."

Before she could step back, Luka grabbed her and lifted her up in the air. It was not a comfortable feeling, but all of Coop's friends seemed to do it. He swung her around twice before setting her down. Both teens headed for the door.

"I'll be back by ten," Coop yelled over his shoulder.

"Have fun."

Ellen gave herself a little shake to make sure nothing had been crushed, then stepped out on her small deck to check out the heat level. The front of the house faced south, leaving the backyard in shade in the early evening. The temperature was close to eighty, but bearable.

The deck overlooked a small patch of lawn edged by fencing. Nothing fancy, but it was hers and she loved it. She quickly wiped off the metal table and dusted the chairs before putting out place mats, plenty of paper napkins and a cut-up lime. She'd already made a green salad to counteract the calories from the fried chicken. Shortly after six, she heard a knock on the front door, followed by a familiar voice calling, "It's me."

"In the kitchen," she yelled as she opened the refrigerator and pulled out two bottles of beer. Dos Equis for him and a Corona for herself. She glared when she saw the extra to-go container in his hand.

"What?" she demanded. "We agreed on chicken."

He held up the KFC bucket. "I brought chicken. Original, because you like it."

"Don't distract me. Are those potatoes? I can't eat those."

"Actually you can. I've seen you. You have no trouble using a fork."

She set his beer on the table. "Do you know how many calories are in those mashed potatoes? I'm not some macho athletic guy."

Keith gave her an unapologetic smile. "I'd still be friends with you if you were." He set down the food. "Stop worrying about it. You look fine." He glanced at her. "As far as anyone can tell."

She ignored that and refused to look down at her oversize tunic and baggy pants. "I like to be comfortable. Loose clothing allows me to move freely on the job." She ducked back into the house to get the salad, then joined him at the table.

He'd already taken his usual seat and opened both to-go containers. The smell of fried chicken reminded her she hadn't eaten since lunch, which felt like two days ago. Her stomach growled and her mouth watered.

Keith put a chicken breast on her plate, then handed her the mashed potatoes. She put slices of lime in both their beers. Their movements were familiar. Comfortable.

Coach Keith Kinne and his daughter had moved to Willowbrook five years ago. He'd joined the faculty of Birchly High as the football coach and athletic director. Washington State might not have the religious fever of Texas when it came to high school football, but there was still a lot of enthusiasm and the six-foot-two-inch, good-looking, darkhaired former NFL player had caught a lot of ladies' attention.

Not hers, though. Mostly because she didn't date—there

wasn't time and no one she met was ever that interesting. So when she'd found him cornered by a slightly aggressive novice teacher from the English department, Ellen had stepped in to save him and their friendship had been born. They hung out together because it was easy and they complemented each other. He'd helped her when she'd bought a new-to-her car a couple of years ago and she went Christmas shopping with him for his daughter.

"Why are you smiling?" he asked, picking up his beer.

"Just thinking that it's nice we're friends. Imagine how awkward things would have been if I'd gone after you when you first moved here."

He frowned. "Don't say that. If you had, we might not be friends now. I was fresh off a divorce and I wasn't looking for trouble."

"I'm not trouble."

"You would have been if we'd dated."

What on earth did he mean? "Trouble how?"

"You know. Boy-girl trouble." He put down his beer. "Speaking of dating, Lissa got on me about my internet relationships."

"You don't have internet relationships. You find women to have sex with."

He winced. "That's what she said. Have you two been talking about me behind my back?"

"Oh, please. We have so many more interesting things to talk about." She'd never understood the appeal of casual sex. It seemed so impersonal. Shouldn't that level of intimacy be part of a relationship? Otherwise sex was just as romantic as passing gas.

"She told me to find someone I wasn't embarrassed by so she could meet her."

"That's nice."

"It freaked me out."

Ellen grinned. "That's because there are emotions attached to relationships and you don't like emotions."

"I like some of them. I like winning."

"Winning isn't an emotion."

"Fine. I like how winning makes me feel." His expression turned smug. "I get emotions."

"You're faking it." She let her smile fade. "Cooper wants to go to UCLA."

"Are you sure? He told me Stanford."

She heard a ringing in her ears as her whole world tilted. "Wh-what? Stanford? No. He can't."

"Why not? They have a better wrestling program. I've spoken to the coach there and he's really interested. I'm working on getting Coop a one-on-one meeting when we visit the school. With his skills and grades, he's got a good shot at getting in."

"I'm going to faint."

"Why? You should be happy."

She glared at him. "Happy? Are you insane? I can't afford UCLA and it's a state school. How on earth would I pay for Stanford? Plus, why isn't Cooper telling me about things like meeting a coach? I should know that."

"Breathe," Keith told her. "If he goes to Stanford, you'll be fine. With what you make, his tuition will be covered. If he gets a partial scholarship, it could go toward room and board. Stanford would be a lot cheaper for you than UCLA."

Her panic faded. "Are you sure?"

He looked at her. "You have to ask me that?"

"Sorry. Of course you're sure. You do this all the time." She picked up her chicken. "Yay, Stanford. Go team."

"You don't have any contact with his dad, do you? Because his income would count."

"No contact," she said cheerfully. "Jeremy disappeared before Coop was born. I hear from him every five or six years for five seconds and then he's gone again. He signed his rights away and he's never given me a penny." She smiled. "I say that without bitterness because I'm loving the Stanford dream."

Keith grinned. "You're saying you can be bought for the price of tuition?"

She smiled back at him. "I can be bought for a whole lot less than that. So why didn't he tell me about wanting to go to Stanford? Why is he keeping secrets?"

"He's becoming a man. He needs his own dreams and plans."

"But I'm his mom and he's my baby boy. Make him stop growing up."

"Sorry. Not my superpower."

She remembered what it had been like when Coop had been younger. It had been the two of them against the world. "I miss being the most important person in his life, but you're right. He needs to make his own way. What are the Stanford colors? Will they look good on me?"

Don't miss what happens next in...

The Friendship List
by Susan Mallery!

*Available August 2020 wherever
HQN books and ebooks are sold.
www.Harlequin.com*

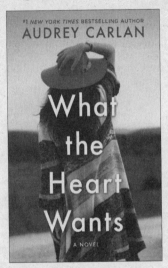